LITTLE FOLLIES

Also by Eric Kraft

Herb 'n' Lorna

Reservations Recommended

LITTLE FOLLIES

The
PERSONAL HISTORY,
ADVENTURES, EXPERIENCES
&
OBSERVATIONS
of
PETER LEROY
(SO FAR)

BY

ERIC KRAFT

CROWN PUBLISHERS, INC., NEW YORK

Grateful acknowledgment is made to the following for permission to reprint
previously published material:

Dover Publications, Inc.; an illustration from *Food and Drink: A Pictorial
Archive from Nineteenth-Century Sources*. Selected by Jim Harter. Third
Revised Edition copyright © 1979, 1980, 1983 by Dover Publications, Inc.

Illustration Credits
Pages 117-119: George Ulrich
Page 170: George Ulrich
Page 213: Steve Terr
Pages 229-232: Susan Gough Magurn
Page 291: Steve Terr
Page 347: Susan Gough Magurn

Publisher's Note: This is a work of fiction. The characters, incidents, diaglogues,
settings, and businesses portrayed in it are products of the author's imagination
and are not to be construed as real. Any resemblance to actual events or
persons, living or dead, is entirely coincidental.

Published by Crown Publishers, Inc., 201 East 50th Street, New York,
New York 10022. Member of the Crown Publishing Group.
Most of the stories were originally published individually by
Apple-wood Books, Inc.

CROWN is a trademark of Crown Publishers, Inc.

Manufactured in the United States of America

Library of Congress Cataloging-in-Publication Data

Kraft, Eric.
        Little follies : the personal history, adventures, experiences &
        observations of Peter Leroy (so far) / by Eric Kraft.—1st ed.
        p.   cm.
        I. Title.
PS3561.R22L53   1992
813'.54—dc20   91-41465
                                           CIP

ISBN 0-517-58543-X
Book design by Eric Kraft
10 9 8 7 6 5 4 3 2 1
First Edition

For Mad

Shed thy faire beames into my feeble eyne,
And raise my thoughtes, too humble and too vile

Edmund Spenser
The Faerie Queene
Prologue to Book One

CONTENTS

LITTLE FOLLIES

Preface

WITHIN A FAMILY, some events that an outsider might consider important are allowed to pass almost unnoticed and are soon forgotten; yet others, which seem trivial to the world at large, may be elevated to positions of such eminence that they acquire the status of milestones. In my family, for example, no one remembers my birthday, but they all remember the day my mother tumbled from her lawn chair.

In the years that followed her tumble, if talk around the dinner table turned to Mr. Beaker, a former neighbor, my mother would often ask, wistfully, I thought, "Do you remember the night he threw his desk lamp through the window? When was that?"

Someone else, usually my grandmother, would answer, "Why, Ella, don't you remember? It was the day you fell out of your lawn chair."

It is comforting, when one feels a bit "lost," to be able to put one's feet up, close one's eyes, and look back, as it were, along the road that one followed from wherever one once was to wherever one may be now, to "retrace one's steps," and find, along that roadside, familiar milestones. It is certainly comforting for me; for if I am feeling a bit "lost," when I begin such a backward ramble, I am often lost during it as well, wandering on someone else's road, or backing out of a cul-de-sac, and it is always a great relief to come upon one of these milestones, or, if you prefer, landmarks. It is a particularly great relief if I stumble upon the milestone that marks the day that, for the rest of my family, came to be known as "The Day Ella Tumbled from Her Lawn Chair" and is, on the map of my childhood memory, labeled "The Day I Was Chasing Kittens," for it is from that day that I date all the rest.

However, I began writing "My Mother Takes a Tumble" not with the aim of commemorating that event but to find a woman for Mr. Beaker.

When I was a child on No Bridge Road, living with my parents in my grandparents' house, Mr. Beaker lived next door, alone. I knew very little about him, and as far as I can recall I never set foot inside his house. He visited my grandparents from time to time, and he always stayed just a

My Mother Takes a Tumble

I think the memory of most of us can go farther back . . . than
many of us suppose; just as I believe the power of observation
in numbers of very young children to be quite wonderful for
its closeness and accuracy. Indeed, I think that most grown
men who are remarkable in this respect, may with greater
propriety be said not to have lost the faculty, than to have
acquired it; . . . I generally observe such men to retain a
certain freshness, and gentleness, and capacity of being
pleased, which are also an inheritance they have preserved
from their childhood.

Charles Dickens
David Copperfield

little too long. He worked for the Babbington Clam Council, writing advertisements. Later, I think, he became president of the council; I'm not certain. He considered himself a fine craftsman with an uncanny knack of echoing, in each of his advertisements, the tone, style, and yearnings of potential clam consumers.

Mr. Beaker relished his work and labored at it longer and harder than was really necessary, often working at home well into the night, when there were fewer distractions and his vast unseen audience seemed to draw in around him, like a group around a campfire, and lean forward, waiting for him to spin a yarn about the succulent mollusk. Between his house and my grandparents' grew a young oak that never fully lost its leaves until the very end of winter; when Mr. Beaker was at work at night, when I was in my crib, the light from his desk lamp would throw the shadows of its branches across my crib, across my parents' bed, and onto the opposite wall, where a door opened into a hall that led into the living room, where Gumma and Guppa and my parents sat listening to the radio or talking, quietly and uneasily, for living together was difficult for all of them.

Whenever Mr. Beaker was visiting and the time had come for him to go home, his face would grow long and dark, and he would begin praising my grandmother's cooking and my mother's figure. "Dudley," my father would say after he had left, "needs a woman."

Years later, I was walking along one fall day and smelled the unmistakable odor of burning leaves. It brought to mind, for reasons I will explain shortly, the years I spent on No Bridge Road, and Mr. Beaker, and all the rest, ending with my father's saying, "Dudley needs a woman." I realized that my father had been right, and that Mr. Beaker had thrown his desk lamp through the window that night because he was alone and hated it; so I created Eliza Foote, arranged a meeting, and let events take their natural course.

Some readers will be interested in knowing the sources of one or two other fabricated details.

My grandfather, Guppa, is a Studebaker salesman in "My Mother Takes a Tumble." In fact, he was not. Making him a Studebaker salesman was, I admit, simply an easy way out of a difficult situation. Let me explain.

The smell of burning leaves made me recall my years on No Bridge Road because it brought to mind quite clearly a fall ritual that began with the raking and burning of leaves: as if in response to some silent bell, men up and down No Bridge Road would rise from their breakfasts one fall Saturday, pull on old sweaters, step outside with rakes in their hands, and

Clams--
the chewy snack in the sturdy pack!

Say, Mom, your family's counting on you! They're counting on you for something *yum-yum good* at supper-time, something that will make up for the *drudgery* of the workaday world of work and the *failures* of the schoolday world of school. Before you start frying that chicken, better stop a moment and think! Is the *same old thing* going to warm the cockles of their hearts? Or will you see *long pusses* all around the table, wearing that chicken-again look? Bring a little *sunshine* into their miserable lives—serve Babbington clams in chowder, steamed, baked, fried, or just as they are in their own handy shells. Look for them . . .

at y<u>ou</u>r favorite store!

The Babbington Clam Council

Free Free recipe book! Yours for the asking! Write
Babbington Clam Council, Babbington, New York.

begin raking leaves into enormous piles on their lawns. Then the children of the neighborhood would jump into these huge piles, run through them, and scatter them. (At that time, any decent leaf pile came up to my waist, and in some I could get buried up to my armpits, but today I am hard pressed to accumulate a pile that reaches to my knees. Either there are fewer leaves now than there were then, or the art of piling leaves has decayed.) The men would rake the leaves into piles again and then begin carrying them to the street. They would make a number of small piles in the street, in the gutter, which was merely a shallow valley at the margin of the roadway, not defined by a curbstone, and burn them, one pile at a time. Up and down No Bridge Road, men would lean on rakes and watch their leaves burn.

The burning of leaves was followed by the second part of the ritual: the crushing of shells. Everyone on No Bridge Road had a clamshell driveway; many people in Babbington still have clamshell driveways, but they are not so widely favored now as they once were. They were cheap and serviceable, and required little maintenance other than a yearly addition of new shells to replace the bits of crushed shell that had been carried away by the wheels of cars and bicycles or the soles of the mailman's, milkman's, and breadman's shoes or washed into the gutter in rainstorms. The men would drag out burlap sacks of clamshells that had accumulated since the last fall and dump them onto their driveways. The children would pick through the shells and set aside a few of the shapeliest, the most clamshell-like; these paragons would be used for ashtrays or made into knickknacks. The others, the not-quite-right, the deformed and broken, the men would spread up and down the driveways. Then, and at last we near the point of this reminiscence, they would drive their cars up and down the driveways to crush the shells.

So vividly did the smell of leaf smoke return the memory of those fall days to me that I could see all the men driving up and down their driveways and hear the clamshells crushing under their wheels. Quite suddenly, I realized something that had never struck me when I witnessed this scene as a child. All the men were driving Studebakers. I looked more closely, straining to see all the way to the corner. There was no doubt about it: every car on No Bridge Road was a Studebaker. This put me into quite a tizzy, because I knew that if I included this remarkable fact without explanation the reader would regard it as gratuitously absurd. So, to make it plausible, I made Guppa a Studebaker salesman, and a very good one, although in fact he was a foreman in the culling section of the clam-packing plant.

In the barroom scene, I have repeated the word *barroom* far too often,
I know. I have no excuse; I repeated the word simply because I enjoy
coming upon it when I read, for I cannot help reading it, no matter how
strong the context, as the word my childhood chum Raskol used to use to
imitate the sound of a mighty explosion: "Boy! You should've seen it
when old Roundass's clamboat got hit by lightning. He's right in the
middle of the bay, minding his own business, taking a break to wipe his
sweaty brow, and thinking that maybe he'll eat a sandwich, when suddenly there's a big flash of light, and then *barroom!*"

One more point. In "My Mother Takes a Tumble," all the houses on
No Bridge Road are stucco. (That is, they are faced with stucco. Such
houses are in Babbington called simply "stucco" instead of "faced with
stucco.") That was not actually the case. All the houses on the *north* side
of No Bridge Road were stucco, but on the south side was a hodgepodge
of small vacation houses and shacks, unevenly spaced and poorly painted,
with no garages and, as I recall, no Studebakers, despite the efforts of my
grandfather. I omitted any mention of the differences between the two
sides of the street because I knew that if I mentioned the difference I
would have to explain it, since if I did not explain it, many readers would
consider my not explaining it significant, nodding knowingly and saying
to themselves, sardonically, as Porky White did when I tried it out on him,
"I see what this is. It's all class differences. Peter is born into the tight-
assed and striving lower middle class, a class that literally lives behind a
thin and fragile facade: stucco." He put his fork down and took a swallow
of coffee. "You know," he said, "the lower middle class is very interesting, if pitiable. This facade they work so hard to erect and maintain is,
well, it's like the frosting on this cake." He poked with his fork at the
slice of cake I had given him. "It's pretty white frosting, but it has no real
flavor; it's just sweet. The good part of the cake, in fact the essence of
cakeness, is the cake itself: its texture, its chocolaty-good flavor, even its
shape. So the people in the class into which Peter is born, to sum up, are
hiding their true vital essence, their essential vitality, behind a sort of icing.
Ahhhh —" He waved his fork at me. "— but across the street Peter sees,
and maybe yearns to join, the haphazard, sweaty, lusty, and fundamentally richer life of the unfrosted sometimes-working class. Right?"

Peter Leroy
Small's Island
April 2, 1982

1

MR. BEAKER LIVED ALONE in a stucco house next door to Gumma and Guppa, my mother's parents, on No Bridge Road. There was, as a sign on the corner cautioned, no bridge at the end of No Bridge Road, though one had once been planned, and rumors persisted that construction would begin soon.

All the houses on No Bridge Road were stucco. Beside each house, on the right as you faced it, was a clamshell driveway that led to a stucco garage. Guppa, a salesman at Babbington Studebaker who never took "no" for an answer, had seen to it that in each garage was a Studebaker.

Under the right conditions, on a winter morning, when snow covered their roofs and glistened in the morning light, the houses looked like the chocolate cakes for which my mother was, within her circle, noted: dark, rich, two-layer cakes covered with shiny white frosting that she pulled into peaks with the back of a spoon.

My mother and father were living in Gumma and Guppa's house then. Gumma taught my mother how to pull the icing into peaks, and Mr. Beaker ate his share of those cakes at Sunday dinners. I first saw one on the day that my mother and I came home from the hospital in South Hargrove. My father swung Guppa's Studebaker into the driveway, crunching clamshells under the wheels. Gumma and Guppa ran from the house, with Mr. Beaker right behind them. My father slid from behind the wheel and dashed to the rear door. Gumma and Guppa ran right up to the car, but Mr. Beaker held back a bit. My father opened the door with a flourish and held out his hand in a gesture usually accompanied by "Voila!"

"Voila!" burst from Mr. Beaker. My father scowled at the driveway.

Gumma and Guppa poked their heads into the car to get their first look at me in natural light. Beyond them, Mr. Beaker was bending this way and that, trying to get a glimpse between them. He was holding his hands behind him and wearing a grin of the sort that usually made Gumma, and later my mother, say, "You look like the cat that swallowed the canary."

At last Gumma and Guppa moved aside, and my father reached into the car to take me off my mother's hands. Seeing an opening, Mr. Beaker stepped up and produced from behind his back, with a flourish, one of the famous chocolate cakes, baked under Gumma's guidance as a birthday cake for me.

"Voila," muttered my father, twisting his foot in the shells.

My mother blushed. "Isn't that nice?" she asked me. "Your first birthday cake."

My father carried me, very carefully, into the house. Mr. Beaker helped my mother from the car.

Mr. Beaker was said to have a college degree, and he may have had one, for (a) he smoked a pipe; (b) on weekends he wore loafers and a cardigan sweater with suede patches on the elbows; and (c) at about the time that I learned to stand up in my crib, he began making a tidy living in a line of work that my father called, shaking his head in grudging admiration, "a swindle that only a college man could have dreamed up": writing letters, as "Mary Strong," to lonely men who from time to time could be persuaded to send the unfortunate Miss Strong some money.

Mr. Beaker drummed up business by running advertisements in the personals columns of small-town newspapers. He ran his first ad in the *Hargrove Daily News,* just to test the waters:

> **Lonely Man** Lovely young woman in unfortunate circumstances wishes to correspond with lonely man. Mary Strong, Post Office Box 98, Babbington, New York.

At that time, Eliza Foote was living in Hargrove and working as a typist at Hackett & Belder, Insurance, the premier firm of its type in Babbington. Guppa recommended them so highly to purchasers of Studebakers that all the homes, lives, and automobiles on No Bridge Road were insured through them, and Mr. Hackett saw to it that Guppa had a steady supply of liquor and turkeys.

When Eliza came home from work each evening, she read the *Daily News* straight through while she sipped bourbon from a juice glass. Sometimes she read aloud, so that her room would not seem so empty. Mr. Beaker's ad caught her eye just as she was swallowing the last little sip. She choked, gasped, and choked and gasped again. For a moment, she saw Mary plainly, somewhere across town, maybe in one of the rooms at the River Sound Hotel, sitting at a table, sipping from a glass of bourbon, reading and rereading her ad, hoping that someone else was reading it too. Eliza began rummaging in her pocketbook for a pen. After a few minutes she remembered that Mr. Hackett had borrowed her pen to print his name on the stub of a raffle ticket he had bought from a pushy high school girl who just wouldn't take "no" for an answer, and rarely gave it either, if Eliza didn't miss her guess. In a kitchen drawer she found a pencil, which she sharpened with a paring knife. She sat at her table and began to write, but she hated the way the pencil lead looked on the nice stationery her sister had sent her for Christmas, so she went next door to Mrs. Mitchell, who had to repair typewriters in her spare time to make ends meet, because Mr. Mitchell had not given much thought to death when he was alive, and had left her ill-provided-for when he died, though God knows he had sent enough money to that brother of his. Mrs. Mitchell was happy to lend her a typewriter after Eliza had given satisfactory answers to a few probing questions.

Eliza wasn't the only person to answer Mr. Beaker's ad, but she was the first. She signed her letter "John Simpson," approximating the name of Dan Hanson, the only unattached salesman at Hackett & Belder, a fellow who cut a dashing figure in his fedora and checked jacket and set Eliza's heart aflutter whenever he walked past her desk.

ON THE MORNING that Mr. Beaker found Eliza's letter in his post office box, snow still covered Gumma and Guppa's lawn.

I was sitting in a high chair in the kitchen, gumming a piece of toast, when Mr. Beaker let himself in through the back door, ending the conversation my mother and Gumma were having about the way I ate my toast.

"You see," my mother was saying, "he doesn't like the dry part of the toast much—I think because it hurts his pink little gums and the roof of his little mouth. But he doesn't like the slobbered part much either—I think because it's revolting. So what he does is turn the toast as he eats it. See that? Dudley says that—" My mother chewed on her lower lip a moment while she tried to remember just what it was that Mr. Beaker had said about the way I ate my toast. While she was ruminating, Mr. Beaker burst into the room.

"Dudley!" exclaimed my mother, breaking out in a smile. "I was just talking about you and what you said about the way Peter eats his toast. How does that go again?"

Mr. Beaker was holding an envelope in front of him, at arm's length, dangling it between two fingers as a boy might dangle a small fish, a killifish or mummichog, say, that he had caught with an old hook and a piece of bacon, sitting on the bulkhead somewhere along the estuarial stretch of the Bolotomy River. He was wearing the same grin that he had worn when he had stood at the end of the driveway with a chocolate cake behind his back.

"It's something about nibbling at the elusive, ever-receding twilight line of this moment, ahead of which lies an abrasive future, and behind which we leave a messy past, isn't it?" my mother asked.

"Yes, yes, something like that," Mr. Beaker answered impatiently. He waggled the envelope and cleared his throat. Gumma poured him a cup of coffee.

"Why, Dudley," said my mother, her mouth falling open and her eyebrows rising, "why aren't you at work? Are you playing hooky?"

"Ladies," Mr. Beaker said, flapping the envelope with great vigor, "I have caught one. I have here a letter written by a shy insurance salesman in response to Mary Strong's advertisement. My new career is launched, and so is—" He pulled the letter from the envelope, unfolded it, and read the signature. "—John Simpson's. He doesn't know it yet, but he is going to become the first of Mary Strong's epistolary sugar daddies. I have quit my job—"

Gumma's face fell. "You quit your job?" she asked.

"Yes, indeed." He adopted a conspiratorial tone and put his arm around Gumma's shoulders. "To tell the truth, I never liked that job. Every morning I would sit at my desk and ask myself, 'Dudley, is writing advertisements for clams suitable work for an educated man, a man with imagination and taste, a man who can be struck dumb by a sunrise, transfixed by a hawthorn abloom in the spring, choked up by Venus gleaming beside the moon on a winter night?'"

I tried holding my toast by two fingers, as Mr. Beaker had held his letter, and flapping it with great vigor, but it got away from me and fell to the floor. Mr. Beaker picked it up and put it on my tray. I looked at it. Some cat hairs and a little fluff ball were stuck to it. I tried to push it disdainfully just to one side of the tray, but in those days there wasn't much subtlety in my vocabulary of gestures; the toast flew off the tray and fell to the floor again.

Mr. Beaker picked the toast up and threw it into the trash. "Do not play with your food , Peter," he said.

"I've always thought your ads were wonderful," my mother said. She was dunking one end of half a slice of toast into her coffee; glistening discs of melted butter drifted and merged on the surface. She stared at a spot about midway between her and me, where her memory projected a

Clamshells --
the answer to family boredom!

Say, Mom, your family's counting on you! They're counting on you to come up with something clever to do in the evenings, something that will make them forget, for a few happy hours, the monotony of work and the tedium of school. Before you drag out that old anagrams game, better stop a moment and think! Is the *same old thing* going to pull them up out of the dumps again this evening? Or will this be the night that Dad turns to *drink,* and Junior and Sis start doing *nasty things* to each other in the closet? Bring a little novelty into their lives—get them making *gewgaws, whatnots, knickknacks,* and *bric-a-brac* from empty clamshells. They'll *love* it! And they'll love *you* for thinking of it!

The Babbington Clam Council

 Free Book! 101 Uses for Empty Clamshells! Yours for the asking! Write Babbington Clam Council, Babbington, New York.

retrospective show of Mr. Beaker's advertisements for the Babbington Clam Council, each of which my mother had placed in an album that my father had given her, intending that she would use it for photographs of me. "They're real clever," she pronounced, the show complete.

"Really," offered Mr. Beaker.

"Oh, yes, Dudley. I wouldn't lie to you," asserted my mother. "If I thought they weren't any good, I'd tell you. That's the way I am. I just have to say what I think, even when I shouldn't."

"She's always been that way," said Gumma. She laughed a little and settled into her chair. She dunked her toast, and a reminiscent glaze formed over her eyes. "I'll never forget the time when Billy Whozit's father—oh, what was his name, Ella, that Billy What's-his-name?"

"Not the one we called Billy Lardbottom, the fat boy whose father was a butcher?"

"No, no, no. I mean that Billy Whatchamacallit. I think his father was a handyman or a painter. He was very handsome, I remember—the father, I mean. Well, anyway, one day this Billy Somebody-or-other's father was talking about something—what was it?—he always talked as if he knew everything—and Ella suddenly said something like—"

"I'll have to hear it another time," said Mr. Beaker. He gave Gumma a kiss on her forehead. "I have a great deal to do." He gave my mother a kiss just to the side of her mouth.

When Mr. Beaker got home, he dashed to the room that he had outfitted for work, a room on the second floor, facing my grandparents' house, directly across from the room I shared with my mother and father, where I slept in the crib my mother once used.

He read and reread John Simpson's letter, until he could begin to hear John Simpson reading it to himself to see how it would sound to the lovely unfortunate. He wrote draft after draft, trying again and again to strike just the right note in his reply. He relished this work as he never had any other, and he labored at it long and hard, working on into the night, until he began to feel the distance between him and John Simpson shrink, and began to develop the trait that would make him so successful in this line of work: an uncanny knack for echoing, in Mary Strong's replies to her many correspondents, the tone, style, and yearnings of each of the men who wrote to her. The light from his desk lamp threw shadows of the branches of a young oak across my crib, across my parents' bed, and onto the opposite wall. Later, Mr. Beaker would become quite facile—"a virtuoso of the heartstrings, especially adept at pizzicato," he liked to say—but his correspondence with Eliza Foote was difficult from start to finish.

Dear Miss Strong,

   I can't begin to tell you how much your ad in the
Hargrove Daily News moved me. I would like very much
to correspond to you, for I understand your needs as I,
too, have needs that are, I'm sure, quite similar. Let
me tell you something about myself. Although I am
considered quite handsome and am in the peak of health
and quite generously endowed and very virile, I find
that I am shy with women because I think that I'm not
what they are looking for, since I am a good and decent
sort, and such men are not in demand so much as the
other sort is, the fast and brassy sort, as I'm sure
you know, from bitter experience no doubt. But you see
it all works out for the best, because here is a lonely
guy who is shy who wants to cheer you up.
   In your ad you said "lovely young woman." Or did you
write "lonely" and the Daily News made a mistake (as
they so often do, not only in their spelling but in
their editorial positions) and printed "lovely"? Or
maybe you are both, because a lovely woman can be
lonely through no fault of her own, I know. I can
imagine what you look like. I mean that I know what a
lovely lonely woman looks like, for example the woman
who waits for the bus to Babbington each morning on the
bench in front of Louise's Coffee Shop. On cold mornings she wears a blue cloth coat that is frayed at the
cuffs and hides what I am sure is a breathtaking figure. In her eyes I can see certain yearnings that
could easily be misunderstood by the wrong sort of man,
as I'm sure I could see in your eyes too if I were with
you and could look into them. On many mornings I have
thought of talking to her, I mean saying something more
than just "Good morning," which of course I say just
out of politeness because that's the way I am, even if
only to say "Chin up," but I have thought that I would
sound like a man of the other sort who lounges on a
street corner all day, when in fact I am a hard worker
with a good job that I for one think is important to
do, selling insurance. But it is sad work, because a
man who sells insurance is always thinking about death.
And so I say to you, "Chin up. Now you have a friend

to correspond to." Please write to me soon and tell me
something about your circumstances and also your youth
and loveliness.

Your new friend,

John Simpson

Assistant District Manager

Dear Mr. John Simpson,

   Oh, what a beautiful morning it is! Though the sky
is gray, and the wind whistles through the gaps around
the door of the little hovel in which my unfortunate
circumstances force me to live, for me the sun is
shining and I'm sitting in a modest but comfortable
house, which is all I would ever want, since I don't
need a castle or any of the trappings of wealth to make
me happy.
   The sun shines for me because I'm holding your
letter, which arrived this morning, and I knew even
from the sound of the letter falling to the floor when
the mailman pushed it through the slot that it was
going to be a sunny day, and so I slipped out of the
tub and went at once to pick it up, with only a small
towel around me, which barely hid the gifts that nature
has bestowed on me so generously that I blush to think
of my reflection in the mirror on my closet door when I
stand and look at myself in the candlelight for a while
before I slip into bed.
   I lay in the tub for, I'm ashamed to admit, nearly an
hour, reading and rereading your letter, John, and
whispering your name, John, John, while I ran my sponge
over myself in a transport of bliss. For me, your
letter is the beginning of a new life. We will, I
know, be the best and most constant of friends. I feel
that we already are. You have been here with me, in
your wonderful letter, for only a morning, and already
I feel that I can tell you so much that I've never told
another soul, including a little, just a little, of the
painful story of lust and shame and betrayal that has
made me a recluse, unwilling to show myself to the
world, though not because of any disfigurement or lack
of beauty, for it would be false modesty for me to say
that I am not what the Daily News accidentally said I
am, although who knows, maybe some Higher Power made
them make that mistake, to say what I could not have
said myself, that I am, yes, lovely. There! I've said
it, and I'm glad I've said it to you, though there are
times when I wish I were plain, because that very
loveliness that should be a joy to me is a burden that

you who are not a woman cannot know, though I think you
can understand it, from what you rightly said about
that <u>other sort</u>.

You'll think I'm odd, but when I began dressing I put
your letter under my pillow for modesty's sake, but
then while I was looking in my closet for something
pretty to wear on this very special day and choking
back the tears because nothing there was suitable, I
said to myself, "Oh, this is silly. I don't have to be
ashamed in front of John!" and so I propped your letter
up on my dresser, right in plain sight. Well, I never
did find anything suitable to wear for you. Some of my
things are torn, torn by brutish, forceful hands, John,
the hands of a forceful brute, hands that I still feel
sometimes in terrible dreams, grabbing and tearing at
my clothes, pawing me, grasping forcefully and brut-
ishly at my--

Not yet, not yet. In time I will be able to write
everything for you, everything, everything, and you
will lift some of the shame from me, somehow cleanse me
of the oils left by his fingers when he touched me,
maybe by using cotton balls and some witch hazel, but
not yet, not yet. If only I could afford to buy something very special to wear when I read your letters,
something clean, something that isn't stained by the
past, something lovely like some silk underwear, which
I could probably get for about twenty-five dollars.

Oh, John, I've exhausted myself. There's high color
in my cheeks, from the joy of having you and the shame
of the things I can't yet tell you. Write to me, write
to me.

Your grateful friend,

Mary Strong

My Dear Mary Strong,

    Please do not be offended by the bills that flutter
to the floor when you unfold this letter, possibly
grazing your thigh or some other part of one of your
lovely legs if you are in the state you were in when
you opened my first letter, as I like to think you may
be, or maybe settling on the plump big toe of one of
your lovely small feet, if it does not offend you to
have me say that, because even a nice guy like me likes
to think about a pretty girl. I suppose you don't even
remember that you let slip in your letter that you had
nothing unsullied to wear when you read my letter, but
you did, and my heart went out to you, and so I'm
sending this trifle. I wish it were enough to allow
you to dress yourself from head to toe, but since it is
not please allow me to counsel you to spend it on goods
of the first quality that will last and not to try to
stretch it too thin and buy things that will not stand
up under rough use. You mentioned silk underwear, but
that seems like an extravagance to me, and perhaps a
simple dress would be better, although I can understand
that silk underwear would feel smooth and soft and
fresh against your skin, and would lift your spirits,
so maybe you should get that after all, but as a woman
I'm sure you understand these things much better than I
do, who am just a hard-working fellow who does not have
much experience with women's underwear, if you know
what I mean and you aren't offended by my saying so.
    May I be bold and say that I feel more than just the
feelings for you that any decent person would feel for
an unfortunate young woman like yourself? When you
hinted that some brute had been rough with you, my
hands shook when I read what you hinted. "If I had him
here now!" I shouted to my empty room, and when Mrs.
Mitchell next door whose story is a long and not very
happy one, believe me, knocked on the wall, it brought
me to my senses and I realized that beating and kicking
him and possibly hitting him on the head with a whiskey
bottle that I had thought of wasn't going to change
anything, and I ran from my room into the night where
cold rain was falling and I wasn't even wearing a hat,

and I walked along full of raging emotions as I walked,
snarling at big lewd men, quite rough-looking fellows,
and smiling with my throat choked up at gentle women
like yourself. I walked all night, and when the sun
came up I still hadn't calmed myself, and somehow I
found myself on the corner where Louise's Coffee shop
is, where I always get the bus to go to work, because I
suppose our feet have a mind of their own. Sitting on
the bench was the unfortunate woman in the cloth coat I
wrote you about, and I admit that tears came to my eyes
when I saw her. I walked right up to her and said,
"Chin up--nobody lives forever," which was the first
thing that came to my mind because I guess I was thinking that I should really be getting to work, which is
selling insurance, you remember, and that's one of our
mottoes in the office, not the "chin up" part, just the
other part. When she looked at me I could see in her
eyes something sad or frightened, and I knew that I'd
been right about how she was like you. I pulled a few
bills from my wallet and pressed them into her hand.
"Buy yourself some silk underwear," I said, "something
clean and fresh." I walked off and didn't turn back,
and I felt good and excited about what I had done to
bring a little joy into this vale of tears.

    Please let me know how the underwear fits if that is
what you decide to buy.

                    With deep affection,

                    Jack Simpson

Dear Jack Simpson,

   I'm blushing as I write this because I'm already
thinking of what I'm going to say. I'm sitting on the
only comfortable chair I have, and it's a wing chair
upholstered in pink, but it's worn at the arms and not
as clean as it might be, because I got it for a good
price at an auction long ago, when I used to go to
such things. It's just big enough for me to curl up
in, so I'm curled up in it now and writing this letter.
I'm wearing your gifts and that's all, even if I am
a little chilly. (Do you know what I mean?) When I
got home from the store I was in quite a state. I'm
sure that anyone who saw me hurrying along the sidewalk
as fast as my shapely legs could carry me must have
known that I had a secret. As soon as I was safely
locked inside, I threw off all my old things and slowly
pulled on my new you-know-whats, the thin, soft silk
touching my skin so lightly. I let myself fall back
onto the bed, and I--
   Oh, John, John. I hope you won't think I'm
criticizing you, but I feel so close to you right now,
after what happened, and so I think I can say anything
and you will understand. And what I have to say, and
please don't take this the wrong way, is this--Do you
think you did the right thing, talking to that woman
that way? I'm sure I'm wrong, and she is probably a
very nice woman who needs love and companionship just
as much as I do, but I wonder what she can have in her
mind if she sits on a bench like that where men can see
her with just a coat to cover herself, which I'm sure
she leaves open on warm days, which we are starting to
have some of now, crossing her legs, too, I suppose.
What can I say about a woman who would accept money
from a man on the street? Be careful, John, be
careful.
   Oh, dear. My leg has fallen asleep, and now I've got
a cramp. I guess it's from being curled up in this
chair too long. I should get a sofa, and then I could
stretch out when I write to you, and I'd be able to
write longer and more interesting letters. Well, dream
on, dream on. Of course, my landlady did say that she

had an old sofa that she would be willing to sell at a
good price, maybe twelve-fifty, and I'm sure that I
could put a new cover on it, and maybe at the same time
I could put a new cover on the chair, to match. Well,
someday, when I have about thirty-two dollars and
eighty cents. Or maybe if I sit on a bench in the
rain, a man will run up to me out of nowhere dragging a
sofa and carrying some fabric.

     Yours faithfully,

Mary Strong

Mary, dear Mary,

   You musn't think for a moment that the woman I told
you about who waits for the bus, and whose name by the
way turns out to be Eliza, which is a pretty name, I
think, although many people think it sounds funny
because it buzzes a little toward the end, is somehow
bad or that I meant to hurt you by telling you about
her. I just wanted to show you that a person like me,
who is handsome and good and quite virile, notices a
woman even if let's say she is just a typist waiting
for a bus in the rain, and has probably thought of
running up to her many times to say something to her
but may just be too shy, or not good at making conversation unless it is about insurance. So you see, this
is just one of my ways of saying, "Chin up."
   But I didn't quite tell you the whole truth, and so I
will tell you now because I don't want any untruthful-
ness to come between us and poison the waters as so
often happens between a man and a woman, as I have seen
even in my own family, but that is another story. The
truth is that Eliza works in the same office where I
work, and the bus she waits for is the same bus that I
wait for and ride to work, which is often quite a long
ride because of the heavy traffic, so that a person
usually arrives at work feeling a little queasy from
spending a long time in an overheated bus that smells
of a mixture of unpleasant things and would like to
take a shower right away if there were a shower in the
office, which there is not.
   She certainly does have a breathtaking figure, but I
know she is a good woman because of her modest demeanor, such as the way she looks down at her hands
that she keeps modestly clasped in her lap when she
smiles at me a little bit if I nod at her to say "Good
morning," or "Good evening," depending on whether we
are riding to work or home from work at the end of the
day. Sometimes I worry that she may think I am a
conceited sort of fellow who does a lot of carousing
and can't be bothered paying attention to the needs of
a good woman because of the way that I just nod in the
morning or the evening and don't make any conversation,

although I can't count the number of times I have
thought of saying something to her and am just too shy
and I guess not good at making conversation unless it
is about insurance, which is the only thing we ever
talk about at the office, for example, "Eliza, would
you type up this letter to Mr. Flypaper, who hasn't
paid the premiums on his full-coverage policy with
endowment at age sixty-five for three months?" (There
isn't really anyone called Mr. Flypaper, at least I
don't think there is. I just made that up to make you
laugh, although some of the names of people who take
out insurance are very funny in real life, like Binker
or Foote or Sandstone, which makes me giggle every time
I think of it, because it's a kind of rock.)

Besides, the things I told you about in my last
letter didn't really happen. I was just thinking about
how they might happen, and so I wrote them down.

Here is thirty-two dollars and eighty cents, and I
hope the eighty cents didn't fall out of the envelope
and hurt your cute foote. Please use the money to get
the sofa that your landlady wants to sell, but act as
if you think that it isn't a very good sofa and that it
will take a lot of work and extra money to make it
something that you would want to sit on, because you
can always get something like that for a cheaper price
if you pretend that you don't really want it, and then
you will have a little more to spend on the fabric, and
it is always a good idea to buy the best when it comes
to cloth, so that it will wear well under hard use.

With deepest affection,

Jack

Dear Jack,

   I have started this letter so many times and thrown
away the starts that didn't work out after crumpling
them up into tight little balls that I finally decided
to just start writing and keep on writing no matter how
it sounded or how it came out, so I hope that nothing I
say will offend you, because I am just going to keep
right on writing and say what is in my heart.
   I am so confused after reading your last letter over
and over. Sometimes I think that you want to have two
women who are your very good friends, and sometimes I
think that you are only making up this Eliza so that I
won't think that you're not a man of the world, and
sometimes I think that you just want me to be your
little pen pal who will listen to your exploits with a
woman who is not just someone who writes letters to you
and who is lying on a second-hand sofa reading a piece
of paper but is there <u>in the flesh</u>, if you know what I
mean.
   If it is the first that you want, to have two women
whose hearts beat faster when they say your name, then
that is okay with me because I can understand that a
man like you with a large heart can have many friends,
and I am willing to go along with what you want. But
maybe that is not what you want? If it is the second,
that you are only making up this Eliza so that I will
know that you can make a woman's heart beat faster,
then you can be sure that I understand, but you must
know that you don't have to pretend with me, because my
heart beats faster every time one of your letters
arrives, but if you do want to pretend, why don't you
pretend about me instead of Eliza, which I think is a
pretty name, too, by the way, and maybe when you pretend about <u>being with me</u>, you would like to call me
Eliza, which I wouldn't mind if that is what you want.
But then again, maybe that is not what you want either.
If you want the third thing, to write to me about
certain exploits that you like to write about, I have
to make a confession to you that my heart beats faster
and a little tingle runs all through me when you write
about Eliza and I think of you close to her if you are

in the office and talking to her about a letter or a
policy and maybe you accidentally brush against her
when you are looking over her shoulder at what she has
typed, and it could be that her blouse is not fully
buttoned, who knows? So if you want me to listen to
what happens with Eliza, it is all right with me, Jack.

Meanwhile, something has happened to the heat here in
my tiny hovel, which is so much prettier now with the
sofa that I can never thank you enough for, and I wish
you were here so that I could try with all my might to
thank you enough for it. I should have spent the money
you sent me on the oil bills that I haven't been able
to pay because of my unfortunate circumstances, but I
was just like a little girl and got the sofa which was
more like getting a present for my birthday, which is
next week. Ever since I was a little girl I have had a
tradition of spending my whole birthday in my birthday
suit, and I wish I could do it this year and write you
a long letter all about it, but I guess I won't be able
to keep this tradition alive after they shut the heat
off because of the overdue bills, which come to around
twenty-one dollars, and even though we are having some
warm days, there is a chill here that won't go away.

Oh, well. I've said what was in my heart, and now I
will just send this letter off, and whatever you think
is what you will think. But before I seal this letter
I will kiss it once and let it rest awhile where I
cannot say and then I will heat up some soup, which
will help me feel warm, and then crawl into my bed.

                   With love,

                   Mary

Dear Mary,

I must tell you what has happened, and you must
listen to me and be happy for me, because I have no one
else to tell. Eliza spoke to me, and not about insurance. Wasn't I surprised and pleased that she somehow
knew that I had not been speaking to her much on the
bus that we both happen to ride to work or at the end
of the day home from work just because I was too modest
and shy even though I don't give that appearance if you
look at me because I wear my hat at a jaunty angle and
look like someone who has a good line with the ladies,
even though I am not.
Well, here's how it happened. When I saw Eliza at
the bus stop, I touched the brim of my hat and said,
"Good morning," which is my custom to say out of politeness and because I'm too nervous when I see her to
say much else. And so she said "Good morning" back,
and though I didn't show it, my heart sank because I
thought I knew that today would be like all the others
and I wouldn't say anything more to her, and then we
got onto the bus. There we were on the bus and having
to stand up holding on when a car suddenly shot out of
a side street in front of the bus, and the driver
shouted something that I pretended not to understand.
When the driver slammed on the brakes, all of us on the
bus were thrown this way and that, and as luck would
have it Eliza was thrown against my chest, which is
hard and broad from the exercises I do every morning
and the swimming I love to do in the summer at the
beach, where I laugh a lot and wear a big grin and a
good tan and have to brush my hair back often because
it falls down over my forehead when the wind blows it,
just like a schoolboy who might be the captain of the
football team. Without thinking of what I was doing, I
threw my strong arm around her waist to stop her from
falling, and she said, "Oh, I'm sorry," and she looked
up at me, blushing, and then quickly looked down, out
of her modesty, which is one of the qualities that I
think is best. Do you know how people do crazy things
if they are a little shaken up when a bus driver slams
on the brakes and a young woman that they have wanted

to talk to for a long time with quite a nice figure is
thrown against them--they don't know what they are
doing and feel just like a schoolboy? Well, that is
just what happened to me. Instead of letting her go,
my arm had a mind of its own and held her more tightly,
and I blurted out, "Why I'm not sorry at all, Miss
Foote," bending down to blurt it out softly right into
her ear, so at least no one else heard it.

Oh, why did I say such a thing? Do you think she
will take it in the wrong way? Later, I was thinking
about it, and I thought that maybe she would be thinking about it too, and if she was, she might be wondering why a guy like me would say something like that,
which is an awful lot like what the wrong sort of guy
would say. I don't want her to get the wrong idea,
because then everything would be spoiled after I finally said something to her. I think she will figure
out that I was just in a muddle and blurted out something that I might have heard someone else say, what do
you think?

Please write and let me know what you think, but try
to slow down when you write and be calm, because I was
a little confused by your last letter. Don't take this
in the wrong way, but I know that some people find that
if they have a little glass of bourbon while they write
a letter it helps them calm down.

Here's some money. For goodness sake, pay your oil
bills! You can catch pneumonia if you run around in a
cold apartment without any clothes on, as I have
learned from bitter experience.

                    Your dear friend,

                    Jack

Dear Jack,

   How very lucky Miss Foote was that that reckless
driver pulled out in front of the bus that you ride to
and from work. I guess some people have all the luck
and have a good job and are not forced by shame that
isn't really any of their fault to live alone in
wretched circumstances and have a nice warm coat to
wear when they are flirting with strangers while they
sit with their legs crossed on street corners. And
then fate smiles on them again and sends an impetuous
lad careening out of a side street very conveniently at
just the right moment so that they are thrown into the
arms of a man like you when they just happen very
conveniently to be standing side by side.
   Oh, dear foolish Jack! Open your eyes! Can all this
have been just coincidence? Think about it. Is the
bus that you ride <u>always</u> so crowded that you and Little
Miss Foote have to stand side by side, so close that
she can <u>accidentally</u> brush her hip or perhaps her thigh
or who knows what against your leg or perhaps who knows
what? Has a car ever <u>just happened</u> to pull out in
front of the bus before? Has the bus driver ever <u>had</u>
to slam on his brakes at just the right moment so that
the Very Fortunate Miss Foote is forced to throw herself against your manly chest before? "Ha!" I say, as
I said when I read your letter.
   You can be sure, Jack, that if a woman has enough
money to spend (and God only knows where or how she
earns this money, because certainly she does not earn
that much on a typist's salary, but there are ways for
a woman to make money in her spare time), she can find
plenty of people who will crowd onto a bus for a price,
and a boy who can borrow his father's car will do
anything to earn a dollar, (or perhaps a woman who is
desperate can find an easier way to pay him, since
young boys are always breathing heavily and almost
drooling whenever I happen to see any of them walking
by if I pull back the curtain to see what is going on
in the world). Everybody knows that a bus driver who
is probably of foreign extraction and has a huge family
would drive his bus from here to California if you

pressed a little folding money into his hand! Oh,
Jack, please listen to someone who knows a bit about
the world through bitter experience, and who loves you
very much although we have not known each other that
long. Do not do anything that you will regret.

Oh, how I wish I could tell you these things in
person and throw myself against you to demonstrate how
such a thing can be made to look like an accident.

Beware, Jack, beware. Think of your future at the
insurance office and how you probably have a good shot
at becoming District Manager but how all that would be
tossed away by a breath of scandal if you commit an
indiscretion for a moment's pleasure.

                    Yours in hope and fear and tears,

                              Mary

P. S.

I almost forgot to ask you. Do you think you could
send me twenty dollars? If you could, then I could
help out an old widow who lives just down the street
and is an artist. I have been posing for her for some
very beautiful drawings that she does in pen and ink,
and if you would send twenty dollars, I would buy some
of those drawings from her and send them to you, and
then you would be able to see your faithful friend
wearing the gifts that you bought her and even
stretched out on her second-hand sofa in a very artistic pose wearing only the gifts that nature has bestowed upon her so generously.

                              Mary

My Dear Mary,

   I hardly know what to say to you. Your last letter
shocked me and disappointed me and made me wonder and
also worry. I wonder if being alone and always wrapped
up just in your own thoughts and unfortunate circumstances hasn't made you see things in a way that is a
little bit out of whack.
   First, you are completely, utterly, terribly wrong
about Eliza. She is a good and modest woman, and if
she wants the affection of an honest and decent man,
what of it? Would you begrudge her a little happiness
just because you are miserable? Isn't that rather
selfish of you, if you really sit down and think about
it? What do you want her to do, just keep banging away
at the keys in the insurance office and reading the
newspaper and drinking alone in her room? Is that
fair? While some people are out dancing and eating in
restaurants?
   I will tell you the truth. I feel that I must. I
don't care whether it was by accident or by some plan
that we were thrown together on that bus. I'm glad it
happened, and I'm glad no matter why it happened. And
I'll tell you something more. If I saw her at the bus
stop tomorrow and she had her hair down instead of up
in the modest way she wears it and she struck up a
conversation with me on the bus and just happened to
brush against me a few times and then in the office
took off her coat and accidentally a button or two of
her blouse had come undone or perhaps she had forgotten
to button them in her hurry to get to work on time, so
what? So what? I wouldn't mind it a bit, not a bit,
and there is no telling what I would do. I might say,
"Eliza--I mean Miss Foote--would you come home with me
this evening to have dinner and meet my parents?" I
just might, because a good man has yearnings too, don't
you realize that? And not just yearnings, even desires
that are perfectly normal when you get right down to
it, and sometimes those yearnings and desires can be a
good thing if they loosen his tongue that is tied in a
knot by shyness. Maybe a woman has to do something.
   Maybe that is all I am waiting for, something, some

sign that might just be another accident or might be on
purpose, who knows?

Mary, dear Mary. I owe this all to you, for if I do
not do something then won't I end up like you, sitting
in my room and peering out the curtain at boys with
their reckless ways and smooth cheeks and nice smiles
and writing to strangers through the mail?

I am sending the twenty dollars that you asked for,
but I do not want you to send me those pictures that
the poor widow drew. Buy the pictures from that widow
and destroy them, by ripping them up into tiny pieces
or burning them in a wastebasket if it is made of metal
and will not start a dangerous fire, that is my advice
to you. You should not offer to send such pictures to
a man who corresponds to you, for what do you really
know about him? Maybe he is just saying things to you
that are not true, and is just giving you a good line
in his letters, and he would not look at those pictures
like something in a museum, how do you know?

Perhaps we should not go on this way, writing to each
other. Maybe you should stop hiding yourself away in a
little room at night and drinking bourbon by yourself
that leaves a sour taste and makes your head ache. Why
don't you do something? You have that nice underwear.
Why don't you put it on and maybe one of those old
things that got a little mussed up by somebody in that
unfortunate past that you sometimes mention, but who
knows maybe it is all in the way you look at it? Why
don't you go outside and walk in the sun? Why don't
you get a job?

                    Your friend,

                    Jack

Oh, Jack, my Jack,

You dear, sweet
~~Don't be a~~ blind fool, (if that's her real name) Can't you see that this Eliza
~~catty~~ toy
has only one thing in mind and that is to ~~get you in~~
with you for a little while and then drop you like a hot
~~her clutches and then never let go?~~ Please, please potato?
~~for the sake of all that we mean~~
promise me that you will stay away from her until you
Just give me a day or two,
receive my next letter. ~~Just give me time to pull my~~
for the sake of all that we already mean to each other.
~~thoughts together so that I can help you come to your~~
~~for the my own sake~~
~~senses.~~ Will you promise me that? Can't you just ~~keep~~
do without ignore (?)
~~your hands off~~ her until I have a chance to write you a
and wonderful
long letter about this? I know that you must have a
~~pent up~~ ~~festering~~ seething
lot of love ~~bottled-up~~ inside you that you want to let
will just any woman do?
out in the arms of some woman, but couldn't you just
hold out a little longer and maybe find some relief in
~~Swimming or daydreaming~~
~~self-abuse?~~ Pretend that I'm there. Wrap your arms
sweet,
around your pillow. Whisper passionate things in my
~~Run your tongue~~ You can. You must
ear. Hold out, my darling. I'm working on the best
letter ever.

Dear, dear Jack,

What good and wise advice you have given me! You
have ~~opened my eyes~~ *lifted me out of the darkness / in the sunshine* and shown me how to live. I will
do it! I will! Oh, but how can *How can I walk / among decent people without a* ~~I get a job without a~~
decent modest dress, and now that I spent the twenty
dollars you sent me buying ~~the~~ *those shameful* pictures, which made me
blush *with shame and embarrassment* when I saw them and thought that I was going to
send them to *so good and kind a person as* you even though I was as innocent as Eve
before she fell when I thought of sending them to you *and caused all that trouble*
and didn't think about *how my innocence, which is ** ~~what anyone else would think~~ I *not even one*
don't have any money to spend on a dress that isn't
anything elaborate but is *just* good enough to get a job.
So, look, Jack— Could you ~~send me~~ *get me started in my new life with* another twenty-five dollars, and then
I'll be able to get a job and you will have saved me,
because there's no telling what I might do to myself if
I can't get a job and follow your *good and wise* advice.

* *really just like the innocence
of a young girl, who's never
been penetrated by*

~~lusty~~

My ~~dearest~~ Jack,

~~strong~~
Jack, Honey,
~~Ahhhh, Jack,~~

    Are you sure you wouldn't like ^to have a peek at those pictures? ~~I'll~~

I don't want ~~to~~ brag, but I
bet that if you just took a look at one or two of them,

your eyes would pop and ^ Wow! What a knockout!
you'd say to yourself, "This is something I can't pass

up. I'm going to get the whole set." If you could
    about ~~ten~~ five   pay the widow and
just send me ~~a few~~ dollars, I'd be happy to send you a
          look at ^them in private &
couple of them and then you could ^be the judge. Let me

just describe one of them for you. ~~There~~ I am
lying languidly   the sun through the window
~~stretched out~~ on the sofa, ~~just as naked as the day I~~
caressing my honey-colored body   lies
~~was born.~~ One of my long, shapely legs ~~is~~ stretched
           attractively
the length of the sofa, and the other is bent ^at the

knee. I'm looking right at you, Jack, and my eyelids
~~with long lashes~~   wet, pink   ~~wet, pink~~
are drooping. ^ I'm running my tongue over my lips, as
        ~~wetly deeply with abandon~~
if I were about to kiss you. ~~My left~~ hand is resting
~~left/right~~   ~~left~~ right One   caressing
on my knee, and with my ~~right~~ hand I am ~~squeezing~~ my
~~right~~ ^left   ~~left/right~~ LEFT
~~left~~ breast. My ~~other~~ hand has strayed down to the
luxuriant soft
~~luxurious~~ light brown hair that ~~grows~~   hides ~~frames~~
        ~~sets off~~
        conceals

2

I WAS LYING IN MY CRIB picking at the fur on the back of my teddy
bear's head. The shadows of the branches of the oak tree outside the window began to sway along the wall of my room, and I began to rock with
them, slowly, then faster and faster, until they were hopping and jumping
about in a blur and my crib was shaking and creaking.

I pulled myself up and looked outside to see what was upsetting the
tree. I saw Mr. Beaker at his desk, not sitting at it, but squatting at it,
pounding on it with both fists and hopping up and down. His gooseneck
desk lamp leaped and bounced and shook from side to side in time with
his hopping and pounding. He began sweeping paper off the desk in a
fury. He seemed to have lost control of his gestures, to have become as
graceless and unpredictable as I. I giggled and clapped my hands and said
kitten, my favorite among the words I knew, a new one, one that I understood, from watching Gumma's cat's kittens hop and tumble about, as a
verb, meaning "hop and tumble about."

Mr. Beaker's flailing grew wilder and wilder: he swept letters from his
desk without regard to who had sent them, sweeping away those from
Mary's many doting and generous correspondents along with those from
the difficult Jack Simpson. While he was sweeping the papers, on one of
his sweeps to the left, he struck the desk lamp and hurt his finger. He
drew in his breath. He held it. His cheeks puffed out, and his face reddened. He pounced on the lamp, seized it with both hands, and hurled it
at the window.

The lamp went through the window and hung by its cord, swinging
against the side of the house, sending the shadows of the oak tree's
branches into a mad frenzy. Mr. Beaker leaned across his desk and
looked at what he had done. I think he smiled. The shadow of his nose
flipped from side to side as the lamp swung.

My mother burst into my room to see if I was all right, scaring the
bejesus out of me. I burst into tears and reached toward her.

"There, there, Peter, don't worry," she began. Then she caught sight
of Mr. Beaker, leaning out his window, watching his desk lamp swing.
"Oh, Dudley, poor Dudley, what's wrong?" she whispered. She scooped
me up and carried me into the living room.

Guppa had gotten his pistol out of his sock drawer. Gumma was wrestling with him at the front door, trying to keep him from making a fool of
himself. My father kept poking his head out the door, glancing left and
right, and pulling it back inside.

"It's Dudley," said my mother. "Something's awfully wrong."

"One of those men he writes to has broken into his house," wailed Gumma. "I knew this would happen. I always knew something like this would happen to me or somebody in my neighborhood someday."

"I can handle this," claimed Guppa.

"I'll go," said my father. He stepped back into the room. "Where's my coat? It's gotten chilly since the sun went down, and there's a pretty stiff breeze."

"You're not going without me," said my mother. She held me a little tighter and started out the door.

We moved slowly along the sidewalk, in a tight group, watching Mr. Beaker's windows. I was leading, and my mother was right behind, carrying me. The lamp was still swinging, but slowly, and the shadows were settling down. When we reached the corner of Mr. Beaker's lot, his front door opened, spilling light onto the front walk. The little group shrank back into the shadows. Mr. Beaker stepped into the doorway and stood there, taking deep breaths. A shudder ran through us all.

"Is he bleeding?" asked Guppa. Then Mr. Beaker flung the screen door open so hard that it banged against the side of the house, spat a third of the way down the walk, turned away and let the screen door slam shut.

"Poor Dudley, something's awfully wrong," repeated my mother. She marched herself, and me, right up to the door, and she called through the screen.

"Dudley. Dudley. Are you all right?"

There was no sound for a minute. Then we heard a toilet flush. Mr. Beaker came to the door zipping his fly; his shirt wasn't well tucked into his pants, and his hair was a sight.

"Ella," he said. "Ella." He shook himself and began arranging his hair.

"Do you have a woman in here, Dudley?" my mother asked. She hoisted me up and held me tighter still.

"What?" Mr. Beaker pushed at his shirt, stuffing it into his trousers. "A woman?" He smiled and raised an eyebrow, the left, I think. "What makes you ask?" He chucked me under the chin, brushing the back of his hand along my mother's cheek on the way.

"We're coming in!" shouted Guppa. Mr. Beaker pulled his hand away and took a step back. My mother and I turned toward the front walk. Gumma, Guppa, and my father were standing on the steps, in the light, bobbing this way and that to see if anyone was hiding behind Mr. Beaker.

"What's going on?" asked Mr. Beaker. "Oh," he said, reaching for the door, "the noise. Sorry. I don't know what came over me. I guess I've been working too hard, I —" He flung himself against the door jamb, leaning his forehead on his forearm. He began shaking his head. "He's getting away from me. I don't know what to do. I've tried, God knows I've tried, but I just can't do anything with him. I don't know what he wants anymore."

"Who? Where is he?" demanded Guppa, waving the pistol and poking his head into the room.

"Jack Simpson," moaned Mr. Beaker. "My first, my very first, and now I'm going to lose him, I just know I'm going to lose him."

"You mean there's nobody here?" asked my father.

"Of course there's nobody here," said my mother. She looked around, and then she stepped back and looked down the hall, toward the bedrooms. "There's nobody here, is there, Dudley?"

"No."

"There's nobody here," called Guppa, turning toward Gumma, who was still on the steps. "Dudley is just having some trouble with that Jack Simpson. One of those lonely men he writes letters to."

"I know," said Gumma. "He was the first one. I remember that day when Dudley came into the kitchen, dangling Mr. Simpson's letter like a little fish —"

"Dudley," my father said, smiling and knocking Mr. Beaker on the shoulder with his fist, "you know what you need? You need a drink."

3

NOW DON'T TRY TO SELL anyone a car, Herb," said Gumma. The group was making its way across the clamshell parking lot behind Whitey's Tavern. "The last time Herb and I were here," she said, turning toward Mr. Beaker, who might possibly not have heard the story, "Herb tried to sell Whitey a car, and he—"

"It wasn't the last time, Lorna," Guppa corrected her. "It was a long time ago. Everybody but you has forgotten it, it was so long ago."

"Well, it couldn't have been that long ago, because I remember it as if it happened yesterday," asserted Gumma.

"It was before Whitey bought that jukebox," said Guppa, the hint of a whine in his voice. "That's why he didn't buy the car, because he wanted to buy that jukebox and liven the place up, remember? What he said to me was 'What am I going to do, Herb, park my Studebaker in the barroom? I've got to think of the business. Now look at this—' and he brought out that brochure about the jukebox. I remember it perfectly."

"Wait till you see this jukebox," my mother said to Dudley, starry-eyed. "It's real clever. It has these two peacocks on the front—"

"Oh, of course," said Mr. Beaker. This struck me at once as a nasty remark, a dismissal, and I held it against Mr. Beaker for a long time, for years in fact. To his credit, he regretted it immediately, and told my mother so.

"I'm sorry, Ella," he said. "I didn't mean to belittle your pleasure in the jukebox that way, or rather, I did mean to belittle it that way, but I regret it very much. You'll have to make allowances for my troubled state of mind. I'm afraid I gave in to the childish and self-centered idea that the gloom that envelops me should envelop you too, and that you should not be able to escape it by thinking of a jukebox, since I couldn't—"

"It's all right, Dudley," said my mother, touching him quickly on the arm. "I know you're worried and upset, and I think you've been doing a little drinking."

Mr. Beaker smiled indulgently at my mother. "Thank you, Ella," he said, "but the explanation for what I said isn't that simple. Let me try to explain it again. Behind my remark there lurked the ignoble desire to make my companions share my suffering and unhappiness, don't you see?" He threw one arm across my father's shoulders and the other across my mother's, knocking me on the ear as he did so. "The shameful desire to fill the hearts of one's good friends with the same anguish and misery that fills one's own, so that when they say, 'We know how you feel,' it will be the honest truth. That," he pronounced, "is what we mean by *commiserating*." I began to whimper and rub my ear, but no one noticed.

"I don't know," said my mother. "I guess so. But anyway you'll like this jukebox, Dudley. There are lights that shine through the peacocks, and they change colors—"

"Yes, I'm sure I'll enjoy it," said Mr. Beaker. For a moment it seemed that he would say nothing more, and my mother seemed relieved. Then, almost reluctantly, he asked, "Do you know how that effect is achieved?"

"No," said my mother, dreamily. "It's real mysterious."

"Not really," said Mr. Beaker, driven by a force that he could not control. "Two disks of glass, or perhaps acetate, I'm not certain about that, are scribed with tiny parallel lines. These disks spin behind the peacocks and in front of ordinary light bulbs. Because of the lines scribed in them, the disks act as prisms, analyzing the white light from the bulbs into the spectrum of colors. As they spin, of course, they produce combinations of light in what seems to be an unpredictable pattern, an endless variety of moving colored lights, but is actually, I would think, repetitious, a cycle with a long period, so long that the viewer, who is probably distracted now and then by other things in the barroom, doesn't notice the pattern."

"It's real mysterious," said my mother, with little conviction, straightening my collar.

"Have you been here before, Dudley?" asked my father.

"Never," said Mr. Beaker, surprised by the question. After a moment, when he realized why my father had asked, he added, "There are other jukeboxes like this one, Bert."

My father narrowed his eyes. "I know," he said. "I just wondered if you had ever been here."

"Anyway, it wasn't Whitey, Lorna," Guppa corrected her, raising his voice. "It was his boy, Chester."

"He means Porky," said my mother. She giggled.

"Well, it doesn't much matter which one really," said Gumma. "But what happened was that Whitey decided that he had heard all he ever wanted to hear about Studebakers, so he—"

"Are you going to enter this establishment, Lorna?" asked Guppa, holding the door open and bowing.

"Oh, stop interrupting, Herb. You just don't want me to tell Dudley how Whitey started—"

"Whoa!" called Whitey from behind the bar. "Hide your money, folks, here comes Herb Studebaker!"

"—calling you Herb Studebaker. Isn't he a sketch?"

Guppa put on a smile and strode into Whitey's, pounding friends on the back, friends who slapped their hands over their wallets in mock terror.

"Now don't feel uncomfortable just because everyone's looking at you, Dudley," said my mother. "It's just that they don't know you and they don't see that many people in here that they don't know."

"And isn't that my problem?" asked Mr. Beaker. He sighed a long sigh, an invitation to commiseration. "I just don't know this Jack Simpson."

"It's not really the same thing," said my father.

"Oh?" asked Mr. Beaker. "Don't these people know you? When they see you walk through the door, don't they say to themselves. 'Ah, it's

Bert Leroy. I know what to expect from him. I don't have to worry.'"

"Oh, sure," said my father. "Ella and I come here pretty often."

"I would say regularly," said Whitey, grinning across the bar.

"You see," said Mr. Beaker, "that's my point —"

"Well, it depends," said my father, responding to Whitey. "I would say regularly on Sunday afternoons."

"And often on Friday nights," asserted Whitey.

"Oh, no," May Castle corrected him. "*Frequently* on Friday nights." She turned on her stool and crossed her legs. She smiled at my father and then at Mr. Beaker, waiting for an introduction.

"Well, yeah," said my father. He chuckled. "Frequently on Friday nights."

"*And* on Saturday nights," added my mother, inserting me between May and Mr. Beaker and setting me on the bar.

"Noooo, Ella," scoffed May, giving my mother a playful push. "You're not here frequently on Saturday nights. I'm *always* here on Saturday nights, and I frequently don't see you here. You're only here sometimes. Now *you*," she reached around my mother and patted Mr. Beaker on the shoulder, "you're *never* here. That is, you've never been here before. I'm May Castle."

"I," said Mr. Beaker, "am someone you know nothing about. I am a stranger, a mystery. I'm Dudley Beaker."

"Oh, you are?" May gave my mother a look.

"Are you going to buy me a beer?" my mother asked my father.

"I've heard your name, Dudley," said May. She looked at my mother again. "Frequently."

My father whispered in Mr. Beaker's ear: "Her husband disappeared about a year ago. No, it must be two years. As soon as people started noticing that he wasn't around, May started saying that he had passed away on a business trip, and she's been playing the merry widow ever since. You could do worse, Dudley."

Mr. Beaker turned toward my father with his eyes wide and his mouth open. "Listen, Bert," he said, "I came here to talk—"

May tugged on his sleeve from the other side. "Come here a minute, Dudley," she said. "Did you dress yourself, honey? Your mommy must be on vacation. You're a mess." She began straightening his tie and smoothing his hair. Mr. Beaker looked uneasily around the barroom. He couldn't find the door.

"So," said Whitey. "You people going to drink something, or do you just want to rent these stools?"

May pushed her glass toward Whitey, and Whitey began drawing beer for my parents.

"I'll have a Scotch," said Mr. Beaker. "With a little water."

My father raised his eyebrows.

May had improved Mr. Beaker's hair and tightened his tie. She smoothed his shirt and tucked it into his slacks a little better; then she gave his pants a hike and tugged at his lapels to straighten his jacket, tipping him toward her.

"You don't look happy, stranger," said May, brushing at Mr. Beaker's shoulders. "You look like a man with a problem."

"He is," said my father, smiling.

"Oh-oh," said Whitey. "What'd you do, buy a car from Herb?"

"Yes, but that has nothing to do with it. I'm quite satisfied with the car," said Mr. Beaker.

"Dudley's having trouble writing a letter," said my father, nodding and acting mysterious.

"Ho-ho," said Whitey. "That's something I stay far away from. Letters can get you into a lot of trouble. My father always told me, 'Don't write anything down.'" He called the words across the room, so that Porky, who was refilling bowls of pretzels, would hear them, and so that everyone else in the room would hear them too. It was an old joke, but it got the old laugh, which was all Whitey wanted.

Porky blushed. He was having so little success in getting his hands on the girls at Babbington High that he couldn't imagine what he might write down that could get him into trouble, but every time his father made the joke Porky blushed, and that convinced Whitey that his son was enjoying youth to a degree that he had not.

"I just don't understand this Simpson," complained Mr. Beaker, shaking his head, looking to either side of him to see who was listening. He swallowed the last of his Scotch. My father immediately signaled Whitey to bring him another, which Mr. Beaker began drinking without noticing that it was a new drink.

"You tell me about it," said May.

Mr. Beaker began fiddling with his pipe, poking and pounding at the tobacco with a complicated brass tool that my father suspected was a prop, something that Beaker used only when he had an audience. At home, my father knew, from standing on his toes and looking into Mr. Beaker's kitchen, he smoked mentholated cigarettes and lit them with ordinary paper matches.

My father passed his hand over his mouth, but his eyes were bright above it, and I could tell he was grinning.

"At first," said Mr. Beaker, leaning toward May and holding up his index finger, "I thought I knew what he was after. I figured that he wanted a little flattery, a little titillation."

Whitey raised both eyebrows, as my father had done earlier. I tried it myself.

"This is a family bar," he said. "You have to watch what you say here."

"I assure you," said Mr. Beaker, "that I do not intend to say anything that will upset the hardworking folk who gather here to drink away the memory of each working day."

"I wouldn't exactly say that," said Whitey. "I mean, most of the people you see here tonight only come in on the weekends. I grant you we get a different crowd during the week, but I don't know that I'd call them hardworking."

"I wonder whether Simpson goes to bars," Mr. Beaker wondered aloud.

"What's the name?" asked Whitey.

Mr. Beaker took from his pocket a brass lighter, a miniature reproduction of the sort of torch used in those days to solder copper pipe. At the back, above the little handle, was a lever that could be pumped to raise the pressure in the fuel container. From the top, a nozzle projected horizontally, terminating in a perforated sleeve, and just in front of this sleeve was a striking wheel that, when spun, produced a spark from a flint held just below the wheel in a cylindrical flint-holder. When a valve was opened, fuel was forced through the tiny nozzle under pressure, and the atomized fuel rushed through the sleeve, where it mixed with air drawn into the sleeve through the perforations. This air-and-fuel mixture was ignited by the spark and produced, with a miniature roar, a flame as long as Mr. Beaker's index finger, a flame that Mr. Beaker could count on to capture the attention of everyone nearby. He pumped the lighter several times, opened the valve, and spun the striker, producing the desired results.

"Jack Simpson," he announced.

"That's the guy he's having all this trouble writing a letter to," said my father.

"He doesn't come in here," said Whitey.

"What's the name?" asked May.

"Simpson," said Whitey. "Jack Simpson."

"What does he look like?" May pushed her glass toward Whitey and twisted on her stool so that she faced Mr. Beaker and her knee just touched his leg. Mr. Beaker looked at her for a long time before answering.

"What does he look like? I don't know. I've never seen him."

"Oh, I thought you knew him."

"I thought I knew him, too." Mr. Beaker shook his head slowly from side to side. He rubbed his forehead with his fingers, as if he were massaging away a pain. "I even thought I knew what he looked like. I would have said, a while ago, that he was short, balding, and a little overweight, that he had in his closet a hat with a feather, a hat he had bought after a long period of hesitation, a hat that he had imagined wearing at a jaunty angle when he went to work in the morning, a hat that he had never had the nerve to wear."

"Oh, I know that guy," said May. She held a cigarette to her lips and leaned toward Mr. Beaker for a light. She lost her balance on the stool and had to steady herself with a hand on his shoulder. "I think my husband, who died, used to know him."

Mr. Beaker sighed through his nose and lit May's cigarette with a match from a book on the bar. "I'm not describing him as he is, only as I imagined him to be," he explained. My father signaled to Whitey again.

"Wait a minute," said Whitey. "Let me get this straight. Are we talking about somebody you just made up?"

"If I had made him up," said Mr. Beaker, "I would not have made him so—" he paused, unable to find not only the right word, but any word that would fit reasonably well. He looked at May, waiting for him to finish the thought, and at Whitey and my father, also waiting. Then he looked at his drink.

"Hard to describe?" suggested May.

"Bald?" asked my father.

"Fat," said Whitey.

"Mysterious?" asked my mother.

"—hard to control," said Mr. Beaker.

My father saw the opportunity that he had been waiting for. His hand shook when he raised his glass, and he spilled a little beer on the bar, but he succeeded fairly well in making himself sound as if a small and inconsequential idea had just occurred to him. "It seems to me," he said, "that your real problem isn't Jack Simpson. It's this woman he has his eye on, this what's-her-name."

"Eliza."

"Yeah. See, with this Simpson you've got a problem you don't have with those others—"

"He writes to other men, too?" May asked my mother.

"—you've got competition. Now, you should be thinking about how you're going to match the competition."

"You're competing with some woman for the attentions of this guy who wears a hat with a feather?" asked May. She drew away from Mr. Beaker.

"It's business, May," said my mother, reaching between May and Mr. Beaker again to move the pretzel dish away from me and slide her glass toward Whitey.

"It sounds like funny business to me," said May. She reached around my mother and gave Mr. Beaker a little push on the shoulder. "Is that what you're up to, funny business?"

"If I were you, Beaker," my father continued, "I'd get a look at this Eliza and see what I was up against. Then I'd know what to do. Maybe she isn't really any competition at all—"

"Sure," said my mother, "that could be. Remember how jealous you used to be of—"

"I wasn't ever jealous," said my father, snapping his head toward my mother.

"Bert," said Mr. Beaker, "you've got it."

My father's jaw dropped, but he recovered quickly. "Sure," he said, "this Eliza may be some dumpy, dull-witted—"

"No, no, no," said Mr. Beaker. "You've got it but you don't know it. Eliza is quite wonderful. She's modest, selfless, and quite nice looking, but she's no competition at all—" Mr. Beaker leaned toward Whitey and finished in a stage whisper that fell across the bar like a heavy drizzle. "—because she isn't. She is not. There is no Eliza Foote at all. I've let myself get all upset over nothing, something my mother always cautioned me against." He smiled and pushed his glass toward Whitey with more vigor than he had intended. It slid across the bar and over the edge. Whitey snatched the glass out of the air and began refilling it.

Mr. Beaker began chuckling. "That Simpson," he said. "The wily devil. He doesn't want flattery and titillation; he wants competition, an epistolary battle of wits. Oh, he's a clever bastard. He introduced an unknown quantity, this Eliza, in order to wrest control of our correspondence from me. Next he'll probably start asking for money. Now what do I know about this feigned Eliza? She waits at a certain bus stop each morning, wearing a blue cloth coat." He leaned across the bar and asked Whitey, "Where is Louise's Coffee Shop?"

"Louise's Coffee Shop? That's over on Bolotomy and Main, isn't it?" suggested Whitey.

"No, no," said May. "That's Lucille's Pastry Shop. They do have coffee, though I wouldn't eat the doughnuts there, if I were you. Too heavy, greasy. Try Lucy's Donuts. They make good doughnuts, but you have to get there early, when they're fresh."

"There's Louise's Sandwich Shop, where's that?" asked my mother.

"That's closed," said my father. "Long ago. We used to go there when we were in high school, remember? Wait a minute, am I thinking of the right place? It wasn't Louise's Sandwich Shop, it was Louise's Lunch, wasn't it?"

Whitey leafed through a telephone book. "Louise's," he said. "There's one in Hargrove."

"Hargrove. Yes, that's right," said Mr. Beaker. "I'm off to Hargrove to see for myself that there is no Eliza Foote." He reached for his drink, then rejected it with a scowl and a wave. "Good night to all," he said. "Whitey, you run a very nice place here. Where is the door?"

4

MR. BEAKER INSISTED on walking home alone through the rain that had begun to fall. At the door, he fumbled with the latch for a moment and then stepped into the night.

That was a Friday night. I didn't see him again until the following Sunday, and only years later did I persuade him and Eliza to give me an account of what had happened in the meantime.

We sat in their living room. Mr. Beaker was wearing a cardigan sweater with suede patches on the elbows. Eliza was wearing a gray silk suit. While we talked, Mr. Beaker smoked his pipe, and Eliza smoked several cigarettes. Mr. Beaker drank half a tumbler of Scotch. Eliza drank two martinis.

"It was raining when I left the bar—Whitey's," said Mr. Beaker. "I welcomed the rain; it was cold, but it refreshed me. I didn't walk directly home, but wandered, and while I walked, I thought about Jack Simpson, about how Simpson had nearly felled me in our epistolary jousting, and I plotted, plotted ways to parry and thrust. As I walked, I grew fonder of Jack Simpson, as combatants can grow fond of worthy adversaries. I let myself project our correspondence into the future, imagining the pleasure of turning from answering the letters of Mary's other correspondents, who were, already, beginning to sound much alike, to dueling with Jack Simpson, as I might turn to a game of chess to clear and stimulate my mind. I was so pleased with the prospect of this long and intriguing combat that I found myself chuckling as I walked, and smiling. So agitated was I that I walked for hours, stopping from time to time, for shelter from the rain, at several of the bars along the winding route that I took from Whitey's to No Bridge Road.

"In some of these, while I sipped a warming Scotch, I felt the urge to talk, and found myself muttering, 'If only Jack were here now!'

"At the last bar I visited, this muttering attracted the attention of another patron, who thought me an unfortunate figure, a lonely drinker with no one but himself to talk to. This fellow tried to strike up a conversation, and his attempt made me think that *he* was a lonely fellow with a need to talk. I found myself going on for hours with a perfect stranger about things I really knew nothing about: the ancient struggle to wrest the clam from the bottom of the bay, brother pitted against brother in the competition for choice beds, the best ways of hiding tough old chowder clams in sacks of tender cherrystones.

"When the bar closed, I slapped this new friend on the back, shook hands heartily, and walked home. I was a little drunk, I think. All the way home, I berated myself for not having had the nerve to ask the fellow the one question I had about clams: do they bite? I intended to slip inside the house quietly, but each of my limbs seemed to have a mind of its own, and I stumbled on the steps and then threw the screen door open with such force that it slammed against the side of the house."

"I remember that," I said. "It woke me, and I stood up in my crib, rubbing my eyes. I watched lights turn on and off, and then your house was quiet again, and I went back to sleep. Early in the morning, I heard whistling, and when I looked out I saw you closing your garage door, your Studebaker idling in the driveway. You got into the car and drove off."

"Meanwhile," said Eliza, "I was at my wit's end. The night before, I had let myself be lured to the apartment of the fellow who had been the inspiration for Jack Simpson. I had, naively, thought him a dashing and clever guy, and he had, I admit, set my heart aflutter when he asked me to have dinner alone with him in his apartment instead of in a restaurant, because his apartment was so much cozier and we would be able to talk together quietly (and of course it would also be much cheaper for him, and he had to consider that since he was on a tight budget). Well, there we were in his apartment, and we hadn't been alone for five minutes when all of a sudden his hands developed a mind of their own! One minute he was a nice guy with a boyish smile and a nice conversation, even if he really didn't have much to say except about how he was sure to be district manager pretty soon and how much money he would make, and a few nice things about how pretty my hair looked when it was down and how long my legs were, and then a few minutes later he was all over me and tearing at my things with the hands of a forceful brute. I kept saying 'no, no,' in a strong voice even if I couldn't really yell because it might have disturbed the neighbors who didn't know what was going on and might have caused a lot of trouble, and I said 'no,' but the more I said it the more he thought I was turning on a green light, and I said 'no, no' but he kept right on going and even kept right on going faster, and 'no' I said, 'no,' and when to my surprise a little sound like a squeal jumped out of my mouth he said, 'Jesus, Honey, the neighbors,' which is not a very romantic thing to say, and 'no' I said, 'no,' and then before I knew it, it was all over and it was a big disappointment, let me tell you."

She stopped and lit a cigarette. She threw her head back and blew a long column of smoke toward the ceiling. She threw her arm along the back of the couch and crossed her legs, making the silk suit whisper. She turned toward me again and pursed her lips. "I got a little carried away. Let me see. He fell asleep. I let myself out and walked home. The next day, I felt pretty good, and I looked at myself in the mirror and my cheeks were bright and I had a little spring in my step, so I didn't put my hair up. When I got to the bus stop, there he was, and did he ever look different. He was wearing a jacket that looked as if he had borrowed it from a gorilla or made it himself in his spare time, and I realized that he'd been wearing that jacket for months. He gave me a little wave and said 'Good morning,' and that was all, and I had been expecting some little secret smile because even though I didn't have such a great time, he seemed to enjoy himself plenty, so something came over me and I walked right up to him and stood on my toes and whispered in his ear as if I were whispering some sweet nothings, and he was looking around to see who noticed, and of course everybody did, and very sweetly I said, 'You need practice,' and right then I could have knocked him over with a feather. I could see the blood drain from his face, and I could tell that his knees got weak and rubbery because he shrank about an inch, and I sashayed over to the bench and took off my coat and crossed my legs and grinned.

"I left work early that afternoon. My mind was racing, and all my typing was a mess. I went home and began sorting out my things. I didn't have any plan; I was just cleaning my slate. I didn't realize that I was talking so loudly to myself until Mrs. Mitchell, who lived next door, came over to see what was the matter. I told her. I began heaping old things of mine on her, and it was only when I came to the little white sunsuit that I had bought after a long period of hesitation, a sunsuit that I had imagined wearing to someone's summer house for the weekend, but had never worn at all, that I knew I wasn't just doing my spring cleaning. I was leaving. I got out my suitcases, and I threw in the sunsuit and the other things that I wanted to keep. I spent a fitful night, and when I got up in the morning I got out of there as quickly as I could."

Mr. Beaker let a moment pass to be certain that it was his turn to speak. "I found Louise's Coffee Shop easily," he said. "It was a popular spot in Hargrove at that time. God knows why. I parked on the street, across from the place, waiting for Eliza not to appear. I grew more and more delighted at her failure to appear, until I realized that no one at all had come to the corner to wait for the bus, that in fact no bus had stopped at the corner, and only then did I realize that this was a Saturday morning. I was disappointed, but not terribly disturbed; I was sure that I was right, that there was no Eliza Foote.

"I decided to make a few discreet inquiries at Louise's. I was just about to step out of the car when a woman carrying two suitcases and a blue cloth coat walked around the corner and sat on the bench, setting a suitcase on either side of her. You could have knocked me over with a feather."

"I sat there on the bench," said Eliza, "enjoying the sun and the anticipation of something new. I glanced across the road and saw a fellow sitting in a Studebaker, staring at me with his mouth hanging open. 'Take a good look,' I said to myself, and I stretched out in the sun. Providentially, a warm breeze blew my skirt up a little. I glanced at him sidelong, and I could see that he was staring at me like mad, so I casually looked in his direction and acted as if I had noticed him for the first time. I said good morning and smiled."

"I got out of the car in a trance," said Mr. Beaker. "I had no doubt who she was, but I had no idea what to do."

"He walked up to me slowly, his eyes fixed on mine, and he didn't say anything. He just stood there. Without thinking about it really, I said to myself, 'I'm not going to give this guy my right name.' So I smiled at him and said, 'My name is Mary Strong,' which was the first name that came to mind, since it had been on my mind for so long."

Mr. Beaker leaned forward and spoke rapidly. "I understood it all in an instant. You must imagine as I relate my thoughts that only a second is passing, that if you had been at the corner you would have seen no hesitation between Eliza's introducing herself and my introducing myself. I thought, *My God, could that be? Could this merely be a coincidence? Oh, no. Never. You're not Mary Strong, my dear. I am Mary Strong, and you can't be anyone but Eliza Foote. But how do you know Mary Strong? Has Jack been showing Mary's letters to you, sharing a laugh over her confusion? Or is there no one to share that laugh with you? No one but me?* I held out my hand. 'I'm Jack Simpson,' I said."

Eliza put out her cigarette slowly, tapping at the ashes until nothing was left burning. "The whole thing came to me in a flash," she said. "All these ideas raced through my mind in the time it takes to blink your eyes. I thought, *Wow, could that be? Is this just a coincidence? Oh, no. Uh-uh. You're not Jack Simpson. I made Jack Simpson up, so if anybody's Jack Simpson, I am. So who are you? Who knows about Jack Simpson? Just me and Mary Strong.* I smiled and batted my lashes. 'I think we've got those backwards,' I said."

"We shook hands," said Mr. Beaker.

"We walked over to the car," said Eliza.

"We drove off."

"We went to the beach."

"We walked on the sand."

"We talked."

"We laughed."

"It was nearly dark when we pulled into Dudley's driveway. Dudley didn't even put the car into the garage. He hustled me into the house. We made love, and it was, well, not bad. Let's say that I've suggested a few improvements since then, matters of style mostly."

Mr. Beaker coughed and tamped his pipe.

"Quite a few," he admitted, and he grinned. "I have suggested a few improvements in style myself, style of dress, of speech, of mannerism."

Eliza patted Mr. Beaker on the back of his hand. "He fell asleep," she said. "I unpacked and then poked around. I found the letters, of course, and spent a long time reading through them. I could see that he had real talent, but that there was room for improvement there, too."

"When I woke up," said Mr. Beaker, "she was pulling on my ear and saying, 'Dudley, wake up.' She hadn't a stitch on, and the sight of her as soon as I opened my eyes, well it took my breath away. She was holding fistfuls of letters, and she insisted that we go through them immediately, so that I could see the changes she had in mind."

"I said to him, 'Admit it, Dudley, you've been botching up the sex parts.'"

"And as she went on, I had to admit that she was right. She had several improvements to suggest, and they were all quite interesting. I suggested that she work with me, as my assistant."

"'Nothing doing,' I said. 'Partner or nothing. I could always write to these guys and tell them they've been duped.'"

"I thought of the way that I had come to anticipate with such relish the competition with Jack Simpson, the jousting, the thrust and parry, and I said to myself, 'Why, here you have the creator of Jack Simpson, you fool,' and I agreed."

"And he has never regretted it since," said Eliza.

"I've never been a religious man," said Mr. Beaker, slowly and carefully, "but I've always had the conviction that a benevolent hand nudged each of us toward that corner that morning."

5

WHAT A BEAUTY the next day was, one of those late spring days that make one want to go on living, a June day that, confused, had blundered into April. Everyone slept late. In the afternoon, we were all on the front lawn. Gumma, Guppa, and my parents were sitting in lawn chairs on the half of the lawn near Mr. Beaker's house. On the other half, separated from them by the front walk, I was chasing Gumma's cat's six black kittens. When I caught one, I carried it, often by the tail, to my little red wagon, plopped it into the wagon, and went off after another. The kitten sniffed around in the wagon for a while, hopped out, and wandered away. I brought another kitten to the empty wagon, plopped it in, clapped my hands and giggled, and scrambled off after another. I was having a fine time. If my mother had not tumbled from her lawn chair, there is no telling how long I might have continued happily chasing those kittens without ever caring whether I got them all into the wagon at once, but the innocent and useless pursuits of childhood cannot last forever.

When Mr. Beaker's front door opened, we all heard it. We stopped

what we were doing, turned, and watched a leggy blonde in a white sunsuit start down the steps. Mr. Beaker followed her, grinning, and saying
something that I couldn't quite make out. We watched them every step of
the way from his house to Gumma and Guppa's, for we knew that we
were watching something important, a change, and that we were likely
always to remember this day as the day that Mr. Beaker stepped out of his
house with a blonde.

The kittens soon stopped watching and went back to hopping and tum-
bling about, but I watched the introductions, which were a little stiff, Eliza holding back a bit until Mr. Beaker put a hand on her nates and nudged
her forward. Guppa and my father hopped out of their chairs and offered
them to Eliza, but she wanted to stand, and my father nearly said that if he
had legs like that he'd rather stand too, but he thought better of it and offered Dudley and Eliza a beer. Gumma pointed out the crescent of crocuses in a corner of the lawn; everyone turned at once to look at them, and
there were remarks about their beauty and the beauty of the day. When
Eliza bent at the waist to look more closely at the crocuses, my mother
looked away, turning toward me again. She looked as if she wanted me to
get back to work chasing the kittens, so I did.

"Oh, look, Dudley, isn't Peter cute?" cooed my mother. She twisted in
her folding chair and reached for her iced tea.

"Cute," said Gumma. She clapped her hands in just the way that I was
clapping them and giggled just as I was giggling. I clapped and giggled
back.

"What he's doing is pretty damned stupid, if you ask me," said my father. "Like trying to carry water in a sieve, wouldn't you say, Dudley?"

Mr. Beaker didn't answer, but he did give my father a look of interest
and encouragement.

"Why doesn't he see that he'll never get the kittens to stay in the wagon, and just give up?" my father asked. "That's one of the big lessons in
life, knowing when to quit." He took a long, bracing pull at his beer and
glanced at my mother.

"Kin," I said.

"Kitten," said Guppa, aiming his box camera my way.

"Kin," I said.

"Kit-ten," said Mr. Beaker. "Kit-ten. Kitten."

"Oh, leave him alone, Dudley," whispered Eliza.

"Smile, Peter. Say 'cheese,'" called Guppa.

"Kin," I said, and clapped my hands and smiled into Guppa's camera.

Reaching for her tea but watching me, my mother bumped her hand against the metal folding table that held the tea and her cigarettes and ash tray. The table, poorly balanced on the uneven lawn, tipped away from her. She felt it move and glanced at it. She saw it tipping and knew at once that she would not be able to stop it. If she tried, she was likely to end up on the lawn herself, with her skirt halfway up her thighs and people fussing over her.

With a frantic, desperate effort, my mother lunged for the table.

My mother, her chair, and her table began to fall in an arc, as if the lawn had been a rug someone had yanked from under her. My mother was wearing a white skirt and blouse and a look of surprise. Her arms were thrown out to the side, toward the falling table, and her legs were raised high in the air, flapping out of control. I could see the tops of her stockings and her garters and the pink flesh of her inner thighs. A glass of tea was in the air above the table, and beside it, drifting away from it, floated a clamshell ashtray under a cloud of ashes. I clapped and giggled again. Another kitten hopped out of the wagon.

The table struck the lawn, its circular top resounding like a gong, flying off the base, and rolling toward the street.

"Ye gods and little kittens!" shouted Gumma, clasping her hands over her heart.

"Shit!" expostulated my mother, reaching the lawn herself.

My father and Mr. Beaker ran to my mother at once. Gumma and Guppa struggled out of their chairs and rushed over to help. The tea had ruined my mother's cigarettes and stained her skirt.

Mr. Beaker gripped my mother in the left armpit and began helping my father haul her to her feet.

Eliza ran into the street after the tabletop and was nearly struck by a passing Studebaker. At the sound of its squealing tires, Mr. Beaker turned, saw Eliza holding the dented tabletop, cried "Oh, God, no," and let go of my mother to run to Eliza, leaving my father struggling with my mother on his own. When he got her to her feet and satisfied himself that she had suffered no serious harm, he too dashed out to the street to see if Eliza was all right.

My mother stood still for a moment, looking into the street, where my father and Mr. Beaker were checking Eliza's legs for scratches. There were none. Finally my mother made her way toward the house on her own, clucking at herself and brushing at her skirt.

"I don't know what came over me," my mother said aloud. "I knew that I didn't have a chance of saving the table, but I just had to try—"

She stopped at the front door and turned toward the street again, where my father and Mr. Beaker were still fussing over Eliza. "I didn't have a chance," she said. "I don't know what came over me." She went inside.

Mr. Beaker, Eliza, and my father stood together, laughing nervously. Gumma and Guppa were straightening up the mess my mother had made.

"I think we could all use a drink," said my father. He began opening bottles. When they each had one, they clinked them together, and my father said to Eliza, "Well, at least you won't forget this day."

"You know, Bert," said Mr. Beaker, "I think you're almost right about Peter and the kittens, but not quite."

"Oh, yeah?" growled my father.

"Dudley—" said Eliza.

Mr. Beaker nodded in my direction. "It's not a matter of foolish persistence in pursuing an impossible goal, it's a matter of focusing the attention." He raised his voice. "'True genius,' it has been said, 'lies in the art of focusing the attention.'" He paused to let that sink in, and Eliza took advantage of the pause at once.

"I don't know about that," she said. "It seems to me that a true genius ought to be able to keep a lot of balls in the air at once."

There was a pregnant silence. Gumma, Guppa, and my father stood still, unbreathing. The kittens and I stopped romping. We all looked at Mr. Beaker.

"No, no," he said. "You have an example right in front of you." He pointed his pipestem at me. "Now if little Peter there were to narrow his focus, concentrate on and pursue only one kitten, he could catch it and keep it. You know what we're seeing here, Bertram?"

My father looked at Mr. Beaker over his glasses, raising his eyebrows to say, "What? Go on. I'm listening."

Mr. Beaker began poking and tamping at his pipe.

"What, Dudley?" asked Eliza.

Mr. Beaker tamped and poked until he had put the fire out. He put the pipe tool into his pocket and bent over and began knocking the pipe on the heel of his shoe. When he had finished knocking it, he began refilling it. My father was growing annoyed.

"Damn it, Beaker, what?" he demanded.

Mr. Beaker brought out his lighter, pumped it several times, and spun the striker.

My father clenched his teeth.

"Get to the point, Beaker!" he cried.

While Mr. Beaker directed the flame into his pipe, he looked at my father as if he had not heard him, raising an eyebrow as if he were surprised that my father hadn't figured out what he was talking about. He pointed at me with his pipestem.

"Remember this scene," he said. "Here we see Peter's life, in miniature: this pursuing now one notion (or kitten), now another, this inability to concentrate entirely on one thing (or kitten) for fear that the others will get away, though really he might just as well pursue any one of them as all of them, for the kittens, as you and I can see at a glance, are so like one another as to be indistinguishable, each just a variation on the theme 'Black Kitten.'" He chuckled and jotted something in a little leather-covered notebook. "Do you follow me?" he asked.

My father turned toward me again. I dropped a kitten into the wagon, clapped my hands and giggled. The kitten hopped out, and my father frowned.

I looked at Eliza, and she looked at me. Then she walked across the front walk onto my side of the lawn and began snatching up kittens. She caught five, and I caught one, and we plopped them all into the wagon at once. Then she picked me up and held me on her hip. The sun was still weak, and it was late in the afternoon now and a little chilly, so she may have hugged me so tightly only for warmth.

Do Clams Bite?

The memories of childhood have no order, and no end.

Dylan Thomas
"Reminiscences of Childhood"

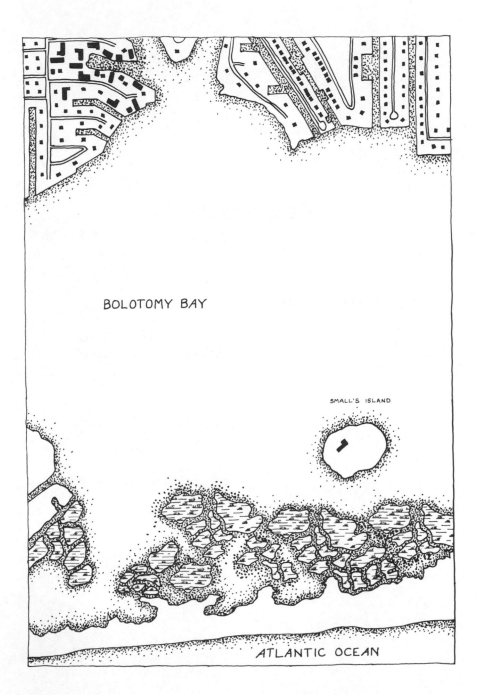

BOLOTOMY BAY

SMALL'S ISLAND

ATLANTIC OCEAN

Preface

"DO CLAMS BITE?" began as a single brief anecdote, the account of my first attempt to dig clams. Briefly, here's how it goes. As soon as I was old enough to keep my chin above water in the clam flats of Bolotomy Bay, my big grandfather, my father's father, took me clamming with him. He was a casual clammer who usually wanted only a few clams for dinner. He "treaded" for clams, walking around in the flats and feeling for the clams with his toes. He walked with a jerky, shuffling step, pushing against the bottom with the balls of his feet. When he felt a clam, he would duck beneath the surface and scoop it out of the sand. He'd bring it up and drop it into the front of his snug wool bathing suit. I watched him go through this routine, filling the front of his bathing suit, then waddling to the boat, his suit distended and lumpy, dumping his catch on the deck and going right back to the hunt. I saw at once that imitating this procedure successfully had something to do with being or becoming a man, but I thought there was a pretty high risk of being unmanned too. I wanted to ask Grandfather, "Do clams bite?" but I knew that if I asked, he would look at me with his smart gray eyes and know at once why I was asking, and that I'd be embarrassed, so I didn't ask, and instead each time I found a clam I pretended that it squirmed out of my grasp before I could get it into my suit.

I had been using this little story effectively at dinner tables for quite a few years. Sentimentalists could release a wistful sigh or two for the innocent little Peter in it, and intellectuals could ride the castration theme for a couple of hours. One evening, early in the telling, just after I had introduced Big Grandfather and Big Grandmother, my father's large and sturdy parents, the realization struck me that over the years, as I had told the story I had distorted the events and characters beyond recognition. It was time, I thought, to strip away the baloney and get down to the truth. The result of my effort to tell it without embellishment, just as it happened, begins in a few pages, but before we get to it I would like to give

you an idea of how I went about reconstructing the incident and to point
out one or two facts that I may have made up.

CONSCIOUSLY TRYING to revisit the past is a little like trying to see
back through a long tunnel or, more accurately, one of those corrugated
metal culverts through which streams are allowed to run under roadways.
Bear with me through this. The culvert itself is the set of your current
prejudices, desires, antipathies, enthusiasms, regrets, and whatnot that re-
strict your view of the past. You peer through this narrow tube and see
only a tiny circle of light, though you are certain that there is more back
there at the other end, beyond what you can see. Apparently, just looking
won't be enough. You are going to have to crawl through the culvert and
see what is back there. If you make it all the way through, you will be
surprised by what you find. You will have the odd sensation of being in
unfamiliar territory and yet recognizing everything.

By crawling through that culvert, I discovered, to my surprise, that I
had first begun using the do-clams-bite anecdote as a boy, just shortly after I had begun going on the clamming trips with Big Grandfather, and
before I was even sure whether clams could bite or not. I was surprised
and pleased to find that even in that very first telling I had altered the facts
considerably.

That first telling occurred one magical night when I sat on the bulkhead along the estuarial stretch of the Bolotomy River, at the end of the
street where Big Grandfather lived, between two moonlit sprites, Margot
and Martha Glynn. That occasion provides the ending for "Do Clams
Bite?" and I have presented it exactly as it happened, except for one or
two small adjustments that I had to make, primarily for structural reasons.
For example, I have represented Margot and Martha as twins, although in
fact Margot is a year older than Martha. The reason is that in that moon-
light-on-the-Bolotomy scene I spend some time swimming in the river
with one of the girls. When I had them read the manuscript, each claimed
to have been the girl described. We spent a long time arguing before I
came up with a change that all of us found acceptable: I made the girls
twins, we flipped a coin to see which name I would use for the girl I described, and I added a passage that introduces some confusion over which
of the girls is which.

For another example, I included in that scene a boy named Raskolnikov, whom I have for years considered my best friend, though I knew him
for only two days, at about the time of the events in "Do Clams Bite?"
One day, when I was visiting my big grandparents, I walked to the food

market in the center of town to get a few things for Grandmother, so that she could make some of the coconut candies that I loved so much. On the way, I met a haunted-, hunted-looking boy carrying a sack. We struck up a conversation, and I learned that he was running away from home because his father and mother simply couldn't get along. His father was an impractical dreamer, who had once wanted to build a lighthouse beside their tract home, and his mother was a beleaguered drudge, who did all the work around the house, struggled to make ends meet, and often screamed at his father, "Grow up!"

As I walked along beside the boy, the possibility occurred to me that he and I might become friends. For a wild moment, I thought of running away with him. Then I thought better of it and tried instead to persuade him to stay in Babbington. I thought that if I took him home my parents would give him some clean clothes and a warm meal and adopt him. He would have none of that. He'd already become a wanderer; he had to keep moving on. He asked me to steal him some fruit and a knife while I was in the market. I had some money of my own, so I bought him some peaches and a paring knife, and I got him a bag of hard candies too, individually wrapped in cellophane, so that they wouldn't stick together in the heat. I told him that I'd stolen these provisions, and I think he was impressed. For the short time that he was in Babbington, we were nearly inseparable, although of course I could not let my parents or grandparents know about him. I did introduce him to my great-grandmother, who lived in a room over Big Grandfather's garage, and it was she who nicknamed him Raskolnikov. He was so taken with her that he gave her the knife I had "stolen" for him, as a gift, after she had given him ten dollars to help him along the road.

Then he simply left. I've had many other friends, but each seems to offer only part of what this archetypal friend offered, just as each of the girls and women I knew before I met Albertine could offer only part of everything I found in her.

ANOTHER CHANGE from actual fact was prompted by good taste, rather than by structure or logic or any of the other considerations that ordinarily influence a writer. I have made two of my ancestors, Black Jacques Leroy and his son Fat Hank Leroy, rather tame: two more or less harmless businessmen, whose interests were limited to beer and poetry. I left a lot unsaid, because I knew that if I had dragged in the tales of Black Jacques's establishing Corinne's Dockside Bordello, his liaison with his son's wife, or his role in the Tong Wars between clamming factions, my family would have suffered considerable embarrassment. It was also a question of taste that made me have Fat Hank sell Leroy Lager, although in fact the brewery is still the cornerstone of the tiny Leroy fortune. The stuff has simply become so anemic that it embarrasses me to admit that I'm connected with it.

AT HEART, THOUGH, "Do Clams Bite?" is not about events or people. It is about fear. It is about several boyhood fears: the fear of saying the wrong thing, fear of sex, fear of oblivion, fear of becoming like one's parents, fear of other boys (especially those who carry knives), and—most of all—the fear of having a hunk of oneself bitten off by a clam. As a boy, I suffered this fear in silence. Only later did I learn that I had not been the only sufferer. Although this fear was not widespread, many boys in Babbington did suffer from it: that group of boys whose fathers or grandfathers were casual clam-diggers, who went right into the water after the clams, feeling for them with their feet, who wore brief woolen bathing suits and stored the clams they caught in the fronts of their suits.

By buttonholing schoolchildren on their way home, I've learned that many still suffer from this fear. (The clam in question, by the way, is *Mercenaria mercenaria*, the hard-shelled quahog, the pinnacle of molluscan evolution, God's own clam. In other areas, I suppose, oysters, mussels, or scallops occasion a similar dread.) Girls fear for their toes, but in boys this pelecypodophobia centers, as so many boyhood fears do, on the penis. At clambakes, I have seen small boys furtively poking at the insides of clams before eating them, to make sure that no part of an unfortunate lad is hidden there, just as I used to poke at clams when I was as young as they and as firmly in the grip of this terror. Once, not long ago, I found myself next to one of these boys at a table full of cherrystones. When I saw him poking at his clams, I leaned over and whispered to him, "Don't worry. They don't bite." I knew at once that he had understood the point of my remark, for he smiled and nodded his head and then laughed a mad, nervous laugh and began wolfing the clams down with horseradish and gusto.

Peter Leroy
Small's Island
July 11, 1982

1

FROM TIME TO TIME, my parents would take me to stay for a weekend with my father's large and sturdy parents, whom I called Big Grandfather and Big Grandmother, or simply Grandfather and Grandmother. My parents stayed just long enough to fulfill an obligation. They would ordinarily leave after dinner if we went on a Friday, and after an hour or so if we went on a Saturday morning. I would stay until Sunday evening. Though I loved my big grandparents dearly, I was never comfortable during these visits, in part because Grandmother and Grandfather were so much larger than anyone else in the family, and in part because all their furniture was upholstered with scratchy scarlet fabric, but mostly because, as soon as I was old enough, if the weather allowed it, Grandfather would take me clamming with him on Saturday and Sunday.

Grandfather clammed in the flats, where the water reached somewhere between his knees and his waist and somewhere between my waist and my chin. He would hunt for clams by "treading," feeling for clams with his toes. When he found one, he would duck beneath the water, bring the clam up, and drop it into the front of his brief wool bathing suit. Soon his bathing suit would fill up with clams, bulging enormously at the front, and he would waddle to his boat, the *Rambunctious*, where he would empty the clams onto the deck. I knew that I was expected to do as he did, but even thinking of dropping a clam into the front of my bathing suit brought a stab of pain between my legs; my stomach grew cold and empty. I was sure that clams must bite and that they were likely to snap at me in there. Every moment of every visit was marked by fear of being bitten if I did as Grandfather did and fear of disappointing him if I did not.

Each of these visits began with a climb up the stairs to the rooms where Great-grandmother Leroy lived, at the very top of the house. I began to move more slowly as I neared the top of the stairs, not out of any reluctance to see Great-grandmother, but simply to adjust myself to the pace of things in her rooms, for in Great-grandmother's rooms everything

moved slowly, and while downstairs events marched on toward the time
when I would have to go out on the bay with Grandfather and suffer
through the squirming anxiety that came with the thought of dropping
snapping clams into my little woolen bathing suit, here at the top of the
house I would be, for a while, outside the rush of forward motion. Great-
grandmother herself had lived so long up here, above things, that she had
slowed to immobility and beyond, had begun to move backward, slipping
farther into the past with each reluctant tick of the old clock that she kept
on the table beside her. From my visits, I had acquired a sense of how
this had happened, and my initial impatience during early visits to Great-
grandmother—to be away, to get downstairs, to be moving, to do something, even to do something frightening—slipped away little by little,
with each succeeding visit, yielding to an insinuating somnolence, a comforting drowsiness. The longer I spent with her there, the thicker the atmosphere became, as if the room were filling with one of the undulating
gelatin desserts my mother was fond of making, and I could relax, stretch
out, float, and drift. But always, sooner or later, my mother would call
from downstairs, and I would have to say good-bye and descend into confusion and haste.

2

THE DOOR AT THE TOP OF THE STAIRS was fitted with glass panes
from top to bottom, and Great-grandmother had hung a gauzy curtain
over it. Through the curtain I could see Great-grandmother sitting in a
chair by the front windows, where she was always sitting when I came to
visit, carving a coconut with a kitchen knife. I knocked lightly, politely,
and then turned the glass doorknob.

"Hello, Grandma," I said.

"Well, Peter," she said. Her voice was small and thin, but strong, and
she had a habit of clicking her teeth in the pauses, so that she sounded as
if she were knitting while she spoke. "Are you here again already?"

"Yes, here I am. I came for the weekend."

"Are you going out on the boat?"

"Yes," I said. I felt my lower lip tremble a bit. "But," I added, by way
of assuring myself that I still had time, that I'd be intact at least while I
was here, at the top of the house, "I'm going to visit you for a while first."

Her rooms were furnished with odds and ends, some from rooms where she had lived before, some just things that Grandfather had found here and there, things that had been in other people's rooms, things with pasts that hadn't included her. She didn't quite trust these strangers among her furnishings. When Grandfather got her a chaise longue from somewhere or other, she had draped it with a worn rug that she knew well so that she wouldn't have it staring her in the face all the time, and once she had had me drag a floor lamp into a closet because she didn't like having it look over her shoulder when she read her mail. The only recent acquisitions she felt comfortable with were the gifts of other children who visited her. She had many little friends around the neighborhood, children I didn't know, since at that time I lived all the way across town, away from the water, and so didn't see any of these children at school. I visited only occasionally and didn't have much time away from the adults when I was visiting. Festoons of paper chains hung over every door and window, and her shelves and tables were crammed with tissue paper carnations in juice glasses and jelly jars, paper baskets, necklaces of painted macaroni, and rows of knickknacks made from clamshells. But pride of place went to the coconuts carved to represent Leroys.

(I mean here not the nut itself, the part of the coconut that one buys at a supermarket and belabors with a hammer and an old screwdriver in an attempt, usually unsuccessful, to draw the milk off cleanly before whacking the damn thing to pieces to get at the meat. The nut has a singularly tough and woody shell that nobody's great-grandmother could carve with a kitchen knife. I mean instead the complete fruit, the outer layer of which, the husk, is, when mature, dark brown, fibrous, and easily carved.)

The carving of these coconuts was a project that she had begun before I could remember, but it was unlikely that it would ever be completed, since she not only kept extending its scope to include more and more distant relatives but regularly revised the carvings she had already done, working to bring the features closer to what she remembered—or supposed—them to be. She had completed heads of all the major Leroys that she had any memory of, and was now filling out the ranks of minor cousins and people related only by marriage; she had not yet carved a head of herself. Whenever I visited, she would quiz me about the exploits of these Leroys, and I had gotten them all down pretty well, but there were gaps in my understanding of what I repeated for her, enough gaps so that the Leroy history as Great-grandmother presented it seemed to me a perilously leaky affair that was likely to sink if the weather got at all rough. Often, when I was reciting for her, I employed a narrative analogue to a widely used technique for keeping afloat a clamboat with a soft bottom, a boat that leaks more or less all the time. One takes the boat out to the clam flats and there crawls under the hull and pokes sawdust into any visible gaps and, for good measure, gives the whole bottom a good coating. Then one drinks a few beers or digs a few clams while the sawdust floats into the cracks and swells with water, stopping, or at least slowing, the leaks. This is not a permanent solution, of course, merely a stop-gap measure, but some boats have been kept afloat this way for years. The hull provides the form, the sawdust the substance, and the result is an artful deception: the illusion of a solid hull, an illusion so substantial that the boat floats. Sometimes, when I was reciting for Great-grandmother, I threw quite a lot of sawdust into the gaps, but she rarely seemed to notice, or if she did, she didn't seem to mind.

Soon, I knew, she would ask me if I wanted a candy. She kept a bowl of hard candies on the table beside her, but the first time that I had tried to take one I had discovered that they were all stuck together. I had tugged on one, then another, and they had all come out in a cluster. I had stood with all the candies in my hand, wondering what on earth to do next. I thought for a moment of smacking them on the edge of the table to break them apart, but I could tell that that would not be the right thing to do up here, so I set the cluster back in the bowl, and popped a candy-size ball of air into my mouth. For the rest of my visit, I made elaborate sucking noises and poked my tongue into my cheek to make it seem that I was eating one of the candies. The deception seemed to work, but I learned from it a truth about lies: once we have injected any little lie into our relationship with someone, it has to be maintained. I now went through this candy-ball charade on every visit.

"Take a candy, Peter," she said.

"Mmmm, thank you," I said. "Cherry—my favorite."

"Sit over there, by the window." She indicated the wing chair where I always sat when I visited her, an old pink one with an antimacassar. "You're not wearing hair oil, are you?"

"No, Grandma."

"Your father always used to wear hair oil, and he made a mess of everything. Does he still wear hair oil?"

"No."

"Do you know which one of these heads is your father?" she asked.

"Yes. It's that one." I pointed to the one that she had identified as my father. All the heads looked more or less alike to me; I distinguished them primarily by location, although I could tell the women from the men because the women wore hats, dusty hats with broken feathers or stained bands of silk.

"Very good. Now which one is Black Jacques?"

"The one in the middle of that shelf."

"You're a good boy, Peter. What was Black Jacques famous for?"

"He invented beer." This was an old routine for us. Some time, much earlier, I had made this mistake, and it had made her laugh, so I had perpetuated it as part of the ritual of naming the ancestors.

"No, no," she laughed. "Not all beer, just the best beer."

"Leroy Lager," I said. "It was a sturdy and honest beer, a drink for sturdy and honest folks, not like the insipid pisswater they try to pass off on people nowadays."

"Right!"

"And on the back of each bottle was a poem, a poem that Black Jacques had commissioned especially for the entertainment, enlightenment, or puzzlement of Leroy Lager drinkers. He paid handsomely for those poems, and they raised the tone of taverns across the land. The period when Black Jacques produced that amber nectar has come to be known as the Golden Age of Brewing."

"And how well did Leroy Lager do in the days of Black Jacques?"

"It depends on how you look at it. It was a great beer, and it had the finest label in the history of beer-bottle-label publishing, but sales were disappointing. Rotten, in fact. You can't sell pearls to swine." I knew that wasn't quite right, but it was close.

"Oh, that's wonderful," she said. "Black Jacques would have liked that. So, who was his son?"

"Great-grandfather. Fat Hank."

"Tell me about him."

"He wasn't always fat. When you first met him, he was quite the fellow. Everybody's friend. You were just a slip of a girl, and he set your heart aflutter when he tipped his hat to you."

"I was young and foolish."

"Yes. And by the time you saw him for what he really was, it was too late. That's the tragedy of your life. If only you'd been born earlier, you might have had the father, Black Jacques himself. Now that was a man! Fat Hank wasn't half the man his father was, and he ruined the business as soon as it came into his hands."

"How?"

"He turned Black Jacques's hearty brew into something so wishy-washy that you couldn't tell it from water, except that you could get drunk on it, and he began accepting flaccid and self-indulgent poems for the labels. In place of a few trenchant and pithy lines on one of the Great Themes, the Leroy label now offered the anguished sniveling of shiftless egoists whose works were so rambling that some of their poems had to be continued onto several labels, leading to the introduction of packages of six bottles and, ultimately, cases of twenty-four. Well, the result of all this was that after a few bottles anybody with a regret, a pang, a fear—any weepy drunk—could write a poem suitable for the once-proud Leroy Lager label. Many more poems were accepted, and the rate of pay for these dropped as the number of poets increased. Sales of Leroy Lager boomed, since poets drink a lot, and every drinker began to consider himself a poet. So, you see, things tend to get worse as time goes by."

She sighed and smiled at me with a mixture of sorrow (because what I'd said was so true) and pleasure (because I'd remembered it so well). "And what was Fat Hank's reward for destroying everything that Black Jacques had worked so hard to build?"

"He made a pile of money." I looked through the doorway into Great-grandmother's bedroom. A picture of Fat Hank stood on her dresser. He was fat; that much was incontestable. Even his coconut was round, with heavy cheeks and a flat base. But he didn't look like someone who had made a pile of money. He was standing in front of a garage with his hands stiffly at his sides. Behind him was a sign that said HONEST SERVICE, and to his left was another sign, only partly visible, with a picture of a tire and the words PUNCTURE PROOF.

"Grandma?" I asked, slowly, hesitantly. I wanted to ask her what had become of the money from Fat Hank's watery brew. I wanted to ask her why Fat Hank wasn't wearing white pleated trousers, a sleeveless sweater, and a white shirt, and standing beside a Packard. I wanted to ask why we weren't rich.

"What, Peter? Do you want another candy?"

"No. No thanks. I'm still sucking this one. They last a long time."

"Longer than I would have thought possible," she said. "What do you want to know, Peter?"

I suddenly knew what I would ask her. The question began to form as I opened my mouth, and pushed aside the other questions that I had thought of asking. It was so big a question that I coughed and sputtered from the size of it, as I might have if I had stuffed too many hard candies into my mouth. It took a moment for me to recover.

"Are you all right, Peter?" she asked.

LEROY, JOHN PETER

"Black Jacques," 1836[?]–1906, American brewer, born Algiers. Among beer drinkers, it is sometimes said of Black Jacques that "He invented beer." Although this is not correct, it is arguably true that he developed the best of beers; this was the legendary Leroy Lager, a sturdy and honest drink, relative only by name to the insipid brew later marketed by his son, John Henry ("Fat Hank"). Often credited (erroneously) with having first marketed beer in pint bottles, Black Jacques did introduce the now widespread practice of printing a poem on a label on the back of each bottle, thus raising the tone of taverns across the land. The period when Black Jacques himself ran the Leroy brewery has come to be known as the Golden Age of Brewing. Sales of the original Leroy Lager were never large, and Black Jacques grew increasingly bitter about its lack of success. Like many another original, he labored under the delusion that something of essentially limited appeal could, as the result of a mutation of public taste, acquire a large and devoted following. In 1894, broken in spirit, he gave the Leroy brewery to his son as a wedding present. Fat Hank, more in tune with popular taste than his father, began brewing a beer that went down more easily than the original, and he launched a promotional campaign that set an industry standard. He continued to publish poems on the Leroy labels, but required that each poem submitted be accompanied by six caps from Leroy bottles, the only requirement for acceptance. At least partly as a result of this practice, the number of poets began a steady increase that has not yet peaked. Another more or less direct consequence was the introduction of the six-pack (q.v.), which put six caps into the hands of the bibulous scribbler at once, in an easy-to-handle package. Fat Hank grew increasingly concerned that his success could not last. He calculated that if sales continued to grow at their then-current rate, by the end of the twentieth century every person in the world capable of holding a pen in one hand and a beer bottle in the other would be spending every evening drinking Leroy Lager and writing poems; foolishly, Fat Hank assumed that this was an impossibility. He sold the brewery, in a move that seemed like mad impetuosity from the outside but that Fat Hank, in his autobiography *Nobody's Fool*, described as the shrewdest decision he had ever made, admitting, however, that his next move fell considerably short of it on the shrewdness scale. He put all the proceeds into a series of service-stations-cum-clam-bars. He claimed to have had a vision one restless night of an endless line of motorcars inching along a paved road, each car filled with a happy family, eating clams on the half shell. "Only a fool," he is said to have said, "could fail to see that cars and clams are the coming things." The story of the failure of this venture is a familiar one. Millions are acquainted with the romanticized version that is the basis of the musical film *The Flop*, and every business school student knows it like the back of his hand, thanks to the lengthy chapter devoted to it in Cartel's basic text, *The Big Book of Business Blunders*. Essentially, blame can be ascribed to three causes: (1) the difficulty of assembling a staff adept at both automobile mechanics and cooking, (2) the incompatible odors produced by automobile maintenance and clam cookery, and (3) Fat Hank himself, who, those in the know aver, began to lose faith in his vision as soon as he had embraced it.   —EF

Black Jacques Leroy

4

WHEN THE CALL CAME from downstairs, it startled me, although I
had expected it.

"Peter. Come on downstairs. You'll miss the boat." It was my mother.
She always called me in the same way.

"I have to go, Grandma," I said. "I'm going to go out on the boat." I
waited a moment, hoping that a tear might form in her eye, that she might
burst out blubbering, imploring me to stay. Had things ever gone right,
she would have said, "I see so little of you Peter, and we've only covered
Black Jacques and Fat Hank. You can't go now. I'll insist. I won't let
them take you out on the bay, I won't, I won't!" She would have thrown
herself on the floor, kicking her feet and pounding with her brittle fists.

Instead, there was a rapid pounding of feet up the stairs, and for a moment I thought my father was coming to tell me that my dawdling was
delaying Grandfather, to tell me to get a move on, to pull me by the shirt-
sleeve if I hesitated. But it wasn't my father who burst through the door
without knocking—it was a boy about my size but a little older. His
mouth was open, to shout a greeting, I suppose, but when he saw me he
stopped himself. We looked at each other warily, with immediate suspicion. He looked to me like a boy who carried a knife. His hair was light,
sun-bleached, and dirty. His face was dirty. His T shirt and his pants
were dirty. He gave up looking me over, and he walked to Great-
grandmother's side. He gave her a kiss, rather a hearty one. That was
something I never did, because she seemed too dry and delicate. "I have
something for you, Lydia," he said.

Lydia. I couldn't imagine even Fat Hank calling Great-grandmother
Lydia to her face.

"You do?" she said. "What?"

She had become animated, eager. The thought struck me that I never
brought her anything, except on her birthday or at Christmas, when I
brought her a box containing a gift that my mother had bought. I was
usually as surprised as Great-grandmother to see what was in those boxes,
and I was often embarrassed, since my mother, who never climbed the
stairs to these rooms, always bought things that were wrong.

"Something you need." He reached into his pocket and pulled out a
knife. It was a small paring knife, with a wooden handle. On the handle
was a small sticker with a price written on it.

"You rascal," said Great-grandmother. "Where did you steal this?"

She had taken it from him and was running her thumb along the blade. "I didn't steal it," he said. "I swear. I bought it off a kid."

"What kid?"

"I don't know. Nobody who lives around here. He was just passing through. See, he was running away from home because his father is a drunk and his mother entertains strange men whenever his father's on a toot, so he needed some cash and I bought a few things off him just to help him out."

It sounded reasonable to me. I wondered how old this runaway was, where he slept at night, and whether he would have to go to school in the fall. Before I could ask, there were other footsteps on the stairs, slower, heavier, and a soft knock at the door. I thought that this must surely be the runaway boy, that I'd get a chance to ask him all my questions, and that this extraordinary appearance would keep me from going clamming with Grandfather, since Great-grandmother would be sure to insist that I make him some sandwiches and warm up a bowl of chowder.

Instead, my father appeared in the doorway. He looked smaller and younger up here, and when he spoke to Great-grandmother his ears turned red and he looked at his shoes.

"Hello, Grandma," he said. "I came to get Peter."

"Why, Bert," she said, "I didn't know you were here. Why didn't you come up to see me?"

"Oh, I was going to, Grandma. I was going to come up sometime before I left. Right now I have to get Peter downstairs. He's holding everything up." He took hold of my sleeve and started backing toward the door.

"Peter can find his way downstairs on his own. Why don't you stay here and talk with me for a while? Look at this," she said, holding the unfinished coconut carving out toward him, turning it so that he could see the profile. "Do you know who this is?"

"I'm not sure," said my father. "I—uh—look—I can't stay, Grandma. I—" He looked at me quickly, and for a moment it seemed to me that he wanted me to tell him what to say.

"I have to go out on the boat," I said.

My father brightened. "Me too," he said. "I'm going out on the boat too."

Great-grandmother's mouth fell open. "You?" she asked.

"Sure," said my father. "I haven't had a chance to go out clamming for a long time. I usually have so many things to do. This is a real treat for me."

5

MY FATHER AND I walked downstairs slowly. I lagged behind. This development, my father's going clamming too, made the prospect even worse. My father hated going out on the boat, I knew, because he felt uncomfortable on the water and he felt uncomfortable with Big Grandfather, who was strapping, leathery, and salty, who considered any inland work not fit for a man, and considered the work that my father did, managing a gas station, a joke.

6

WHEN MY FATHER WAS A BOY, Grandfather had bought him a copy of *The Boys' Book of Boatbuilding*. In that book were plans for a number of boats that any boy might build. My father greeted the gift with an enthusiasm that made Grandfather's heart leap. He got to work on boatbuilding immediately, but his distaste for actually being on the water in a boat led him to interpret the scale drawings in the book as full-size plans, and he built a series of model boats that lined the shelves of his room.

Big Grandfather was annoyed. He had wanted to get the boy out on the water; instead he was up in his room all the time making toys. Grandfather went out and bought the lumber for the first of the boats in the book, a flat-bottomed punt of the sort that one might pole in shallow waters. Overcompensating preposterously for my father's miniaturism, he misread the scale in the drawings, and constructed, in the side yard, with my father as a conscripted apprentice, a twenty-foot punt, which, although singularly graceless, was ideally suited for cruising the shallow clam flats, since it drew very little water. It was not at all suited for crossing the bay to reach the flats, however. It bucked and reared over the smallest wavelets. As time passed, Grandfather added to the punt, which he christened the *Rambunctious*, bits and pieces of other boats in the book that caught his eye. There was a cabin from a trim little sloop, blown up in scale so that it almost seemed suitable. He added a large gaff-rigged sail from a catboat and a centerboard enlarged from the plans for a sailing dinghy. He began to feel a facility for improvisation, and so he undertook on his own the addition of a gasoline engine, an engine that had once powered a small tractor. The engine was never christened, but he was as surely male as the *Rambunctious* was female. The *Rambunctious* was always referred to as she, and the unnamed engine as he.

Starting him, with a crank, occupied a good portion of the time spent in any of the *Rambunctious's* excursions on the bay. Grandfather kept the *Rambunctious* in a slip on the estuarial stretch of the Bolotomy River, about half a mile upstream from the bay, where many other boats were docked. Most of those on the side where Grandfather kept the *Rambunctious* were working clamboats. On the other side of the river, broad lawns stretched out behind large, comfortable houses. Notched into each lawn was a slip, in some cases covered by a boathouse, that held a sloop or a mahogany runabout or both.

Grandfather was a man of great patience and even temper; nothing better illustrated these qualities than his attempts to start him. Grandfather had intended that he would make the trip downriver to the bay quicker and easier than it was under sail, but it was not unusual for us to begin an outing in the early morning and be munching our lunch by the time we chugged past the town dock and reached the bay at last.

While Grandfather patiently cranked and adjusted something and cranked again, I sat in the stern, dangling my legs overboard, playing a game with the undulating surface of the water. I tried to bring the soles of my bare feet as close to the surface as I could without touching it. It was a game that could not be won, a game that my father would have considered like my chasing kittens on the day that my mother tumbled from her lawn chair. I couldn't win the game because I couldn't know that I had reached the point I was after until I had passed it. To make matters worse, I included a forfeit in the game on this day: if I touched the surface ten times before Grandfather got him started, I would brave the clams. I would put some into the front of my bathing suit, just as Grandfather did, and take my chances on their biting.

I had already failed nine times, and he showed no signs of starting. Grandfather had a series of procedures that he would follow, each of which was more severe than the last. He followed these procedures as predictably and precisely as if they had been regulations issued by the tractor manufacturer, printed on a little card that Grandfather had put in a black frame and screwed to the cabin bulkhead between his clamming license and the *Rambunctious's* registration:

    1. Let him rest for a while.
    2. Curse at him.

3. Remove his air cleaner (that's the piece of window screen that keeps any really large pebbles from falling into his carburetor) and try choking him with your hand.
4. Squirt some gas right into his carburetor. (It's a good idea to keep an oil can with gas in it handy.)
5. Pull his spark-plug wire off and clean it with your shirt.
6. Repeat procedures 1 through 5 until you're convinced that stronger measures are required.
7. Change his spark plug.
8. Smack him with the crank handle.

Grandfather had already changed his spark plug. If we were to get underway before the water kissed my feet again, he was going to have to get going fast.

"Hit him with the crank handle!" I shouted.

"Hey, take it easy," said my father. "Hitting a machine never does any good. This isn't something alive, you know, it's a machine. You have to respect it. You shouldn't ever take your anger out on a machine."

Grandfather snorted and whacked him a couple of good ones with the crank handle, then stuck the handle onto his crankshaft and spun it once. He coughed into life immediately, and Grandfather snorted again.

A stone landed in the water near my feet, disturbing the surface of the water enough so that it hit my soles, too late, however, to require me to stuff clams into my bathing suit. I looked around and saw the boy who had interrupted my visit with Great-grandmother, the one she had called "rascal." He was standing on the bulkhead, smiling at me. I smiled back and waved. When I saw him there, I saw also the possibility of having a friend, someone to hang around with. Seeing the possibility, I felt the need—for a boon companion, a roarer, a rowdy. I thought of asking Grandfather if the boy on the dock could come out clamming with us, but we were already past jumping distance from the dock, and Grandfather was never willing to turn back once one of these voyages was begun. I gave the boy another wave and watched him grow smaller as we chugged away.

Behind the boy, two suntanned and leggy little girls, blond girls, so alike that I blinked and rubbed my eyes when I saw them, came walking into view, turning the corner from the street where Grandfather lived. They were wearing tiny white shorts and yellow halter tops. When they saw the rascal, they nudged each other and whispered. I knew at once what they were plotting; they were going to push him into the water. He was watching the *Rambunctious*, and they were so stealthy that he didn't seem at all aware that they were sneaking up on him. I began making signs to warn him. I tried to be subtle, so that my gestures wouldn't attract their attention. I cupped a hand and pointed my finger into it. That was supposed to mean "Look behind you." He looked into his hand. I made a pushing motion with both hands. He looked at both his hands. I stood up on the stern and made the same motion. He repeated it. I made a much more exaggerated version of the shoving motion and then took the role of the victim, pantomiming losing my balance, waving my arms in a vain attempt to recover it, and falling into the water.

"Peter!" shouted my father. "Hey, Dad! Stop! Peter fell in!"

I was surprised, when I came up with a mouthful of water, to find that the water was sweet and clean. I looked across the river and noticed a small stream. The tide was going out, and I thought I could see the water from the stream flowing out on top of the receding mix of Bolotomy and bay water. It was smooth, soft, a coat of quicksilver poured over the gray-green and turbid water below it. I paddled around a bit, sampling the water from time to time. I heard applause, and found the rascal standing between the girls at the edge of the bulkhead, laughing and applauding me. I smiled and waved at them.

"Peter! Grab hold!" called my father. He was holding a crab net out toward me. The *Rambunctious* was still chugging downriver, toward the bay, but Grandfather had throttled back so that she was barely moving. I knew that this was as close as he would come to turning back.

"Maybe I should swim to shore," I said, hoping that Grandfather would think that this was a good idea, since he would not have to interrupt his progress toward the flats, and the clams.

"Don't be ridiculous," said my father. "Just take a couple of strokes, and you'll be able to reach the net."

He was right. Reaching the net would be easy. I was able to imagine myself taking one, two, perhaps three strokes, and grabbing hold of the net. I was as easily able to imagine myself doing nothing. I could stop treading water and simply slip below the soft and silvery fresh water into the dark water of this stretch of the Bolotomy, fouled by so many boats. It was the darkness of that lower water and the certainty that the bottom would be a sticky ooze littered with rusting cans that made me decide against letting go. I began to take my strokes, and with each one I found myself repeating the question, "Do clams bite? Do clams bite? Do clams bite?"

"There!" said my father. I had taken hold of the net without noticing, and he was pulling me alongside the *Rambunctious*. He helped me aboard and handed me a towel. I began drying myself. I saw the rascal standing on the dock between the girls, an arm around each of them. I wondered how that felt. He grinned suddenly, out of one side of his mouth, and the girls giggled. I felt doomed.

7

I HAVE SOMETIMES had the feeling, since that time, that the future held nothing that I wanted to face, that I was moving downriver toward some equivalent of having to stuff a hungry clam down the front of my bathing suit, and that I would be better off, on the whole, jumping overboard and letting myself slip beneath the surface, but the thought of the bottom—the slime, the rusty cans—has kept me on board.

8

I WENT UP TO THE BOW and sat there watching the docked boats, the waterside houses, the Flying A station, and the Municipal Dock slip past. It was always a pleasure, however mixed with fear, to see the bay suddenly open before us when we passed the dock, where boys my age sat fishing safely. It was a clear day, and I could see across to the flats.

The flats were a broad expanse of the bay where the water was waist-deep or lower for Grandfather, depending on the spot and the tide. In the flats were numberless small islands, some just dots of land, others large enough to hold a shack. They scarcely rose above the surface of the water. In fact, what height they had was largely an illusion, since it was composed mostly of grasses, not the sand in which the grasses grew. As much as I disliked the flats at the time, I loved the islands, and as much as I feared clamming I loved crabbing with Grandfather along the network of narrow waterways that ran among them. Grandfather slowly, silently rowed the *Rambunctious's* dinghy while I watched for a scurrying crab along the overhanging edges of the islands, a flash of white in the shadowy water, so quick that I reacted not to the crab itself but to the memory of it, and darted my net at where it had been, much as I'm rowing the waterways of memory now, snatching at flashes in the shadows. I liked the pace of crabbing too: the lazy pace, barely more than drifting, and the whispered conversation, which wandered as we did, in and out and around the islands. If, just then, I had been asked to choose a perfect life for myself, that is what I would have chosen, and Grandfather and I would be there now, whispering, barely moving.

9

OF ALL THE ISLANDS, my favorite was the largest, Small's Island. On Small's there was an old hotel, Small's Hotel. Small's had, in its day, been quite the spot. It was abandoned now, and it fascinated me. It was exactly where I wanted to live. I knew nothing of its history at the time, and I was embarrassed to ask my grandfather about it because he was likely to see beyond my questions and realize that I wanted the hotel, the whole island, for my own.

10

GRANDFATHER RAISED THE SAILS, and we began the slow haul across the bay. It occurred to me that a heavy fog might roll in, obscuring the flats, making it impossible for us to find them, impossible for us to clam there. A dark, angry line of thunderclouds might appear on the horizon and bear down on us, and Grandfather would have to turn back. The *Rambunctious* might spring a mighty leak, and we would all have to crowd into the dinghy and row to shore. Instead, the day stayed fair, and the *Rambunctious* leaked no more than usual. We arrived at the flats in due time, Grandfather dropped the sails, cranked him up again, and stood in the bow holding the anchor, looking for a promising piece of bottom, while my father took my usual job, holding the tiller steady, and waiting for word to kill him. I looked over the side, watching the bottom move slowly toward the stern, unrolling like a story. It was, depending on how I saw it on any particular day, seaweed interrupted by patches of sand or sand interrupted by patches of seaweed. On this day it was seaweed interrupted by patches of sand. Now and then I'd see a fish swimming along, a crab crawling across one of the sandy spots, pieces of broken shell, jelly fish, an eel. I always hoped that Grandfather was looking for a wide sandy spot while he stood in the bow, since the sand was much nicer to stand on than the weeds, and I had a better chance to see what was sneaking up on me if it came across the sand than if it came skulking through the weeds.

"Kill him!" Grandfather shouted. A family, fifty yards or so off starboard, looked up at this shout. They had a small motorboat anchored in the flats. The father was doing some clamming, using a rake. The mother was sunning on the tiny deck forward. Two children were paddling around in inner tubes.

"OK!" called my father. He grabbed a screwdriver and shorted the spark-plug lead to the block. He coughed a couple of times and died. I let out a scream and fell to the deck in the cockpit.

"What are you up to, Peter?" asked my father. "He's dead," he called out to Grandfather. I raised myself on one elbow and peeked over at the family. Father and the children were scrambling for the boat. Mother was tugging at the anchor line. Soon they were planing toward the mainland, ahead of a wide, white wake, and we had a broad expanse of the flats to ourselves.

11

A DIGRESSION on the techniques and equipment necessary for clamming. The getting of clams is an ancient undertaking that varies somewhat from place to place and species to species. Of all, the most romantic, the most emblematic of mankind's relationship with the sea, the most persistently attractive mythologically, is the hunting and gathering of the elusive quahog. In Babbington when I was a boy, the methods varied primarily according to the aims of the clammer.

The professional, the clammy, took to the bay in a broad-beamed clamboat. Some of the newer ones had been built in basements or back yards specifically for motorized clamming. They were, as a group, homely and unpretentious craft, roughly rectangular, rising slightly at the bow. Placed near the stern was a small cabin, just large enough to allow the clammy to get out of the sun or the rain for a while, to eat his lunch and drink his beer. Others were converted sailing craft, relics of the days when men were men and clamboats had no motors. These broad-beamed, shallow-draft boats had had their masts and centerboards removed, and now had engines. A few clamboats of both types had engines that were specifically designed for marine use, but most had marine conversions of engines from worn-out cars. Typically, the engine would simply be dropped into the hull, transmission and all. The exhaust was routed upward through a straight stack alongside the cabin, and a galvanized bucket, the same bucket that was used for washing down the deck at the end of the day, was inverted on this stack when the boat was idle, to keep rainwater out. The driveshaft went to a prop, and only first gear and reverse were used. The radiator was eliminated, and bay water was circulated through the block for cooling. Since all clamboats leak, the savvy clammy also made a provision for drawing bilge water through the block and emptying it into the bay, so that the engine bailed the boat while it cooled itself. A simple hand valve switched between bay water and bilge water. I have known many clamboats, and owned a couple, in which this valve was left permanently in the bailing position.

All clamboats had wide, unobstructed decks that ran all around the perimeter of the boat. The clammy would stand on this deck and lower a pair of tongs or, in the technical vocabulary of the profession, sticks, into the water. These sticks could be had in lengths ranging from eight to twelve feet or so. Their long wooden handles were pivoted near the bottom end. At the bottom of each stick was a sturdy wire basket, and at the very bottom of each basket was a row of sturdy metal fingers or teeth. The clammy worked the handles back and forth, raising and dropping the sticks, opening and closing the basket. Each bite scooped up some sand or muck, shell, weed, and, if the clammy had picked the right spot, clams. By shaking the closed baskets vertically, the clammy could wash out the sand and weeds before raising the closed sticks hand over hand, bringing up the catch and dumping it on the deck. The clammy would then take a step to the left, or right if that was his habit, and begin again, so that he would gradually work his way around the deck and, aided by the slow shifting of the boat in the wind and current, cover a broad section of the bottom pretty well by the time he returned to his starting point.

This sounds simple enough, but the subtleties of the art took years to master. Let me give you a single example. A really good clammy could tell just what was in the basket as he shook out the sand and weed. When I was small, I thought that they got their information by weight or sound or vibrations through the sticks. After I had done some clamming myself and spent some time with real master clammies, I learned that a clammy, working his sticks open and shut, rocking swaybacked in the hot sun hour after hour, standing with his feet apart, shifting his weight constantly on a rolling deck, squinting into the sunlight rippling on the waves, attains an exalted state of awareness that allows him to *see* what is in the basket at the bottom of the bay, and that the best of them can not only drop the shells out, but even let the big, tough chowder clams go and keep the small, sweet, valuable cherrystones and littlenecks.

Tonging for clams was hard work, tiring work. Much less tiring, and much more fun, was treading for clams. The tonging clammy worked in the deeper parts of the bay, but the treader worked in the flats, standing in water that was about waist deep. Treading took less skill than tonging; all the treader did was walk around, on the balls of his feet, feeling for clams with the toes and the ball of the foot itself. When he found one, he would duck beneath the surface and pull the clam out of the sand by hand. For treaders with experienced feet, judging the sizes of the clams they found was an easy matter. The casual treader, just gathering a few hors d'oeuvres to have with the evening cocktails, might pass up the larger clams completely, but people who treaded seriously, and there were quite a few, would harvest everything. All serious treaders, and many casual treaders, put the clams they caught into a peck basket that they had inserted into the open center of an inflated inner tube. With this container floating handily beside them, they didn't have to make frequent trips to the boat to empty the catch. My grandfather disdained this eminently sensible contraption. Serious treaders would spend all day at the hunt, so they had to protect their feet in some way. Most used extremely unattractive gray rubber booties.

Both tonging and treading required the clammy to actually go out on the bay in pursuit of the clams, but at the time of my clamming trips with Grandfather, a few visionaries were already experimenting with a new method: avoiding going out on the bay entirely and raising clams at home. Since that time, the popularity of home clam farming, in tanks built especially for that purpose, in swimming pools, or even, on a small scale, in discarded bathtubs, has increased enormously. The main reason, as Porky White put it once, is that "There's no size limit on home-growns. You can gorge yourself on tender little darlings if you want."

12

ONE MORE SHORT DIGRESSION, this time on the sizes of clams. When the day's clamming is over, the clammy culls the clams, sorting them by size. There are four sizes of *Mercenaria mercenaria* in the wild: seeds, littlenecks, cherrystones, and chowder clams.

If you have an adult hand and close your thumb and forefinger to make an oval, you will have defined the approximate size of a littleneck. Littlenecks are the youngest, tenderest of the legal sizes. They should be eaten as they are, raw, or cooked only very briefly. No one with a sense of the fitness of things would ever use them for chowder. Anything smaller than a littleneck is a seed, a clam too young to take. The culler should throw those back into the bay, but many a clammy will tell you that the little ones go very nicely as a snack with a beer. The shells of littlenecks have few practical uses, but they are perfect for crafting handsome whatnots to fill the shelves in your living room, and they make nice jewelry.

If you form another oval with your thumb and forefinger, leaving a gap of about an inch this time, you will have defined the upper limit of a cherrystone. Cherrystones are good for everything. You can eat them raw or steam them or use them in a sauce for pasta, and you can use them in chowder if you're expecting company, elegant company: tall, slim men in dinner jackets, long-stemmed and angular women in silk. The shells are really a little large for earrings, and a little small for ashtrays, unless you're having an elegant little dinner party with the people mentioned above. Most cherrystone shells end up as driveway topping, but quite a few are made into knickknacks and whatnots by people who have somewhat larger knickknack or whatnot shelves than the people who make their knickknacks and whatnots from littleneck shells.

Anything larger than a cherrystone is a chowder clam, and as its name suggests, it is really only good for chowder, and only everyday chowder at that. Now everyday chowder is nothing to sneer at, and there are many occasions when it is just the thing—cold, blustery, rainy days, for instance. Many clam fanciers consider chowder clams the most flavorful and littlenecks almost insipid; others, of course, find the littlenecks sweet and subtle and think that a mouthful of chowder clam is a lot like a mouthful of rubber bands. The shells of chowder clams are widely used as ashtrays.

At Corinne's Fabulous Fruits of the Sea, one of the places where I conduct my research, Porky White, slurping down a few necks flavored with some pepper and lemon one night, said to me, "You know, they're a lot like women, clams. The older ones are kinda tough and wily, but they have real flavor. Those in their prime are sort of the standard, the ideal, but since they're what most people want, the real connoisseur generally wants something else. Now the younger ones, well, they are tenderer, and there are times when tenderness is all, but after a few you find yourself wanting something that you can chew on. And the ones that are too young are a guilty pleasure; you know that you shouldn't even consider them, but every once in a while, when no one's looking—"

The pepper must have gotten to him. He broke off and blew his nose in his napkin.

13

GRANDFATHER slipped over the side into the water. My father stood around with his hands in his pockets, whistling and looking out over the water at the islands.

I sat in the stern, with my legs dangling, playing my game with the surface of the water again, hoping that, since Grandfather had my father to clam with him, I might go unnoticed and not have to get into the water at all.

"Bert," called Grandfather, "are you going to dig some clams?"

"Oh, yeah," said my father. "I was just looking at the islands and wondering how they were formed. Do you ever wonder about that?"

"Nope," said Grandfather

"They probably started out as just sand bars, wouldn't you say?"

"Probably," said Grandfather.

"And then they grew, little by little."

"Guess so," said Grandfather.

My father seemed to have run out of things to say about the islands. He began unbuttoning his shirt, slowly. He spotted me in the stern. "Hey, Peter," he said. "Let's get a move on. Let's not sit around. I want to see you in the water. You must be quite a little clammer by now."

I gave him a sickly grin and started unbuttoning my shirt, more slowly than he. Unbuttoning one's shirt, removing one's trousers, adjusting the string tie on one's little woolen bathing suit—these are tasks that one can't stretch out forever. Eventually my father and I were ready to get into the water. We let ourselves over the side.

I stood near the *Rambunctious*, in water up to my shoulders, watching Grandfather, standing in water up to his waist, shuffling along with short steps, probing the sand with his toes. When he felt a clam, he would duck beneath the surface and scoop it out of the sand. He'd bring it up and drop it into the front of his snug wool suit. Slowly, reluctantly, I began an imitation of his shuffle. I was scared to death: with my father and my grandfather both watching me, today was going to have to be the day.

14

ON MY FIRST CLAMMING TRIP with Grandfather, I had watched him go through this routine, filling the front of his bathing suit, then waddling to the *Rambunctious*, his suit distended and lumpy, dumping his catch on the deck and going right back to the hunt, and I developed a deep admiration for Grandfather's sangfroid that has never left me. I had seen at once that popping clams into one's bathing suit was the manly way of carrying the clams one had caught, but, I thought, "If the little devils bite, then doing the manly thing may be the cause of my being unmanned." I didn't think exactly that, but I thought along those lines. I wanted to ask Grandfather then, "Do clams bite?" but I knew that if I asked, he would look at me with his smart gray eyes and know at once why I was asking, so I did not ask, and instead I began a halfhearted imitation of his shuffle, worrying all the while about what to do with the clams I found, if I found any. Should I take the awful risk? "I'll be unmanned if I do, unmanly if I don't," I thought.

Almost at once, my toes struck something hard, something that could only be one of the tasty bivalves.

Slowly, resignedly, I took a breath, dipped beneath the water, and dug it out of the sand. I stood up slowly.

"You got one," called Grandfather. He beamed at me. "I think maybe you've really got the knack. Now your father—"

"Yah! Woo! Hey!" I shouted.

Grandfather's mouth fell open. He watched me thrashing in the water, rolling around, holding the clam with both hands, twisting, turning. Soon enough, a hefty chowder clam flew from my hands and fell into the water, baloomp, some distance away.

"Damn!" I cried, smacking the water with my open hand. "It got away!"

Grandfather looked at me for a little while, and I thought he was going to say something. He opened his mouth, then closed it without a word.

"It's harder than I thought," I said. "I'll get the next one."

I went through the rest of the afternoon without, apparently, finding another clam. Now Grandfather was a very savvy clammer, and when he stood in the bow of the *Rambunctious* while we glided across the flats looking for a likely spot, he must have been able to see the clams through the sand, for he invariably picked a spot so loaded with them that I couldn't take a step without feeling a couple, but I rarely admitted finding any that day, and by the end of the day I was committed to another fiction, harder to maintain than the hard-candy one. I was passing myself off as hopelessly inept at clamming. Whenever I did call out that I had found one—just often enough, I thought, for verisimilitude—it got away.

15

SINCE MY FATHER WAS CLAMMING TOO, I thought that it would be a good idea to find a clam early and have it get away, put on a good display of disappointment, throw in a little self-denigration, and see if I could coast on that for the rest of the day, not finding another. My father and I were shuffling along side by side, and I had already felt several clams, though my father showed no signs of having found a single one. Then, suddenly, and with greater glee than I'd seen from him before, he sang out, "Hey, Dad, I got one!" He was smiling like an idiot, I thought. He threw himself beneath the surface and almost at once seemed to be locked in a life-or-death struggle with something huge and frightening. His legs shot into the air, his feet flailing. Spray shot out from the place where he fought so desperately. Twice he lifted his head above the surface and gasped for breath. At last he stood upright, with his hands still beneath the surface, as if he were throttling something. Then, as if propelled, his hands shot out of the water, and from them flew a clam. It sailed through the air and landed, baloomp, in the water about ten feet away.

"Son of a bitch!" he shouted. He smacked the water with his fist. "It got away. I guess I'm no better at this than I ever was."

I had seen the clam in the air, followed it in its arc. It was a very young one, probably not legal size.

My father and I shuffled around for the rest of the afternoon, but my father apparently never found another of the elusive little devils, and I ignored all the ones that I felt, though the spot seemed to be paved with them. Grandfather brought up a mess of them; he was a master. He snorted quite a bit and rarely looked our way.

16

WHEN WE RETURNED HOME, the house was full of the smell of the coconut candies that Grandmother often made. They were spheres the size of marbles, made of a butter-and-powdered-sugar concoction that was more buttery than sweet, and they were covered with strands of grated coconut. That smell lingered in the house long after Grandmother died.

17

AT DINNER, my father kept up a rapid chatter, yakking with unusual enthusiasm about this and that. My parents rarely ate dinner at Grandmother and Grandfather's, and their presence made the evening seem a little like a party or a holiday gathering.

May Castle, a longtime friend of my grandparents who was friendly with my parents too, had been at the house when we returned from the bay, and Grandmother had invited her to stay for dinner. May had insisted that she would stay only if Grandfather made cocktails, Manhattans. Everyone was in high spirits by the time we sat down, but my father talked and laughed most and loudest. I had caught his volubility, and I filled any gap that he allowed me to fill with stories about my playmates, stories that included plenty of sawdust. These stories rarely went very well at the dinner table at home, since most were of the you-had-to-be-there type, but they were enjoying great success here, especially with

May, who laughed uproariously at some and squeezed and tickled me after each. Since that time, I have seen other survivors of near-disasters react as my father and I were reacting that night to our having survived the clamming expedition. They go on and on in an uproarious manner. We were eating the clams that Grandfather had gotten, fried.

"You know, we ought to sell our house and buy something closer to the water," my father suddenly said to my mother. Eyebrows went up around the table. "I really miss it." Grandfather snorted and went on eating. My father got up to get another beer.

He usually drank a beer called Bendernagle's Old Bavarian, a beer widely advertised on billboards that depicted a smiling blond barmaid with breasts like prize-winning cantaloupes, wearing a Bavarian costume, leaning toward the potential Bendernagle customer, and pouring a can of Old Bavarian into an enormous crockery stein that, miraculously, she was filling to overflowing, foam sloshing over the lip and dripping onto an invisible floor. This woman played a prominent role in a series of dreams I had begun having. You will probably not be surprised to learn that in these dreams I was wearing my little woolen bathing suit, stuffed full of clams, and that I was quite uncomfortable.

"If only Fat Hank hadn't sold Leroy Lager," I said, or, in my enthusiasm, shouted, "we'd be rich, and we'd be driving around in a white Packard, and we could buy Small's Island and fix up the hotel and live there." I beamed around the table, expecting that people would jump into my fantasy, and that we'd spend a happy hour rehabilitating the hotel and assigning rooms to one another, but only May had any enthusiasm for the idea.

"I've spent many a happy night there," she said.

"May—" said Grandmother. May raised her glass to Grandmother, as if she were toasting something, and said no more. From the expressions on the faces of the others, I saw that I had said something wrong.

"Peter," said my mother, "you shouldn't talk about things that you don't know anything about, and even if you do, you shouldn't make fun of people who are dead, and especially not your ancestors."

I wasn't quite sure where I had gone wrong. I had supposed, when I made the remark, that I was on safe ground with Fat Hank, and that the only risky part was my desire for the island.

"What do you know about Fat Hank?" my father asked me. The table was quiet now, and I had everyone's attention. I swallowed once.

"Well, he was the only child of Black Jacques, the dashing and swarthy Algerian, who invented beer." I waited the briefest of moments for a laugh, but I could see quite quickly that there wasn't going to be any. "Not beer, but Leroy Lager. It was a really great beer, sturdy and honest, not like the insipid pisswater that they try to pass off on you now—"

"Peter!" interjected my mother.

"—and there was a poem on the back of each bottle," I said, trailing off at the end to a whisper.

My father burst out laughing, but not as he had been. This was a dark laugh.

"Where did you get that?" he asked.

"From Great-grandmother," I said.

My father made a sober face and rumpled my hair. "Don't believe everything you hear up there," he told me. "You know, Peter," he said, "your great-grandmother is pretty old."

"I know," I said. Of course I knew. Everything about Great-grandmother was old. The paint in her rooms, the curtains, and she herself were yellow and brittle with age; the paint cracked in intricate networks and curled away from the wall in places, stiffly, in one spot forming the shape of an owl that watched and listened to the talks we had together; the threads in the curtains had grown so brittle that they had cracked in the breeze, and Great-grandmother's hair had become as stiff and brittle as the hair on a coconut. I worried every time she shifted in her chair. I was afraid that she would break and I'd be blamed for it.

"Well," he said, speaking as slowly as Great-grandmother herself, picking each word carefully, "she doesn't remember things quite the way they really happened. She, uh, changes things a little."

"You mean she makes things up," I said.

"Not on purpose. She just doesn't remember the way they really happened, so she says what she thinks should have happened or what she wishes had happened—"

"Or hadn't," May mumbled.

"—instead of what she remembers. Understand?"

"Yeah," I said. I didn't believe a word he was saying.

May leaned toward me and whispered through a mist of Manhattan, "She's not the only one—I do it myself," and kissed my ear.

"May—" said Grandmother again.

"Let me tell you about Black Jacques," my father said. He drew a long breath and took a pull at his beer. He glanced at Grandfather. When he looked back at me, I looked hard into his eyes, and I said to myself, "He's going to make this up." May put her hand on my knee and gave it a squeeze.

"Black Jacques," my father said, "was a clammy. He was a short, fat man with black hair and a black beard. That's why he was called Black Jacques. He worked hard, when he was sober. You have to give him that," he said, to the others, turning from me for a moment. "Now, as far as beer goes, he was well known for drinking it, and I imagine that he did make quite a lot for his own use, but he was not in the beer business, and there wasn't any Leroy Lager, and Black Jacques didn't hang around with poets and that kind of crowd."

"Well—" said May.

"All right, all right," said my father. "In a way he did, I guess. His cronies liked their beer as much as he did, and you will find, Peter, when you grow older, that people start to behave in lots of funny ways when they have too much to drink. Some of them decide that they're God's gift to women. Those are usually the ones who are too loaded to get it up."

"Bert!" said my mother.

"Hmmmmm. How do you know that, Bertram?" asked May

"Let me speak my piece," said my father. "Other ones decide that they're great poets. Those are usually the ones who are too drunk to hold a pencil. So, if you like, you could probably say that Black Jacques hung around with a lot of great poets and famous lovers. So much for that. Now this beer of his—"

Grandfather snorted.

"If you want to get technical about it," said my father, "he did put up some beer in bottles, but this wasn't any sort of real business. It was just a guy brewing some beer so that he could drink it with his friends. And these poems that keep coming up, they were just some obscene—"

Grandfather had been eating throughout my father's talk, contributing only the one snort noted above. He was passionately devoted to the fried clam. He ate them slowly, with his fingers, as we all did, for that was the only effective way to eat the clams he cooked, which crunched spectacularly and were likely to snap in two and fly off the table if you tried to cut them or stab them with a fork. Every time I fry up a batch of clams now, following Grandfather's instructions, and sit down to eat them, I take on his single-mindedness. I want to eat through that plate undisturbed, undistracted, undiverted. If Grandfather was asked a direct question while he was eating, we would have to wait until he was between clams for an answer, and even then it would be reluctant and brief. Now, he stopped with half a clam in his hand and half in his mouth, and he said, smiling, with his skin crinkled at the edges of his eyes, "They were great." He meant that to be all he would say, but before he could take another bite of the clam, a chuckle took control of him, and he paused again. "Great," he repeated.

"That's a matter of opinion," said my father. "Anyway, it was Henry Leroy, my grandfather, who wound up having to support Black Jacques, and in fact you could say that he had to work from the time he was a boy to support his father's habits, and what did his father do to thank him? He—"

"That's enough, Bert," said Grandfather, very quietly, as he might have told me that he had seen a crab when we were rowing slowly in and out among the grassy islands in the flats.

A silence followed. I looked down at my plate and let my eyes drift out of focus, blurring the food into an unappetizing lump. May ran her hand up and down my thigh and now and then gave me a little pat, as if to say, "Chin up. This won't last long. It's part of growing up."

"Well, anyway," said my father after a long while, turning to me again, "the point is that Black Jacques isn't anybody to look up to."

He stopped. I waited to find out why Black Jacques wasn't anybody to look up to, but my father seemed to think he had said all he needed to say.

"Why?" I asked at last.

"That's something that will have to wait until you're a little older," said my mother. There was a strong tone of relief in her voice, as if she thought it likely that I would never be a little older, and that the matter was, therefore, and thank God for it, closed. I was embarrassed. I knew that if it was something that had to wait until I was a little older, it had to be about boys and girls. Being embarrassed made me feel small and powerless, but when I raised my eyes, surreptitiously, without raising my head, I saw that except for May, who was grinning, they were as embarrassed as I. I had no way of realizing then why they were embarrassed. I didn't realize, couldn't have realized, that the boy-and-girl business went right on being embarrassing when people got older. Only very much later did I realize that this embarrassment was a source of power. Studying the uneasy faces, I could see, however, that the uneasiness, the embarrassment around the table, offered a little opening for me, a little chink through which, before I started to cry, I could strike a blow for Black Jacques, that tall, dark, well-muscled Algerian who was standing somewhere in my mind holding an overflowing stein of Leroy Lager, his arm around the Bavarian barmaid, reciting a bawdy poem. I didn't hesitate an instant, and in my ignorance I tapped that source of power.

"When Great Grandma was a girl, she liked Black Jacques better than Fat Hank," I said.

"You said it," burst from May.
"Peter, go to bed," said my mother.
I started sniffling.

18

I DID GO TO BED, upstairs, where I always slept when I visited Grand-mother and Grandfather, in the room my father had had when he was a boy. It was still a boy's room. On the walls were maps of faraway countries and charcoal sketches of boats. A tall bookshelf was filled with boys' adventure stories and aviation magazines. A cupboard and a set of shelves above it were filled with ship models, the models that he had built from *The Boys' Book of Boatbuilding*. A couple of these were half-finished, as if my father had been at play, working on his models one day, when there was a knock on the door and someone had barged in, caught him playing, and said, "Stop that, now. You're grown up," and he had never returned. I always stayed in this room, but he never came upstairs to visit it. I sometimes thought of finishing the models, but they were too complicated for me then, and they bored me later.

The room was in the front of the house, with three windows along the front wall, above the roof over the porch that ran the length of the front of the house, and one on a side wall, facing west. Below the west window, Grandfather had built a small desk, where my father must have done his schoolwork. Beside the desk was a set of drawers. In the top drawer were a student's supplies, abandoned, old, and useless: yellowed sheets of paper, a grammar book, pencils with hardened erasers, pens and nibs, bottles that held the dried remains of ink and mucilage.

In the second drawer was equipment for adventures: a compass, hand-drawn maps of Babbington, the bay, and the course of the Bolotomy, a code book, several coded messages, a book with its middle pages cut out to make a secret compartment (empty), a whistle, a camera, a telescope, a magnifying glass, and a burnt cork.

The third drawer seemed to be filled with a hodgepodge of souvenirs: rocks, shells, postcards, ribbons, newspaper clippings, booklets, badges, and the like. From investigation, however, I knew that at the bottom of this drawer were guilty pleasures: a corncob pipe, a half-empty package of Lucky Strikes, and a dozen photographs of a nude woman.

She was at the ocean, romping in the surf, standing at the edge, running into the water, running from the water, throwing sand at the photographer, imitating September Morn, sticking her tongue out, striking a bathing-beauty pose, lying in the surf, standing with her hands on her hips, toweling herself dry, and finally, holding the towel at her side, draping it on the sand, just smiling at the camera, a little chilled, with goosebumps on her skin, so very happy that my heart leaped each time I reached the last picture. The pictures were clear and sharp. My father had taken a passionate interest in photography for a while; these pictures had been printed with great skill and care.

I WAS IN BED, examining the pictures with the magnifying glass. There was a knock at the door. I shoved the pictures under the covers, just as the door opened and May slipped in. She was holding a finger to her lips and wearing a conspiratorial look, her eyes squinted half shut, her brows knit, and her lips pursed. She made a bit of business out of looking over her shoulder into the hall to see if she'd been followed, tiptoeing into the room, and closing the door with exaggerated caution. In a napkin she had some of Grandmother's coconut balls. She sat on the bed, spread the napkin, and picked out half of the balls for me.

"I'm supposed to be taking these up to your Grandma Lydia," she whispered, leaning close to me, enveloping me in a cloud of Manhattan. "But I thought I'd just stop by and give a few to my favorite Peter." She giggled and leaned forward and nuzzled me.

"Thanks," I whispered, joining in the little conspiracy.

She took my right hand and began patting it rapidly. "They're not really upset with you, you know," she said. "Don't you worry. By morning they will have forgotten all about it." Then she shrugged and said, "Then again, on the other hand, perhaps they won't have forgotten all about it." She snickered and put a coconut ball into my mouth. I chewed and swallowed it while she studied me. Then she held my chin with her thumb and forefinger and turned my head this way and that, examining me with great care. I thought for a moment of offering her the magnifying glass. "There's a little Black Jacques in all the Leroy boys," she said. She dropped her hand to the covers between my legs and patted me there as she had patted my hand before. She looked around the room. "Some of them lose it or have it knocked out of them, as if Fat Hank caught them having fun one day and said, 'Stop that now. You're grown up.'"

She sat still, rubbing me through the covers, looking at the wall above

"Oh, yes," I said, wiping tears from my eyes. "I swallowed my candy, that's all."

"This must be quite a question that you want to ask, if it chokes you on the way out. Is it about boys and girls?"

"Oh, no. I know about that." I didn't, but I thought that I was supposed to. "Grandma, do clams bite?"

She looked at me for a while, not, as I had feared, with disgust, as if I had asked a question that only a timid little boy would ask, but with surprise and bewilderment. After a long time, she said simply, "I haven't any idea."

3

LATER, AS A YOUNG MAN, I went to work as an editor on the staff of *The Young People's Cyclopedia*. This compendium of useful facts, historical anecdotes, brief lives, practical instruction, oversimplifications, and misinformation was compiled first in a small office above Jack's Twenty-Four Hour Jokes, on the corner of Bolotomy and Main, in the heart of Babbington, and later, when it had become an institution, in a concrete castle, one of those structures that businesses build to show their nostalgia for feudalism, outside town in a spot that had once been a potato farm and now held many industrial and office buildings and was called, preposterously, a park. The entries were written by a network of experts, amateurs, teachers, and housewives who were assigned topics to develop within strict limits of space. To add a little to the salary I received there, I wrote some entries myself, borrowing as a pseudonym the name of a good friend, Eliza Foote. As Eliza Foote, I wrote many entries in *The Young People's Cyclopedia*, including entries for most of the Leroys, points of interest in and around Babbington, bivalves, and friends and acquaintances who deserved, it seemed to me, a little space on a library shelf. For the entry on Black Jacques, I used some of what Great-grandmother had told me, and lots of sawdust.

my head. I was looking closely at her mouth, at the parentheses around it and at the vertical lines along her upper lip.

"I have to go," she said. She gave me a squeeze and left.

19

SHE WAS RIGHT about the influence of Black Jacques, or of some strain that began before Black Jacques and reached its full flowering in him, but I wasn't sure then just what it meant to be like Black Jacques or like Fat Hank, and I'm still not sure, because they have turned out to be more complicated than either my great-grandmother or my father presented them. I think that Big Grandfather, sitting silently, eating his clams while my father talked, may have understood them better than any of the others, or perhaps Big Grandmother did, for she joined him in his silence, and she ate with great gusto.

Broadly, being like Black Jacques means, I think, letting yourself be seduced by your dreams, pursuing them, sending them flowers, and never noticing, or caring, that people are laughing at you behind their hands, never even quite noticing, at last, that you've made a fool of yourself. And being like Fat Hank means being ashamed of a dream, sneering at it, pushing it away, abandoning it as foolishness, and having it haunt you, having it leave a cold, empty spot right behind your breastbone, as if you had swallowed an ice cube when you drained your drink. But the two strains have become so mixed and confused along the Leroy line (if they were ever really distinct, for there was some Hank in Jacques and some Jacques in Hank) that the voices of Black Jacques and Fat Hank sometimes speak to me at once, and I can't always tell which is which.

Even my father, who had been so disturbed when he watched the Black Jacques in me pursuing the kittens on my mother's parents' lawn, still had a little Black Jacques in him. I had seen it, though I hadn't recognized it for what it was at the time, after my parents and I left my mother's parents' house and moved into a little house of our own, one of thirty-six nearly identical houses thrown up one summer in the northwest corner of Babbington, on a piece of land that wasn't good for anything else.

My mother wanted my father to finish a corner of the attic as a bedroom for me. All she wanted was four plasterboard walls and a solid floor. My father began working at night on plans for the room, and on many nights he worked on into the morning, leaving for work late and red-eyed, rushing off without breakfast. But he was smiling, and the house was full of excitement. Late at night, when he finally put his pencil down and went to bed, he and my mother would wake me with their laughing and squealing and jumping about. He began to whistle. At last, one evening after dinner, he spread the plans out on the kitchen table for us to see. The room he planned would fill the whole attic, from one end of the house to the other. The attic stairs would be torn out: I would reach my room by climbing a rope ladder from the kitchen, and in the morning I would slide down a fire pole to the hall outside the bathroom. A model railroad would run completely around the perimeter of the room, through mountains, alongside a river, and through a miniature Babbington that would fill the corner that my mother had thought would serve as the entire bedroom. Painted on the walls behind Babbington would be the bay, the clam flats, the islands, and the sea and the sky, receding to a thin, precise horizon. Painted on the floor would be a chess board, where I would be able to play living games with my playmates in the neighborhood. At the center of the room, a helical staircase would lead to the top of a lighthouse that would grow from the center of the roof like a cupola gone mad. I would be charged with the responsibility of seeing that it was always lit at night.

My mother and I were ecstatic. It was a magnificent conception. I would become, in a stroke bold beyond anything that the neighbors might have dreamed, the envy of all the kids on the block. The three of us dragged a stepladder to the roof and set it up with its legs on either side of the peak, just where the lighthouse was going to emerge. We took turns steadying it for one another so that we could stand on the top step and look out over the lights of Babbington, the bay, the flats, the islands, the sea. It was breathtaking.

On the following weekend, my father bought a case of beer and assembled a crew of friends, and they cut a circular hole in the center of the roof. Storm clouds gathered, and there was a high-spirited scramble for tarpaulins and tents that they patched together to cover the opening. While the rain fell, my father and his helpers drank the beer and studied the plans. I could see that my father was already the envy of all *his* friends. After a while, since the rain kept up, the friends drifted off, and Black Jacques, thinking that there was a pretty good chance that they'd be stopping at a tavern, slipped off with them. Somehow, while the door was open and no one was looking, Fat Hank got in.

My father went upstairs, with the plans in his hand, and stood under the canvas, listening to the drumming of the rain and shaking his head. He worked every evening during the next week to close the hole and patch the roof, and on the following weekend he put up plasterboard walls in a small corner of the attic and laid a floor of linoleum tile. This corner became my room. Once, later, at night, when my parents were out, I put a ladder up to the back of the house and climbed it to the roof. I walked to the center of the roof and stood where the hole had been, on my toes, looking out toward the bay.

20

WHEN MAY HAD GONE, I took the pictures out from under the covers and bent over them with the magnifying glass. In the pictures, May was quite a few years younger, and there was no sign of the vertical lines along her upper lip. I could see the parentheses around her mouth though, and a spray of lines shooting out from her eyes, because she smiled so much. But the closer I looked, no matter how much I tried to persuade myself that I was wrong, that the shadows were deceiving me, the more I had to admit the truth: May had no penis.

I wished that I had had the nerve to ask her, while she had been sitting with me, how she had lost it and whether it had hurt, but I wouldn't have known how to console her if she had broken down in tears, and it may have been the certainty that if she did break down in tears I'd be blamed for it that kept me from asking. Still, she was so happy in the pictures, running in the surf. If she'd been hurt, she had recovered. On her face I could see a kind of joy that could not be faked. These were not pictures of someone who was making the best of a bad deal. She was happy. Maybe, I allowed myself to think, it didn't matter all that much. Maybe it was no worse than losing a tooth.

21

WHENEVER I BEGAN TO GO TO SLEEP after a day on the *Rambunctious*, the bed in my father's room would toss and roll, replaying the trip down the river and across the bay. Sometime before I reached the flats, I would usually be asleep, but that night, shortly after I passed the town dock, I heard a scratching at the window screen. I lifted my head and found myself looking into a boy's face flattened against the screen. His nose was bent to one side and pressed white, with dimpled squares of flesh projecting through the interstices. His lips were curled into a snarl, and he was holding his hands beside his ears and clawing with his fingers against the screen, playing the part of a large, white-faced cat that would go for my throat if it could get in. It was the boy who had burst into Great-grandmother's room, the one she called "rascal," crouched on the roof over the front porch.

Recently, when I read to him the foregoing description of his snarling at the window screen, he said, "I think I realized even then that making friends is an odd and delicate business, full of opportunities for disaster, for losing face, and for rejection. At some point, in some way, you have to declare your intentions, to say, 'I like you. I want to be friends.' This is much harder to say than 'I love you,' because friends give up much more to each other than lovers do. I suppose that's why few lovers are friends. I'm certain that's why making friends, for many boys anyway, often begins with a threat. The boy needs to establish antagonism as a base from which to build the friendship, so that if anything goes wrong, if the possible friend laughs at his name or catches him in a lie, he can fall back on the antagonism and pretend that he was only kidding about the friendship."

That may be, but it struck me at once when I saw him that he had come to make friends. He pulled his face away from the screen and smiled. I opened the screen, and he climbed through the window onto the bed.

"You're Peter," he said. "Right?"

"Yes," I whispered. I was fascinated by the grid left on his nose and the side of his face by the window screen.

"My name's Rodney," he said. He paused a moment. He was looking at me with unblinking eyes. "You think that's funny?"

"No," I said.

"I think it's the stupidest name I ever heard of, and so does my father," he said. "My mother thought it up. But nobody calls me that anyway. Everybody calls me Raskolnikov. It's a mouthful, isn't it? My uncle started calling me that, on account of the haunted look I have. What do you think?" He clamped his jaw and tipped his head downward so that he was looking up at me, his eyes glinting from deep hollows. "It's the name of a character in a book. A real son of a bitch. Carries an ax." He stopped to let that sink in. He was chewing gum. "Anyway, everybody calls me Raskol."

"Oh," I said, "that's what Grandma called you."

"Yeah," he said. "Your great-grandmother, you mean. She's a peach, isn't she?"

"Yeah," I said. I tried to sound as if I agreed enthusiastically, but I wasn't sure that I liked having this fellow call my great-grandmother a peach; in fact, I wasn't sure that I liked his knowing my great-grand-mother well enough to have decided that she was a peach. Things were not off to a very good start, I thought. Still, I had decided that I liked him, and I wanted him to like me.

"Move over," he said. "I've got somebody else with me."

"Is it the boy who sold you the knife?" I asked. "The one who ran away from home because his father is a drunk and his mother is an enter-tainer? He probably needs a place to sleep. We can put some blankets on the floor and fold up some towels to make a pillow. Did he have any lunch or dinner? I could probably sneak down into the kitchen later, when I'm sure everybody's asleep, and make him some sandwiches."

He had started to turn toward the window. Now he turned back toward me, but he looked to one side of me and the dimpled squares on his cheek reddened. He said nothing.

I felt like a fool, a naive fool, a little boy, next to this little man. Why hadn't I realized that the runaway had been stitched up out of whole cloth and stuffed full of sawdust? Why hadn't I kept my mouth shut? I sup-pose that I looked wistful and disappointed, for I felt that I had lost the chance to make the right impression on this fellow, who would have made so good a friend. I was trying like the dickens to think of something clever to say that would get both of us out of this awkward spot, get things moving again, but I couldn't think of a thing, and the moment seemed as if it would freeze as it was and become one of those damned moments that persist and persist, rising from the memory now and then like heart-burn, but then Raskol's face lit up. For an instant he seemed about to grin, but then he tightened his mouth. He shook his head resignedly.

"Oh, him," he said. "Nah, he's gone. Now *there* was a haunted char-acter. I really feel sorry for that kid. I know how you feel; I felt the same way you do about him. I figured that if I brought him home my parents would probably give him a warm meal and then adopt him, but he wouldn't have any of that. He just wanted to keep moving. I never even got his name."

"That's a shame," I said, "a real shame," and I was grinning from ear to ear and so was he. It was going to be all right.

"Anyway," he said, "I brought somebody much better than him. I brought these two sweeties."

He leaned out the window and hissed. The two girls that I had seen sneaking up behind him on the dock appeared, and they climbed through the window and onto the bed.

22

I AM THIRTY-SEVEN years old now. Margot and Martha, the Glynn twins, who climbed through the window that night, are now thirty-nine. Raskol is forty. The events that I have been relating took place early in the summer after I had finished the fourth grade. I had skipped the third grade, and my birthday wouldn't come until the fall, after the school year had started, so I was, when the Glynn twins came through the window, not yet nine. I'll let you work the rest of the ages out for yourself. If we had been clams, you would have had to throw us back.

I followed the three of them out the window, along the porch roof, and down a maple tree at the far end of the porch. As I slid along a branch that overhung the porch, light from the living room fell on me, and through the window I could see my grandparents, sitting on the scratchy furniture, reading. We walked along the road to the river, and along the river to Raskol's father's clamboat. The night was warm. Clouds slipped across the face of the moon. Raskol began undressing as soon as we reached the clamboat, and I saw that we were going to swim in the river. He was in the water quickly, and I wasn't far behind. The tide was out again now, so the soft, sweet water from the stream flowed out over the dark Bolotomy. I turned onto my back and watched Margot and Martha undress on the flat deck at the stern of the boat, two shadows against the white cabin, bending over, sliding their shorts down to their ankles and stepping out of them, grabbing the hems of their shirts and shooting their arms upward. Then the clouds moved aside, and for a moment before they dove into the water everything glowed with moonlight: the sumptuous skin of the water, like pewter, and Margot and Martha, side by side, before the fluorescent white cabin, two smooth sprites, their hair as soft and bright as the moonlight, and between their long thighs, no penises.

Their dives were sleek and silent, and they swam underwater quite a distance before coming up. During the time that they were underwater, I figured it all out. They were girls. May had been a girl. They had all been girls from the very start. I understood the whole thing, more or less.

A head rose out of the water next to me.

Her features—their features—were still just sketches of what they would eventually become, except for their large eyes, their large watery blue eyes, and their long lashes.

"I'm Martha," she said, just so that I'd know. She already had the unsettling habit of looking steadily, unblinkingly into my face with those lovely, wide, incredulous eyes. We were treading water, looking at each other, and that steady, doubtful look made me think, as it so often has since, that she was waiting for me to say something, that she probably wouldn't believe what I said, but that she had expected me to say something, and wondered why I hadn't come out with it yet. So I came out with it.

"I like the way you look," I said.

We swam in the river for a while, paddling around, talking, whispering. Whenever a car went by on the road that ran along the water we clung to one of the boats, and to each other, hiding in the shadows. Incidentally, she would place her hand on the small of my back and apply a little pressure to guide me into the shadows; I would put my arm around her waist and hold her close to me, because in her shimmering reflection I thought I'd seen her shiver. After a while, our hands began to wander, and soon we had pretty well satisfied our curiosity.

We swam across the river, to the mouth of the stream, on the side of the river where there were no clamboats, where a large house stood back from the water, separated from it by trim lawns. Raskol and Margot were there, and the four of us stood up in the stream. Even in the shifting light, I could see how very alike Margot and Martha were.

"Let's go up this stream," I said. "I want to see where it comes from."

"You can't go very far," said Raskol. "It runs between these houses, and then you come to the street."

He was right. Whispering and giggling, we walked along in the stream bed, the water barely up to our ankles. Willow trees grew on either side, and the stream was so narrow that their branches mingled and hung in a tangle overhead. We could look into the lighted houses as we passed. We hadn't gone far before we came to a metal culvert, hardly large enough for us to crawl through.

"See?" said Raskol. "There isn't much to it. I've been through there, but it's a tight squeeze, and it's not worth squeezing through. You know what I used to think when I was little? I used to think that this stream came from another world. My brother told me that. He told me that he had crawled through the culvert once and come out in another place like

this, but different, different in a way that he couldn't explain. He made a
lot of noise about how I was probably too scared to go there, so one morning I crawled in, and I *was* scared. I've never been so scared. I could see
some light, way down at the end, and I thought that must be the other
world, so I started getting excited, and I crawled along faster, on my
hands and knees in the water. When I got to the end, I thought I had made
the biggest discovery anybody ever made. There it was, right there in
front of me, this other world that looked just like this one, but a little different. I had to sit down because my heart was pounding so hard. When I
got my breath, I started exploring around. And what did I find? The
other world was exactly like this one. There were houses just like regular
houses. There was a Bolotomy River just like our Bolotomy River.
There were clamboats just like real clamboats. There was even a clamboat just like my father's clamboat, and on it there was a guy just like my
father wiping his nose on his sleeve the way my father does. It was
spooky. There was something wrong about it—I can't explain it, but I
knew I didn't want to stay there. So I ran back to the end of the culvert
and crawled back through, and when I got back out I felt safe again because I was back home."

We had started back down the stream, and we walked along quietly for a
while pondering the implications of Raskol's story. Then Margot spoke up.

"Our father used to tell us something like that," she said. "We used to
race to be the first one out the door to play, and we'd wind up squeezing
through the door side by side. He wanted to get us to stop racing for the
door by having us take turns being first, so he warned us that every time
we squeezed through the door side by side we would change into each
other. Martha would become Margot and Margot would become Martha.
If we wanted to stay who we were, we'd better start going through the
door one at a time."

"We believed him, too," said Martha. "He told us in such a serious
voice, as if he had just noticed what was happening and was worried
about us."

"We spent almost a whole night trying to figure out how many times
we had already been through the door side by side, so that we'd know
who was who so far."

"In the morning we decided that it didn't make any difference, so long
as neither of us wanted to switch."

"So we never squeezed through the door again."

We giggled at that while we swam across to Raskol's father's boat.
While we were dressing, Margot and Martha turned those unblinking eyes
on me, and I thought that I should say something.

"That's nothing," I said. My mouth began filling again, as if I had taken too many of Great-grandmother's hard candies. I swallowed hard and went on. "When I was little, I used to think that clams could bite." I laughed uproariously, and they chuckled a little, tentatively.

"I would go out clamming with Grandfather, and I would stand in the water watching him shuffle along. When he felt a clam, he would duck under and bring it up and drop it into the front of his bathing suit. He'd keep dropping clams in until his suit was all lumpy, and then he'd waddle over to the *Rambunctious* and empty them onto the deck. I knew he wanted me to do the same thing, but I was sure that the first one I dropped in there would bite—"

I hesitated a moment. I didn't quite have a word for what I wanted to say.

"—me," I said, using a word that came closer to the essence of my pelecypodophobia than I knew.

"I wanted to ask him, 'Do clams bite?' but I knew that if I asked, he would figure out why I was asking and know that I was afraid, so I didn't ask. I just did what he did, and hoped that all the clams I caught would be asleep. Well, I caught a lot of clams, and none of them bit me, so I figured it out for myself. Clams don't bite. Girls are just born that way."

I have often wondered, of a Sunday morning, what imp made me say the things I said on Saturday night. As soon as my last sentence was out, I wondered why I had said it. I blushed, and they laughed. Raskol clamped a strong hand on my shoulder and said, "I knew I was going to like you the minute I saw you fall into the water."

Life on the Bolotomy

The pleasures of my earliest youth have become the inheritance of other men.

Henry David Thoreau
A Week on the Concord and Merrimack Rivers

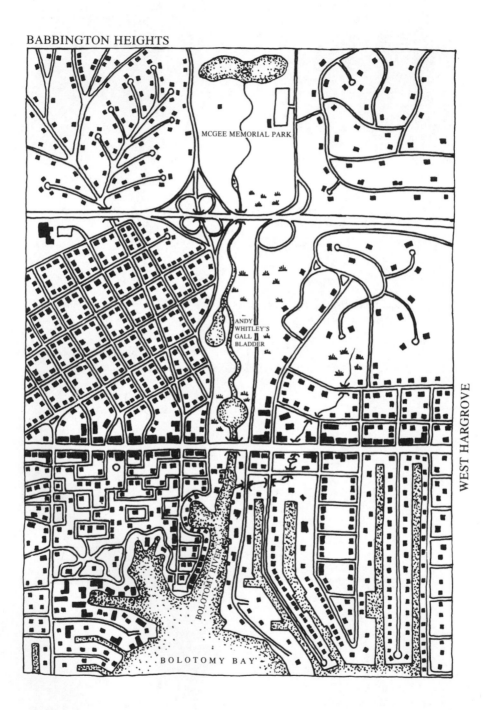

BABBINGTON HEIGHTS

MCGEE MEMORIAL PARK

ANDY
WHITLEY'S
GALL
BLADDER

WEST HARGROVE

BOLOTOMY RIVER

BOLOTOMY BAY

Preface

It has often seemed to us that life, in several respects at any
rate, is much like a river.

Susanna and Elizabeth Christensen
Boating on the Bolotomy

I KNOW THAT many people agree with the Christensen sisters, but it
has always seemed to me that life, in several respects at any rate, is more
like clam chowder. My development of the exposition of this notion
reached its zenith one evening not long ago when I was chatting with
Porky White, the entrepreneur responsible for the Kap'n Klam chain of
bivalve-shaped fast-food huts, and Congo Red, the bartender at Corinne's
Fabulous Fruits of the Sea.

A surprising snowstorm had struck Babbington in the morning, and
Red was complaining about how long the trip from Hargrove to Babbington had taken on the Hargrove-to-Babbington bus.

Suddenly, Porky poked me on the shoulder and asked, "It's a lot like
life, isn't it? A bus ride, that is."

"Mmmmm?" I asked.

"Sure," he said. "Just think about it. You're always on your way from
one goddamned place to another, and you have to pay for the trip, and
nobody cares whether you get there or not, and you feel miserable the
whole time, and when you get there nobody's there to meet you, and like
as not you step off the bus into some dog shit."

Porky and Red collapsed into phlegmy, racking laughter. I thought
about what Porky had said.

"It seems to me," I put forth, "that life is more like clam chowder."

They stopped laughing and regarded me with some curiosity.

"Some people's lives are the kind of chowder made with cream," I
said, "which is quite acceptable, but others are the kind made with tomatoes, which can be superb, especially with a little cayenne. Each life is

like an individual batch of chowder: some have too many potatoes, and others have too much cayenne. Each has its high points—"

"The clams!" suggested Red.

"Of course," I said. "And each has its low points—"

"The potatoes!" offered Porky.

"Mmmmm—not necessarily," said Red. "What about the grains of sand that collect at the bottom of the bowl?"

"Oh, yeah, I forgot about that," admitted Porky.

"Those may be the dark, gritty bits at the bottom of any life that one would really rather forget," I suggested. "Any dark, gritty bits at the bottom of your life, Porky?"

"Well—"

Red and I enjoyed a little snickering at Porky's expense.

"Of course," I said, pushing my empty glass toward Red, "some lives have no sand at all, because they're made with *canned* clams, but they're a bland bunch. Now here comes the real secret to a good chowder or a good life—a good broth. Why? Because in any life, even the richest, one finds so very many moments that are neither high nor low, those times when you scoop up a spoonful of broth without any clams or potatoes or dark, gritty bits at all."

"Amen," said Porky, and I knew that he was convinced.

And yet, the Christensen sisters and all the people who agree with them may be right. I will admit that part of my life, my youth, has had at least a geographic resemblance to the course of the Bolotomy River.

The Bolotomy flows from a spring-fed pond several miles north of Babbington. This pond is at the heart of the Mayor Harvey ("Heavy Harv") McGee Memorial Park. At the center of the pond is a tiny wooded island where, I believe, I was, on a January night, during a skating party, just beyond the light and warmth of a bonfire, conceived.

In its early stretches, the Bolotomy is narrow and shallow, barely a stream, but at one point, suddenly and surprisingly, the river broadens and deepens, and for a short stretch it is an idyllic swimming spot. When I was a boy, I often rode my bicycle to this spot from my parents' house. There the water was pellucid and cold, the bottom was covered with small rounded stones, and the bank on one side was flat and grassy. This spot was supposed to be a secret. I was taught its location by a neighbor, an older boy who later broke my foot for me by jumping on it. To reach the swimming spot, one rode or walked along a well-used trail to a certain place where the sides of the trail seemed to be closed by impenetrable bushes; then one stopped as if to tie a shoe, looked over one's shoulder and, if no one was in sight, parted one pair of bushes carefully to open the way to another trail, a narrow, damp one that led to the secret spot.

From time to time, the spot would be violated by older boys and girls, who smoked and drank and frightened the rest of us, and once a family arrived and spread out a blanket and ate a picnic lunch, but most of the time children my age were the only swimmers.

Later, as a boy, and even more as a young man, I spent a lot of time along the estuarial stretch of the Bolotomy, learning things, talking, working, and wondering about the world outside Babbington.

And now, as I write this, some time after youth, I'm on an island in Bolotomy Bay, surrounded by the river's water, though by the time it reaches this island the river water is no longer part of the river. From where I work, I can look back across the bay and a little way up the Bolotomy, back toward my beginnings.

I began planning "Life on the Bolotomy" while I was sitting where I am sitting now, looking across the bay and up the river. I remembered that I had wanted, as a boy, to travel the length of the river and see what I could see. It would have been a perfect trip for Raskol and me. I was taken at once with the idea of making the trip now, of traveling up the river to find out where it began, how it became what it was. If I were to make such a journey, I thought, I would need a boat, a specialized boat, one that could navigate the narrow upper reaches. I began sketching such a boat at once.

Peter Leroy
Small's Island
December 17, 1982

1

If, as we suggested at the start of this book, life is like a river, then old age must be a period of loss of control, of foul-smelling discharges. Certainly this is the case with the Bolotomy. If one judged the river by its final stretch, one would have no notion at all of its earlier, upriver, beauty, for here it has been made to submit to the demeaning demands of men: its course is defined by wooden bulkheads, docks and piers intrude into it, and the offal of commerce fouls its waters. As if in despair, its vital force sapped by these affronts, here the river ceases its constant forward motion and surrenders to the ebb and flow of Bolotomy Bay. Here the river can be said to die.

Boating on the Bolotomy

RASKOLNIKOV AND I had become good friends in a short time. As often as I was allowed to do so, on weekends or during school vacations, I would ride my bicycle from home, our tract house in a corner of Babbington far from the bay, to stay with my big grandparents, and while I was staying with them Raskol and I would hang around together.

Many of the days of youth are sweet, but the sweetest of all may be those that friends, friends who are determined that they will be friends forever, spend doing nothing but sitting and dreaming, as Raskol and I were on the day that we decided to journey up the Bolotomy.

Imagine, please, the lassitude of a summer day along the estuarial stretch of the river. The sun is stuck in place directly overhead and seems to yawn there, dozing. Heat is suspended in the air like fog. The river is lying at slack tide, as relaxed and unhurried as a boy lying on his back and watching the clouds drift by, dreaming. On the water, the sunlight collects in pools like the pools of melted butter that form on your cocoa when you dunk your toast in the morning, after your father has gone off to work, while your mother is dusting in the living room, when you can pretend for a while in the quiet that the house is yours, that you live alone.

Gasoline and motor oil shine on the water in rainbow swirls like those on the marbled endpapers of a fine book. Across the river, a dark-haired girl about your age, a beauty in a white bathing suit, with eyes that even at this distance make your heart stop for a moment, lies on the deck of a lean blue sloop, stretching her legs out, turning her face to the sun, dozing, dreaming, going nowhere.

Raskolnikov and I were sitting on the bulkhead on just such a summer day. With my finger, I was tracing the grain in the weathered planks, weathered to the color of dust. I was following one of the channels formed where the softer wood had worn away. As I ran my finger along the channel, as if downriver, I pictured on the plank the landmarks that I knew downriver along the Bolotomy: empty slips where the clamboats that were now out on the bay docked, a few pleasure boats, the Flying A marine gas station, Whitey's Boatyard, where Big Grandfather was at work, Dutch's New 'n' Used Boats, Curly's Marine Supply, Frenchy's Nautical Knickknacks, Corinne's Fabulous Fruits of the Sea and Corinne's Dockside Bordello, the clam processing plant, the ferry slip, the municipal dock. I stopped to pull a splinter from my finger, then brought it back to its starting point and started upriver, past Leech's Son's Boatyard, and beyond it to the bridge where Main Street crossed the Bolotomy on the way to South Hargrove, and there I stopped. It occurred to me that I had no idea what lay beyond the bridge. I stood up on the bulkhead and shaded my eyes, but I couldn't even see past the boatyard, for there was a bend in the river there, and what lay upstream was hidden, unknown, mysterious, and inviting.

"Raskol," I asked, "what's past the bridge?"

"Mmmm?" he asked. He had been studying the dark-haired girl. "What's past the bridge? I don't know."

"Let's find out," I said.

"Sure," he said. Some time passed before he added, "Let's go."

Neither of us moved.

"We'll need a boat," I said.

"Yeah," Raskol agreed.

It would be fun having a boat of our own, I thought. After we had completed the Bolotomy River trip, we could do some exploring a little farther afield. Suppose we built our own boat! If we did, we'd be able to brag to other boys our age that we had not only traveled the length of the Bolotomy but had done it in a boat that we had built ourselves.

"We could build a boat," I said, hesitantly, careful not to let my eagerness show.

"You bet," said Raskol.

It would be the most beautiful boat on the bay, or at least on the river. Of course, it would be small, but it would stand out.

"We'll paint it in bright colors," I said. "It'll look great."

"Mmm," said Raskol.

There was a lot of planning to do, I realized. For a moment, I felt nearly overwhelmed, but I told myself that if I went about it methodically I could get everything done in good time. The first thing, clearly, was the boat, but it wasn't too soon to start thinking about the things we would need on the trip. Clothes, a tent, camp knives, maybe the machete that my father had bought at the army-navy store for clearing brush, food—

"We'll need plenty of food," said Raskol.

"And not just that," I said, all my thoughts bursting from me. "We'll need maps, and a compass, extra socks, lots of stuff. How long do you think it would take to go all the way up the river, all the way to the place where it starts?"

"The source."

"What?"

"The source. That's what you call the place where a river starts."

"How long would it take to get to the *source*?" I asked, adding a special emphasis to the last word, since it made me feel already intimate with the river, now that I knew a part of its vocabulary.

Raskol thought for a while, then sucked air through his teeth, then squinted at the water, then pursed his lips, and then said, "Don't know."

"We'd better figure on three days' worth of food," I said.

"Bring five days' worth, just in case," said Raskol.

As if a breeze had blown over me, the whole sequence of the trip swept past me—the excitement when we announced our plans, designing the boat, building the boat, launching the boat, the shakedown cruise, our departure, the trip itself, the surprises and discoveries, the hardships and struggles, the climactic thrill of arriving at the source.

"It's not every kid our age who can build a boat, paint it, stock it with provisions, and travel all the way to the source of a river in it," I said.

"That's true," said Raskol.

"We'll probably be the first kids our age to have done this ever," I cried, slapping my hand on the planks, "or at least in hundreds of years. People will be amazed when we tell them what we're going to do."

"My father especially," said Raskol.

"This trip is going to create quite a stir," I went on, and I knew that I was getting a little carried away, but I knew too that Black Jacques would have been proud of me. "We'll be the talk of the town. When we start out, people will line the bulkhead, cheering us and wishing us well."

I stood up and swept my hands out toward the bay. Raskol looked where I indicated, and the dark-haired girl across the way stirred when I raised my voice.

"There will be bands playing," I said, "and all the boats along here will be decked out with pennants and crepe paper and banners. The mayor will give a speech from a barge decorated with flowers, and pretty girls will be throwing flowers into the river."

The girl across the way propped herself on an elbow and watched me with some curiosity.

"Then we'll come paddling by, and all the clamboats will pass by us in a line, as a salute. Reporters will take our picture, and everyone will wonder how we got the nerve to take such a trip, and they'll marvel at all the work that went into building the boat and planning the menu. We'll be in the paper, and we'll be famous."

The girl across the way stood up, picked up her towel, and walked toward the house where she lived.

2

On the right bank, as you drift toward the bay, note the
occasional rude dwelling on stilts. These quaint huts are, like
the people who live in them, vestiges of a simpler past.
Boating on the Bolotomy

RASKOL'S MOTHER staggered through the kitchen door, carrying an enormous kettle of chowder with both hands. As she struggled toward the table, the kettle swung, and bits of the chowder splashed out onto the floor.

"Ariane!" she shouted. "Get a rag and wipe this up!" To the rest of us she shouted, "Soup's on!"

The Lodkochnikovs, Raskol's family, lived in a small shingled house that stood on pilings at the very edge of the river, set back from the road behind a thick growth of cattails. At high tide, the water was only a foot or two below the floor, and Raskol's mother would often drop a fishing line through a small trapdoor in the kitchen to see what she might come up with for dinner. At low tide, the house stood out of the water, over a slick slope of black muck and two generations of Lodkochnikov trash. From the day that I first set foot in it, Raskol's house seemed to me a place outside the world that I knew. Even getting into the house was different from getting into the other houses that I knew: instead of the cement walks that led to the front doors of my other friends' houses, the Lodkochnikovs had a long, springy plank, weathered to gray. When Raskol and I ran along the plank, we set it bouncing. Whichever of us was first, usually Raskol, felt as if he were flying, his steps amplified to soaring leaps by the spring of the board, but the second runner, usually me, found the plank going up when he was going down and sometimes fell off into the muck below.

The Lodkochnikovs themselves were as different from one another as they were from the families of my other friends. When I first visited them, I thought that a few people from the neighborhood must be visiting too, because no one seemed to resemble Raskol enough to be related to him.

Raskol's father was a squat man with dark flyaway hair. He grinned a lot, but wasn't often happy. He was always on the lookout for something that he didn't like, his eyes shifting from side to side while he talked or listened or ate. His ears wiggled while he chewed, and he seemed to me to be turning them this way and that as a rabbit or a cat would, listening for something disturbing. At dinner, if one of his boys made a remark that he didn't like or did something that annoyed him, the grin disappeared at once, and he reached for the length of broom handle that he kept beside his place on the table. After I had visited a few times, Mr. Lodkochnikov told me that I would could walk into the house without knocking because he thought of me now as one of the family. From that day on, though I never did walk into the house without knocking, I was very careful about what I said and did at the table, because I was certain that being regarded as a member of the family meant that if I said something that rubbed him the wrong way he would use the broom handle on me, too. It lay to the right of his plate, as easy to reach as his spoon.

Raskol's mother was half again as tall as Raskol's father, and she had similar flyaway hair, but it was red. When they faced each other from opposite ends of the table and began wolfing their food, each holding a fork in one round fist and a spoon in the other, they looked as if they were engaged in a contest, a battle of some kind, with the smart money on the big redhead. Even though they seemed so mismatched physically, they were completely suited to each other, and so attached to each other that one without the other would have been as awkward as a single andiron.

Raskol's mother laughed loud and often, and she often flew into screaming fits when something annoyed her, as many things did, especially Raskol, his brothers, his sister, and his father. She had a boundless fondness for me, and this was manifested in attempts to fatten me up at dinner and to squeeze me to death whenever I entered or left the house.

Raskol's brothers, Ernie and Little Ernie, sat at the table on packing crates, because when they were much younger they had, in a fight over the relative sizes of the last two corn fritters on a platter that Mrs. Lodkochnikov had been quite fond of, broken their chairs and the platter, and their father would never let them sit on chairs or eat corn fritters again.

Once, Ernie had told his father that he wanted to get a clamboat of his own instead of continuing to work for the old man. Mr. Lodkochnikov had leaped up from his chair and grabbed the boy from behind, twisted his ears, and lectured him a bit on the subject of paternal respect. Ernie listened pretty politely for a while, but his father's arguments were apparently not convincing enough, for when he had finished, Ernie stood up, lifting Mr. Lodkochnikov, who still had one arm locked around his head, and ran backward against the wall repeatedly until the old man let go and fell to the floor. Then he told his father that from now on he intended to do whatever he damn well pleased. Mr. Lodkochnikov said nothing. The table was cleared in silence, and the mood in the house that evening was murky. At night, when Ernie was asleep in the attic with Little Ernie and Raskol, Mr. Lodkochnikov crept up the stairs and tied a note to Ernie's toe. The note said:

> If you behave rudely again,
> I'll cut this off.

In the morning, Ernie went out clamming with his father as usual, and from then on an uneasy truce prevailed between them.

Little Ernie had none of his older brother's ambition, and would never have challenged his father's authority in any case, I think, but I know that the note tied to Ernie's toe impressed him powerfully. I know it because, about eight years later, I learned that he had kept the note. At that time Little Ernie did me what he considered a favor. I had taken the Glynn twins, Margot and Martha, to a party at the Babbington Yacht Club, and when I pulled into the parking lot a very beefy and very drunk fellow, a stranger to me, reached into the car that I had borrowed for the occasion and pulled me out of it, without opening the door. He shook me around by the neck for a while, then banged my head against the windshield a couple of times, punched my nose a bit with his free hand, brought his knee up into my groin smartly four or five times, and tossed me back into the car. After a while, when I could move again, I drove the Glynn twins home, since I felt that I'd really had enough for one night, and went home to sleep for a couple of days. When I was out of bed and ambling around town again, I happened to narrate the events of that night to Little Ernie, and I may even have embellished them a bit to make certain that Little Ernie, who had some trouble catching things on the first run-through, grasped the full extent of the injuries to my person and pride. "Jesus shit," he said at last, and I felt that he understood. The next morning, the beefy fellow was found in the parking lot at the municipal dock, much the worse for wear, naked and unconscious, with a note tied to his penis, the very note that Mr. Lodkochnikov had tied to Ernie's toe years before.

Despite my apprehensions about Mr. Lodkochnikov's temper, I felt comfortable in the Lodkochnikov household, and I would have wanted to return to it again and again even if Raskol hadn't had a sister. As it happens, he did. Her name was Ariane. She lurked in the shadows like a dream. Her hair and eyes were dark, and the aura of sexual desire when she was in the room was so strong at times that it filled the air like scent and made my head reel. I'm not sure whether it came from her or me.

Mr. Lodkochnikov kept Ariane on a short tether. She was permitted to go to school only because Mrs. Lodkochnikov insisted that she go. But she was something of an outcast there, and one of the prime objects, perhaps *the* prime object, of the drooling, uncouth lust that high school boys have down so well. Though Mr. Lodkochnikov allowed her to go, he insisted that she come directly home each day immediately after school, and her mother had to report to him the time of each day's return. Ariane knew what happened if her father was annoyed, so she was generally at home on time. Once in a while, a boy from school would walk her home, or follow her home. If either of the Ernies saw him, the fellow was made to listen to a disquisition on the respect that ought to be accorded Lodkochnikov women and generally didn't show up again.

As I recall, on most of my visits Ariane would be prowling around the house in a slip, rubbing against door jambs or running her hands over her hips and purring. In hot weather, she wore tiny cotton underpants and a sleeveless undershirt. It was that outfit that she was wearing now, while she cleaned the spilled chowder from the floor.

Mrs. Lodkochnikov set the kettle in the middle of the table, and we served ourselves, using a saucepan as a ladle.

When Ariane finished cleaning the floor, she sat down beside me on the little bench that she and I shared whenever I stayed for dinner, wiggling into a spot that wasn't really big enough for her, on the end of the bench, squeezed against Ernie's packing case. Ernie wouldn't move, out of sibling stubbornness, and I wouldn't move because I wanted to feel the pressure of Ariane's hip against mine during the meal.

I was so eager to announce the plans for our river trip that I spoke right up as soon as everyone had a full bowl.

"Raskol and I are going to travel the whole length of the Bolotomy, by boat," I said.

Raskol's father had been about to take a drink of beer from the large, heavy glass that he used. He stopped when I spoke and looked at me with surprise. Then he banged his glass on the table and leaped up from his chair. His eyes were wide, and he was breathing hard through flared nostrils. I thought he was going to knock me on the head and send me home. I cringed. He came around the table and lifted me out of my seat and crushed me against his chest.

"A journey!" he bellowed. "A voyage of discovery! Terrific! A great idea!" He carried me around to the other side of the table, where he lifted Raskol out of his seat. "By God, I didn't think you had it in you!" He knocked our heads together playfully and dropped us onto the floor. "A journey is just what boys like you need." He poked a stubby finger toward the Ernies. "You two should have done something like this. A river journey should be part of growing up! Think of Thoreau and his brother, whatever his name was, and what about Huck Finn and his old pal Jim, and I don't know who else, river travelers all. Why, why," he spluttered, and his eyes bulged, "growing up itself is like a journey. You understand what I mean?" His eyes bulged at me, and I nodded my head enthusiastically so that he would see that I had no intention of doing anything that he might not like.

"You understand?" he repeated.

"Oh, yeah," I said, smiling like crazy and praying that he wouldn't ask me to explain it.

He picked up his glass again and stomped around the room, gesticulating, flinging beer onto the wallpaper. "You start out," he said, "as just a little trickle, and you go here and you go there, and you grow bigger and deeper, and you have to turn this way and that to get around rocks, and you have some grand times, and you have some awful times, and eventually—"

He swallowed hard, and his eyes misted over.

"—eventually, you come to the sea, and your journey is done, and you're a river no more."

The room was silent, except for Little Ernie, who snuffled and blew his nose into his napkin.

"Yes, sir, boys," said Mr. Lodkochnikov at last, "a journey downriver is sort of, well, shit, it's practically a universal metaphor for life."

"Oh," I began, "we're not going to—"

"Yow!" screamed Ariane. She pushed herself back from the table with such force that she fell off the bench and onto the floor.

"What's going on?" demanded her mother.

"One of those bastards kicked me!" cried Ariane, rubbing her shin and pointing across the table at Raskol and Little Ernie.

"Don't you ever call your brothers bastards again," bellowed Mr. Lodkochnikov, wearing a menacing look and reaching for his broom handle.

"I didn't mean it, Daddy," said Ariane, her eyes wide.

"All you kids are the fruit of my loins, and don't you forget it," he bellowed.

"Oh, yeah, we know that. Of course! Never any doubt about that," and the like burst from each of the children, and it seemed prudent for me to join in, so I did.

Ariane squeezed herself back onto the bench, and she raised her leg over mine so that she could rub her bruise better. I let my hand fall onto her thigh by way of comforting her, and she rubbed her shoulder against mine.

"What were you saying, Peter?" asked Mr. Lodkochnikov.

"Hmmm?" I asked, with barely any notion now of anything in the room but the smooth inside of Ariane's thigh, the flattened oval where our shoulders were pressed together, the smell of her hair, and the whimpering sound that came from somewhere deep in her throat.

"What were you saying about 'We're not going to—'?"

I looked at him with an empty smile. I had realized why Raskol had tried to kick me. Since his father had invested so much effort in elaborating the metaphor of a downriver journey, he hadn't wanted me to tell Mr. Lodkochnikov that we were planning to go upriver, not downriver. I should have been able to think of something else to say, but I couldn't concentrate very well, and so the only thing that occurred to me was: "We're not going to take Ariane with us."

For a very brief moment, Mr. Lodkochnikov looked flabbergasted. Then he said, "Damn right you're not."

"I just didn't want you to worry, or anything," I said, shifting away from Ariane and sitting up straight.

Mr. Lodkochnikov squinted his eyes and looked hard into mine for a few heartbeats. "We'll get to work on a boat right away," he said at last. "You came to the right man, boys. We Lodkochnikovs have been boatmen since time immemorial."

3

In Babbington you will find one or two yards where passable
craft are built, but you will find no relics of a once-proud
boatbuilding industry, since the boatbuilding industry here has
never been proud. Boatbuilding in Babbington has since time
immemorial been a haphazard affair. If one needed a boat,
one built one, and most of the boats used for clamming could
have been built by almost anyone.

Boating on the Bolotomy

WITH MY MOUTH FULL of Gumma's fricasseed chicken and dumplings, I announced, "Raskol and I are going to travel the whole length of the Bolotomy, by boat." My mother told me, as she often had before, not to talk with my mouth full, but Guppa had understood me through the chicken and dumpling just fine, and his eyes lit up at once.

So much of the pleasure of any project comes from the planning. I've passed many a happy hour at the little table on the lawn in front of the hotel here on Small's Island drinking my coffee and smoking a few cigarettes, drawing plans for bookshelves, outlining fat books, marking maps for trips, compiling menus and guest lists for dinners. I keep all these plans in labeled folders, arranged in file cabinets, lined in ranks in a room of their own on the third floor, and when I have the time, someday, I'll get down to work on one of them, I guess, but I've already enjoyed them all.

The planning of the boat that Raskol and I would use to journey up the Bolotomy was such an enormous pleasure that I didn't feel right in keeping it to myself; I had to share it; I had to give some of the pleasure to the two people I knew would enjoy it most: Guppa and Big Grandfather.

I told Guppa, through that mouthful of chicken and dumpling, one Sunday, when my parents and I had gone to visit Gumma and Guppa for dinner. Those Sunday dinners at Gumma and Guppa's were slow and luxurious affairs, with hours spent at the table and hours afterward spent

sitting on the porch when the weather was warm or in front of the fire
when it was cold. Sometimes Mr. Beaker and Eliza would come over,
and the affair would become a sedate party, with a continuous chatter as
cozy and comfortable as the plump sofa Gumma sat on in front of the fire,
drawing me to her when I sat beside her, snuggling me against her and
rubbing my back until I began to doze.

Guppa could hardly contain himself. He put his fork down and looked
as if he would start giggling. "I know just the thing," he said. He jumped
up from the table and struck the paneled wall behind him with the flat of
his hand. One panel swung open, revealing floor-to-ceiling bookcases
that held all of Guppa's copies of *Impractical Craftsman,* a monthly
magazine chock full of plans for single-seater folding airplanes, concealed bookcases, inflatable rubber garages, and the like. He stood up on
his toes and ran his finger along the spines. In a moment he had found the
issue he wanted, and it took him only another moment to find the page he
wanted. "Just the ticket!" he announced, beaming. He spread the magazine in front of me, opened at instructions for building an "Adventurer's
Bubble" from materials found around the home, scrounged from dumps,
or ordered by mail from large industrial supply houses. The Adventurer's
Bubble was a sphere within which the adventurer hung in a sling as in a
breeches buoy. The sling was suspended from an axle that ran along a
diameter of the sphere. The adventurer's feet rested on the inside of the
sphere itself, and by walking he or she propelled the sphere. The axle was
made of hollow tubing and served as an inlet for fresh air, but the sphere
was otherwise entirely enclosed, so the adventurer could travel in it over
virtually any terrain, including, of course, water.

Guppa sat down again, smiling, the skin around his eyes crinkling.

"Now, Herb—" cautioned Gumma.

"Oh, now, Lorna," began Guppa, his smile fading a bit and a whine
coming into his voice, the whine of a boy who's been told that he must
not, absolutely must not go into the water so soon after eating.

Gumma smiled indulgently. "He's just like a little boy," she said to
Mr. Beaker and Eliza. To Guppa she said, "Very well, but you must finish converting the Studebaker into a vacation trailer before you start on
this."

"I promise," he said. "I'll finish that right up and then Peter and I can
start in on this."

Adventurer's Bubble
Opens High Road to Adventure

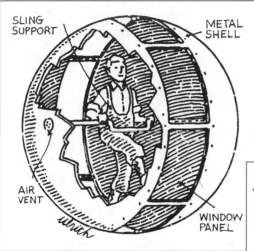

The drawing at left will give you a pretty fair idea of the way the "Adventurer's Bubble" will look when she's completed. Note the clever sling support, sturdy metal shell, handy air vent, and circumferential window panels. This drawing is what we here at *IC* call a "cutaway drawing." Do *not* actually cut the side panel away as we've done, though, or you'll be in big trouble.

At right, we see an adventurer on his way, off on the high road, undeterred by Nature's hazards, oblivious to the many little annoyances that might otherwise accompany a trek in the wild.

THE DREAM of adventure has whispered into the ear of each of us, yet few of us dare respond to its siren call. We are deterred by the thought of slogging through muck or fording icy rivers, by the anticipation of the whining mosquito's proboscis and the lumbering porcupine's quills, are we not? Well, here you are, adventure fans. Thanks to the ingenuity of Arnold Benson, part-time inventor, armchair explorer, and lifetime reader of *IC,* even the most timorous of us can now answer the call to adventure without getting his feet wet.

Impractical Craftsman

Benson's remarkable invention, which the gang here at *IC* has christened the Adventurer's Bubble, shields the explorer from the nastier side of nature inside a sturdy metal sphere. Why not build a number of these bubbles and run some cross-country races this summer? They are simple and inexpensive, and just about anyone can build one in a short time.

All the Adventurer's Needs Are Supplied

The adventurer sits comfortably inside the bubble in a clever sling-type arrangement. Close at hand is an ingenious set of closed cabinets and crannies (adapted from *IC* Plan Set 3355) that hold the essentials for any journey. Here you will find a first-aid kit, fishing gear, collapsible cookstove, nesting utensils, food lockers, built-in water cans, short-wave sending and receiving set, quadrant for celestial navi-

gation, map table, uncanny collapsible latrine outfit, and a deck of playing cards. Don't look for a tent, though! You won't find one because the adventurer won't need one. Like the turtle, the adventurer travels inside his shelter! (Want to build a tent anyway, just for the hell of it? Send for Plan Set 185 or 987).

Materials Are Easily Obtainable

The scrap heaps behind your local heavy industries should yield most of the materials needed for the bubble, but if you do encounter any trouble acquiring the needed supplies, be inventive! If you followed last month's instructions for making a convertible out of your sedan, you've got a spare roof on your hands! That sheet metal would go a long way toward the construction of a bubble. Think about starting a home sedan-conversion business. If you convert your neighbors'

Impractical Craftsman

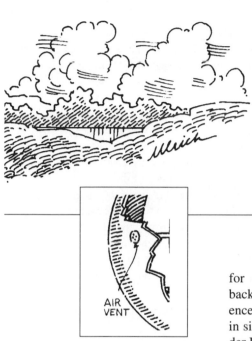

AIR
VENT

Construction is simplicity itself, and the handyman will find that the Adventurer's Bubble also opens the possibility of a home business!

sedans, you'll have plenty of sheet metal for your bubble and a few extra bucks in your pocket besides.

Construction Is Simplicity Itself

With just a few simple tools, such as a hammer, chisel, saw, drills, and portable welding outfit, you can build a bubble in those wasted evening hours after work. (No tools? With Tool Outfit 326, you can fit yourself out with a neat workshop in the garage or barn where you can build a bubble without annoying disturbances from your loved ones. Don't have a garage or barn? Order Plan Set 6024 for an inflatable rubber garage or Plan Set 2214

for a barn constructed of laminated back issues of *IC*. No welding experience? You can learn welding at home in six short months of spare time. Order Home Study Course 319.)

Panels can be shaped by hand over a simple wooden mold, or they can be formed much more quickly through the use of a hydraulic press. (A good hydraulic press for home use is the Bulldog model manufactured by Whitworth Novelties of Chicago, Illinois, which will produce a force of 2,500 pounds per square inch.) It is possible to form the metal panels entirely out of empty food cans, but a sturdier and more durable bubble will result if galvanized sheet steel is used, and aluminum panels would add the virtue of lightness, which will be much appreciated over the course of a long journey.

(Continued on page 194)

Impractical Craftsman

4

In Babbington you will find no shortage of fellows who will
tell you a good lie for the price of a beer. We have collected a
number of their tales. Our favorite concerns the clamdigger
who became lost in a fog on the bay one day while chugging
along in his boat hunting for a bed of clams worth digging.
He kept chugging and hunting, and before he knew it he was
far out at sea. Well, he figured that since he was already on
his way he might as well continue on to the South Seas, where
he had dreamed of going since he was a boy. A year later, he
came chugging back into the bay full of tales of the islands
and their women and the unusual clams that flourished there,
Antigona lamellaris and *Tapes literata*. So seductive were his
stories that they have been passed along from generation to
generation. Even today, many a male Babbingtonian gets a
faraway look in his eyes if the name of one of the islands in
that area—say Pago Pago, Puka Puka, Rarotonga, or Disappointment—happens to come up in conversation.

Boating on the Bolotomy

BIG GRANDFATHER, my father's father, was at first much less enthusiastic about the trip than Guppa had been. I told him on a Saturday,
while he was mowing his lawn and I was sitting in the crotch of an enormous weeping willow that grew behind his house. Windblown dust had
accumulated in the crotch over the years until it had become a layer of
soil. Then windblown grass seed had lodged in the soil and sprouted, and
now the crotch was padded with soft grass and made a comfortable seat,
where I sometimes whiled away afternoon hours by myself. Since
Grandfather was moving up and down the lawn, pushing his mower, and I
was stationary, I had to get the essential information out in short bursts as
he trundled past, short bursts shouted over the whirring of the mower
blade against the cutting bar.

"Raskol and I are going to travel the whole length of the Bolotomy, by
boat," I shouted.

"No kidding?" he said. There was grandfatherly indulgence in his
voice, I thought. He pushed on down to the end of the lawn and turned
back toward me. I thought he looked skeptical.

"We've got it all planned," I assured him.

"Great," he said.

I watched him move on, and his nonchalance about what to me seemed an adventure, a considerable undertaking, especially for a boy my age, brought a sinking disappointment to my heart. Only later did the thought occur to me that he had heard this sort of thing before, that my father, trying to please him, had planned voyages on the bay and elsewhere and perhaps had even proposed the very trip that Raskol and I intended to make, but that my father had never taken any of them, and that Grandfather, nobody's fool, had hardened his heart against such boyish schemes. At the time, I could only think that he didn't consider me capable of making the journey, and I was hurt. I wanted to show him how much work I was going to put into this.

"We're going to build our own boat," I shouted as he pushed past.

He snorted. He pushed on and turned at the edge of the driveway. He started back toward me, looking at the line of his last cut, concentrating on making his path straight.

"We're not quite sure what kind of boat we should build," I shouted on his next pass.

He said nothing, and I thought of giving up, but when he turned at the fence and began moving toward me again I could see that he was smiling and his eyes were bright.

"It ought to be good and sturdy," he shouted as he went by, and I knew that he was hooked. I watched him move back and forth, cutting swaths farther and farther away from me. His mouth was moving: he was discussing boat plans with himself. From time to time he'd snap his fingers or smile at a particularly happy idea. When he had mowed about two-thirds of the lawn, he stopped, left the mower where it was, and walked away. He went to his workshop in the cellar, and no one saw him for hours.

After Grandmother and I had eaten dinner, she made a plate of sandwiches, and I carried them to Grandfather, down the steep, worn wooden stairs that led to the cellar, where a coal furnace stood squat and staunch in the middle of the cement floor that Grandfather had poured, a floor level and smooth and swept clean. Grandfather's workbench stretched the length of one wall. Above it was a shelf that held a row of jars, each labeled, holding nails, screws, nuts, bolts, washers, and the like. Grandfather was sitting at his drawing table. He hardly noticed me when I came down the stairs. He was bent over the table, smiling, drawing rapidly on wrapping paper. He had *The Boys' Book of Boatbuilding* and a worn atlas beside him. He was drawing plans for a boat. Other large sheets of paper lay around him on the floor, earlier versions that he had rejected or aban-

doned. I picked one of these up. It showed a tidy rowboat, neatly drawn
in a steady hand, with some additions in a heavier, hastier hand. I picked
up another. It showed a larger sailing vessel, far too big to navigate the
upper reaches of the Bolotomy. When I set the sandwiches down, I stood
a moment at Grandfather's side, looking at what he was drawing. He was
bent so close to it that I couldn't make out much, but I did catch sight of
the words CREW'S QUARTERS lettered on one section, and in the upper
right corner of the sheet he had listed:
    Pago Pago?
    Puka Puka?
    Rarotonga?
    Disappointment?

5

> As you approach Babbington, note the large and unattractive
> water tower rising from the center of town. Topped by a
> winking red light, this tower serves as a beacon for ships at
> sea, much as a lighthouse would, though God knows a
> lighthouse would have been much quainter and more attrac-
> tive, and one can't help but wonder why, if a water tower had
> to be constructed in the center of the town, those responsible
> for it could not have had the good sense to disguise it as a
> lighthouse, or an obelisk, or a tree, or something.
> *Boating on the Bolotomy*

CAP'N ANDREW LEECH lived alone in a shack under the water tower
that dominated the skyline of Babbington. The tower stood on four thick,
tubular legs, up one of which a small and fragile-looking ladder ran. At
the top, the tank, an enormous sphere, slightly oblate, rested on the legs.
Around its equator was a narrow walkway. The names of daring adolescents were painted all over the sphere, those of more recent generations
obscuring those of boys who had long ago become men and, in some
cases, legends. Largest of all, still discernible in fat black letters beneath
the newer names, running all the way around the sphere, was

BLACK JACQUES LEROY

which Black Jacques had painted on the day the tower was dedicated, Au-

gust 13, 1905, when he was sixty-nine and probably should have been beyond such pranks. Except where it had been painted with names, the
structure had gone unpainted, since there were no daring adolescents in
the Babbington Department of Public Works to climb the rickety ladder.
The tower had rusted to a ruddy orange, and in the setting sun it was a
magnificent sight, as magnificent as the sun itself. A boatman on the bay,
when the day was done and the desire to be at home and at rest became so
tangible that he could feel the cold glass in his hand, would see the tower
above the roofs of the town, burnished by the late sunlight, more magnificent in its way than any cathedral—earthy, not ethereal, speaking of the
simple comforts of this life, of home, a shower, a comfy chair, a full glass,
a full stomach.

Raskol took me to visit Cap'n Leech one night when he was delivering
half a peck of chowder clams to him. Raskol's father, like many another
clammy, sent the Cap'n a sack of clams now and then, and once in a while
a few dollars too. When he was younger, Cap'n Leech had owned the
boatyard at the end of the street where my big grandparents lived, the
boatyard that was now run by his son: Leech's Son's Boatyard. "Cap'n"
was an honorary title.

It was dark when we reached the shack. A dim light showed through
the one window. When Raskol knocked on the door, the whole shack
shook.

"Hey, Raskol, take it easy," I whispered.

"What's the matter?" he asked.

"You're being too rough. Look—the whole place shakes when you
bang on the door like that. You're going to knock the shack down, and
then we'll be blamed for it. My father would go wild if I ever got into any
trouble like that. The police would arrest us, and the whole story would
be in the paper:

YOUTHS DESTROY HOVEL

BABBINGTON—Police remain baffled this morning as to the
probable motive behind the senseless destruction of the humble
shack that was all Captain Andrew Leech, retired, could call
home. The Captain, discovered beneath the rubble, was also at
a loss to explain why two unidentified youths had flattened his
modest hovel. (Continued, with photos, on page 18.)

"Ye gods, I can see my father now, tromping up and down the living
room, waving the paper at me and raving:

"'What's the matter with you? Huh? Answer me that! What's the

124   LITTLE FOLLIES

matter with you, knocking down a poor old geezer's only home and shelter from the elements! Just what is the matter with you?'

"And he'd never let me go on the boat trip—"

The door flew open, and a skinny old man in boxer shorts, a sleeveless undershirt, and a blue cap stood outlined by the feeble light.

"Who the hell is out there?" he demanded.

"It's me, Cap'n," said Raskol.

"Oh, hello there, boy. Who's this lunatic you have with you?" He looked me up and down. I seemed to worry him. I think he thought I might fly out of control and begin breaking things. "Where are those little girls?"

"The Glynn twins?" Raskol asked. "I'm sorry, I forgot to tell them that I was coming to see you." The captain's face fell. "But I've got some clams for you, and Peter and I want to talk to you about the trip."

Cap'n Leech brightened at this. "I've got your boat all built," he cried. He cackled with pleasure and waved at us impatiently, urging us into the shack. "Come on, come on," he said.

Inside, the place looked worse than it did from the outside. If I had kept my room the way Cap'n Leech kept his hovel, my mother would have thrown me out of the house. For furniture, he had a few burlap sacks stuffed with what I guessed was shredded paper. These served as chairs and beds. He had some packing crates here and there. One was an end table, another a coffee table. Two made a kitchen counter, on which he had a tiny gasoline-fired burner, a small version of the one that Gumma and Guppa used when they went camping.

"Now," the captain said, taking the clams and tossing them aside impatiently, "let's talk about the kind of boat you need. It's got to hold two boys your size—"

"—and their gear," I said.

The captain and Raskol gave me looks.

"You know, food, tent, first-aid kit—"

"Yeah," snapped the captain. "It's got to hold two boys your size and their gear. It's got to be narrow enough to squeeze between the banks in the upper reaches of the Bolotomy—"

"That's right," I said. "That's why I was thinking that a canoe—"

They were giving me looks again. I shrugged and kept quiet.

"It must draw very little water," the captain went on, in a much louder voice. "It must be light enough for two boys your size to carry around or over obstacles."

Raskol and I waited for him to say something else, but for a while he did nothing but giggle and rub his hands together. I wouldn't have been surprised if he had vanished in a puff of smoke, leaving behind the dying echo of his giggle. Finally, he shouted, "I've got just the thing!"

He spun around and began throwing junk out of a low pine box, about eight feet long, two feet wide, and two feet deep. It was a rich mix of junk, but because socks, underwear, and torn shirts made up the majority of it, I decided that this box must be his dresser. The top of the box was propped behind it. Stenciled in a corner of the top was

IMPRACTICAL CRAFTSMAN
SHELTER KIT 6403

and

Merry Christmas Dad Your Son Raoul

was written across the top in red crayon.

"I've been saving this box to use as a coffin," said the captain, "but there's no reason why you boys can't use it in the meantime. Grab hold, and we'll bring her out into the light."

Raskol and I grabbed the box by the ends and lifted. He got his end up, but his face began turning red. I couldn't lift mine.

"Heave!" shouted the captain. Raskol let his end fall to the floor with a crash.

"It's too heavy, Cap'n," said Raskol.

Cap'n Leech rubbed the gray stubble on his chin for a bit, and then he climbed into the box and stretched out on his back. "I'm pretty thin," he said. "This is a lot deeper box than I need. I'd say she's a little less than two foot deep. Now suppose you cut off about a foot from the top part of the box. That'd leave me about nine inches depth, which should be plenty, because I don't eat as much as I used to, and by the time I need the box I'm likely to be thin enough to just flatten right out in it."

Raskol and the captain snapped a line around the box, and we took turns sawing off the upper foot or so. The captain made a watery chowder from the clams, an onion, and a couple of potatoes, and we ate this from cups while we worked. When we finished, we had a long shallow box that Raskol and I could carry, some spare lumber from which the captain promised to carve a pair of paddles, and lots of sawdust, which I swept through the cracks in the floor.

6

> The boats employed in the harvesting of clams from Bolotomy
> Bay are painted in shades of gray, and are as little distin-
> guished from one another as are the men who captain them or
> the clams that they hunt. Though all imaginable gradations of
> gray are represented, the most popular is a brownish gray,
> much the color of the bay itself. What a delightful contrast the
> gaily colored pleasure boats make, each as it were a frolic-
> some Pierrot, flitting about among the clumsy, mirthless,
> working boats.
>
> *Boating on the Bolotomy*

RASKOL AND I rummaged in Grandfather's cellar, and found a few half-empty cans of paint. None contained enough to cover much area, so a debate ensued between us on the subject of the best way to paint the boat with what we had. I suggested stripes, but Raskol wanted to take the easy way out.

"Here," he said, "I'll get a bucket, and we'll mix all the paint together, and then we'll have enough to cover the whole boat, and we can get started on the painting right away."

I was against that.

"Wait," I cried. "Don't do that. You'll wind up with a drab, joyless muck. We want something bright, gay, optimistic. Watch this."

I poured a little of each color of paint onto the lid of one of the cans and stirred the colors together with a stick. The result looked much like the muck beneath the Lodkochnikovs' house.

"What's wrong with that?" asked Raskol. He looked at me with genu-ine surprise. "That's my favorite color," he said. "Taupe. It's quiet, and it goes with almost anything. Most of the clam boats on the bay are that color, haven't you ever noticed? The clammies like it because it doesn't clash with anything. Say you paint your boat yellow instead, and then you go out to buy rain gear. You buy yellow rain gear and take it back to the boat, and the first time a storm blows up, you pull the rain gear out and put it on. Well, the chances are very good that the boat and the rain gear won't be the same yellow, and they'll look just awful together. Your whole day is ruined. Not only is it raining, but your colors are clashing. You look like a jerk. You feel like a jerk. You might as well call it quits and go back in. But if you paint your boat taupe, then just about anything looks pretty good with it, and a little splash of color seems to kind of stand out."

7

> The Bolotomy, like most rivers, is said to be haunted by all
> manner of sprites and goblins and witches, some benign, some
> malevolent. What is it that makes people who live beside
> rivers think that they see things at night —disembodied faces
> floating above the water and the like? Is it the purling of the
> water that drives them mad?
>
> *Boating on the Bolotomy*

WE DECIDED to take the boat on its shakedown cruise at night, so that none of the adults, seeing the boat, would see how small our boatbuilding talents and aspirations were. I knew that Big Grandfather had already ordered a lot of lumber for the schooner he was planning, and Guppa had bought a second-hand welding rig and was furiously working to finish converting the Studebaker into a vacation trailer so that he could start right in on the Adventurer's Bubble. Raskol's father hadn't done much of anything yet, but there was a strong likelihood that he'd consider our boat not suitable for a voyage of such metaphoric importance anyway.

There was another reason for trying the boat out at night, a reason that neither of us admitted to the other, though I'm certain that Raskol considered it as important a reason as I did. Testing the boat in the daytime, with an anxious crowd of onlookers following us in craft of several descriptions, watching us through binoculars, taking notes, arguing about the box's river-worthiness, calling out advice, standing ready to fish us out of the water if anything untoward should occur, would not have been an adventure, and the point of the trip was that it was to be an adventure.

I slipped out of my grandparents' house and found my way to Raskol's. We had chosen the perfect night. Fog lay over the bay, so thick that it drifted past us in the breeze like rain turned sideways. From the spot in the cattails near Raskol's house where we had hidden the boat, we couldn't even see the river. We carried the boat toward the sound of the water, and when Raskol cried "Shit!" and I heard a splash and felt his end drop, I knew that we had launched her.

With the paddles that Cap'n Leech had carved, we got the boat off-shore a little way. In the night and fog we were nearly invisible. Our taupe boat was indistinguishable from the water and the fog, and Raskol and I were wearing watch caps and navy sweaters that we had bought at the army-navy surplus store, so we disappeared too, except for our faces.

"Where do we go from here?" I asked Raskol.

"I haven't got any idea," he said after a while. "I've lost track of which way is downriver. Let's just paddle for a while. We're pretty likely to run into one bank or the other."

We paddled for a while, slowly and quietly.

"Where do you think we are now?" I asked Raskol in a whisper. It seemed right to whisper in the fog.

"I have no idea," he answered. Our voices had a curiously hollow, echoing quality.

"Do you notice that strange echo?" I asked.

"Yeah," he answered. "You know, this is going to sound pretty un-likely to you, but I think that we—"

With a jarring thud the boat struck something hard, and I fell over-board. I sank below the surface of the water into darkness darker than the fog, and when I came up I couldn't find Raskol, or the boat, or anything.

"Raskol!" I called. My voice echoed back, muffled and distorted, but loud.

"Peter!" he answered. To find each other, we kept calling and pad-dling toward the sound, but the echoes misdirected us, and what seemed like ten minutes passed before our flailing hands touched. Then we set out to find the boat. We had just begun looking when I heard what sounded exactly like a door opening very near me, just in front of us.

"That sounded like a door," I whispered.

A deep voice in front of us demanded, "Who's there?"

A flashlight beam shone suddenly on Raskol, and I caught a glimpse of him, or rather of his face, floating in the fog over the water as if it were attached to nothing. Then there was a really terrifying scream, the kind that people have in mind when they say "a blood-curdling scream," the kind that makes your blood turn to soft, mushy lumps, like cottage cheese. Whoever had been holding the flashlight, the same person who had screamed, dropped the light into the water and ran off, still screaming. In the moment that the light had shone on us, I had been able to see that we were inside a boathouse, probably one of the ones across the river from where we had launched the boat. The flashlight continued to shine from under the water, and it gave enough light for us to find the boat, scramble into it, find our paddles, and get started back across the river. For a while we could see the dim glow of the flashlight, before the fog absorbed it.

"That's a pretty good flashlight," Raskol said after a long while. "Waterproof. Do you think that they have that kind at the army-navy store?"

8

If you are planning an extended trip on the Bolotomy (or on any other river for that matter, and there is many another that you might prefer to travel), it is wise to travel light. Don't pack more food than you can eat, for a surplus of food around the camp is an open invitation to raccoons, skunks, and the down-and-out.

Boating on the Bolotomy

"I DON'T CARE what kind of food you bring so long as you bring plenty of it," Raskol said when I asked him for suggestions for the menu.

I began the planning by listing all my favorite meals. The trouble with most of them, I saw at once, was that they required having my mother or one of my grandmothers along to cook them. For a while, I thought that it might be possible to persuade them to meet us at points along the river, for breakfast, lunch, and dinner, and whip up the things that I had in mind. But I soon thought better of it. For one thing, I couldn't predict just where we would be at each of those times. For another, I didn't think that I'd be able to persuade them to do it, indulgent as they were. For yet another, the picture of Gumma crashing through the brush with a picnic basket followed by Guppa lugging his collapsible camp kitchen didn't fit with the picture of two intrepid lads, full of pluck, exploring the shadowy and mysterious upper reaches of the Bolotomy. If no one was going to cook for us, then cooking was out. I had tried my hand at cooking over an open fire once and had no inclination to try it again. So I cut my list down to those of my favorite foods that I enjoyed eating cold. I knew even at that time that a good meal is like a musical composition. A successful meal on a grand scale is as complex a composition as a symphony. It must have balance. It must have a theme. It must have variation. It must

have pace. It must build to a climax. A successful meal on a boat trip up
a river may be more on the order of a popular song, but it is still no simple
matter. I knew that I had my work cut out for me, and I was determined
to make the meals memorable.

9

If you are determined to make a trip on the Bolotomy, summer
is the best time for it, but be sure to avoid the weekend of the
Babbington Clam Fest, the town's annual salute to the bivalve
on which its economy depends. For the sophisticated traveler,
this molluscan hoopla is likely to be simply an embarrassment.
                                        Boating on the Bolotomy

THE DAY WAS FINE and clear. I dressed and left the house before my
mother and father were stirring. I packed my old red wagon with the food
and equipment for the trip and tied it behind my bicycle. I set off for
Raskol's, weaving and struggling along the street, with the wagon wandering this way and that, independent of my steering, like a curious child
holding his mother's hand. The part of Babbington where I lived, outside
the center of things, was still quiet, and I didn't see another person until I
was downtown, riding on Main Street. There excitement was in the air.
At street corners, high-spirited auxiliary policemen stood eating doughnuts, drinking coffee from paper cups, and poking at one another's bel-
lies. I saluted these fellows as I rode past.
  "Nice morning!" I sang out to some. "Great day for traveling!" I
called to others. I pedaled past them, and behind me I could hear some
references to me that I couldn't quite make out, perhaps praise for my
pluck, perhaps expressions of envy, of nostalgia for lost youth, for its discoveries and adventures, who can say? The Babbington High School
Marching Band had begun to assemble at the corner of Bolotomy and
Main. These boys and girls, so much older than I that they seemed to me
already to have become men and women, shuffled around in disarray,
kicking at pebbles on the pavement, tuning their instruments, and making
one another giggle with remarks that I could not begin to imagine. I
stopped for a moment at the edge of the river, near Leech's Son's
Boatyard, to look at the clamboats gathered there, covered with flowers,

waiting for the grand procession. The clammies were standing on the
decks, dressed in Sunday suits, shouting friendly insults to one another,
drinking coffee from paper cups or beer from brown bottles, spitting into
the river, and hoisting their pants up from time to time. I thought for a
moment of going over to them to try walking from clamboat to clamboat,
which looked like fun, but I pushed on instead, because Raskol and I had
decided that if we weren't in the water early enough, people were likely to
see us wobbling under the weight of the boat when we carried it to the
water, and the photographer from the paper was sure to consider that a
cute shot, take it, and use it on the front page, making both of us look like
idiots. We had decided that we, and the boat, would look much better in
the water than on our way to it, so we planned to paddle out into the bay a
little way, just around the Municipal Dock, then reverse course when we
saw that the crowds had gathered on the dock and paddle past them with
style and grace.

10

The Clam Fest, of course, includes a Queen, an adolescent
who is made to wear an abbreviated costume and ride, at the
head of a procession of clamboats, on the boat belonging to
the oldest of the clamdiggers, in the bow, as far forward as
possible, with her legs dangling overboard. Since the oldest
clamboats were once sailing vessels, she is likely to be
straddling a bowsprit, in a display that is really too much for
words.

Boating on the Bolotomy

RASKOL AND I waited beyond the Municipal Dock, on the bay side,
away from the crowds on the river side, and there we went unnoticed.
After an hour or so, we heard a murmur rise from the crowd, and soon we
could hear, over the murmurs of the crowd, the Babbington High School
Band, playing the Bergomask from Ottorino Respighi's *Ancient Airs and
Dances for the Lute,* scored for marching band by Babbington High's
own Timothy J. Courtney, a prodigy of some note.

"That's our cue," I said. We pushed off. I saw, approaching us, the
Agnes My Dear, the oldest clamboat on the bay. In the bow, straddling

the bowsprit, was a girl with yellow hair, shining in the sun. She was waving and smiling, and I was certain that much of her waving and smiling was for me. I thought that I could see in her smile a little dreamy admiration for a fellow as young as I was who had such pluck. I waved and smiled back at her. Arranged along the deck were other girls, also waving and smiling. Behind the boat full of girls was a barge, on which the band was standing, playing away and performing some drill routines. People were lined up along the banks, many holding cameras. In some places I could pick out whole families, sitting on folding chairs, with bright umbrellas stuck in the ground beside them. Small children were waving tiny flags. Here and there were girls my age, in ruffled dresses, throwing flowers into the river, and boys my age, awestruck and envious, throwing stones into the river and being cuffed by their parents.

After the barge came the clamboats, decked out with flowers and banners. The mayor stood on one, and Raskol and I saluted him as our boats passed each other. He called out "Good luck, boys," or something similar, as we passed. A motorboat full of news photographers wound in and out of the procession.

The band was charging into the grand, swelling, soaring conclusion to the Bergomask. Raskol and I had nearly reached Leech's Son's Boatyard, and the end of the beginning of the journey. I was ecstatic. I had been elevated by the music and the crowd. I stood in the boat and waved my paddle to them all. In my enthusiasm, I waved a little too wildly, and for a moment I could imagine myself falling into the water as I had in "Do Clams Bite?" It would be, I thought as I struggled to keep my balance, my luck to have the photographers come cruising by, with most of the formal procession past now and only the least attractive clamboats still to reach the dock, looking for some human interest shots, something like a couple of boys in a homemade boat, and capture this moment with their expensive cameras. In the photograph I would be half in the water, my right half hidden below the surface, my left arm and leg flailing, my mouth and eyes wide, my paddle in the air above me, Raskol hiding his head in his hands.

But I recovered, and by shifting my weight and using my paddle as a counterweight I kept myself upright, and I let myself down carefully into the boat again. My ears were burning. I bent to the work of paddling the boat, and looked straight ahead, upriver, until we were past the boatyard and out of sight of everyone.

I cleared my throat. "Do you think anybody noticed?" I asked Raskol.

He burst out laughing. "Probably," he said.

I could feel the blood rise to my face, and I could imagine the headline in the *Babbington Reporter:*

Clam Fest Almost Marred by Near-Tragedy
Boy Nearly Falls from Crude Boat

We paddled the boat under the bridge, and left the music and the crowds behind us. My embarrassment passed, and my heart swelled with excitement and pride. Ahead of us lay a pond, nearly circular, with cat-tails around the edge. This pond was the end of the estuarial stretch of the river, the Bay's farthest penetration into the land. The pond caught the fresh river water flowing downward and the bay water flowing in with the tide.

"There's a nice spot, over there," said Raskol.

I turned back toward him, and he pointed out a sandy spot on the shore, a break in the cattails.

"That *is* a nice spot," I said. I was gushing with excitement and enthusiasm. I would have agreed with anything. Raskol began heading us toward the sandy spot.

"What are you doing?" I asked.

"I'm heading us over there," he said, "toward that nice spot."

"Why?" I asked.

"So we can eat our lunch," he said, a note of surprise in his voice.

"Eat our lunch?" I cried. "We just got started. It's only about nine in the morning."

Raskol was silent for a while, but he stopped paddling. "Did you eat breakfast?" he asked at last, and this time there was a note of concern in his voice.

"No," I said. "I was too excited to eat, and I had to get over to your house early, remember?"

"Hey, you must be starving," he said. "It's not a good idea to start a journey like this on an empty stomach. You got anything packed for breakfast?"

"Not for today's breakfast," I said, frowning. I could see what was going to happen. "Just tomorrow and the next day."

"Hmmm," he said, his brows knit. He looked the way Gumma did when she was about to tell me that I was looking a little peaked. "We'd better get something to eat. We've got a lot of work ahead of us. Tell you what. Why don't we beach the boat over there and walk into town and get something at the diner?"

I sighed, but I didn't argue. We paddled the boat to shore, hid it in the cattails, and walked downtown to the Babbington Diner, where Raskol had fried eggs, home fries, bacon, toast, and coffee. I had a doughnut and a glass of milk.

11

> The only decent fishing along the Bolotomy is found at a spot
> known as Andy Whitley's Gall Bladder because of Whitley's
> fame as an angler and the spot's resemblance, on maps and
> aerial photographs, to a gall bladder.
>
> *Boating on the Bolotomy*

A SHORT WAY UPSTREAM from the pond, the river bulged out oddly on our left, and there we saw a fellow sitting with his back against a tree, fishing with a bamboo pole. He wore a battered hat, a dark shirt with the sleeves rolled above the elbows, and dark trousers, with the cuffs rolled above his ankles. He had taken his shoes and socks off, and he had his legs stretched out along the ground so that his feet were in the water. When we came into sight he raised his hat to us.

"How d'you do, boys?" he greeted us.

"Very well, thank you," I answered him, hoping that he'd ask us where we were headed.

"Where are you headed?" he asked.

"To the source!" I called out proudly.

He considered that for a moment, then asked, "Where exactly would you say that is?"

"We don't know," I sang out, full of glee, standing up again. I felt the boat rock under me and sat down again quickly. "But we're going to find out!"

"A voyage of discovery, eh?" he said. He fished in his pocket and brought out a pipe, which he filled and lit while we talked.

"That's right!" I said. I was grinning from ear to ear, so proud of Raskol and me for being on this voyage that I couldn't contain it.

"And when you find the source of this mighty river, what exactly would you say that you will have found?"

This question made no sense to me. "What do you mean?" I asked.

"Well, will you have found the place where the river begins?" he asked.

"Sure," I said, wondering to myself how he could have missed the point of everything I had said so far.

"And I suppose you think that you will have found something out about life too, when you find the place where you think the river begins."

"Well—" I said. I had wanted to say, "Nah, I don't expect to learn anything about life from this trip. I just want to find out where the river begins and eat a few of my favorite meals along the way and look at the scenery and become famous." And I wanted to add, "Please don't tell me that life is like a river, because I'm sick of hearing that life is like a river." However, I had a sneaking suspicion that he was going to tell me that life is like a river, and I didn't want to offend him, so I just let my "Well—" hang in the air and waited to see what he'd make of it.

"Well what?" he said.

"Well, I don't know," I said.

"You don't know what?" he asked, and I thought that it was really rather annoying of him to ask such penetrating questions of a kid, a kid who had just happened to paddle by in a homemade boat, minding his own business.

"I don't know if life is like a river," I said. He burst out laughing, and Raskol began paddling away.

"No, wait. Wait!" the fellow called. Raskol stopped paddling. "Why don't you boys stay and have some lunch with me? I'm sure I have more than enough for the three of us. I have ham sandwiches." Raskol began paddling again, but toward shore. We beached the boat, and the fisherman pulled about six sandwiches from a knapsack.

"How come you have so much food?" Raskol asked.

"Because one takes what one can get when one can get it," the fisherman answered. "Yesterday I did a little gardening for a woman, not far from here, and after I finished work a certain lightheadedness swept over me, and I fell at the good woman's feet, in what looked a lot like a faint. After I came to myself again, she dragged from me the information that I hadn't eaten in days, and she insisted not only that she pay me more than we had agreed upon, but that I take this stack of sandwiches with me."

"You're a bum, aren't you?" asked Raskol.

"Yes," the fellow said, smiling with what looked a lot like pride.

He tossed each of us a sandwich, and we began eating.

"So you're not sure whether life is like a river," he said to me. I didn't know what answer to make, and my mouth was full, so I just shrugged.

"Well, it's not," he said. "Life is like the whole water cycle. Do you know what that is?"

"You bet," I said. "We had that last year in science."

"Ah," said the fisherman, "but did you have it in metaphysics?"

"Not yet," I said. "Maybe we'll get that next year."

"Well, let me give you a jump on the other boys and girls—"

This is great, I thought. *Here I am out having adventures, and now a real bum is going to tell me something that the other kids don't know yet. I'm having the time of my life.*

"Since we are here, at this late point in the river's course," he said, "let's begin here. In that direction, the river flows on, toward the sea, where it dies. What does it mean to say that the river dies? It dissipates, it mingles its waters with the vastness of the sea, it loses its identity, it ceases to exist as a river, although—" (He drew the word out and pointed his finger into the air and then waited until Raskol and I were leaning forward to hear what would come next before going on.) "—although it does not cease to exist as water. It loses its form, but something of it remains: its substance. And then it is released from the sea. It evaporates. Evaporation, boys, is the exaltation of water. It rises, free of the tug of all that is low and base and mean, and it rises further, leaving all its dirt and impurities behind. It is purified. It is distilled! It drifts as tiny particles among other tiny particles. It is water, but it is not differentiated from the air. It is of the air, but it is not the air. It has no identity, no self. It is united with all creation. In this state, it approaches as near as anything may in these times to the blissful primeval chaos. And then, little by little, it joins together with its companion particles in clouds. Clouds. Big, fluffy clouds. What do they look like? Lambs. Big, fluffy lambs. And from clouds comes what?"

"Rain?" I offered.

"Right," he said, and I felt pretty proud of myself. "Rain. And the rain washes over us like what?"

"Like what?" I asked, stalling.

"Yes, like what?" he asked. "Think. If the clouds are like lambs, then the rain is like what from lambs?"

I reddened. I thought I knew the answer, but I wasn't sure how to put it to a grown-up. "Urine?" I whispered.

"Blood!" he shouted. "The rain washes over us as if it were the blood of lambs. From the old lambs the new lambs are born, and the blood of the old will become the blood of the new—"

"I've heard some of this before," I tossed in, brightening—but he kept right on rolling, and I kept quiet.

"Rainwater is the newborn, the reborn, the babe of the water cycle. It freshens the earth, as each new birth freshens us, brings hope to all of us stuck here in misery, mud, muck, and mire. It is a new beginning. It drips from the leaves of the forest. It washes the city sidewalks. It runs into the mountain rivulet and the city gutter. It gathers with the runoff from other leaves and sidewalks, and it becomes what?"

"A flood," I suggested, pretty sure of myself.

"A stream," he cried, rolling right on, "the childhood of a river. And the stream flows on and it picks up dirt and mud and bits of dead and decaying animals, and it is fouled by sewage and tainted by young boys who piss into it, just as young boys and girls are tainted and spoiled by their experiences. And tributaries, other streams, spill into it and swell it, and what do they stand for?"

I really wanted to get another one right. "Eating?" I suggested.

"Sexual contact!" he roared. "The bodily oils that rub off other people. Contact with the world of other bodies, other odors, other fluids."

He leaned back against the tree, satisfied with himself. Raskol and I got up. It was time for us to get going again.

"Thanks for the sandwiches," said Raskol.

"Don't mention it," said the fisherman.

"And thanks for the conversation," I added.

He pointed at me with a long and callused finger. As we shoved off, he said, "You just remember that life is bigger than a river, and much more complicated. Of all that life is, only a person's childhood is anything like a river. For the essence of a river, like the essence of childhood, is a moving on, from one place to another. And if the essence of a river is its flowing on, its moving toward a destination, the essence of the sea is its tidal vacillation, its leaning now this way and now that way and going nowhere. Although most of childhood is like a river, a flowing on toward somewhere, toward being grown up, much of being grown up is like the sea, being tugged this way and that and going nowhere."

We pushed the boat into the current, and were swept a little way downstream before we laid into our paddling, overcame the seaward motion of the water, and began making progress toward the source again. When we had gone on upstream for some distance, I heard the fisherman call out, "And another thing—if this journey of yours is going to have any metaphoric value at all, you should, I think, be going the other way."

12

Rarely does one eat with as hearty an appetite as when one is
on a riverine excursion. There is something about the combination of outdoor air and the flowing, babbling waters of a
river that makes one ravenous. We feel quite safe in saying
that on a river journey one could eat anything with gusto.

Boating on the Bolotomy

"WHAT DID YOU BRING for lunch?" Raskol asked after we had
paddled on for a while.

"Are you still hungry?" I asked.

"No," he answered. "Just curious. I was wondering what we would
have had if we hadn't run into that bum with the ham sandwiches."

"Tuna-noodle casserole," I said brightly. "And biscuits."

Raskol was in the bow. He stopped paddling and turned around. He
wore a look of boundless incredulity. "Tuna-noodle casserole?" he
asked. "Cold biscuits?" He sat just staring at me for a few minutes, and
he seemed to have trouble swallowing. "When I think of cold biscuits,"
he said, "all the moisture in my mouth disappears. Eating a cold biscuit
would be like chewing on a piece of sheetrock."

"They're not so bad," I said.

He didn't answer. He turned forward again and began paddling with
fierce, silent determination. So did I.

Rain began to fall late in the afternoon, and Raskol began to complain
about having to sleep in the tent. We paddled on through the rain for a
while, until it was falling so heavily that we had a hard time seeing the
banks of the river.

"Let's head for the shore and see if we can find a place to get out of the
rain," Raskol shouted over the din of splashing drops.

"Maybe we can prop the boat up with forked sticks and spread the tent
out over it," I suggested cheerily, while we dragged the boat up onto the
bank.

"Forked sticks," grumbled Raskol, and from the way he said it I could
tell that he didn't think much of the idea. "Tuna casserole," he added.
"Cold biscuits."

I didn't know quite what to say. A friendship is much like a river journey, I think. At least, I thought so then. I sensed that Raskol and I had
reached one of those perilous rocky stretches in the course of our friend-

ship, when the boatmen should be alert and paddle with vigor but are, for one reason or another, distracted or disaffected and so are inattentive or reluctant, and for one or the other reason do not get through the rocky stretch successfully. Their boat strikes the rocks. They are shocked from their distraction or disaffection. Too late. No effort now would be enough. Their vessel founders. They swim for shore separately, and when they pull themselves from the water find that they have swum for opposite shores and stand now, soaking wet, looking at each other across a distance. Their friendship has run its course, though life and time flow on like the river between them.

These thoughts made me horribly melancholy. Something had to be done. Something had to happen to snap Raskol out of this mood that he was in.

I set about propping the boat up with forked sticks to protect our food and gear, while Raskol worked at pitching the tent. In a little while, I had turned the boat into a lean-to, and Raskol had broken both tent poles over his knee in anger over the fact that the tent would not allow itself to be pitched as he imagined it should be. I had learned from experiences before this one that the wise person did not point out to Raskol during one of these difficult periods any small shortcoming in his methods—say, for example, that the tent was inside out. I let him go on, and in time he had the tent draped pretty adequately between two young trees. When he finished, he sat inside, tired, wet, grouchy, and hungry.

"So," he said, and I think his teeth were clenched, "what are we eating for dinner?"

"Plenty," I said. "Wait till you see."

I spread out the tablecloth that my mother had made me bring along, and on it I arranged two place settings. Then, with no little pride, I set the main dish in the center.

"What's that?" asked Raskol.

Those two words can be spoken in several ways. One can imagine a naturalist, observing an odd polka-dotted lizard scrambling up a tree trunk somewhere along the Amazon, asking a colleague "What's that?" with a tone vibrant at once with real curiosity and the dizzying excitement that accompanies a discovery that may change one's life, almost the tone that the same naturalist, after returning to the States in the full flush of fame after word of his lizard discovery has spread, might use at a cocktail party for the words "Who's that?" when he spots a woman poised on the threshold of the room, a woman in a black dress, wearing a small black hat with a veil and a long black feather. That, however, was not the tone Raskol used. Instead, he used the tone one might use if one had been offered the same polka-dotted lizard, roasted, on a platter with new potatoes.

"It's baked Spam," I said. "Doesn't it look nice the way I scored it in a diamond pattern and studded it with cloves and put a pineapple slice on top?"

Raskol looked at me in amazement. His eyes were wide, and his jaw had fallen slack.

"Of course, it's cold," I explained, "and it would look a lot better if it were hot, which is the way we usually have it at home, but this is made just the way my mother makes it, so it should be good even cold."

"What else did you bring?" he asked. His forehead was puckered between his eyebrows, and he spoke now not with the tone of curiosity that his words suggest on the page, but with a note of concern, such as my mother used when she put her cool hand on my forehead and asked, "Do you feel feverish?"

"Well," I said. "I've got plenty of biscuits, and some of the onion sandwiches that Guppa and I like so much, and some buttered lima beans, and for tomorrow night I've got spaghetti."

"Cold spaghetti," he said.

"Yeah," I said. "With tomato sauce."

"Cold spaghetti," he repeated.

"And meatballs," I added.

Raskol said nothing. He was moving his lips noiselessly, as if he were saying grace.

"Maybe you'd rather have the spaghetti tonight," I said. I got the cardboard bucket that held the spaghetti out of the duffle bag that I used for carrying the food. The rain and the tomato sauce had softened the bucket so that it no longer held its shape well. I pried the lid off and looked inside. At once, I saw what I was holding as if through Raskol's eyes. It looked a lot like a poor dumb woodland creature that had been dead for a while. Scavengers might have been picking at it, tearing away at its flesh and exposing its tangled innards. Since I had nothing else to offer in place of the Spam, I held the bucket out toward Raskol. Tentatively, he looked inside. He meant to say something about the spaghetti, I think, for he opened his mouth and emitted a small sound, but at that moment both of us were distracted by the sound of snapping twigs, coming from somewhere near us.

"Somebody's coming!" I whispered.

"Yeah," said Raskol, swallowing hard. "I hope it's somebody with food."

The sound came nearer and nearer. It was certainly someone walking through the woods, approaching our tent. A light played across the canvas.

"A flashlight," I said.

"Yeah," said Raskol.

The footsteps stopped. My heart was pounding. In the stillness I could hear Raskol's stomach growling. Then a voice called out, "Do you mind if I come in out of the rain?" It was May Castle.

"May!" I cried. "Hello, Peter," she said, smiling devilishly. "How goes the adventure so far?"

"Great!" I said. I glanced at Raskol. "Well, pretty good," I said.

May squeezed into the tent and settled herself on the checkered tablecloth. She had with her a large picnic hamper, covered with a slicker. She set it down and gave me a big hug and a sweet, sticky, lipstick kiss. Then she turned to Raskol and introduced herself.

"I'm May Castle," she said. "I am a very good friend of Peter's grandparents, on both sides, and I think I'm a pretty good friend of Peter's too." She turned toward me again and asked, "What do you say? Am I a pretty good friend of yours?"

"Yes," I said, and for some reason I blushed.

"Well," she said, turning to Raskol again. "And I hope I'll be a pretty good friend of yours, too. You're this Raskolnikov, aren't you? But your name is Rodney. Now why don't you use Rodney? I think that's a perfectly dashing name, Rodney. Did I know a Rodney? No, I think not. I think I knew a Roderick. Or Broderick. But Rodney is just fine, I think. Sounds like a name for a good horseman, Rodney."

Raskol wasn't smiling.

"No Rodney, eh?" said May. "All right, then, Raskolnikov it is."

She chucked him under the chin, and he didn't wince. He grinned. "What have you got with you?" he asked.

"Dinner!" she said. She threw off the slicker and began removing dishes from the basket. She had an enormous dinner with her: turkey, mashed potatoes, sweet potatoes, stuffing, gravy, apple pie, and more. The aromas rose from the basket and filled the tent at once. She brought out a cocktail shaker, a glass cocktail shaker with a red plastic top. The top was in three parts. The lowest of these was threaded and screwed onto the glass shaker. The topmost part was a cap that slipped onto the middle part and was removed for pouring. The middle part was attached to the bottom part by an axle, so that it could be rotated freely. Through a window in the middle part, recipes for drinks, which were embossed on the bottom part, showed. I can see the cocktail shaker through the haze of

memory with the odd vividness that a small detail from the past sometimes assumes, so sharply and clearly that I can read the recipe showing
through the window in the top. It was for a drink called "Between the
Sheets." To make this drink, one was instructed to combine equal parts of
rum, brandy, triple sec, and lemon juice. May next brought out a
stemmed glass, with a band of red and a gold rim, and a little bottle of
cherries, with stems. From the cocktail shaker she poured herself a Manhattan. While she drank one or two or three of these, Raskol and I ate.

"May," said Raskol when we had finished, "how did you get this food
here without having it get cold?"

"I drove," she said.

"You drove?" I asked. "Do you have a Jeep?"

"A Jeep?" she asked, laughing. "Do I look like a woman who has a
Jeep? Certainly not. I drove my Chrysler."

"Through the woods?" I asked.

"No, not through the woods," she said, leaning over and squeezing my
cheek, as if she were going to add, "you cute little fool, you."

"Where are we?" asked Raskol.

"You're right near Route 13," she said. "If the rain weren't so loud,
you'd be able to hear the traffic."

"How did you guess that we'd be here?" asked Raskol. He was smiling at May with admiration.

"I didn't have to guess," she said. "I knew. This is as far as I got on
the first day of the trip up the Bolotomy when I made it, quite a few years
ago, with a little friend of mine. Of course, Route 13 was just called
Hargrove Road at that time."

"Was your little friend a boy or a girl?" asked Raskol.

May laughed and poured from the cocktail shaker again.

"Hmmmmm. A boy or a girl. I think that I won't answer that," she
said. She smiled, took a sip, and went on. "It was a summer night, much
like this, but without rain, thank God. We were able to lie on the
riverbank on our backs and look up at the stars. You know—well, I'm
sure you don't know, but one day you will—a memory will blur with time
until only the most general outlines of things remain, like the unidentifi-
able people in a fuzzy photograph, and yet, off to one side, some tiny detail will stand out crisp and clear and sharp, as if a single ray of light had
caught it just right and burned it onto the film. Years from now, some
detail may remain from tonight, if you're lucky."

"I'll bet there's some sharp detail that shines in the memory of your
night here," said Raskol. His voice startled me. He sounded like an adult.

"Yes," said May, very softly, "there is."

"What?" asked Raskol.

May sighed and lit a cigarette. I wanted very much to hear what hard, bright detail remained of May's trip up the Bolotomy, but I had been nodding for a while, and before she spoke I was asleep.

13

Just north of Hargrove Road is a spot that we must admit is lovely, where the river runs clear and cool and deep through a small clearing. On a summer day, with iridescent dragonflies gleaming in the sun, it can be an idyllic spot for a cooling swim. Unfortunately, the locals know all about it, so the traveler is likely to have to share the idyll.

Boating on the Bolotomy

THE NEXT DAY DAWNED still and hot. May was gone, and Raskol had traces of her lipstick on his mouth and cheeks.

I ate quickly. I had some Spam on one of the biscuits that I had brought along. In a snit, Raskol crashed off through the bushes; eleven minutes later, still in a snit, he crashed back through the bushes, carrying a cardboard cup of coffee.

All our provisions were a mess. We threw the wet things into the boat and pushed it out into the river. Here the river was shallow and not much wider than the boat. Bushes grew right to the banks on both sides, making the space above the water narrower than the river itself. We pushed the boat into the middle of the river and climbed in. The boat bottom crunched on the river bottom.

Raskol sighed. "We've got to jettison some of this rubbish," he said. He reached for the nearest bag and tossed it over the side.

"Hey, wait!" I cried. "Don't just toss things out indiscriminately. We're going to need some of this stuff. We've got to go through each of the bags and sort out the essentials from the inessential items. Then we've got to figure out a plan for rationing our food and water so that we know how much we can do without."

"All right," he said. "Here's the plan—we'll throw out all the food and trust to luck."

I sighed. I began picking through the supplies and packing the nonessentials into one of the bags. Raskol sat in his end of the boat and watched. When I came to the machete, his eyes lit up.

"Where'd you get this?" he asked, snatching it from me.

"It was in the cellar at home," I said. "My father bought it at the army-navy store. He uses it for clearing brush."

"Now this is the sort of thing we're likely to need," he said. He gave me a nod and a grin, and I could see that some of his faith in me had returned. He stuck the sheath into his belt and practiced flourishing the machete while I finished lightening the load. When I had us down to the bare necessities, I loaded the boat again. We pushed it out into the stream. We climbed in. The boat floated.

The water purled along the banks, dragonflies flew alongside the boat, and water striders skittered out of our way. We began pushing ourselves along, pushing with our paddles against the river bottom, and at once we began to sweat.

"This is going to be a bitch of a day," predicted Raskol. He peeled off his shirt, soaked it in the water, wrung it out, and put it back on. He did this with such verve, such style, that I knew he'd learned it along the docks, and it looked to me like the savviest bit of clammy know-how that I'd ever seen, so I did the same. My wet shirt stuck to my back and chest and chafed my armpits while I worked at pushing with my paddle, and as the cloth dried it became stiff and rough and chafed worse and worse.

Raskol pushed along in grim silence. I was sure that he was angry with me for having gotten him to agree to come along on this trip, and that he was taking his anger out on the river. His pushes were strong and regular, and he spoke only when he had to, to warn me of a rock or a low-hanging branch.

The river began to narrow. We made our way now through a tunnel of overarching bushes, and in the tunnel the heat lay like fog, heavy and unmoving. The leaves overhead were pale, translucent green, sunlight burning through them. The interstices between the leaves flamed with pale, lemon fire. Sweat ran from me continually now. It ran from my hair, down my back, down the sides of my face, across my forehead, and into my eyes. Mosquitoes buzzed around my head. They had bitten the upper curve of my ears so often that I looked like a pixie. While Raskol kept pushing on, staunch and rhythmical, I squirmed and twisted, slapping mosquitoes and wiping the sweat from my eyes, and when I did get a push in, it was a clumsy and ineffective effort, my paddle striking the side of the boat or catching the river bottom too early in the stroke, so that I was actually working against Raskol.

The sun rose higher, the heat and light grew stronger. I began to feel lightheaded and dizzy.

"Whew!" cried Raskol. "It's too hot to keep this up. Let's take a break. We'll pull the boat out over there."

He headed for the bank. I was too hot and tired and sick to answer him or to help push the boat ahead.

When the boat was out of the water, Raskol looked me over with some concern. "Peter," he said, "you don't look right. Lie down on the bank here and put your feet in the water. Rest for a while. I'm going to look for a place to buy some lunch. You rest and cool off for a while."

I heard him walk off through the woods. After the sound of his footsteps had passed away, woodsy sounds—birds and locusts and the river—rushed in around me. The river water, flowing along the banks, burbled. It was a soft and cool and soothing sound, as pleasant as a chuckle. Every once in a while I'd catch another sound from the river, at a higher pitch, more like a giggle than a chuckle. While I lay there listening, the giggles seemed to increase in number and to draw nearer to me. Curious to know what caused these sounds, I thought of sitting up and opening my eyes, but I did not, partly because the heat still pressed me to the ground like an enormous hand, and partly because the thought struck me that it would be amusing first to make a good guess about the origin of the sounds, and then open my eyes to see whether my guess was correct. This I did. I decided that the sound probably came from the random collisions of a number of small wooden objects, such as twigs, spools, or billiard balls, that had entered the river somewhere upstream and were washing past me now.

I sat up and opened my eyes. The giggling sounds were coming from a dozen or so beautiful young girls who were bathing in the river. Their clothes lay in piles on the opposite bank, but they had made their way across the river, and they stood in the clear water only a short distance from me. In my memory, they are all lovely, but you know how it is in a situation like that—the surprise at seeing them there when I opened my eyes, the sunlight playing over them through the leaves, their wide eyes, my fatigue and dizziness, may have made some of them a little lovelier then than they would ever be again. One of them, however, has always been as beautiful as she seemed that day. She was the only one that I recognized; she was the dark-haired girl about my age, who had been lying on the deck of a lean blue sloop, stretching her legs out, turning her face to the sun, dozing, dreaming, going nowhere, on the day that Raskol and I decided to journey up the Bolotomy.

She—or perhaps it was another of the girls—reached out toward me

and took my hand. She pulled me, tugging me toward the water. Soon
they were all tugging at me and urging me to come into the water with
them, and I decided that I would. It would be cool. It would refresh and
relax me. It would probably be just what I needed.

From behind me came the sound of crashing footsteps. The girls
looked up with alarm. They scrambled for the opposite bank, clambered
out of the river, snatched up their clothes and disappeared into the woods.
The dark-haired one paused for a moment, I think, just a moment, before
she too slipped out of sight. Raskol burst from the bushes. He had woven
leaves and branches into his hair as camouflage, and he was holding the
machete in his teeth.

"Raskol," I said. "You won't believe what—"

He said something.

"I can't understand you when you talk with a machete in your mouth,"
I said.

He took the machete out of his mouth. "We're almost there!" he
shouted. He was grinning with delight.

"Almost there?" I asked.

"Yeah," he said. "Our journey is nearly over."

I looked upriver. The Bolotomy disappeared into a mass of greenery.

"But I thought it would take much longer," I said. I was smiling, because I didn't want Raskol to know that I was disappointed. I had
planned for three days and two nights, but in my heart I had been hoping
that it would take us four days and three nights, and that for one night and
day we'd have to live off the land.

14

The upper reaches of the river are not navigable by any but the
most specialized craft. Those interested in exploring these
areas might be better off on foot, wearing some of those
funny-looking waders that fishermen wear.

Boating on the Bolotomy

IT IS NOT WISE to try to prolong an episode that is approaching its natural end—best not to try to fan the embers of a dying conversation; best
not, when dinner is over and the wine is gone, to call for another bottle. I

thought for a moment of suggesting to Raskol that we just hang around where we were for a couple of days, living on a diet of nuts and berries, before we finished the trip, but I could see that it wouldn't be right to do so, and I resigned myself to having the journey end.

The stream—too narrow, really, to be called a river here—flowed from a tangle of vines and bushes, bearing no traces of the constraints of civilization, emerging small and clear from the vital chaos of the wild. The stream was so small and shallow, the vines so thick, the shadows so dark, that I was sure that within this tangle, hidden, cloistered, must lie the source. Raskol and I plunged into the thicket, pushing on our paddles with all our might, and came to a halt at once.

"What's the matter?" I called forward.

"I've got to go to work with the machete," he said. "These vines are like a wall."

"A wall," I said, and a philosophical inclination swept over me, like a breeze. Something like a chill ran down my back, and I shuddered. "Yes. The wall that Nature builds to hide her mysteries, the veil she keeps before her lovely face. How many of us are content to look at the veil; how many of us mistake it for the face of nature herself. Few dare tear the veil aside, to bare the inner beauty."

"Get out," Raskol commanded. "We're going to have to push the boat through."

We climbed out and got behind the boat. We pushed against the tangled vines and felt them yield, but when we relaxed, the boat sprang back against us.

"Try again," said Raskol. "One, two, three, heave!"

We pushed the boat against the vines again, and again it penetrated partway and then sprang back against us. We pushed again. Again we failed to penetrate the vines.

A cry came from the woods. "Come on, let's give 'em a hand." Dozens of boys ran crashing out of the woods, and they ran into the water and gathered around the boat, pushing and shoving for a spot where they could get a grip on it. I was squeezed out of contact with it. There was no room for my hands. Many of the boys were wearing caps, and on the front of the caps were the words

BABBINGTON CLAM COUNCIL
FAMILY DAY

Grunting with each exertion, each thrust, the mob of boys pushed the boat with a mighty effort, and the vines were rent asunder. The boat thrust through the snug opening, and the boys fell back, self-satisfied. Raskol and I stepped through the opening they had made and into blazing sun. The Bolotomy lay ahead of us, running for a hundred yards or so as an ornamental stream. On the banks were trim lawns and topiary plantings, commemorative statues, and benches, maintained by the Babbington Department of Public Works.

Neither of us looked at the other. We walked along in the stream bed, leaving the boat behind. Ahead of us, water spilled over an artificial waterfall, embellished with concrete Cupids, and above the tiny waterfall, contained by a grassy embankment, lay a pond. On the surface of the pond white swans drifted lazily, and to one side little children threw bits of bread into the water and called "Here, ducky, ducky." The fat swans ignored them and drifted along.

A crowd was gathered on the other side of the pond, and a banner was suspended above them, hung between two trees. Raskol and I exchanged glances, and I stopped a moment to tuck in my shirt. Though I'd dreamed of it, I hadn't really believed that we'd get this kind of reception. I was surprised that word had spread so far and fast. We drew ourselves up to full height and marched toward the crowd with the boat between us.

As we got nearer, I began to be able to make out the words spoken by a man in the middle of the crowd, standing above them, on a platform.

"Life," he was saying, "as the Christensen sisters so aptly put it, is like a journey down a river. We know not what lies before us when we start out, what perils we shall encounter, what rapids, mosquitoes, or other riverine terrors lie ahead, but we know one thing with certainty, and that is that every river winds somewhere to the sea. And from that knowledge we can take heart, for we know that at the end of our journey we will come at last to the great gray rolling mother of us all, and rock in bliss and comfort, when she draws us to her soft and ample bosom."

The Static of the Spheres

We are all obliged, if we are to make reality endurable, to
nurse a few little follies in ourselves.

Marcel Proust
Within a Budding Grove
(translated by C. K. Scott Moncrieff)

Preface

OF THE DIFFICULTIES that arose during the writing of "The Static of the Spheres," no other posed so intriguing a set of challenges as the need to create a preoccupation for Guppa, something that he could do in his living room of an evening, in the quiet hours after dinner, that would be the equivalent of his practicing culling clams.

Guppa's clam-culling skills were legendary. When he had worked on the line at the clam-packing plant, he had been an inspiration to anyone who worked beside him, and at the annual Clam Fests he had won the culling competition for twelve years in succession, a record that stands to this day. When he became foreman of the culling section and retired from active day-in-and-day-out culling, he practiced at home in the evenings to keep his hand in, so that when a new culler joined the crew or when Guppa thought that the work was slowing, he could step over to the galvanized table where the clams were dumped and put on a display of speed and accuracy that was still dazzling, still inspiring.

So that he could practice at home, in the privacy of his own living room, while listening to the radio, and later while watching television, he would arrange in a semicircle in front of his favorite comfy chair a set of peck baskets into which, while blindfolded—or at least, during the television years—without looking, he would toss clams that were randomly arranged in a bushel basket between his feet. Arranging the clams randomly again after Guppa had culled them became my job as soon as I was old enough to perform it.

At first, immediately after Guppa had retired from active culling, he had used clams straight from the bay, but these quickly became too smelly for Gumma to tolerate. For her part, Gumma liked to spend an evening curled up on the sofa with a slide rule and a book of recreational mathematics problems, very much as I have described in the pages that follow. She said that the stink of the clams made it hard for her to think straight, that the clams reeked and her head reeled. So Guppa and I undertook a project that threw us together for long and happy hours in the cellar, at his workbench. We constructed practice clams. Guppa would open the clams and remove the edible portion. I would scrape the insides of the shells clean and wash and dry them thoroughly. Together we mixed mortar to use as ballast in each clam, so that the heft would be realistic. Guppa measured varying amounts of the mortar for each clam, so that each would vary a bit from the average weight for clams their size, which Gumma calculated, throwing herself into the problem with great intensity, covering sheets of paper with notes and numbers. Guppa spooned the right amount of mortar into a clean valve, and then after the mortar was dry I glued the opposite valve to it.

The memories of the time that we spent in the cellar, working together, are among the most pleasant of my childhood. I would gladly have related them just as they were, and would probably have called this work "The Cement Clams," but in "My Mother Takes a Tumble" I had made Guppa a Studebaker salesman rather than a foreman in the culling section of the clam-packing plant, and now I felt that I was stuck with that story, just as I found myself stuck with the little lie about the hard candies that my great-grandmother offered me in "Do Clams Bite?" So, I worked out a comparable kind of practice for a Studebaker salesman of the first rank: categorizing potential buyers according to the sales pitch most likely to succeed with each—culling of another sort.

So far, so good. I thought that I would call this "All in the Cards." Ah, but then when I tried to imagine Guppa and my ten-year-old self passing happy hours in the cellar at work filling out note cards, I realized that it was not a project that would have held my attention for the long periods that constructing practice clams had, and so I cast about for something else that Guppa and I could do together in the cellar. I put myself back in Gumma and Guppa's living room and looked around for something that might inspire me. To my surprise and relief, the solution came to me at once. I found myself twisting the dials on Gumma's magnificent multiband radio and wishing that I had one like it. Guppa and I would build a shortwave radio.

THE SECOND MOST VEXING PROBLEM arose after I wrote the sentence that now stands as the last one in the bathroom scene. At once, I began to have misgivings about the whole scene. I meant to go on, and I meant to be quite frank, but I hesitated, because I realized that the scene would succeed only if it were at once frank and delicate. I didn't want to seem prudish, but I didn't want to embarrass myself either. I didn't want to describe the bathtub shenanigans that I had concocted for Eliza and me in a way that would mean injuring Eliza or disturbing the perilous balance that I had in mind for this work.

I went downstairs to the lobby, where Albertine was behind the desk, working on the accounts. I lit a cigarette and began pacing up and down. Al didn't look up. I began sighing whenever I passed the desk, but still she didn't look up. I began muttering "damn-damn-damn" under my breath. Al put her pencil down and leaned on the desk.

"Okay," she said. "I hear you. What's the matter?"

"Oh, I don't know," I said.

"I'll give you two minutes," she said. She went back to work.

After about a minute and a half, I said, "Well, I'm having doubts about a scene in which Eliza is giving me a bath. I think it's very important, because it leads to the confusion of motives for my wanting the shortwave radio—the mixture of sexual desire, jealousy, pride, anger, and my simple ingenuous hankering for a shortwave radio. But I'm afraid that if it isn't handled just right it will look like an unnecessary sex scene and that it will embarrass Eliza to boot."

"Why don't you ask Eliza what she thinks?" she suggested.

My jaw dropped. Al and I have been married for more than twenty years, but still there are times when I am not sure whether she possesses a surpassing understanding, an uncanny percipience, or is just not listening to me most of the time.

"There is no Eliza," I said. "I made her up."

Al looked at me as if I were a nitwit and went back to work. I trudged back upstairs. At least half an hour passed before I decided what to do. I dialed the desk from the phone in my workroom.

"Small's Hotel," answered Al.

"Al," I said. "Will you be Eliza?"

"Will you take me to lunch?" she asked.

"Okay," I said.

"Sure," said Al.

I TELEPHONED ELIZA AT ONCE to invite her to have lunch with me. Eliza is now sixty-three. After Dudley Beaker died, she stayed on in the stucco house on No Bridge Road, at the end of which there is now a bridge.

"Hello?" she said, in the small and tentative tone she uses to answer the phone, as if she expected a call from a creditor or a grasping relative.

"Eliza," I said. "It's Peter."

"Peter, darling," she said, switching at once to the voice she uses with friends, a voice like velvet or cognac or *pot de crème*.

"Eliza, will you have lunch with me?" I asked.

"Oh, I think that would be delightful," she said. "When would that be?"

"How about one-thirty?"

"Oh, you mean today."

"Yes."

"Oh, well, yes, fine. I wonder if I have anything that I can wear? I'm standing here in a Chinese robe. You don't think I could wear that, do you? No. I know what, why don't you and the gorgeous Albertine come here, and I will fix you some lunch?"

My heart stopped for a moment, though I was certain that the offer wasn't genuine.

"Nonsense!" I said. "I insist that I take you out somewhere—just you and me. Al is otherwise engaged."

I held my breath.

"Oh, well," she said. "Fine. I think I can put some outfit together."

I let a long sigh out to one side of the mouthpiece, and I was sure that I could hear a similar sigh from the other end of the line. Both of us were relieved. None of the domestic arts was ever an interest of Eliza's, because, she said to me once, "Not one of those activities gets you anywhere. After cleaning a house, you're merely back to where you were before the place got dirty. After you've cooked, eaten, and cleaned up after Thursday's meal, you can't say that you are anywhere but where you were after you had cooked, eaten, and cleaned up after Wednesday's meal."

I suggested that we eat at the Manifest Destiny Diner, a favorite haunt of mine, which I like for its Wild West motif, its thick 'n' juicy Vanishing Buffaloburgers, and its frosty mugs o' beer, but she wanted to try Pussy's, a new place downtown, where the sign that directs one to the toilets says Litter Boxes, a hamburger is called a Cat's Meow, soup is served in heavy earthenware bowls that say CAT on the side, and the staff smiles relentlessly.

"Something from the bar?" asked a waitress, before we had quite settled in.

"Yes indeed," said Eliza. "Drinks."

The waitress smiled but did not laugh.

"Vodka and soda," said Eliza. "No ice."

"I'll have a martini," I said. "Straight up, with an olive."

Al stepped out of character for a moment. "I'll have the same," she said, "but with a twist. Forget the vodka and soda."

While we were having our drinks, Eliza read what I had written so far
of the bathroom scene. She handed the manuscript back to me and asked
me to order her another vodka and soda. She winked when she said it, so
I ordered her another martini. She asked, "Well, Peter, what comes after
this?"

"That's what I wanted to ask you," I said.

The waitress brought Eliza's drink, and I decided that I'd have another
too.

"Well," said Eliza, "of course, it's up to you, but I think that, if I were
you, I would not include anything explicitly erotic. I would think that it
would be much—better—more effective—to just provide pretty much
what you have—or maybe just a little more—some disconnected sensory
details that would invite the reader to imagine an erotic—situation—taking either your part or mine—*chacun à son goût,* don't you think? Just
mention in a list—say—the smooth, wet, and slippery body of a boy of—
ten, I think—a cotton blouse, damp with steam, clinging to the breasts of
a voluptuous woman of thirty-four—her blond hair pinned up—a strand
or two falling over her forehead—droplets of steam on the mirror and the
white tiles—the tiny sound of popping bubbles—millions of tiny popping
bubbles—hissing and crackling—like champagne or static—muffled by
the clouds of steam—the light diffused by the steam—vague highlights
on the boy's smooth, wet skin—her hands in the warm water—the warm
water enveloping the boy's body—the slick, smooth skin along his
thighs—his wet hand along her arm— the rounded tops of her quite lovely breasts when she leans over the edge of the tub—the firm pressure of
the tub against her belly—her hand brushing against his smooth thigh—
that sort of thing."

THEN CAME THE THIRD PROBLEM: the flood. I had nearly finished
the manuscript when nature interrupted my work and divided my attention. Most of the material was there, though a few things were still out of
place and there were still some unanswered questions and some voices
that I could not quite hear clearly. Rain began falling one night and continued to fall for eight days. Throughout that time, Babbington was nearly invisible: it was only a set of vague gray shapes beyond the rain. The
water level in the cellar of the hotel rose steadily, and there was nothing
we could do to stop it. We worked for hours each day bringing endan-
gered tools, supplies, and mementos up to the safety of the ground floor. I
was so concerned that my jars of nuts and bolts and the like would be
disorganized that I insisted that we place things around the hotel in the

same positions that they had occupied in the cellar. When the waters receded, I set up in the cellar every fan that we had, and in a couple of days the place was more or less back to normal. We carried everything back to the cellar and arranged it as it had been.

Then only the last and most perilous of the difficulties was still to be overcome: doubt. It was as if, while I was distracted by the flood, Fat Hank had moved into my workroom.

At about the time that I began work on "The Static of the Spheres," Albertine brought home two large cartons of wood from which she planned to build a miniature of Small's Hotel. She had in mind a true miniature, not just a representation of the exterior. She would build with miniature framing, tiny nails, sheathing, and clapboards. Best of all, she had bought a set of tiny, precise tools: a square, a plane, saws with teensy teeth, a mitre box, and so on.

She was at work on her small hotel throughout my work on this, and I suppose that the rhythms of her miniature construction—the tap-tap-tap of her little hammer, the back-and-forth whisper of her little saw—underlie some passages. But that is by the way; I want to say something about the materials themselves.

When she brought all the stuff home, we spread it out neatly on the tabletops in the dining room and spent quite a while just handling all of it and looking at it.

"You know, Al," I said to her, "this is just like the moment when Guppa has all the parts of the radio lined up on his workbench. I have the same anticipatory feelings, the same mixture of excitement, eagerness—and fear. I sense, in all this cute stuff you brought home, what I should sense in the parts of the radio when they lie in ranks on Guppa's workbench—the presence of a potential magnificence, something that I've found in the parts of other things before they're assembled. The components might be—oh—a clutter of memories, boxes full of thin slabs of basswood and slender dowels, or ranks of vacuum tubes, resistors, capacitors, transformers, and the like. Sleeping in these things is the capacity to become a book, a dollhouse, or a shortwave receiver. One has the feeling that merely by gathering the parts, one has made a step toward realizing the end.

"'Ah,' one is tempted to say, 'the pieces are all there. Now all I have to do is put them together.'

"But—" I said, dramatically, "—it may be better, sometimes, to leave the pieces as they are, unassembled, for the potential book crackles with wit, the shutters on the potential dollhouse are straight, and the signals picked up by the potential receiver are clear and strong, but the actual book is going to have its passages of half-baked philosophy and weepy sentimentality, some of the shutters on the actual dollhouse will hang at odd angles, and the receiver may bring in nothing but a rising and falling howl muffled by a thick hiss."

Al laughed at me and told me to get upstairs and get to work, and I did.

Peter Leroy
Small's Island
March 18, 1983

1

AT HOME in my parents' house in Babbington Heights, in the corner of
the attic that was my bedroom, I had, on a table beside my bed, a small
Philco radio. It was made of cream-colored plastic. The radio had seen
years of use on somebody else's bedside table before I got it for my room.
Over the years, the heat from the bulb that lighted its dial had discolored
and cracked the plastic in a spot along the rounded edge of the top, right
above the dial. On winter nights, when the attic was cold, I would bring
the radio close to me, onto the bed, under the covers, and rest one hand on
the warm, discolored spot while I listened.

Of all the programs that I listened to on that radio, I can remember
only one clearly: one about a boy about my age who lost everyone who
was dear to him—his mother and father and grandparents and a clever
younger sister with a voice like a flute—in a shipwreck, and was left
alone, entirely alone, on an island somewhere warm and wet and windy,
and called out for them in the night, calling against the persistent, over-
powering sound of the wind and the sea, and listened in despair for the
sound of their voices through the crashing surf and howling wind. I hud-
dled in my bed, with the blankets pulled over my head, and trembled
when the sound of his voice and the wind filled the little cave that I had
made. This program so terrified me that I wanted to cry out for my own
parents, to run downstairs for some comfort from them, at least to reas-
sure myself that they were still there, but I couldn't run to them because I
was listening to the radio at a time of night when my mother didn't allow
me to listen, since the programs that were broadcast at those late hours
were, she had told me often enough, the sort of thing that scared the wits
out of young boys.

Though I remember only that one program, I can remember as clearly
as a memorized poem or a popular song the susurrous and crackling static
that accompanied everything I heard on the little radio. Over the course
of time, this insistent sound has pushed its way from the background of

my radio memories to the foreground, and the private detectives, ship-wrecked travelers, cowboys, bandleaders, and comedians who once were able to shout over it now call out only faintly and indecipherably, like voices calling against the roaring of the sea and the wind.

Then Guppa bought a Motorola console radio as a Christmas gift for Gumma, and at once the Philco became a pedestrian radio. The Motorola had several bands, and it could pull in programs from places so far removed from Babbington that their names alone, printed at intervals along the dial, were enough to bring to mind notions of places so remote and exotic that I had to work to convince myself that they were real places, places where people worked, slept, ate meals, listened to radios, places that I could, someday, actually visit: Balbec, London, Macondo, Moscow, Paris, Tokyo. It was as if the Motorola were more worldly, more sophisticated, more knowledgeable than the Philco, as if the Philco were naive, untraveled, because it knew only Babbington and the surrounding towns and cities that everyone knew. Not only could the Philco not detect the signals from far-flung places, but it seemed to me that the little radio was ignorant of the notion that these places even existed.

2

AS SOON AS I HAD LISTENED to Gumma's Motorola, I wanted—no, I needed—a more sophisticated radio. It was a familiar sequence: seeing the lack of something, one feels the need for it.

Even now, when I have reached an age when, I tell myself, I should be beyond such feelings, I find myself in the grip, now and then, of an irresistible desire to replace a perfectly good turntable, amplifier, or tuner with a newer and more complicated one. I consider myself, on the whole, a mature and sensible fellow, and I expend no little effort in trying to talk myself out of these periodic attacks of electronic lust, but—as Porky White has said to me so often—"Look, it's like a fight. One guy comes into the ring in a gray pin-striped robe and across the back in small black letters it says REASON. He's wearing glasses, and his hair is thinning. Into the opposite corner leaps a guy in a robe of scarlet satin, and across the back in orange and purple letters it says THE IRRESISTIBLE URGE. He looks like a bull, and there's foam at the corners of his mouth. Where you gonna put your money, kid?"

Still, I think that, even at ten, I might have talked myself into being content with the little Philco if I had not spent the New Year's Eve that followed with Dudley Beaker and Eliza Foote at Gumma and Guppa's, and my desire had not become so mixed up with other, baser emotions—lust and pride—that I could not separate them, as one sometimes cannot separate the overlapping signals of weak radio stations.

3

IT WAS NOT UNUSUAL for Eliza and Mr. Beaker to look after me for an evening when I was spending a weekend at Gumma and Guppa's. For many years, they would stay with me on Saturday nights while Gumma and Guppa went out to play bridge with friends.

I was, throughout my childhood, required to take a bath sometime between dinner and bedtime, and Eliza took on the responsibility of bathing me when she and Mr. Beaker were taking care of me on one of those Saturday nights during my earliest years. Mr. Beaker left this responsibility to her gladly, and he would spend my bath time in the living room, smoking his pipe and reading. Eliza invented a number of bath time games over the years. My favorite of these was making soapsuds landscapes. We would work up a lather of suds in the tub together, enough so that the suds covered the water entirely. We would spend some time smoothing the layer of suds so that it completely and evenly covered the water, with the exception, of course, of the spot where I, sitting, projected through the layer of suds. Then, moving and shaping the suds with our hands, we would create a landscape around me. There might be mountains in the distance near my feet, a winding road, conical evergreens, a river. The renderings of the features were never very precise, and they began to decay as soon as they were constructed, from the bursting of the soap bubbles and the pull of gravity. By the time the little village in the valley had been constructed, for example, the mountains had sunk to the level of the plain, and the river would be nearly indistinguishable. To appreciate a completed soapscape, one had to be able to see the mountains as they had been when they were new and to imagine that they were better formed than they really were.

As I grew and aged, the pleasure that I took in soapsuds landscapes and Eliza's other bathtub games began, as one might expect, to shift from the aesthetic to the erotic.

On that important New Year's Eve, my parents were going to a celebration in our neighborhood, and Gumma and Guppa were going to some kind of wingding that someone in their set was throwing, perhaps a New Year's Eve bridge tournament. When Eliza learned about their plans, she volunteered to stay with me at Gumma and Guppa's.

"We won't be going anywhere anyway," she told Gumma. "Dudley thinks that New Year's Eve celebrations are not at all the right way to usher in the new year. He says that in the Orient people make a point of planning, as the old year wanes, what endeavors they wish to undertake in the coming year, and then in the first moments of the new year they do a lick of work on each of these undertakings, thereby ensuring that they will prosper throughout the year, and this, he feels, is a much wiser way of beginning a year than a lot of drunken whoopdedo."

So it was that on New Year's Eve Eliza and I were in the bathroom, shaping a soapsuds landscape, while Dudley was in the living room, making a list of endeavors that he hoped would prosper in the coming year. Eliza and I had been at work for a while. The room was steamy. Droplets covered the mirror and the chrome fixtures. The droplets commingled and grew and ran suddenly down erratic courses. Eliza's cheeks were rosy with the heat. Damp strands of her blond hair fell across her eyes. She blew up at them to get them out of her way or pushed them up with the back of her hand, keeping the soap out of her eyes. She bent over the tub, working at shaping the soapsuds. Her damp blouse clung to her breasts. Her hand grazed my thigh while she was shaping suds into a peasant cottage, and we glanced at each other simultaneously. There was a look in her eyes that I had never seen before.

4

FLUSHED AND GIGGLY, Eliza and I returned to the living room after my bath and settled ourselves in front of the new radio. I was wearing a white terrycloth robe. Eliza tousled my hair and hugged my shoulders. Mr. Beaker looked up from his lists, acknowledged us with a smile, and went back to work.

Eliza turned the radio on, and began twisting the dial, exploring for signals. For much of the time while she explored, she was between stations, and the living room was full of the noises that lie between stations on a radio dial, noises that are drowned out when we come upon a strong

signal. Some of those noises come from within the receiver itself, produced by the operation of the receiver's circuits, noises from within the
machine. Other noises come from outside the receiver. The sources of
some of those are local, familiar, homely. These may, for example, be
produced by the ignition systems of passing Studebakers or by the motor
in a refrigerator or by a toaster. The sources of others, however, are distant, exotic, intriguing. These may, for example, be produced by stations
too far away for a clear signal to reach us, stations calling from God
knows where, with voices as weak as that of a boy calling against the
wind. Or they may originate in electrical discharges from the sun, from
other stars, other galaxies: the pervasive and indecipherable, eternal and
inestimable noise, the static of the spheres.

While Eliza and I are curled up on the floor twiddling the dial, search-
ing for a signal, let me pause for a moment to plant in your mind the notion that our senses, like radio receivers, pick up lots of noise, and that in
our perception of events the truth is sometimes nearly buried by static.
Let me suggest, too, that in remembering the things that have happened to
us, the people who have spoken to us, the things that they have said, we
introduce new static, and that as time goes by we may even find, as I did
with the whine from my little Philco, that the noise has become stronger
than the signal.

"Oh, I know what we can do," cried Eliza suddenly. "We can follow
the new year as it approaches us, and then follow it across the country."

"Calm down, you two," said Mr. Beaker. He stood up from his work
and stretched. He chuckled indulgently. "You seem quite worked up.
Look at you. You're flushed and giggly."

Eliza looked at me and reddened a little more. So did I. We giggled
again. Mr. Beaker walked over beside us and rumpled Eliza's hair. He
took another log from the wood box and drew back the mesh curtain that
hung in front of the fire.

"Peter," said Mr. Beaker. His back was toward us. He was working at
the fire, using tongs to rearrange the logs. There was, it seemed to me,
something stern, something menacing in his voice.

"Yes?" I answered. The word leaped from me like a small frightened
animal. My heart began to beat quickly, and my voice seemed to tremble.
I threw a wild look at Eliza. She made a motion with both hands, as if
pushing against a plump, resilient pillow of air, and I could tell at once
that she meant, "Slow down. Calm down." I cleared my throat, and
asked again, in a steadier voice, "Yes?"

Mr. Beaker spun around to look at me. The fire blazed suddenly, and the room filled with its heat. Perspiration formed on my forehead and upper lip. "Is something wrong with you, Peter?" he asked. "You sound odd. You almost sound frightened."

I smiled at him. The smile was meant to be that smile of amused incredulity that we adults have learned to affect when we are caught doing something that we shouldn't. For some reason, we continue to expect that smile to work for us, even though, as soon as we see it on anyone else, we say to ourselves, "This guy is as guilty as sin." I thought that I had shaped it pretty well, but Mr. Beaker's look remained one of concern, and when I look at this scene now in my mind's eye, the smile on my face, the trembling lips, the blinking eyes look as if they belong on a plucky fellow with a noose around his neck.

Mr. Beaker reached toward me suddenly. I raised my hands to ward off the blow that I thought was coming. He reached between my hands and felt my forehead.

"I think he's running a fever," he said to Eliza.

"Oh, it's nothing," she said. "He's still warm from his bath. The whole room was—steamy—very steamy—in there." She took Mr. Beaker's hand and held it against her own forehead. "See?" she asked. "I'm a little overheated myself."

Mr. Beaker smiled and caressed Eliza's forehead. He leaned forward and kissed the top of her head.

"I was thinking, Peter," he said, turning to me, "that you ought to do as I am doing. You should decide what you would like to accomplish in the coming year and then, as the year turns, make some small start toward accomplishing it."

"Maybe he already has," said Eliza. She looked steadily at me for a moment. The fire was yellow and bright. It flared again, and the heat rushed over me. I thought that there was a good chance that I would either faint or throw up if I didn't do something—move around a bit, take some deep breaths. I stood up quickly, as if inspired by Mr. Beaker's suggestion.

"That's right!" I cried. "You know what I want? I want—" I had spoken too quickly. I had a few ideas about what I wanted—vague ideas, certainly, but ideas just the same—but of the ones that came to mind, none were things that I could announce, or confess, to Mr. Beaker. I certainly could not have said to him, "I want Eliza," and if somehow I had found it possible to say that, I would not have known how to say to him why I wanted Eliza or exactly what for. My mind hissed and crackled, much like a radio between stations. Now and then a strong, but inexpressible, desire came through as I looked wildly around the room, and at last, to my relief, something came through strong and clear: Gumma's radio. "—I want a radio like this," I said.

"That's good, Peter," said Mr. Beaker, beaming. "Now you have a goal. Of course, a radio like this is a little beyond your reach, but it is a good sign, I think, that you set your goal high. Now let's see if we can bring it down to a point where you can, if you extend yourself, if you really stretch out, grasp it. How would you like a small radio that you could keep on a bedside table at home? If you were to begin working at odd jobs—"

"I already have a radio on my bedside table at home," I said. A great many emotions had run through me while Mr. Beaker had been talking. First, there was passion, a passion that I could not express because there was no acceptable object for it. Then there was fear, the fear that the passion would be discovered if I didn't hide it somehow. Next there was pride, pride that arose when Mr. Beaker told me that a radio like Gumma's was a little beyond my reach, as if he were saying that a woman, a grown woman like Eliza, was a little beyond my reach. And then there was surprise, for I discovered after I had said it that I really did want a radio like Gumma's. I now burned with a desire for such a radio, so passionate a desire that it surpassed anything I had felt for Eliza.

"Ah," said Mr. Beaker, "but suppose that you were to build a radio yourself. That would be something quite different from the radio that you have at home."

If I were responding to that remark now, I would say, "No, it wouldn't, Dudley. It would be essentially the same: it would be the same in purpose and in function. It would pull in the same frightening programs about shipwrecked boys, the same music, the same comedy programs, and I have no doubt that it would pull in the same annoying static. I know why you said what you did, Dudley, and I'm surprised, surprised and disappointed, for I know that what made you make that remark was the same crazy idea that inspires those people who praise a thing—a dining-room table, say—simply because someone has made it himself, attaching to it a value that is not derived from any improvement in form or function over any other dining-room table, a value derived merely from the way in which it was made. What did you take me for, an idiot? I may have been just a kid, but I could see, even then, that any radio that I would build for myself, if I could even imagine building a radio for myself, would differ from the little Philco at home only in being a sloppier job."

At the time, however, I said, "I want a radio that gets different programs."

Mr. Beaker began an elaborately simple explanation of the way a radio works, apparently thinking, from my remark, that I imagined that the programs I heard on the radio came from within the radio, and that a different radio would, simply because it was a different radio, play different programs.

"Dudley," interrupted Eliza, "I think you misinterpreted Peter's remark, and I think you're underestimating his understanding."

"Oh?" said Mr. Beaker. "Am I, Peter?"

"Yeah," I said. "What I meant is that my radio at home can't get all the programs that this radio can get."

"Oh, well—" said Mr. Beaker.

Ah, Beaker, I wish I had you here now. The conversation would be considerably different today from what it was then.

"As I see it, Dudley," I would say, "a radio is a lot like a pair of ears. With my ears, I can't hear everything that there is to hear. For one thing, my ears aren't sensitive enough. Some things are too quiet for me to hear most of the time—for instance, the cat's stomach. Usually, I don't hear the cat's stomach at all, but if I lie on the floor and put my ear right against the cat's stomach, I can hear a sort of wheezing and rumbling."

"That's not a good idea, Peter," you would say. "Cats generally have fleas—"

"There's another example," I'd interrupt. "Fleas make noise too, but we don't hear them. Little bits of dust crashing into each other when they float in the air would make a hell of a racket if we could hear them."

"I see what you—"

"Other sounds," I'd say, firmly, "are too far away to hear. My equipment—my receiving set of ears—is not powerful enough to pick them up. You and I and Eliza, while we were sitting in the living room that New Year's Eve, knew that Gumma and Guppa were probably laughing and telling stories or playing bridge at the same time, but we couldn't hear their laughter or their stories or the snap of the cards, could we?"

"Of course not. We—"

"And in the farthest reaches of the heavens, in distant galaxies, stars were exploding, but we couldn't hear those either, could we?"

"No."

"And, more important than any of that, something was happening to Albertine at that time, at that very moment when you and I were going on about the radio, someone was talking to her, or she was thinking about something, or dreaming about something—something was happening to her, Dudley, that would contribute to making her the sweetie she is today, and we didn't know anything about it. There was no apparatus that would allow us to tune in to the Albertine Show and find out what was happening to her."

Heh-heh-heh. Oh, I am rolling now, Dud. I can feel myself taking the upper hand, I can feel your grip loosening with each word. Where was I? I did sensitivity. I did power. Range. Range.

"Finally, Dudley," I would say, "some sounds are outside the range of frequencies of sound that my ears can pick up, just as—"

"Calm down, Peter—"

"—just as some stations were outside the range of the little Philco. Do you understand?"

"I understand."

But at the time, Mr. Beaker just went on and said, "—then what you want is a shortwave radio."

"I do?" I said, playing the part of naive child as well as it has ever been played.

"Yes, of course," said Mr. Beaker. "With a shortwave radio, you will be able to pick up conversations among people all over the globe. You'll hear the babble of many tongues. You may even pick up a few useful phrases."

He was right, and I knew it, and the prospect of making contact with all the mysterious people out there sold me at once on the idea of a short-wave radio, a radio that would allow me to eavesdrop on the conversations of people in all the quaint countries I had heard about, people whose habitual preoccupations I had come to understand from the phrases that I had heard repeated about them, phrases that classified them according to their national passions: Japanese beetles, French bread, Irish coffee, Spanish fly, Mexican jumping beans, Chinese checkers, British steel, German beer, Russian roulette, Canadian sunsets, Turkish taffy, Swiss cheese, Italian loafers, Polish jokes, Hungarian goulash, Cuban cigars, Siamese twins, Panama hats, Greek statues, Dutch uncles.

5

"GUPPA COULD build me a radio," I said.

"I'm sure he could," said Mr. Beaker. He turned toward Eliza, and from the way his ear twitched, and from the flash of anger in Eliza's eyes, I knew that he had winked.

"And I could help him," I said, through clenched teeth.

"I'm sure you could," said Mr. Beaker. He began loading his pipe. He wore a small, twisted grin. It was not until several years later that I learned the word *supercilious,* but when I did, I found that I already knew exactly what it meant.

I was furious. Mr. Beaker took his pipe tool from his pocket and began tamping his tobacco. If I had been holding the poker, I might have hit him with it. Instead, it occurred to me to use another weapon: Eliza.

"You know, Mr. Beaker," I began, in a tone that startled me, "Eliza and I—"

Eliza had been looking into the fire. Now she snapped her head around to look at me, and there was on her face an expression of terror so striking that my throat caught when I saw it. She looked as frightened and helpless as I imagine the marooned boy in the radio program must have looked when he realized that he was alone. A chill ran through me, and I actually shuddered. Instantly I lost all desire to hurt Mr. Beaker, because I wanted instead to comfort Eliza.

"Eliza and I could look through Guppa's magazines," I said, looking into her eyes as I said it. "I bet one of them tells how to make a shortwave radio."

Mr. Beaker looked at his watch. "I think it's a little late for that sort of thing," he said. "You really should be in bed."

"My mother said that I could stay up until midnight," I said.

"And you have," said Mr. Beaker. "It's twelve-eighteen."

6

I PROPOSED the project to Guppa the very next night, while he and Gumma and I were sitting in the living room after dinner.

Guppa was working on what he called his pigeonholes. One reason that Guppa was so phenomenally successful a Studebaker salesman was that he developed individual sales pitches to suit each potential customer. He didn't wait for those potential customers to walk into the showroom, either; he went right out into the field after them and ran them down. In later years, I realized that Big Grandfather was disdainful of Guppa's occupation because it was so definitely landbound, just as my father was landbound in his gas station, and I know that Big Grandfather didn't think much of that. He would snort at the mention of anything automotive. Guppa, however, considered the hunt for Studebaker buyers every bit as exciting and demanding as the hunt for clams. If it wasn't man pitted against nature, it was man pitted against man, and the reluctant Studebaker buyer could be a warier and more elusive prey than the wily bivalve.

To make certain that no potential buyer was overlooked, Guppa kept a card file with information about everyone in Babbington who might eventually be made, in one way or another, to become a Studebaker owner. Guppa had a lot of confidence in himself and in Studebakers. He would eliminate a person from the file only if he was convinced that there was no hope whatsoever of an eventual sale. I know, for instance, that he kept a small stack of cards with the names of the crippled and blind in the pocket of his Sunday suit, and he would take these out after communion and say a silent prayer for the cure of each.

Guppa believed that every one of the people in his active file would buy a car from him sooner or later, and that belief was the real secret of his success. It was, as he saw it, just a matter of catching the prey at the right moment or using the right lure.

Of an evening, Guppa would set himself up in the living room to do his pigeonholes. He would bring a straightback chair in from the dining room and put it in front of his comfortable chair. On the seat of the straightback chair he would prop a large, shallow, cardboard carton that had in it a number of compartments formed by interlocking cardboard dividers. This carton might have been used originally to ship apples or glassware or electrical equipment. Guppa would sit in his comfortable chair, listening to the radio, or, in later years, watching television, and pull out a batch of his cards. He'd shuffle them, turn the top card, read his notes on it, and mull the situation over. After some time, he'd come to a decision about the prospects for selling a Studebaker to the person described on the card. He'd deal the card into one of the pigeonholes in the cardboard carton. Each pigeonhole represented a strategy. They were labeled in Guppa's wavy style of block lettering. Some of the labels made sense to me, but others made sense only to Guppa:

THE IRON IS HOT

WAIT 'N' SEE

RATTLE SKELETON

PROD

WHEEDLE

CAJOLE

and so on. It looked like fun, this process of pigeonholing Babbingtonians. I had a small part in it. As soon as I was able to handle the cards
without damaging them, Guppa would let me scramble their order for
him. He liked to begin his pigeonholing afresh every month or so, yank-
ing all the cards out of their holes, scrambling them, and reconsidering
each. He would pull all the cards out of their pigeonholes and give them
to me. My job was to put them into random order. Since I wasn't nimble-
fingered enough to shuffle them, I would spread them out all over the living room floor and then walk around picking the cards up in another order. I got into the habit of squatting to read the cards as I went along, and
this habit has stayed with me throughout my life. Now, when I am about
to do some painting and squat to begin spreading newspapers on the floor,
or when I am building a fire and squat to stuff a crumpled sheet of newspaper under the kindling, something comes over me with the act of squatting, something left from the days when I used to rearrange Guppa's
cards, and I begin to read whatever article is in front of me, reading for
that small but useful piece of information about a person that would have
held the key to the sale of another Studebaker.

   I was pleased and thrilled to discover, the first time I did this work for
Guppa, that there was a card for me, with my own name lettered across
the top in Guppa's wavy block letters.

   After the cards had been randomized, Guppa would spend evenings
during the next month going through them and reconsidering each one.
As soon as I was able to print neatly enough to satisfy Guppa, I got even
more responsibility: Guppa would save the birth announcements and obit-
uary notices from the *Babbington Reporter,* and I made out cards for newborn Babbingtonians and drew black borders around the cards of the de-
ceased. Guppa didn't discard the dead prospects' cards, however. He
used them to warm up before he got down to serious pigeonholing, pulling a card or two from the stack of black-bordered ones and thinking
about what he *might* have done to snare the pigeon before he or she had
dropped off. Now and then during these warmups, he would heave a sigh
and his eyes would mist over if the sense of loss or of lost opportunity
became too great.

   I also copied the data from old, worn, and dirty cards onto clean new
ones. This work, which I did for several years, spending some time on it
whenever I visited Gumma and Guppa, gave me some familiarity with a
large random sample of people in Babbington, at least with many of those
who were even remotely likely to purchase a Studebaker someday.

   While Guppa was working with his pigeonholes, Gumma liked to pass the time manipulating large numbers with one of her slide rules. Gumma's affection for the slide rule began when she took an off-season job in one of the slide-rule factories in Hargrove. She had worked at one job or another for nearly all her married life, but her work at the slide-rule factory was, as far as I knew, the first that she had ever really enjoyed. Before that, she had worked because Guppa was either selling too many Studebakers or too few. When he was selling too few, she worked to bring the income up to the budget, and when he was selling too many, she worked to help him keep up with the demand. Selling Studebakers in Babbington was a seasonal business, like clamming. Since the economy of Babbington was so dependent on the clam and clam by-products, such as gewgaws and driveway topping, most businesses in Babbington slipped into a torpor in the winter, when the bay was cold and choppy, and the air stung, and fewer clammies were at work. With fewer clams coming in, the work at the Babbington Clam packing plant and at Bivalve By-products, the by-product plant, would slow. Less money circulated around town, and most shopkeepers stood at their windows most of the day, looking at one another across the slushy streets. Most people in Babbington, in every line of work, expected this winter lull and considered whatever work they did seasonal. Only a few occupations—schoolteaching and bartending come to mind—provided steady, reliable employment throughout the winter, and the few people in these occupations were courted during the cold months by anyone who tried to make a living selling something. Only Guppa, the most senior of the salesmen at Babbington Studebaker, worked the year round; the others did one thing or another to make ends meet during the winter. And even Guppa, skilled as he was, found the pickings lean during the cold months. So, Gumma worked during the winter to help make ends meet.

During the summer, on the other hand, when the sun was strong and the breezes were warm, the ranks of clammies would be swollen by vacationing college students, moonlighting milkmen, and many others. The clam-packing plant would go onto three shifts, working day and night, and a person could find work there just by showing up at almost any time. Then Babbington bustled, people felt flush, and Guppa would say that selling a Studebaker was as easy as shooting fish in a barrel, although when I asked him how exactly shooting fish in a barrel was done and how the fish got into the barrel in the first place, he admitted that he had never tried shooting fish in a barrel and that it might actually be pretty difficult for all he knew. During the summer, Babbington Studebaker would take on extra help, and Gumma often pitched in then just to help Guppa out.

However, as soon as she began working on slide rules, Gumma fell in love with them, and she worked at a slide rule factory year-round for many years thereafter. A slide rule, which is today merely a curiosity, a relic of a simpler and cruder past, the mechanical analogue of an electronic calculator, has three main parts: the stock, the slide, and the cursor (see diagram).

Gumma was fondest of the cursor. From her first off-season job installing screws in the shiny little metal frame that holds the cursor in place on the stock, she had worked her way up to chief checker in the cursor department.

Despite the effort that Gumma and her dedicated crew put into making the hairlines in the cursors fine and straight, the slide rule remained an imprecise device. For discovering the final digits of an answer, the user had to rely on interpolation, on imagination. It was this quality of the slide rule—its bringing the user not to an absolute, indisputable answer, but only within the realm where the answer could be more or less accurately imagined—that won Gumma's affection, that made working with the rule as intriguing a pastime as reading detective stories. What Gumma understood at once—and she was always just a bit annoyed by the fact that she couldn't get anyone else to regard this fact with quite the awestruck reverence that she did—was that the hairline in the cursor did not reveal the answer to a problem: it concealed it. The edges of the hairline defined the limits of the range within which the answer lay; therefore the answer itself was under the hairline somewhere.

Gumma reserved for herself the best of the cursors that were produced there in the cursor room, the ones with the smoothest action, the ones with the finest and straightest hairlines. Each member of her crew would bring her any that seemed especially good pieces of work. If Gumma accepted

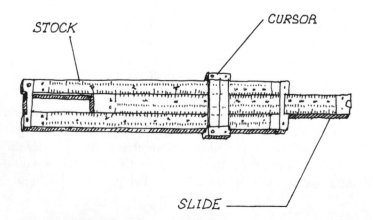

STOCK   CURSOR

SLIDE

one of these for her own, her having accepted it was a greater reward than the thanks she gave for it. But when she sat curled up on her sofa in the evening, working at recreational mathematics problems, even when she bent over the largest and finest rule in her collection, with a jeweler's loupe in her eye, she was only working at the edges of accuracy, she was only making tiny steps toward a more correct answer, the way the toast in her toaster made tiny steps from breadness to toastness.

7

SO THERE WE WERE, Gumma and Guppa and I, sitting in their living room after dinner on New Year's Day. Guppa had a fire going, and he was sitting in his comfortable chair doing his pigeonholes. Gumma was curled up on the sofa, working with her slide rule. I was on the floor in front of the fire, with a stack of birth announcements from recent issues of the *Babbington Reporter* and a stack of clean white cards. The room was cozy and quiet, with just the crackle of the fire, the flutter of Guppa's cards, the swish of the slide moving through the stock of Gumma's slide rule.

"Is it okay if we listen to the radio?" I asked.

"Of course, Peter," said Guppa. "I'll tune it in for you."

"Oh, don't get up, Guppa," I said. "I can tune it in by myself. Eliza showed me how to work it last night."

I went over to the radio and turned it on.

"This is a wonderful radio," I said. Neither Guppa nor Gumma said anything. "Gumma, you sure are lucky to have a wonderful radio like this," I said.

"Mmmm," said Gumma.

She bent over her slide rule and made some notations on a piece of paper. I switched to one of the international bands, and the room filled with a foreign howl. I twiddled the dial.

"Boy, it would be great to have a radio like this at home," I said.

The flutter of Guppa's cards.

"It wouldn't have to be as fancy as this," I said. "After all, I've already got a radio that gets the regular stations."

"Mmm-hmm," said Guppa. He knit his brows and bit his lower lip while he puzzled over one of the cards.

"What I need is a shortwave radio!" I said, as if the idea had just popped into my head from the ether. "If I had a shortwave radio, I'd be able to listen in on people's conversations from all over the place. I'd hear the rabble speaking in tongues. I might even pick up a few useful phrases."

"Yes, that's true," said Gumma, but I could tell that she was responding only to my tone of voice and that she hadn't really heard anything I'd said.

"I'll bet you could build a shortwave radio, couldn't you, Guppa," I said, loudly and proudly, very nearly shouting in his ear.

"What?" he asked, startled, looking up from his cards at last.

"You could probably build a shortwave radio, couldn't you?" I repeated.

"Well—" he began, and Gumma responded to *his* tone of voice as surely as she had responded to mine. She caught in the way he said "Well—" what might be the first note in a crescendo of self-deception that would end with his being committed to something long and complicated.

To tell the truth, I caught it too, and my heart beat a little faster and a smile came onto my face. I threw my arms around Guppa. "Oh, thanks, Guppa," I said. "This is going to be great fun!"

"Peter," said Gumma. "I'm not sure that your grandfather has the time to build a radio for you."

"Now Lorna," said Guppa, tousling my hair.

"Oh, Herb," said Gumma. She was smiling when she said it, and so was Guppa, and so was I.

8

WE WENT THROUGH back issues of *Impractical Craftsman* that evening, that first evening of the New Year. We found plans for many radios that might be suitable, but then Guppa came upon the one that was just right. The article began: "Here's a project that offers hour after interminable hour of baffling precision work, one that's sure to bring you an almost enervating sense of satisfaction when you've finally finished, one that is guaranteed to make your loved ones admire your stick-to-itiveness, your determination to see a difficult job through, your conviction that there is a right way of doing things, your unwillingness to cut corners."

"This sounds like the one for us," Guppa said.

9

OUR FIRST WORKING DAY was a Saturday. My father had driven me to Gumma and Guppa's on Friday night. I passed the night in restless impatience, eager for the work to begin, eager to be sitting beside Guppa in the cellar, to be working with him. I woke several times in the night, and was disappointed each time to find that the sun hadn't risen yet, to hear Guppa still snoring in the next room. Finally, enough gray light spread through the room so that when I climbed out of bed and stood close to the wall I could make out the branches and cherry blossoms on the wallpaper. I decided that morning had arrived and that things should get under way, so I dressed quickly and went to the kitchen to make some toast.

Gumma and Guppa loved to sleep late on weekends. When I was at home and wanted to talk to them on the telephone, I would have to wait until noon before I could call them. When I was spending a weekend with them, I knew that I had to be quiet until they were up, but there was always something interesting to look forward to on those weekends, something that made me impatient and restless, something that made me get up early. Gumma and I might be going to plant bulbs or bake bread or fry doughnuts. Guppa and I might be going to build a submarine out of oil drums or buy a Geiger counter and see if we could find any uranium deposits in the back yard or spread a new batch of clamshells on the driveway or just drive around town in the Studebaker looking to see if anybody had thrown away anything interesting. I would always be in a hurry to get going on these projects, so I would wake early. I would get up on my own and wander around the house for hours until Gumma and Guppa woke up.

I filled these morning hours by playing with their cat, by drawing pictures at Guppa's desk, and—when I was old enough—by making toast.

This morning, I had already played with the cat. I had even fed him, given him fresh water, and let him in and out of the house several times. I had drawn several pictures, each of which was a landscape that featured a pond (because I had just learned to draw ponds with pretty convincing perspective and particularly enjoyed complicating their shorelines with points and lagoons), clouds (because I had also just learned to draw nice, plump, billowy cumulus clouds), shadows (because I got a kick out of using the side of the pencil point to shade things), a disproportionately large duck (because Guppa had a nice little cast-metal Merganser paperweight that I wanted very much to learn to draw), and the transparent moon that sometimes graces the daytime sky (because I had begun to develop a fondness for it that still persists). I had made myself three slices of toast and eaten one with butter, one with butter and peanut butter, and one with butter and strawberry jam.

I was lying on the living-room rug in the light that fell through the windows in the front door. There were four diamond-shaped windows, themselves arranged in a diamond. The door was black and massive, made of wood, with iron strap hinges that ran nearly its entire width. It was rounded at the top. January sunlight fell in shafts through the windows, and in the shafts of sunlight, dust was dancing.

Why, I wondered, *does the dust dance that way?*

After some experimentation, I thought that I had found the answer. The dust was alive. (I did not believe this, of course; I was merely passing the time until Gumma and Guppa got up.) From the conclusion that the dust dancing in the air was alive, it was not a great leap to the idea that the dust on the floor must be dead. There wasn't a lot of dust on the floor; just enough. I picked up a little on my finger and blew it into the sunlight. It leaped and danced with more vigor than the dust I had been watching. I had been wrong! The dust on the floor was just resting, sleeping late, like Gumma and Guppa.

(My morning wasn't being wasted: I was exercising the faculty of human reasoning. I had accumulated some information and I had detected in it or pretended to detect in it certain patterns, and from them I had drawn a couple of conclusions. Then, as happens as often as not, along came some new information, and I was forced to recognize that the conclusion was wrong or not quite right. I took the old information and the new information, shook them well together, and poured out a new conclusion. I had to do quite a lot of this while I was growing up, and I found, frequently, that my conclusions made adults (and even older children) laugh, so when a private opportunity to practice arose—as this one had—I seized it. However, the affection that I had developed for any of my old conclusions was likely to persist strongly enough to leave its mark on a new one, and over the course of time I've found that I grow fonder and fonder of certain of the *old* conclusions and wearier and wearier of accommodating new information.)

I had decided that the dust on the floor wasn't dead; it was just resting. Perhaps I was on to something. I'd have to gather more information. I went down to the cellar, where there was plenty of dust. I ran a series of tests. A lot of the dust down there turned out to be just resting too, even the sawdust. I sat down and thought. The idea came to me that everything, everything I saw and touched, even the air I moved through, was moving, was in a sense alive.

"Peter, are you down there?" It was Gumma, calling me from the top of the cellar stairs.

"Yes, Gumma," I called. "I was just—"

I hesitated. Was I going to say that I was just looking at dust? I had enough experience with adults to know that that probably wouldn't be well received.

"— waiting for Guppa," I said.

"You have to be patient, Peter," said Gumma. "You have to remember that Guppa works very hard all week long, and he needs his rest on the weekends. It's the only time he has to sleep late."

I'd gotten myself into a mess. "Oh, I know that," I said. "That's why I was being so quiet, and I was sweeping up dust in the cellar to help him out."

"You're a good boy, Peter," said Gumma, in a voice as warm as a hug. "Come on up and help me make breakfast." She knew that this was a reward, since I liked helping her with any kitchen work, though I especially enjoyed using the toaster.

The smell of coffee and bacon drew Guppa out of bed soon enough, and he arrived in the kitchen as bright-eyed and eager to begin work as I had been when I awoke, hours before.

"Well, Peter," he said. "Up 'n' at 'em 'n' eager to go, are you?"

Some of my enthusiasm had worn off while I waited. I had made the mistake of imagining what work we would do, imagining my excitement, imagining the parts in my hands, Guppa's voice reading slowly through the instructions, and I had become a bit bored by the day's work. I was, after all, going to have to go through it for a second time.

"Yessiree!" I said, but my eagerness was forced, and it gave to the whole undertaking, before it had even really begun, the insidious suggestion of error, of something wrong enough at the start that it can't be put right by the end. If this feeling were an odor, it would smell like wet wool.

10

"FIRST we have to read the directions carefully," said Guppa. "Before you begin any project like this, you've got to read the directions a few times, until you know them pretty well. Then you can start to work, but you don't just jump right in and start doing the first thing. Understand?"

"Oh, yeah, I understand," I said, wanting for all the world to jump right in and start doing the first thing, whatever that might be. I pulled my metal stool up to Guppa's workbench, moving in as close to him as I could. Here we were, working on a project together, and we were going to do everything just right, just the way it should be done. First, we'd read the directions carefully, several times.

Guppa bent over the old issue of *Impractical Craftsman.* He moved his finger along as he read the directions, and now and then he commented to himself under his breath.

"Ah-ha!" he might say

Or, "Hmmph!"

Or, "Well, well, well."

Sometimes he would underline something with a flat red carpenter's pencil.

I read along too, and now and then, to make certain that everything was done right, I commented to myself under my breath. Sometimes I asked Guppa a question.

"What's this mean—*superheterodyne?*" I asked, pointing to the word in the second paragraph, where it had stopped me cold.

"Ah-ha!" said Guppa, and he underlined the word with his pencil. "That's what kind of radio it will be, when we're finished," he said.

"What about *triode?*" I asked a little later.

"That's got something to do with it too," Guppa said, "but it's not really as important." A moment passed. "Well, come to think of it, it might be pretty important at that," he said. He went back and underlined it. He read on. I tried to keep up with him, but I ran into so many words that I didn't know that I gave up trying to read and put my effort into daydreaming about the real work of building the radio, the work that would begin after we had read the directions a few more times, and into saying "Ah-ha!" and "Gosh!" and "Hmmmm" under my breath.

When Guppa had finished reading the directions, he began reading them again, and I began turning on my stool and looking around the cellar. When he had finished reading the directions a second time, he began reading them *again,* and I began fooling around with the wringer on Gumma's washing machine. When he had finished reading the directions for the third time, he straightened up and rubbed his back and then flipped back to the start again.

"You hungry, Guppa?" I asked. He turned to me with a look of some surprise, as if he had forgotten that I was there.

"Hungry?" he asked. "No, not yet, Peter."

"When do you think you'll want lunch?" I asked.

He looked at me and smiled. "Oh, in a little while, I guess," he said.

"Maybe I should go upstairs and help Gumma make some sandwiches," I suggested.

He looked at me for a minute before he said anything. "Maybe you should," he said at last.

Gumma and I worked together on lunch. We made Guppa's favorite, raw onion sandwiches, on toast, with butter. Gumma sliced the onions, as she always did, and she was a marvel to watch. With her old knife, worn by sharpening so that the blade arched upward, she cut uniform slices, with the precision of one of the women in the ruling room at the slide-rule factory. I got to make the toast, and spread butter on it, and lay the slices of raw onion on it, and I carried a tray with two glasses of milk and a plate of the sandwiches to the cellar. They were delicious.

11

GUPPA DROVE HIS STUDEBAKER slowly along the highway, watching for Two Regular Joes Electrical Gadgets, the store where we would buy the parts for the radio. We were more than half an hour west of Babbington, in an area where I had never been before. The road was crowded with cars. Now and then a driver would pull out from behind us and rush past honking his horn and shaking his fist, but Guppa ignored all of them, and I tried to ignore them too. My heart beat quickly with the excitement of this adventure, of being in unfamiliar territory, on an unfamiliar errand.

"There it is, Guppa!" I cried. It was a large cement-block building, painted yellow. The name was painted in enormous black letters along the side and repeated in a huge neon sign on the roof and again in metal letters above the front windows.

Guppa pulled off the road and parked in front of the building. When I got out of the car, my knees were weak with excitement.

Hand-painted across the door was the motto, "If we don't got it, you don't need it," and as soon as we entered the store, I knew that it was so. The place was entirely filled with things that I had never seen before. Most of what was for sale there did not even resemble anything that I had seen before. Not only was everything unfamiliar, but none of it gave, from outward appearance, any hint of what it was supposed to do or how it might be used. Among stores, Two Regular Joes Electrical Gadgets immediately leaped to the foremost spot in my affection, dropping the Babbington Army-Navy Surplus Store to second and Arnberg's Hardware and Sick-room Supply to a distant third. The mystery, the subtlety of these gadgets won me immediately; a nail and a hammer give themselves away at once, but a soldering iron and a capacitor do not. I stood inside the door for a few breaths, just looking around, and I think my mouth was hanging open. I know that when I looked at Guppa *his* mouth was hanging open.

Guppa opened his *Impractical Craftsman* to the list of materials for the receiving set. He looked at the list for a while, muttering to himself, and then he looked up and down the rows of shelves.

Directly in front of us were some gadgets made of black-painted metal, roughly rectangular, with an open section in the middle filled with a cylinder that seemed to be made of brown paper. Shiny, coppery wires projected from the bottom of the paper cylinder. These things came in several sizes, and they had a nice heft to them. The paper part was coated with or soaked in wax, and so felt soft and sticky. I hoped that we'd need a few of these.

"Do we need any of these, Guppa?" I asked.

"Hmmm, let's see," he said. He stared at the list for a while. "No, I guess we can do without those," he said.

"How about just one?" I asked.

"Peter," said Guppa, "why don't you just look around for a while? I'm going to have that clerk help me find some of the things we need. That'll save some time."

"Okay, Guppa," I said.

Guppa walked over to a counter where a thin, dark-haired man, probably one of the two regular Joes, was reading a newspaper.

"Morning," said Guppa.

The man looked up. "Do something for you?" he asked.

"My grandson and I are going to build a shortwave receiving set," said Guppa.

"Great," said the man. He began chewing on his thumbnail.

"We're going to need some parts," said Guppa. "Wire, for instance, and, well, that sort of thing."

The clerk raised an eyebrow and smiled with only the left side of his mouth. I tried doing it myself. "You got a list?" he asked.

"Right here," said Guppa, and he released lots of air with the words.

He opened the magazine on the counter.

The clerk looked at the list and said almost at once, "Sure, we've got all of this stuff."

"I want only the best," said Guppa, in a louder voice. "And all new. I don't want any rebuilt triodes or any of that."

The clerk laughed and shook his head. Guppa knitted his brows for a moment and stared hard at the clerk. Then he relaxed and laughed too.

"Heh-heh-heh," he laughed.

"Heh-heh-heh," the clerk laughed right back.

I began examining with minute care some mud-brown cylinders with wires sticking out of each end and bright painted bands of red, yellow, and orange along their sides.

12

I DRAGGED the metal stool up to the workbench and climbed onto it. I did not know then, and could not have known then, how much time I would spend on that stool in that cellar.

Guppa rubbed his hands together and reached for one of the several brown paper bags that he had brought home from the electrical gadget store. "Well, here we go," he said. He began pulling strange and wonderful objects from the bags and arranging them in a neat array on his workbench.

A few things have reappeared at intervals throughout my life, like motifs, like variations on a little phrase in a sonata. Among these are clams, of course, and a particularly unattractive plaid that first appeared on a bathing suit my mother bought me during the fat period of my childhood, and workbenches. I've always taken great pleasure in seeing anyone's workbench, for a workbench is, I think, a window on one's aesthetic soul. To be permitted to see a person's workbench is, for me, a sign of great intimacy, particularly if the workbench is in the cellar, because merely to be invited to the cellar is a token of close affection.

Guppa's workbench was small and old. It was certainly less than half the size of Big Grandfather's workbench. Both grandfathers kept neat, orderly workbenches, but Guppa's style of neatness and organization differed from Big Grandfather's. It was a case of a difference in degree producing a clear difference in style. Along shallow shelves above Big

Grandfather's workbench stood rows of identical jelly jars, each labeled to describe its contents, and each containing only items that were quite precisely alike. Big Grandfather's level of categorization was highly refined. One jar, for example, contained only brass screws one inch long; another contained only blue steel tacks one-half inch long. Any item that Grandfather did not feel comfortable putting into an existing jar had to have a new jar of its own. As a result, many of the jars held a single item.

Guppa, on the other hand, kept his supplies in large cans and large categories, such as "screws," "springs," and "string." Whenever he needed a brass screw one inch long, he would dump all the screws out onto his bench and poke through them for a pleasant interval, whistling with the carefree pleasure of this simple task, until he found the screw he needed.

The screw supplies of both grandfathers also offered vivid evidence of the strongest of the many attitudes that they had in common: frugality. Each grandfather had a great many screws that had been removed from household objects in the course of repair work or, if the objects were beyond repair, removed as part of a stripping operation before they were thrown out. The screws had been removed at the expense of no small labor, yet most of these salvaged screws were unusable. Their slots were so filled with paint or worn over that driving one of them into a hole would require great effort and concentration and an incredibly high tolerance for frustration. These qualities both grandfathers possessed in abundance. I do not. If I encounter difficulty in driving a screw into a wall to hold a shelf, for example, I am likely to abandon the project, to drive the screw in with a few vicious blows from a heavy hammer, or to tear the half-hung shelf off the wall and throw it through a window. And yet, in my cellar there are jars chock full of screws that are entirely unusable. Whatever it was that made it so hard for my grandfathers to throw a screw away they passed along to me.

My father's workbench was quite a different matter. It was so cluttered with tools and scraps that no work surface was exposed anymore. Since the workbench had become storage space, any work on a project had to be performed on the cellar floor or on a couple of planks thrown over a couple of sawhorses. If you had seen my father's workbench, you might have thought that its clutter was a sign of a sloppy mind, but it was not at all; it was merely an expression of a workbench aesthetic different from my grandfathers'. My father knew more or less precisely where everything on the workbench was; he could, for example, reach behind him while he was measuring a board and grab a carpenter's pencil with very little groping, and of the several cords that were entwined among the clutter, he could most of the time pick out the one that belonged to the tool he wanted and follow it from the plug on up to the tool itself.

The two aesthetics—neatness and clutter—are at war within me, and from the state of my workbench one can tell at any time which has, temporarily, the upper hand. I was surprised and delighted to find, when Albertine and I first thought of buying the place, that Small's Hotel had a fine, large, solid workbench. Things have a way of accumulating on this bench until the clutter resembles that on my father's workbench, though it never quite comes up to that standard. When it reaches a certain level of clutter, a level that I can recognize quite precisely even though the contents of the clutter are never the same, I swing in the direction of my grandfathers and spend a day or two putting things in their proper places and putting old screws and nails into jars and plastic containers. Al is always delighted to see the grandfathers beginning to get the upper hand again, and while I bustle around in the cellar it is not unusual to hear her playing something sprightly on the piano in the ballroom just above me.

As Guppa removed the wonderful gadgets from the paper bags, he arranged them in ranks by type, and I helped out by arranging them within the ranks by size.

13

FROM ONE OF THE BAGS Guppa pulled a couple of the hefty rectangular objects that I had admired at the store.

"Oh, great," I said. "You got some of those." I held one in either hand and enjoyed the weight of them. "Thanks, Guppa," I said, and I gave him a hug. "It's going to look a lot more solid with a couple of these on it."

Guppa chuckled and patted me on the head.

"What should I do?" I asked.

"Well," said Guppa, "we have to make a chassis out of this sheet metal."

Make a chassis out of sheet metal! Wow! I had no idea what a chassis was, but I could see that the sheet metal was, by its very nature—its precise rectangularity, its hardness, its smoothness, the whoomp-whoomp sound it made when I flexed it in my hands—going to be lots of fun to work with.

"I'll get started on that," I said. "What do I do?"

Guppa looked at me and tightened his lips. When he spoke, he used the soft voice that he used when he told me that it was time for bed. "Well, Peter, we have some things to do that you don't know how to do yet. You'll just have to be patient for a while and watch me. After I show you how to do things, you can try them, okay?"

"Sure!" I said. It seemed like a fair enough deal to me. I wanted to work on the radio, of course, but I didn't want the results marred by the sloppy sort of work that an untrained kid like me would produce.

Guppa began fabricating the chassis. It turned out to be even more fun than I had imagined. It involved lots of sawing with a hacksaw that went scree-scree through the metal, sending thrilling chills up and down our spines, plenty of whanging and banging at the metal while it was clamped in a vise, a good deal of drilling with Guppa's hefty electric drill, which squealed through the metal and threw bright, sharp-edged helixes all over the workbench and onto the floor, and quite a bit of cursing, mostly under the breath, but occasionally loud enough to bring Gumma to the cellar door to call out, "Are you sure you know what you're doing, Herb?"

It also involved some sweeping up, and that's what I did.

14

I WILL NOT make you sit through each step in the building of the radio. We began, you will recall, in January. By the time the crocuses began to pop up in corners of Gumma and Guppa's lawn, the chassis looked quite complete from the top. There were handsome black sockets that would hold the tubes and coils, and there were stocky transformers and some shiny things that looked like little cans. On the front of the chassis were six knobs in a row and a shiny toggle switch that would, one day, make the tubes light up and send unfamiliar sounds into the earphones. Looking underneath, one got an idea of how far we still had to go. Each of the gadgets mounted on top bristled with prongs and lugs underneath, and even I could figure out that all of those had to be connected with some of the wire that Guppa had bought. There were still lots of gadgets, most of them pretty small, lined up on the workbench, and I supposed that all of them had to go in there somewhere. I had developed a deep admiration for Guppa's stick-to-itiveness that persists to this day. We had made two more excursions to the electrical gadget store to find out what some of the things lined up on the bench were and to replace tubes that had rolled onto the cellar floor. I had assumed for myself the job of sweeping the cellar while Guppa worked, and there was by this time so little dust left that I had to get down on my hands and knees and work at the floor with a whisk broom to fill the dustpan. I had taken to wearing the earphones while I worked and imagining the strange and wonderful things I would hear through them when the radio was ready.

By the time the first tomatoes ripened in Guppa's garden, the underside of the chassis looked like my father's workbench. Wires of many colors connected most of the prongs and lugs, and most of the colorful resistors and drab capacitors were hooked in there somehow too. Gumma had taught me how to bake bread, and I had become nearly as precise as she at slicing onions for onion sandwiches. I had swept dust from the walls around the cellar, and then, with no more dust available, had given up sweeping the cellar, and had sat on the metal stool beside Guppa, watching him solder connection after connection.

When Thanksgiving arrived, Gumma taught me to make chestnut stuffing, and Guppa and I believed that we had the radio licked. Everything was in place, except for a few extra resistors and capacitors, but on another trip to the gadget store one of the Regular Joes assured Guppa that these leftovers had been included in the parts list only as spares. Guppa brought the radio up from the cellar after Thanksgiving dinner and plunked it down in the middle of the table, where it occasioned as much oohing and ahing as the turkey had. Well, perhaps not as much as the turkey, but at least as much as the Waldorf salad. Guppa beamed. He pushed his chair back from the table and took a cigarette from my father's pack. He gave an account of the labor that had been involved so far, and I could see that everyone admired his stick-to-itiveness.

"All we have to do now," he said, "is wind the coils."

15

THEN CAME THE FLOOD. Gumma and Guppa lived near Bolotomy Bay, about half a foot above sea level. Every fall, during the hurricane season, high tides during storms would send a couple of inches of bay water into Gumma and Guppa's cellar. This year had been without hurricanes during the usual season, but a whopper of a storm struck during the weekend after Thanksgiving.

When I got up that Saturday, the whole world was howling and whining. The house felt cold, the cat wouldn't come out from under the living room sofa, and the toaster wouldn't work. I had taken to inspecting the radio alone in the mornings before Guppa woke up. I opened the door to the cellar and started down the stairs. When I got two-thirds of the way down, I was up to my knees in water.

Anything buoyant bobbed lethargically on the surface of the water, including, here and there, the vacuum tubes that were supposed to go into the radio. I knew that I was up to my knees in a disaster. My first thought was that the radio was doomed. It would never be completed now. Disappointment mingled with an odd sense of release. There was a lump in my throat, but my mouth was twisted into a strange smile, not unlike the one that I had seen the Regular Joes use on our visits to their store.

When Guppa saw the damage, he sprang into action at once. He had, years ago, built a powerful pump from parts of a cement mixer and an outboard motor, for just such an occasion. He improvised a ramp and wheeled the pump into the kitchen. By the afternoon he had pumped the cellar dry, flooded No Bridge Road, and filled the kitchen with oily soot.

Gumma and I worked at cleaning the kitchen, while Guppa rigged up the fans that he had built for drying out the waterlogged contents of the cellar. ("Surplus Wind Machine Makes Neat Rig for Drying Waterlogged Cellar Contents," *Impractical Craftsman,* Volume XVIII, Number 3, pages 48–52.)

By the following weekend, Guppa was back at work on the radio, and I was sitting on the metal stool watching him. He began winding the coils.

16

ON CHRISTMAS EVE, Guppa was bent over his workbench, winding loop after loop of fine varnished wire around a core of purple Bakelite, straining his eyes and his patience. He worked slowly and carefully, and as he worked he counted the windings, muttering the count to himself, repeating and repeating each number so that he wouldn't lose it in the foggy tedium of the winding. I was doing all that I could to help him: first, I was being very quiet, trying as hard as I could not to create any distraction that would make him lose track of what he was doing, nothing that would make him lose count of the windings on the coil; second, I was trying, by smiling a lot and holding my eyes wide, to show how delighted and amazed I was by the work that he was doing, how impressed I was by his stick-to-itiveness.

It was almost time for dinner. In the morning, right after an early breakfast, much earlier than Guppa was accustomed to on a day that was not a workday, seven hours and twenty-two minutes ago, we had come down to the cellar, and Guppa had begun trying to wind this, the final coil. Guppa had not even taken a break for lunch. I had tiptoed upstairs and made some onion sandwiches for us, on dark bread, bread that I had baked myself, and had brought the sandwiches and two glasses of milk to the cellar, stepping carefully down the stairs so that the scraping of my shoes wouldn't make Guppa lose count. Guppa's milk and sandwiches lay untouched on the plate. The bread had curled as it dried.

Guppa's work on the receiving set since January had, little by little, step by step—some steps forward and some steps backward and some off on dead-end side streets—transformed a couple of bags of electrical gadgets into something that was now very nearly a radio, but that would not cross the threshold to radio-ness until this last difficult coil was complete. Until it was successfully wound, all the effort throughout the year would only be effort expended in an *attempt* to build a radio; but with the completion of this coil, the effort would become effort expended in the *building* of a radio. I had stuck with Guppa throughout all the effort, all the time, that he had been at work on this, except for time that I spent upstairs making sandwiches or helping Gumma with other chores, and even that work was indirectly helpful, I like to think. My situation, waiting for Guppa to complete the almost magical transformation of these electrical gadgets, was a lot like that of a child who has put a slice of bread into a toaster and sits, still sleepy-eyed, waiting for the toaster to transform the bread to toast.

Most children do not have a good sense of the amount of work required to build a radio from scratch or of the amount of time required to do it or—for that matter—of the passage of time itself. For most of them, time is like a dotted line, with unequal sections of the line itself (events) and unequal interstices (non-events, the periods of waiting for something to happen that make up much of a person's childhood). I blame this misconception on the type of toaster used in most households: the pop-up toaster. In operating a pop-up toaster, one inserts a batch of bread (usually a slice or two) and lowers it into the toaster. For the child who watches this operation, the lowering of the bread is apparently the last event that occurs for some time, since the string of small events that add up to the toasting of the bread—the real work of toasting the bread—takes place out of the child's sight. Therefore, the toasting itself becomes one of those interstices between events, a nonevent, a period of waiting that varies, both in real and in apparent length, according to the hunger of the child, the thickness of the bread, and random fluctuations in the voltage of the electrical service to the toaster. When the toast pops up, the child at last witnesses another event, which terminates the period of waiting for something to happen.

What effect, we might ask ourselves, does the pop-up toaster have on the intellectual development of the child who sits beside it, morning after morning, waiting with his plate and peanut butter? Bread goes in as bread and comes out, after an interval, as toast. Put in bread. Wait. Get out toast. Surely, the child who watches this happen over a period of time comes to think of bread as *either* bread or toast, to think of time as discrete intervals, and to think of being as being in some one form or in some other, with intervals of waiting, intervals between states when, apparently, nothing happens. Such a child would ask his grandfather to build him a radio (that is, lower the bread into the toaster), wait for some interval, and then expect his grandfather to hand him a radio (that is, expect the toast to pop up). When they grow up, these children are immediately attracted to the quantum theory, digital watches, and electronic calculators.

I was not such a child, because Gumma and Guppa did not have a pop-up toaster. Their toaster was a chrome-plated metal box about as long as three slices of bread lined up side by side. At each end of the box was a slot a little higher than the height of a slice of bread and a little wider than the thickness of a slice of bread. Inside the box was a tunnel through which the toast moved from the left end of the toaster to the right. Along the bottom of the tunnel was a set of toothed rails linked by an armature to a motor. The motor made the rails raise the toast, move it a short distance to the right, and set it down again on the stationary base rail. On either side of the tunnel were resistance wires that provided the heat to toast the bread. Little by little, as the bread marched through the toaster, it browned; that is, it became toast.

Now here comes the best part. The manufacturer of this toaster, clearly nobody's fool, had provided a small circular window in the side, so that one could watch the rhythmic rightward shuffle of the slices of bread and their progress from bread to toast.

From a very early age, I loved watching—and listening to—the operation of this toaster. As the toaster operated, it produced a repetitive sound from somewhere inside the machine, from the scraping of some parts against others, a sound that I interpreted as words, the words *Annie ate her radiator,* repeated over and over while the bread toasted. I would sit and watch and listen to the toaster and watch the bread through the little window and try to decide where in its passage from left to right it became toast. And from that toaster I learned to think of time as a belt, to think of being as being in transit, and I laid the groundwork for a persistent nostalgic affection for the wave theory of electromagnetic radiation and round-faced watches and slide rules, and I developed a sense of time's passing.

During the forty-six weekends that I had so far spent with Guppa in the cellar working on the receiving set (not counting the time that we had spent pumping the cellar out and drying its contents after the flood in November), my sense of the passing of time had developed to a point where, although it may not have been as acute as my sense of sight, it was at least as sharp as my sense of smell.

When Guppa and I had begun work on the receiving set, we had, each in his mind's eye, pictured a similar tableau: grandfather and grandson bent to the work together, youth and age, experience and enthusiasm, harnessed in tandem. We had glowed for a while with the flush of a mutual overconfidence in what an enthusiastic grandson might be able to accomplish, guided by his grandfather's hand. That glow had faded pretty early in the course of the work, as soon as we had come to see that there was very little that I could do that Guppa would not have to undo or redo later. My helping had degenerated into my keeping out of Guppa's way and keeping him company, demonstrating by my presence, and by displays of enthusiasm, that I was grateful for the effort that he was making, that I was impressed as could be by his stick-to-itiveness, and that I was still crazy about the idea of having a shortwave receiving set, although in fact I had begun to think, halfway through our third day in the cellar, that I would have been a lot better off if I had asked Guppa to make me something quick and simple, like a scooter, just as I was sometimes struck by the thought, while watching a slice of white bread move through the toaster, that I would rather have had raisin bread.

17

LET ME EXPLAIN these coils that were giving Guppa so much trouble. The reason one radio can pick up signals that another cannot is that each

of them is tuned to a different range of radio frequencies. The radio that
Guppa was building for me would detect signals in the range of frequencies that are called "shortwave." Now within that broad range lie narrower "bands." The receiver would be able to receive signals in many of
these bands, depending on which coil was plugged into its circuit. To
change from one band to another, all I would have to do was unplug one
coil and plug in another. The coils were to be wound on hollow Bakelite
forms with pins projecting from their bases that could be inserted into
sockets like those into which vacuum tubes were inserted.

When Guppa and I were looking through his back issues of *Impractical Craftsman* to decide what sort of radio we would build, we had found
other, simpler radios, but Guppa had liked the notion of winding these
coils by hand, and the thin, shiny wire had appealed to him as soon as he
saw it in the electrical gadget store, but what had really persuaded him
that this radio was just the one for us to build was the description of the
work that appeared in the article: the hours of baffling precision work.

18

GUPPA HAD SPENT forty-six weekends in the cellar at work on the radio, discounting the time that he had spent pumping the cellar out and
drying its contents. He had put eight hundred twenty-eight hours into the
project. I had put in four hundred fourteen hours in the cellar and another
seventy-eight making onion sandwiches and pouring coffee. I had made
one hundred thirty-eight onion sandwiches, not counting the one that a
boy from across No Bridge Road, a boy that I never knew by any other
name but Frankie, left half-eaten on his plate when he came over one Saturday at noontime to see if I wanted to climb trees with him.

"There!" said Guppa at last. He turned toward me, raising the finished
coil, the final coil, in a shaking hand. He had aged a great deal during the
time that he had been at work on the radio. His eyes were red and teary,
and the skin below them hung in dark, flaccid folds. His lips trembled
and twitched with the effort to form a grandfatherly smile.

"That's great, Guppa!" I cried, with deep, genuine enthusiasm. The
coil-winding was at last complete, the receiver was at last complete, a
phase of my life had come to a crisp and clear conclusion. There was no

ambiguity, no fuzzy line, no indeterminate point like that between breadness and toastness in Gumma's toaster, no need for interpolation. This
moment marked the end of the work on the radio, and anything to follow,
whatever it might be, would be a post-radio-construction event.

"This was the hardest one of all, wasn't it?" I asked. I knew that it had
been; I had been able to see that it had been, even though I avoided
watching Guppa too carefully and hoped that he did not know that I knew
how many times he had unwound the coil and begun winding it again
when he lost count of the windings.

"Well, yes, it was," he acknowledged.

I could see him gaining in strength now that the winding was done,
now that everything was done. He was beginning to allow himself to feel
proud.

"A job like this has got to be done just right," he said, raising the coil a
little higher in a steadier hand. "If you're not ready to do what has to be
done the way it should be done, then you're not ready to do it at all. Now,
you take this coil. I could probably have been off by a few turns and it
wouldn't have made all that much difference, except to me. I'd know that
it wasn't right. That's why I had to stick to it until it *was* right."

Now he was glowing. His hand was firm, and he drew in deep breaths
of the damp cellar air. He could relax now. He and I would be able to
straighten things up on the bench, put the few remaining leftover parts
into the electrical gadget jar, go upstairs to the kitchen, smiling so that
Gumma would say that we looked like the cat that swallowed the canary,
tell her about the progress we had made, then surprise her with the finished radio, listen to a few foreign broadcasts, show the radio to my parents when they arrived, eat dinner, sit in the living room and listen for a
while longer, and then go to bed, content.

I heard the door at the top of the stairs open, and I heard rapid, brisk
footsteps coming down the stairs. Mr. Beaker popped around the corner.

"What industry!" he cried. "You two haven't seen the light of day
since breakfast, I understand."

He leaned back in an exaggerated pose and scrutinized us with exaggerated care.

"Hmmmm," he said. "From the fact that you got up so early, Herb,
and from the little grins that you two are wearing, I'd say that you're getting very close to the end of this project. How's the work going?"

With pride, I announced to him that Guppa had wound all the coils and
we would be listening in on the babble of foreign tongues any minute now.

"Take a look at this," I said. I picked up the coil that Guppa had finished. "This was the toughest one of all. It has the finest wire and the most windings."

"That is quite a piece of work," said Mr. Beaker. He took the coil from me and held it in front of him, raising it to eye level as if it were a jewel. "Quite a piece of work," he repeated. He looked closely at the coil and said, "Mm-mm-mm." He compressed his lips and nodded his approval. "How many windings does this have?" he asked Guppa.

Guppa had been smiling, standing with his hands in his pockets and rocking on his heels. Mr. Beaker's question had a visible effect on him, the same effect as a sudden increase in the mass of the earth would have had. All of Guppa seemed to slump.

"How many windings?" Guppa asked.

"Yes," said Mr. Beaker. "How many windings?"

My throat became dry, my palms moist. I knew that something was terribly wrong. I didn't want to look at Guppa, but I couldn't look away from him. He pulled his hands from his pockets and swept them through his hair, pushing it back from his forehead.

"It's got about—"

He looked at me. I gave him a jaunty smile that I intended to mean "I have every confidence in you, Guppa. You're my hero." He squinted his eyes and peered at me as if he had forgotten who I was.

"I don't know," he said. "It was in the hundreds—I know that." He turned toward the plans, open on his workbench, then turned away quickly, as if looking at the plans would have been cheating. "I'm sure I got it right," he said. He seemed to be pleading.

"Me too!" I said, with great verve and the conviction that came from a heartfelt desire not to have him wind the coil again.

"I'm sure that a few turns more or less won't make enough difference for anyone to notice anyway," said Mr. Beaker. He put the coil down on the bench.

Guppa picked the coil up and peered at it, as if by looking closely enough he would have been able to remember exactly how many turns of that fine varnished wire he had made. He sighed. "We'll try again tomorrow," he said. "What do you say we quit for the day and get something to eat?"

"Oh, yeah!" I cried. I dashed toward the stairs and pounded up them. I had to get away from Guppa. There was a lump in my throat, and I could feel the tears forming in my eyes. I felt horribly sorry for Guppa, who so wanted to please and impress me, and I felt sorry for myself, too, for I was now going to have to spend God knows how much longer sitting on the cold metal stool beside Guppa watching him rewind that damned coil.

19

BUT I DIDN'T HAVE TO, thanks to Gumma. When I told her what had happened, she got her slide rule and marched downstairs. She had Guppa and Mr. Beaker and me count and recount the number of windings we could see on the outside of the coil. She looked through the instructions and mumbled to herself. She measured the thickness of the windings on the coil and the thickness of the wire itself. Then she went to work with her slide rule. Guppa, Mr. Beaker, and I held our breath. If my heart hadn't been thumping so loudly, I would have been able to hear the slide whispering through the stock.

Gumma took a deep breath. She smiled and let the breath out.

"It's exactly right," she said.

Mr. Beaker looked puzzled. "How many—" he began.

"Exactly right," Gumma repeated in a soft voice that reverberated through the cellar as if she had shouted.

"Yahoo!" I cheered.

Gumma gave Guppa a big hug, and so did I. Mr. Beaker gave him a pat on the back and said, "Well, you'll want to celebrate without me, so I'll head for home." No one said anything to him, so he left.

Gumma went back upstairs, and Guppa turned toward the workbench, but he was not close enough to it to read the instructions. I walked over to the workbench and closed the magazine.

"I'll help you straighten up, Guppa," I said, "and then we can go upstairs and try it out."

He didn't say anything. Hesitantly, I looked at him over my shoulder. He stood with his mouth in a rictus.

"I'll go put the magazine back," I said. "Why don't you clean the radio up with a rag so that it's nice and shiny when we take it upstairs?"

I walked upstairs with the magazine, and at the head of the stairs turned left, toward the back door, instead of right, toward the dining room, where Guppa had built the concealed bookcases that held his back issues of *Impractical Craftsman*. I went outside, onto the back porch, down the porch steps, and over to the trash cans. I lifted the lid of one and dropped the magazine in.

20

"CLOSE YOUR EYES, GUMMA," I said. "We're bringing it upstairs."

I opened the cellar door and peeked around it to make sure that Gumma had her eyes closed. She was holding her apron up over her eyes with both hands. The kitchen was full of the smell of turkey. I held the door open for Guppa, who was holding the radio in front of him in both hands. He set it on the kitchen table and plugged it in.

"Okay," I said, "you can look now." My skin was tingling all over with pride in Guppa, with affection for the radio itself.

Gumma looked at the shining radio with wide eyes, and she began clucking and exclaiming over it. Guppa beamed, and so did I. At last, Guppa said, "What do you say we put it to the test?"

Gumma and I sat down at the table, silent and eager. Guppa switched the radio on. The tubes began to glow with tiny, intricate lines of orange light. Guppa put the earphones on and began twisting the dials. Gumma and I tried to read his expression. His smile slipped away, and he wrinkled his forehead and pursed his lips. He twisted the dials some more, and he tapped at a couple of the tubes. He wiggled the coil in its socket. Then he pulled the coil out and put in another.

"How is it, Guppa?" I asked. He looked at me, but I could tell from his expression that with the earphones on he hadn't made out what I had said.

"How is it?" I asked again, in a much louder voice. Guppa flashed a smile and nodded. Gumma put her arm across my shoulder. Guppa began twisting the dials and tapping the tubes again, and he began to frown. He pulled the second coil out and put in a third.

"Can I try?" I asked. I had to go to the bathroom, but I didn't want to leave the scene of all the excitement, so I was squeezing my legs together and bouncing up and down. Guppa didn't seem to hear me. Gumma tapped him on the shoulder, and he turned toward her with a start.

"What? What's the matter?" he asked in a loud voice.

"Peter wants to try listening," said Gumma, speaking with exaggerated precision.

Guppa looked at me, and he seemed terribly tired. My expression was beyond my control. I was smiling so completely that I couldn't speak when Guppa handed me the earphones. I slipped them on and fussed with them until they felt right or at least didn't hurt my ears too much. I cupped my hands over them and held them to my ears. The sound seemed to come at once from within me, from the earphones, and from someplace far away.

From a great distance came a sound like wind through willow trees, the rustle of the hanging branches of a weeping willow, the sweep of the branches along the ground. Winding through this was a deep and indecipherable murmur, like the voices of my parents and Gumma and Guppa when I had heard them talking together at night, years before, when I lay in my crib. And rising and falling through it all was a metallic sound, like the operation of a machine, very much like the scraping sound that Gumma's toaster made.

I looked at Guppa, who was looking at his shoes, and at Gumma, who was looking at me. Her lips were tight, and she was wringing her apron in her hands.

"It's just right, Guppa!" I said, and of course, with the earphones on and the static hissing in my ears I shouted it so loudly that Guppa looked up with a start and Gumma burst out laughing.

I twiddled the dials, and the rushing hiss faded and the murmur became a howl, the metallic scraping began to echo, and an irregular ticking began somewhere far away.

Gumma said, "Oh, Herb, I'm so proud of you," and Guppa shrugged and smiled. Gumma got up and poured Guppa a glass of beer and then went back to making dinner, and Guppa went off to the living room. Neither of them asked to try the radio, and I didn't offer. When my parents arrived I showed the radio to them but didn't let them listen to it, and then we ate dinner, and after dinner I insisted on taking it to bed with me.

21

GUPPA DIED when I was twenty-five, of a heart attack. Gumma died when I was twenty-eight, of cancer. I still have the radio. I keep it in the cellar, on an old maple table that was here when Al and I bought Small's Hotel. Beside the table is a wobbly straightback chair. Sometimes, when I wake up in the middle of the night, I go to the cellar and put the earphones on, turn the set on, and sit and listen to the static. I know that, in a sense, the radio doesn't work, but I know too that in the night, sitting there alone in the cellar, dark except for the glow of the tubes, I can sometimes pick up, through the static, the flutter of Guppa's note cards, the whisper of Gumma's slide rule, the crackle of the living room fire, the scree-scree of Guppa's hacksaw, the Annie-ate-her-radiator-Annie-ate-her-radiator of the toaster, one of those sighs that Guppa let out while he worked on the coils, or the sound of my own footsteps scraping on the wooden stairs, when I came down to the cellar carrying a tray with two glasses of milk and a plate of onion sandwiches.

The Fox and the Clam

Nothing is miserable except when you think it so, and, vice versa, all luck is good luck to the man who bears it with equanimity. No one is so happy that he would not want to change his lot if he gives in to impatience. Such is the bittersweetness of human happiness. To him that enjoys it, it may seem full of delight, but he cannot prevent it slipping away when it will. It is evident, therefore, how miserable the happiness of human life is.

Boethius
The Consolation of Philosophy
(translated by V. E. Watts)

Preface

I FIRST TOLD THE STORY that follows to Porky White, the fast-food clam-bar mogul, one stormy spring afternoon while we were bailing a leaky clamboat in the middle of Bolotomy Bay, but one could say that the story was conceived in a conversation with Porky the evening before, when Al and Raskol and I dropped in at Corinne's Fabulous Fruits of the Sea. A couple of months before that evening, Albertine had decided that she could attract more honeymooners, young lovers, and adulterers to our hotel on Small's Island if she had a cozy cottage or two to offer them, set apart from the hotel itself, where they could feel quite sure that no one would blunder in on their moonlight trysting. Al found an appropriate cottage for sale on the mainland at a good price, and she and Raskolnikov worked out a plan for moving it to the island on a platform constructed atop four clamboats.

In the weeks that followed, Al was extremely busy. She negotiated for and purchased the cottage. She solicited bids on moving it to the island, and she chose an outfit called Three Jolly Tinkers to do the work. Their advertisement in the *Babbington Reporter* ("We'll do anything to the best of our ability") had caught Al's eye, and their bid was by far the lowest. They were three former schoolteachers who distinguished themselves from other jolly tinkers and most other former schoolteachers by wearing derby hats on the job. Al took to them at once. They moved the cottage to Raskol's boat yard and constructed the platform.

On the evening when we ran into Porky White at Corinne's, the three of us were excited, even bubbly. The cottage was sitting on the platform, and the voyage to the island would begin the next morning.

Porky, however, was down in the dumps. He was sitting alone, wearing a long face. He had a platter of onion rings in front of him and a glass of beer in his hand.

"Porky!" cried Al. She threw her arms around his neck and gave him an extravagant kiss. "Why the long puss?" she asked.

Porky didn't answer. He just frowned and shook his head and stuffed a couple of onion rings into his mouth.

Al sat down beside him and snuggled up to him. She turned his face toward her. "Tell me about it, Porky," she said.

Porky took a swallow of beer and ate another onion ring before he spoke.

"Well," he said, "it's like this." He wiped his mouth with a napkin and cleared his throat. "I suppose it happens to all of us from time to time: we feel utterly miserable for no clear or sufficient reason, you know what I mean? Even those of us who think of ourselves as essentially happy people find that our essential happiness is, at these times, in danger of drowning, as it were, in a sea of misery."

Al, Raskol, and I looked an one another. Raskol went up to the bar to get us some drinks.

"Most often," Porky went on, "the misery—almost despair—is brought on not by a tragedy but by an accumulation of small problems. I think it's the smallness of these problems that makes them so deadly, because if you think about it you'll realize that our lives are full of small things that *could* go wrong, and when one of them *does* go wrong, we're suddenly threatened with the collapse of the whole Tinkertoy framework of our lives, you get me? When the freezer broke down in one of my Kap'n Klam Family Restaurants today, it made me think there's a good chance that the freezers in all the rest of them will break down tomorrow. Happiness is a fragile commodity, kids. You get a little crack in it, and the next thing you know it's in pieces all over the floor."

Porky went back to work on the onion rings. Al gave me a worried look. Porky wiped his mouth again and went on.

"At such times as that, when a little crack shows up in my essential happiness," he said, "I respond very badly. I try to resist the despair, and I try hard. I use all the right arguments with myself, and I actually work at fighting the despair, but little by little my strength slips away. It's like trying to row a boat across the bay into a fierce headwind—can you get that picture in your mind? I'm in this rowboat, and I'm rowing like blazes, but I'm not getting anywhere. The rain is lashing against my back. The wind is stronger than I am. I'm getting more and more tired. The boat is filling with rainwater. In fact, I think it's starting to leak. I know what I should do—press on, Porky, press on. But I ask myself—why? Why go to any more trouble? I stop rowing. I sit there, exhausted, miserable, leaving myself at the mercy of the wind and the rain."

I reached for one of Porky's onion rings, but Al slapped my hand.

"In a perverse way," Porky continued, "I enjoy these periods of misery. I think I enjoy them because they give depth and texture to my life,
to my character, you know? I wouldn't want to be happy all the time, to
have people pass me off as one of the grasshoppers rather than one of the
ants. Periods of brooding, it seems to me, show that I'm serious, that I'm
sensitive to the pain of modern life, that I'm not unaware of how fragile
the fabric of a happy life is."

Porky sat in silence for a moment. None of the rest of us could think
of anything to say. Finally Porky spoke. "Hey, Shirley!" he called out.
"How about another beer and some more onion rings?"

THE NEXT DAY, at noon, Porky and I were standing on the front porch
of the cottage. We were about in the middle of Bolotomy Bay, pushing
into a headwind, a driving rain, and a nasty chop. Al had suggested that
Porky join us in the transbay voyage, because she had thought it would
cheer him up. The two clamboats on the port side, the *Kitten's Paw* and
Means to an End, were taking on water, and the engine in the *Alice Blue
Gown* had quit. The Three Jolly Tinkers were bustling around the platform, checking the lines that held the cottage in place, clucking and looking gravely concerned. I was eating a tuna fish sandwich and worrying
about whether we'd make it to the island.

Al opened the door to the porch. It got away from her, but she caught
it again and threw herself inside.

"This is rotten weather," said Porky.

"Yeah, you said it," I said.

"It's not the rain and cold I mind so much as the wind," Al said. "Listen, Raskol says we've all got to start bailing or we're not going to make
it to the island."

We scrambled down to the *Kitten's Paw* to start bailing. On the way,
Al stopped Porky for a moment and made him take a good look at one of
the clamboats nearby, on which Serge de Nimes stood in the rain and
wind, clawing at the bay bottom with his tongs. "Now there's something
that should cheer you up, Porky," she said. "You ought to be glad that
you're not one of those guys, out here all day in all kinds of weather."

Porky didn't say anything, but I could see that he was thinking, deciding whether the fact that he wasn't Serge or any of the other clammies
ought to cheer him up. When the three of us were bent over in the *Kitten's Paw,* bailing like mad, he spoke. "You know, I'm not so sure that I
wouldn't be happier as a clammy," he said. "It's not an easy life, I grant
you, but it has more of an aura of romance about it than being a giant in

the fast-food industry has, you know what I mean? I mean, sure they're out here in some rotten weather, but after their day's work is done they gather in a bar along the docks somewhere and tell stories about their close calls on the unforgiving bay, embellish the tales of the legendary clammies, and that kind of thing. It's like living in a beer commercial. It seems exciting to me."

"Well, that's true," admitted Al.

Porky went on. "And I guess they all must have the feeling that some-day, after they're gone, other clammies, their sons and the sons of their friends, and their sons' sons and their friends' sons' sons, will tell stories about them, that they won't be forgotten, that they might become legends themselves, you know?"

He stopped bailing for a minute and rubbed his hands together.

"I can just see my kid telling stories about me when I'm gone," he said.

A thrill ran through me, the electrifying thrill that comes from recog-nizing a theme in a setting where one doesn't expect to find it. "This is like the fox and the clam," I said.

"Oh, yeah?" said Porky.

"Yeah," I said. "Keep bailing and I'll tell you the story."

I told Porky the story that appears on the following pages. It kept him bailing, and we got the cottage to the island safely. When I had finished the story, Porky smiled and pounded me on the back. "Thanks, Peter," he said. "I guess I'm just a sucker for a happy ending."

THE NEXT MORNING, I began writing the story down. I think that I might have been able to complete it very quickly if I hadn't tried to verify some of the facts. When I did, I found to my surprise that I had made up two essential ingredients.

As part of the story as I told it to Porky White, I had included the ver-sion of the fable of the fox and the clam that I remembered from the first real book that I owned, *The Little Folks' Big Book.* Before I began writ-ing, I went downstairs to the library to see how accurately I had remem-bered the fable. When I opened the *Big Book* I was surprised to find that the fable of the fox and the clam was not in it. I had been certain that I had first encountered it there. I had read and reread the *Big Book* so often as a child that I could recite most of the stories in it, and the memory of the fable of the fox and the clam returned to me with such clarity and force that I was sure it had been one of the stories I had memorized from the *Big Book.*

A little shaken, I searched through my class photographs from grade

school to find a picture of Matthew Barber, a boy who figured prominently in the story as I had told it to Porky. He was not there.

I was rattled. These discoveries were terribly disturbing, because they
demonstrated to me that the memories, fabrications, and unrealized desires from my past were in even more of a muddle than I had thought. If I
couldn't separate them from one another, then I really didn't know any
longer who I was. Fabrications from my Personal History, Adventures,
Experiences & Observations were invading the territory that had once
been held pretty securely by memories from my life. Dazed and confused, I wandered absently to my workroom and stood at the window,
staring.

After weeks of introspection, during which I spent much of each workday standing at the window of my workroom watching the Jolly Tinkers
build a foundation for the cottage and move it into place, I came to understand why I had fabricated my memories of Matthew Barber and the fable
of the fox and the clam.

So that the reader may be spared the time and effort required to come
to a similar understanding, I include here a summary of my conclusions.

TO UNDERSTAND the relationship between experience and imagination, one must be familiar with the paint-by-number canvases that were
popular when I was a boy. These were canvases or canvas-textured
boards on which were printed, in pale blue, the outlines of portions of a
picture, each portion to be filled in with paint of a color indicated by a
numeral within the outline. It was often not immediately obvious, from
looking at the pale blue outlines alone, what some parts of the picture
were supposed to depict, but when all the oddly-shaped pieces had been
filled with paint, one could see the whole picture—if the painting had
been done with care and the viewer stood a considerable distance from it.

It seems to me that my earliest experience with something creates, in
my mind, a sketch like the pale blue sketches on those paint-by-number
canvases. This sketch then becomes a framework for all my subsequent
experiences with similar things. In most of my later life, I've been putting paint into the oddly-shaped segments of a picture that I sketched very
early. However, as time has gone on, I've run out of space on the canvas
of experience, and in order to accommodate new experiences I have had
to paint over some of the older ones. You can, no doubt, imagine the results. The outline and the earliest experiences are soon obscured. The
picture grows more distorted as time passes, at least in the sense that it
departs more and more from the original outline. However, since the ear-

lier experiences have been obscured by the later ones, I am forced to rely on memory and on the assumed congruity of the later and earlier experiences to reconstruct the earlier ones, and that reliance has been the source of several illusions.

Take, for example, my understanding of the *Big Book*.

From the *Big Book,* right from the start, I got the idea—or the pale blue outline of an idea—that all the characters in the *Big Book* lived in the same place, a place that was as comfortable a home for talking squirrels as it was for dashing knights. Over the course of the years, this childish idea has persisted, although as a young man I came to regard it with the patronizing indulgence that so many of us, as soon as we become young men and women, feel for ourselves as children and our childish misconceptions, and I felt embarrassed by the idea, as I did by many other ideas that seemed like unbecoming baggage for a young man, the intellectual equivalents of hand-me-down cardboard suitcases plastered with stickers from one's parents' travels. But after I had finished being a youth I rediscovered my affection for the idea and began painting away at it.

I have now a fond affection for the idea that all the characters in books live in the same place, the *Big-Book* place, and I've painted in so much of it over the years that I have a picture of a well-populated town, where, with Albertine on my arm, I sometimes walk along a shady street on a summer morning and pause to watch the talking squirrels gather nuts in Emma Bovary's front yard while Tom Sawyer paints her fence.

At the same time, I seem to have been expanding and distorting the memory of the *Big Book* itself to include every story that I've ever enjoyed, or every story that has had a strong effect on me. Therefore, it isn't surprising that in the picture I formed of the *Big Book* I included the fable of the fox and the clam, although in fact it was never there. Nor is it surprising that in the mental pictures I had of my early grade-school years, I painted in the pale and dour face of Matthew Barber, though I didn't meet Matthew until I entered high school.

Peter Leroy
Small's Island
July 28, 1983

1

ONE QUIET MORNING, a Saturday, in the spring, when I was three, while Dudley Beaker was sitting on his porch drinking a cup of coffee and reading the morning paper, the thought struck him that it was time I learned to read.

Mr. Beaker was wearing a tan satin robe that my mother had made for him, though she had presented it first to my father, who never wore such things, as a birthday present. After a month or two had passed and my father had not worn the robe, my mother asked why he didn't wear it on Saturday mornings when he sat in the kitchen drinking a cup of coffee and reading the paper. My father told her, sheepishly and gently, that he was really sorry he hadn't worn it, but that a tan satin robe wasn't his style, that he didn't wear that sort of thing. My mother admitted that he was right and said it seemed a terrible shame to have a perfectly good robe go to waste and that it was too bad she couldn't think of somebody else to give it to. My father struck himself on the head with the heel of his right hand and said that he had a perfect idea. They could give the robe to Dudley Beaker, whose birthday was coming up in just a week or two. At first my mother didn't seem to think much of this idea. She said that Dudley's birthday wouldn't come up for months, but my father consulted the small book in which my mother listed birthdays and anniversaries and showed her that Mr. Beaker's birthday was, in fact, just around the corner. My mother declared that she must be losing her marbles like poor Mrs. Barber, the widow downtown, and scampered off to rewrap the robe, using the original box, paper, and bow, which she had saved on the topmost shelf of her closet, in the back, behind a hat box. When she gave the robe to Mr. Beaker, he said that it was just his style, just the sort of thing he would enjoy wearing on a spring morning, when he drank his coffee and read the morning paper on his porch.

The idea that it was time for me to learn to read struck Mr. Beaker so powerfully that he put the paper aside at once, scrawled a note for Eliza, who was sleeping late, left his coffee, and went off to buy me a book.

There was no bookstore in Babbington at that time, but Lydia Barber, who ran a used furniture store on Main Street, liked to arrange the furniture in her shop as it might be arranged in a house, so she kept a good supply of props to lend verisimilitude to the arrangements, including antimacassars and doilies, knickkacks and books, and these were also for sale. Among the books at Mrs. Barber's shop was a used, foxed copy of *The Little Folks' Big Book,* an anthology of fables, maxims, poems, cautionary tales, and lighthearted stories for children. Mrs. Barber was the widow to whom my mother referred when she said that she must be losing her marbles. Like many other young Babbington matrons at that time, whenever my mother thought of Mrs Barber, she took a deep breath and thanked her lucky stars that she was not in her shoes, and she made a mental note to call her on the telephone or drop into the shop for a chat.

Mrs. Barber had one child, a son named Matthew, who was about my age. It was Mrs. Barber's custom, while she tended the shop, to keep Matthew in the back room, which was full of dusty furniture, antimacassars and doilies, knickknacks and books, or, in good weather, to let him play in the tiny yard behind the shop. When Matthew grew tired and cranky, Mrs. Barber would read to him from one of the books that she had for sale, and this habit gave her a reputation for having lost her marbles, since Matthew, although he could hear her perfectly well from the back room or the yard behind the shop, was invisible to the passersby who glanced through the store window and saw the slight woman reading aloud, apparently to no one.

Among the books that Mrs. Barber read from was *The Little Folks' Big Book.* However, Matthew didn't seem fond of the *Big Book.* If anything, listening to his mother read from it seemed to make him more tired and cranky. Mrs. Barber was not, therefore, unwilling to sell the book to Mr. Beaker, who decided that it was just the thing for teaching me to read.

Mr. Beaker had Mrs. Barber wrap the book. Then he drove directly to my parents' house.

When he arrived, my mother was in the kitchen, making breakfast. My father was in the bathroom, shaving. I was sitting at the kitchen table, eating a bowl of graham crackers and milk. My mother was wearing a terrycloth bathrobe and fuzzy slippers. My father was wearing blue boxer shorts. I was wearing a fresh pair of flannel pajamas with pictures of romping, drooling dogs all over them. Mr. Beaker suddenly appeared at the back door, rapping on the window, smiling.

My mother was quite startled. "Dudley!" she cried, and began patting her hair into place. She opened the door and let him in. "Dudley!" she said again. She blushed and smiled and turned her cheek toward Mr. Beaker for a kiss.

"Good morning, Ella!" said Mr. Beaker, full of hearty good humor. He was holding both his hands behind him and smiling. He leaned forward and kissed my mother and rubbed his cheek against hers.

My mother giggled. "Why, Dudley," she said, "you look like the cat that swallowed the canary." She took a step back and studied Mr. Beaker's smile. "What have you got there, Dudley?" she asked. She stepped toward him again and tried to look behind him. He turned so that she couldn't see. She turned the other way. "What are you holding behind your back?" she asked. She grabbed his arm and tried to turn him around. He twisted away. Her bathrobe fell open. Mr. Beaker drew a sharp breath. My mother blushed and pulled her robe closed. Mr. Beaker turned toward me.

"I—have—something—for—Peter," he said, advancing toward me and releasing one word with each step.

"Oh," said my mother. She let her arms fall to her sides. "Isn't that nice. Isn't that nice, Peter?" she said.

Mr. Beaker brought the package from behind his back and put it on the table in front of me. It was wrapped in brown paper and tied with cord. Slowly, he began to unwrap it. My mother tied the belt on her robe and came over to watch.

Before Mr. Beaker had folded the paper back enough for my mother and me to see what was inside it, my father peeked around the corner and said, "Oh, it's you, Dudley, I thought I heard your voice." He came into the kitchen in his shorts, with shaving cream on his face and a razor in his hand.

"Berrrrt," said my mother, dragging the name out into a complaint, "you're not dressed."

"Oh," said my father, looking at his shorts. Then he frowned and shrugged and said, "Oh, so what? I'm sure Dudley isn't shocked by a guy in his shorts. Look at you—you're not dressed either."

My mother blushed again and pulled her bathrobe tighter around her. "I'll go throw something on," she said. "Don't open the package without me."

My father looked at the half-unwrapped package. "What've we got here?" he asked. He walked toward the table, raising an eyebrow and pointing at the package with his razor.

"Some—thing—for—me," I said, in much the way that Mr. Beaker had. I finished with a little flourish of my spoon that sent a piece of limp graham cracker flying over the package onto the table.

"Peter!" said Mr. Beaker and my father precisely in unison. They snapped their heads toward each other, and my father knit his brows. Mr. Beaker cleared his throat and turned away. He got a napkin and wiped up the bit of graham cracker.

"Don't play with your food," said my father. Mr. Beaker opened his mouth, and I thought that he might say something. My father must have thought that he was going to say something too, since he turned abruptly toward him. But Mr. Beaker just smiled at my father and said nothing.

"Okay," called my mother. "Here I come." She ran into the kitchen, wearing the red robe that my father had given her for Christmas. She had put on bright red lipstick too.

"Go ahead, Peter," said Mr. Beaker. "You finish opening it." He tugged at the paper a little to show me what he wanted me to do.

I looked at my bowl and at the package. I looked at my father. Very carefully, I picked up the bowl and held it out to him. He took it. The lather on his face had dried and cracked like peeling paint.

I pulled the wrapping paper off the book and lifted the cover. The book was placed on the table with the binding away from me, so that I opened it as I would have opened a box, lifting the cover up and away as if I were lifting its lid.

When I opened the book, it released into the kitchen a rich, earthy, damp odor that I have ever since associated with reading, an odor that I've come to expect to smell when I'm about to begin reading a book, an odor that produces an anticipatory thrill and an appetite for graham crackers and milk. Of course, the odor is missing from new books, which smell only of paper and ink, and even from most used books, those that have been treated with care. But from time to time I find a used book with that evocative odor, and when I come across one of these, I buy it at once, regardless of its subject or author. As a result, I have a number of books—*The Piezoelectric Properties of Wood* comes to mind—that I've bought for their odor alone.

I looked at the endpapers, where swirls of brown, purple, blue, and gold swam—swam, it occurs to me now, like the colors made by gasoline and oil on the surface of the estuarial stretch of the Bolotomy. The swirling colors and the odor of the book made a heady, intoxicating mix, and for a moment I thought I was going to be sick. But I knew that I was getting a gift, and I knew that I should be grateful for a gift, so I looked up at Mr. Beaker and smiled.

"Here, Peter," he said. "Open it this way." He turned the book and
flipped the first few pages. The paper was thick and deckle-edged. Mr.
Beaker stopped at a place with a color plate. The left-hand page was
handsome and intriguing but indecipherable. It had on it only blocks of
print, squared off along the sides, indented in paragraphs, with irregular
lines of type that looked like rows of dark houses silhouetted against a
light sky, and intriguing rivers of white that ran along surprising courses,
cutting across the lines at angles and changing direction unexpectedly.
The right-hand page had a smoother, whiter piece of paper glued to it, and
on this paper was a picture, a color picture of a fox in a rowboat, the first
picture I had ever seen of a fox in a rowboat.

My father looked over my shoulder at the book. He rubbed his chin,
and flecks of dried soap fluttered onto the picture. I swept them off with
my hand. My father walked over to the stove and poured himself a cup of
coffee.

Mr. Beaker drew a chair up beside me and sat down. "Now, Peter," he
said. "I'm going to read to you."

My mother stood behind me with her hands on my shoulders, leaning
over me so that she could see the page. My father sat at the far end of the
table with his coffee.

"This ought to be as good a place to start as any," Mr. Beaker said. I
looked at the open book, and Mr. Beaker began the story.

The Fable
of the
Fox and the Clam

NE EVENING, a poor fox was on his way home. The fox lived on an island, as all foxes did at that time, so to get home the fox had to use a rowboat. His route took him across some clam flats. In his mouth the fox was carrying a nice dinner for his family, a leg of lamb, dripping with gravy, that he had snatched from the dinner table of a farmer while the farmer and his family were saying grace. While the fox was rowing, he began to feel sorry for himself.

First he compared the misery of his existence with the joy that he imagined other animals felt. Day after day he risked life and limb to bring food home to his family, and yet when he arrived home, his heart still pounding with fear, he was greeted not with looks of admiration but with gluttony and drool, and every night he fell asleep with the thought in his mind that tomorrow he would have to do it all again.

Next the fox began to think about his past life, to weigh what he had done against what he had once hoped to do. It seemed to the fox that he had done nothing commendable, nothing memorable. He decided that if, one day, he did not return home, he'd be forgotten the day after.

A profound weariness spread through the fox. He stopped rowing and just let the boat drift. The evening was still, and the boat barely moved. The fox sank into a sapping despair that lasted for days. A number of other foxes happened to be watching from the island, and, as the days passed, more and more gathered along the shore to watch the drifting, brooding fox, who quickly acquired a reputation as a deep and complex thinker. Finally, on the third evening, while the fox was brooding and thinking about himself, his troubles, and his unhappy lot, he chanced to think about the clams, cozy in the sandy bottom below him.

"Jeez," wailed the fox.

He meant to go on to say, "You clams lead a great life. I bet you're happier than I am." However, when he opened his mouth, the leg of lamb fell into the water. The fox tried to grab the leg of lamb, fell in after it, struck his head against the gunwale, and drowned.

To the foxes watching from the shore, it seemed as if the fox must have thrown himself into the water deliberately, after days of deep and complex thinking. They trudged home with long faces.

As time went by, the foxes talked among themselves about the miserable life of foxes in general and the wisdom and sensitivity of the poor fox who had thrown himself from the rowboat, and so the poor fox lived on in the memory of foxes, respected and admired as the one fox above all others who understood the absurdity and pain of a fox's lot.

ow it happened that, in the mucky bottom of the bay, there lived a clam, in a bed with lots of other clams. This clam—like most other clams at that time—hated the life of a clam, which seemed to him a cruel joke. One minute a clam would be sitting around minding its own business, feeling all right, eating a few diatoms and dinoflagellates, and then—just like that—be scooped up and carried off, never to be seen again. Under such conditions it was hard for clams to make long-range plans.

Whenever the fox had rowed across the bay, the clam would watch with envy and curse his lot. "If only I had been a fox," the clam would sigh.

On the day when the fox fell into despair, when the fox had first stopped rowing, the clam said to himself, "Hey, what gives? What's the matter with that fox?"

The clam watched the fox with great interest throughout his ordeal. When the fox finally dropped the leg of lamb and fell in after it, the clam was thunderstruck.

"Holy mackerel," thought the clam, when the fox had stopped struggling and floated, lifeless, on the surface of the bay. "One never knows how well off one is, does one? I see now that the life of a fox is no bed of roses. All in all, I'm pretty lucky to be a clam."

This was so sustaining a thought that the clam remained essentially happy for the rest of his days. As it happened, the rest of his days added up to only four, but during those days the clam wore a smile and whistled a happy tune. When one of life's misfortunes occurred, the happy clam would shrug and say, "It could have been worse," and after a while he would be smiling and whistling again and telling the other clams funny stories to try to cheer them up. The other clams decided that he had lost his marbles, since he no longer seemed to understand that a clam's life is absurd and miserable.

When, after four essentially happy days, the clam was dug up and perished in a chowder, the other clams began to tell stories about him and his wacky ways. In these stories, the clam was a figure of fun, a clown, a buffoon. The clams who told them and the clams who heard them would snicker and chuckle at the happy clam's simplemindedness and the zany things he did. These stories were handed down from generation to generation, and each generation concocted new ones, and to this day, especially on long winter nights when life in the muck is almost unbearable, the clams still snicker and chuckle at the stories of the happy clam and his zany antics.

2

"WELL, PETER," said Mr. Beaker, "what did you think of that?"

"It was funny," I said. I was studying the picture of the fox in the row-boat. I wondered how Mr. Beaker had gotten so long a story out of that one picture, and especially how he had been able to imagine so clearly the hilarious figure of the fox grabbing for the falling leg of lamb and losing his balance. When my father cleared his throat, I was aware that all three of them were looking at me, waiting for me to say something more. When I looked at them, I saw that they wore long faces. There were tears in the corners of my mother's eyes, and Mr. Beaker and my father looked gravely concerned. I was smiling.

"The fox fell down," I said, and pointed to the picture to show them what I meant, because it seemed to me that the whole story was somehow contained in the picture, and that my mother and father must be able to see the fox falling just as Mr. Beaker had. "He was a silly fox," I said. I looked at them again. I could see that they didn't agree.

"What about the clam, Peter?" asked Mr. Beaker.

"He was a smart clam," I said. I began to feel embarrassed. I could tell, from the quiet, patient tone Mr. Beaker used, that I was not answering correctly, that Mr. Beaker thought I didn't have all my marbles.

"Don't you think he's a little young for a story like this?" asked my father.

"Oh, yes," said my mother. She hugged me from behind and ran her hands over my chest. "He's much too young, Dudley. Don't you remember telling me that childhood is like a moment on a mountaintop in the sunshine before we descend into the vale of tears?"

"I don't remember that," said my father. "When did he say that?"

"Oh, one time," said my mother. "I forget when."

"I suppose you're right," said Mr. Beaker. He chucked me under the chin and looked straight at me and frowned. "Smile while you can, Peter. Enjoy that moment on the mountaintop in the sunshine."

"Why don't I remember that?" asked my father.

I looked at the picture of the fox again. I still didn't get it. The fox still seemed like a laughable jerk to me.

"Let's read it again," I said.

3

SO DELICIOUS was the pleasure of listening to adults read to me that I resisted learning to read for a long time. Mr. Beaker came to my parents' house a few times a week to read to me and to try to teach me to read. He would run his finger along the lines of type as he read to demonstrate that it was from them that he was taking his words, and I soon began to understand that he was just repeating what was already in the book, that he wasn't improvising the stories from the pictures, and I began to think that Mr. Beaker wasn't as smart—as clever—as I had thought. He would point out words to me and have me repeat them, and if a word appeared several times on a page he would have me point to each occurrence of it. But when he asked me to try to read, I would return to the pictures, to my memory of the story as he had read it, and to whatever popped into my head, and I would improvise. I'd try to concentrate on the type, but my eyes and my mind would wander. I used the written words that I could read only as I used the pictures—as prompts for memory, spurs for imagination.

Finally, one day Mr. Beaker asked me to read the fable of the fox and the clam, which he knew was my favorite. "One sunny day the silly fox hopped into his rowboat and set off to see his friend the farmer," I began.

"I give up," said Mr. Beaker, and he did. But by that time my mother had grown fond of the stories in the *Big Book,* and she read to me from it every night when I went to bed. Inevitably, I began to be able to decipher the blocks of print, but when I read, whenever I came to a spot that I didn't like or a place where something seemed to be missing or where something seemed to be wrong, I would make an improvement, an addition, or a correction. I did this when I read to myself, and I did it when I read aloud for my mother. She became concerned, and she asked Mr. Beaker to listen to me read once more and decide what should be done. He did. When I read the words on the page, my mother and Mr. Beaker smiled. When I added or changed anything, they frowned.

I loved my mother dearly, and I wanted Mr. Beaker's approval. I wanted to please them, and I was trying to please them. I had gotten the idea, and it had become an unshakable conviction, that the writing in the book was only part of the story, and the thinnest part of it at that. It seemed to me that it was an outline, that it was just supposed to get you going, that the best parts of any of the stories were waiting in the spaces where your mind was free to wander, to decide what the fox's children

were doing and what his house looked like, to make up the stories that
were told about the clam.

"Peter," asked Mr. Beaker, "why did you say that about the fox's children fighting over the toy lamb?"

"He says that every time," said my mother.

"Why do you say that, Peter?" Mr. Beaker asked again.

"Because that's what the children do," I said.

"Do you think that's part of the story?" he asked.

I wasn't quite sure how to interpret this question. Either Mr. Beaker
was insulting me or he had begun to lose his marbles. Hadn't I just read
the story to him with the fighting over the toy lamb in it? Didn't that
make it part of the story? If I put it into the story, it was in the story,
wasn't it?

"Yes," I said, warily.

Mr. Beaker gave me a pat on the head, and he began talking to my
mother in whispers.

My mother and Mr. Beaker decided that I had memorized parts of the
stories, and that I was making additions and changes to cover up for my
not being able to remember other parts. In short, they decided that I
couldn't really read at all.

My mother worried about me. In consultation with the other mothers
in our neighborhood, she decided that I had serious intellectual deficiencies that should be corrected before I began kindergarten. She wanted to
enroll me in the Misses Leighton's Nursery School. She enlisted Eliza
Foote as an ally, and together they persuaded Mr. Beaker to endorse the
idea. The Misses Leighton's Nursery School was much less practical
than what Mr. Beaker would have liked, but it was the only school that it
was possible for me to attend, since there was no other nursery school in
Babbington, and it would at least be a beginning. I would be, at least for-
mally, a student. When my father seemed hesitant, Mr. Beaker offered to
pay half the cost, and the matter was settled.

The school was conducted within the Misses Leighton's house, a large
and comfortable frame house where the two women—Emily and Louisa—had for some twenty years attended their ailing mother. When she
had died at last, the daughters, released from their responsibility well into
middle age, had spent their small inheritance on a trip to Greece, where
they acquired an enormous number of fascinating miniature plaster repli-
cas of classical statuary, and where Emily learned to play the bouzouki,
though not well.

When they returned, they opened the little school, which emphasized the visual arts (mostly coloring, finger painting, and modeling in clay), dance (which consisted of having the children put on shifts made of cheesecloth and romp around the lawn behind Louisa while Emily played the bouzouki), and literature (which consisted of our sitting in a circle and listening to one or the other of the Misses Leighton read aloud).

Most of our instruction took place on their porch. The porch had been enclosed with windows and knotty pine. In my memory of the time I spent there, the sun is always shining. Miss Emily, large and soft, is wearing a white cotton dress with a billowy skirt. She is constantly moving, bustling from one pupil to another, giving out squashy hugs, and

The Misses Leighton's Nursery School was much less practical than what Mr. Beaker would have liked . . .

from time to time she bursts into operatic passages that make Louisa, a wiry, wan woman with fine, dark hair, wince.

Miss Emily paid particular attention to one of the other boys, who was so plump and soft and pale that the rest of us thought of him as a marsh-mallow. He was a sad little boy who wore a look of disappointment nearly all the time. He didn't laugh, but neither did he cry. He was so uncommunicative that the rest of us gave up trying to talk to him after a while, though Miss Emily continually urged us to talk to him, to play with him. This was Matthew Barber. All of the rest of us knew that Matthew sometimes stayed at the Leightons' after we left. His mother would come to get him later, when she closed her shop. I had heard my parents talk about how big-hearted the Leighton sisters were, how fortunate Mrs. Bar-ber was that the Leightons allowed Matthew to attend the school for nothing, how fortunate the poor boy was that he had this opportunity.

Outside the porch, behind the house, was a wide lawn, surrounded by lilacs. Surely these lilacs cannot always have been in bloom while I was at the Leightons' school, but in my memory they are. Perhaps I am re-membering the lilac cologne that Miss Emily wore.

During the morning we would draw, paint, or model in clay. Then we would eat lunch. All of us brought lunches from home. When it was time to eat, we would gather together in groups of friends. Periodically, Miss Louisa took us aside, one at a time, and reminded us that Matthew was not a happy boy, that he had no father, and that we should share our lunches with him because he didn't have any money. Once, I traded sandwiches with him. The sandwich I gave him was tuna fish, and I was fond of tuna fish sandwiches. The sandwich he gave me was lard, just lard. With the first bite I decided that I'd been duped. I looked at him. He was wolfing down the tuna fish sandwich, but he paused to smile at me. It was not a pure smile. It was more like a sneer.

During the afternoon, we would dance, hurl the discus and javelin, play follow-the-leader, or act in skits. Then at the end of the day, our little group would sit in a ring around Emily or Louisa, who would read to us. On cool days we would sit on the porch, but on warm days we would sit outside on the lawn. After the day's reading, our parents would arrive, and we would go home.

Most of the time, my mother drove me to the school and picked me up at the end of the day. She was always deferential toward the Misses Leighton, who quite bowled her over. Sometimes, though, my father picked me up, and he was always nervous around the Leighton sisters. He would stand with his hands in his pockets for most of the time. He looked at the ground or the floor, or he looked quickly at the drawings and finger paintings I had made, but he almost never raised his eyes to look directly at Emily or Louisa, and since he spoke, when he spoke, in the direction of the floor, neither of them had any idea what he was saying. When we rode home together in the car, he would sometimes ask me questions about what went on at the school, but he seemed more interested in knowing whether the boys and girls changed into their cheesecloth shifts in the same room at the same time than in what I had made out of my ration of clay that day.

One afternoon, at reading time, we settled onto the lawn, and Miss Louisa opened a book and said, "Today I'm going to read you a story called 'The Fox and the Clam.'"

"I know that story," I blurted out, surprised and thrilled. A new feeling arose within me, a warm and pleasant feeling. It was pride. I had already read the story of the fox and the clam, but the other children, to judge from their blank faces, hadn't; that meant that I was in an elevated position, closer to Miss Emily and Miss Louisa than any of the others.

"I know it, too," said Matthew. The sound of his voice stunned everyone. It attenuated my warm and pleasant feeling. Miss Emily recovered first; she bounded to Matthew and scooped him up.

"Oh, good, Matthew," said Miss Emily. She enveloped him in one of her pillowy hugs. "And you, too, Peter, good for you." She had Matthew squashed in her arms, with his head bent to one side, but nonetheless I could see when he looked at me that he wore the same malevolent smile he had worn when he'd palmed that lard sandwich off on me.

"Now, Matthew and Peter," said Miss Emily, "since you and I already know the story, we'll have to be very quiet while Miss Louisa reads, so that we won't spoil it for the others, won't we?"

"Yeah," I said, crushed. Not until she had told me that I was going to have to be quiet did I realize that I had been hoping to parade my familiarity with the story, that I had intended to keep interrupting with "Here comes a good part," or "Wait'll you hear what happens to the clam!"

Miss Louisa began.

"Once upon a time, a fox was on her way home to her family. She had spent all day scrubbing floors in the palace of the lion, who was the king of all the beasts."

I had been wearing a big smile and the condescending look of the cognoscenti, but now my heart began to pound and I broke out in a sweat because the story Miss Louisa was beginning was clearly going to be wildly different from the fox-and-clam story I knew. I felt, at the same time, three kinds of anxiety. The first was the anxiety one feels when one is watching an actor in a difficult role, a musician playing a difficult piece, an athlete attempting a difficult feat: it seemed to me that Miss Louisa was undertaking a stupendous effort of improvisation, and I was afraid for her, afraid that she couldn't bring off the spontaneous construction of so vastly different a version of the story, afraid that she was going to make a fool of herself. The second was the anxiety one feels when one has pretended, in conversation, to have read a book that one has not and sees in the expression on the face of one's interlocutor genuine interest, interest that is already forming into a question that one will not be able to answer: it seemed to me that, since I had claimed to know the story, Miss Louisa might at some point ask me what was going to happen next, and I would be the one to make a fool of himself. The third was entirely new to me: it was anxiety born of rivalry. I looked at Matthew. His expression had reverted to his habitual look of disappointment, and from it I couldn't get any idea of what he was thinking. Since he stayed with the Leightons after the rest of us left, I wondered whether he had perhaps already heard Miss Louisa's story, whether perhaps he already knew what Miss Louisa was going to say. Since he and I were the only ones who knew anything about the story, we were competitors, but it might well be that he had an advantage, inside information on Miss Louisa's version of the story of the fox and the clam.

Miss Louisa went on. "Her knees were sore, and her hands were rough and chafed. Her body ached from the hard work she had to do. Her heart ached too, because she knew that she would have to go on doing this work until she died. 'Oh,' she wailed, 'A fox's life is a sorry life. I wish I could be some other animal.'

"Just then a fairy popped out from under a toadstool. 'Your wish is granted,' said the fairy, who had the power to grant wishes. 'You may be any animal you choose to be.'

"The fox's heart leaped up, and she skipped along, thinking about what animal she might become. While she skipped along, a small bird flew past her, and the fox said, 'Oh, I think I might be happy if I were a bird like you. It must be wonderful to fly through the air instead of scrubbing floors.

"'Does my life look good to you?' asked the bird. 'All day long I have been flying back and forth with worms in my mouth to feed my babies, who scream all the time. If that sounds good to you, then why don't you take my place?'

"The bird's life didn't sound very good to the fox, so she went on. After a while, she saw a rabbit hop across the path in front of her, and the fox said, 'Oh, I think I might be happy if I were a rabbit like you. It must be wonderful to spend all day hopping through the woods, so blithe and nonchalant.'

"'Does my life look good to you?' asked the rabbit. 'Right now I'm running from a farmer who saw me eating cabbage in his cabbage patch. If he catches me, he's going to impale me on the pitchfork he's carrying. If that sounds good to you, then why don't you take my place?'

"The rabbit's life didn't sound very good to the fox, so she went on. After a while, she came to a bay, and the fox said, 'I'll bet there are clams in this bay.' And she called out to the clams, 'Oh, I think I might be happy if I were a clam like you. It must be wonderful to spend all day resting in the sand.'

"'Oh, yes,' called a clam. 'It is wonderful. We don't have to hunt for food—we just stick our necks out and eat whatever comes along. We never have to bring food to our children, as the birds do—in fact, we never give any thought to our children at all. We never get chased by farmers, as the rabbits do. We don't have any work to do for the King, as you do, and we don't ever get sore knees, since we don't have any knees. However—'

"The clam's life sounded so very, very good to the fox that she didn't wait for the clam to finish. She cried, 'I wish to be a clam,' and jumped into the bay. By the time she reached the bottom, she had become a clam, and she was happy.

"But just then, along came one of the Royal Clamdiggers, and he dug up the clam who had once been a fox. He took her to the Royal Cook, and that night she ended up in the Royal Stomach."

Miss Louisa closed her book with a bang and looked around at us with a big smile, as she always did when she finished reading. I looked back at her, beaming. I was tremendously proud of her. She had turned in a magnificent performance. She had brought it off so smoothly, apparently effortlessly, without hesitation. I clapped my little hands together and said "Yay! yay!" as if she'd just set a new record for the high jump.

I was the only one clapping. I looked around at my fellow pupils and I discovered that they, for some reason, were beginning to blubber. Matthew, however, was not. He sat there in Miss Emily's lap nodding his head, his mouth twisted into that sneering grin.

Miss Louisa's face fell. Miss Emily looked terrified. She began gathering children to her bosom. "It's all right," she repeated as she ran around the circle trying to give a hug to each of them. "It's only a story."

"It's not just a story." said Matthew. "It's the truth." His voice surprised everyone. We all looked at him, and the other children stopped crying. "I heard another story about the fox and the clam," he said, "and it was just as bad."

"I know a different story about the fox and the clam, too!" I said, smiling again, thinking that I might get a chance to tell my version.

Matthew looked straight at me. "How come you're always smiling, Peter?" he asked.

I stopped smiling. I thought about the question, but I couldn't think of an answer. I looked at Matthew, and then I looked around at the other boys and girls, at Miss Louisa and Miss Emily. They were all looking at me, waiting for an answer. None of them was smiling. I began to feel empty, stupid, and sad.

"I'm not always smiling," I said, and I wasn't.

The mothers and fathers began arriving. One by one their children ran to them, weeping, inconsolable. When my mother arrived, I ran to her at once and took her hand and started tugging her toward the car. When we were nearly there, I turned back to look at Matthew. He was staring at me, and after a moment he stuck his tongue out at me. He looked so silly with his red tongue sticking out of his white face that I couldn't help myself. I laughed.

4

THE FOX-AND-CLAM EPISODE cost the Leightons several pupils. I was one of them. My mother spent much of that afternoon on the telephone. Most of the time, she just listened to the mothers of children who had been upset by the story—children who were lying on their beds, wringing their little hands, staring at the walls—but by the time she had listened to the fourth anxious mother, she had herself become anxious.

Over dinner, she told my father what she had learned. "I think it isn't the right atmosphere for Peter," she said when she had finished. "I think we should take him out of the school."

"But I thought you said that the story didn't seem to bother him," said my father. He hadn't finished eating. He had been listening to my mother throughout her account of the day, taking bites in between nodding and saying "Mm-hmm" and "Hmmm." Now he put his fork down and ran his hand through his hair.

"Yes," said my mother, "but if they're going to be reading that sort of story, I think it's just not the right sort of atmosphere for a child." Several of the mothers were using the same phrase that evening. It had originated with Mrs. Hosmer, who, entirely by coincidence, had been reading a magazine article on the importance of the right atmosphere in child-rearing on the very morning of the fox-and-clam incident at the Misses Leighton's School.

"I think childhood is important to a child," said my mother. My father sneaked in a quick bite of meatloaf. "There's time enough later for them to see the misery and unhappiness of life. They should be allowed to spend some time on that mountaintop, in the sun—"

"Yeah, I know," said my father. "Before they descend into the valley of death." He frowned.

"The vale of tears," said my mother.

"Right, right," said my father. "I don't have any objection to taking him out of the school. I think those two old gals are kind of funny anyway."

"Then it's settled?" asked my mother.

"As far as I'm concerned," said my father.

My mother went straight to the telephone, and my father had to pour his own coffee. He and I sat at the table, not looking at each other. I stirred the last of my peas into my mashed potatoes. I could hear my mother talking on the telephone to one of the other mothers. She was saying, "We decided that it just wasn't the right atmosphere—"

5

I DIDN'T SEE MATTHEW BARBER again until the first day of kindergarten, and then only at the very end of the day, on the school bus.

It had been an exciting day, and each of us on the bus had a handful of drawings to show mom and dad and a headful of strange events to tell about. Each of us was in his or her own sort of daze: puzzled, overwhelmed.

I rode along, sitting beside a window, on one of the seats toward the back of the bus. I was looking out the window, but I wasn't really noticing anything. I was letting the things I'd seen and heard and done during the day drift through my mind, re-experiencing them and rehearsing the way I would tell about them when I got home. Time passed. From time to time the bus stopped. Each time it did, there was a group of mothers waiting for it. Some children would recognize their mothers and get off at once. Others would remain sitting much as I was, mouths open, eyes blank. Some, I suppose, were rehearsing their stories as I was. Others, I suppose, were just baffled.

A scene often repeated went something like this: a girl sitting staring at nothing suddenly started when a woman who had come onto the bus touched her on the shoulder. She looked up, blinked, and said "Mommy!" Mother and daughter laughed, and the girl began talking as fast as she could, spilling out snippets of the day at random, and pushing papers at her mother, who, beaming, was guiding the child down the aisle toward the door of the bus.

More time passed. The bus emptied. I looked around. There were only two children left, two boys. One was a boy I recognized from the classroom. His name was Mort Grumbacher. He was sitting directly across the aisle from me. The other was Matthew Barber. He was sitting in the seat behind Mort, his head down, staring at the floor.

Mort was looking around wildly, and he had crumpled his papers into a tight ball in his hands.

"They're all gone," he said to me.

"Yeah," I said.

"They all went home," he said.

"Yeah," I said.

His eyes were wide, but he wasn't really looking at me, he was looking far beyond me, at his future.

"We're going to die on this bus," he said, "I'm never going to see my mother again."

"What?" I said. "What?" I looked around the bus again. There really were no other kids left. I looked under the seat, along the floor. There were plenty of drawings left behind, but I didn't see any little feet dangling down from the seats.

"You're probably right," said Matthew. "The rest of them are all at home right now," he said. "They're sitting on their mothers' laps."

"Uh, yeah," I said, "probably."

"But we're not going to get home," said Matthew. Mort's eyes were bulging. His mouth hung open in stupefied horror.

"Sure we are," I said. "We're going to get home. It's just a longer ride for us."

Matthew gave me his twisted grin, pursed his lips and rolled his eyes, dismissing me as a ridiculous naïf.

"Nah," he said. "We're lost."

"Lost?" I said. "Lost?" I turned back toward the window. We were passing houses that I didn't recognize. We *were* lost.

"I knew this was going to happen," Matthew said. "As soon as we drove up to the school, I had a feeling. I felt sick."

So did I, I remembered. "So did I," I said.

"Me too," said Mort. He swallowed hard. It looked to me as if there was a good chance he would be sick right then.

"I knew that if my mother left me there I'd never see her again," said Matthew. "I screamed, I cried, I kicked. But she left anyway." He sighed and stared out the window, wistfully, remembering his mother. As I remember him now, he seems so drooped, so sagging and world-weary that I'm surprised he didn't pull a half pint of Jack Daniel's out of his pocket and light up a Lucky.

"Yeah," I said, but I didn't admit having done anything similar. Mort just kept looking wildly back and forth at Matthew and me, swallowing hard and nodding his head.

"And now," Matthew said, "the other kids are showing their mothers the drawings they made—"

Mort looked down at the tight, sweaty ball of drawings in his hand. Matthew gave another of those twisted grins, shook his head slowly, and sighed. He crumpled his own drawings into a ball and tossed the ball over his shoulder. Mort looked at him and moaned. He looked at his ball of papers again and then let it fall to the floor. It was the most hopeless gesture I'd ever seen.

"—and they're eating cookies too," Matthew added.

Then he laughed a mad, desperate laugh. My heart nearly broke. My mother had told me that she'd make chocolate chip cookies for me to have when I got home. When I got home! When I got home!

Mort and I burst into tears at the same time. A voice boomed from the front of the bus, "Hey kids! What are you doing here? Did you miss your stop?"

The bus came to a halt, and a fat, sweaty man wearing a brown suit and a derby hat lurched down the aisle toward Matthew, Mort, and me. Mort and I gave each other looks of terror. I think it was the first time that either of us had realized that somebody had been driving the bus. We had just been riding along as passengers on a bus beyond our control, a bus that could have been traveling on its own. Now it dawned on us that this big and frightening character with a little mustache right under his nose was in control of the bus, in control of our destinies. I imagine that Mort had the same thought I did at that moment: that our not having gotten home was proof that this guy's intentions were not good. Matthew simply sat, unmoved, wearing the same impassive look that he had worn most of the time in nursery school.

"Don't cry, kids," the driver said. "Stop crying. I'll get you home. Don't worry." I was ready to take heart at this, ready to trust this wheezing stranger as soon as he said the word *home*. I looked at Matthew to see what he thought about this, and my hopes vanished. He was giving me another of those twisted grins, and I took it to mean that everything the fat man was telling us was a lie, that we were doomed.

The man went back to the front of the bus and sat in his seat. He turned around and called out to us, "Stop crying!" I took this as an order and did my best to stop. I was past crying anyway. I was sniffling and gasping for breath, shaking with the desperate sobbing that comes after the tears are gone, choking, hardly able to breathe, but through my fears the idea came to me that we should try to escape this demon and find our way home.

I dashed across the aisle and sat beside Mort. I beckoned to Matthew, and he stood up and stuck his chin over the back of the seat.

"We—we—we should try to get out of here," I said. "If we can get the man to stop, then we can run away and find our way home. Let's tell him that we have to go tinkle."

Matthew looked at me with undisguised contempt. "'Go tinkle'?" he asked.

"You know what I mean." I said.

"Yeah," he said. "'Go tinkle,'" he repeated, and he laughed a hollow laugh. "Anyway," he said, "it's no use."

"We could try," I said.

"I'm telling you, it's no use," Matthew said.

"He's right," said Mort. Mort had stopped crying. He wiped his eyes, leaving behind feathery streaks of dirt that swept out along his cheeks. They made him look like a tired old man. "It's too late," he said. There was no emotion at all in his voice now. He sounded like Matthew. "My mother has probably got another kid by now. Even if I could get off this bus and find my way home, when I got there I'd see some other little boy on her lap eating cookies, and she wouldn't even remember who I was."

A thrill ran through me, the electrifying thrill that comes from recognizing a theme in a setting where one doesn't expect to find it. "This—this—this is like 'The Fox and the Clam,'" I said. All I really meant was that our situation was as miserable as the fox's.

Matthew looked at me and opened his mouth. He had that look of disdain again. "Shut up, Matthew," I said.

Mort looked at me without saying anything. His face still looked drawn and tired, but in his eyes was a wild look of hope.

"Did they get home?" he asked.

"Yeah, Peter," said Matthew. "Tell us. Did they get home, the fox and the clam?" There was, I thought, a tremor in Matthew's voice that he hadn't been able to hide. I started to tell Mort that getting home wasn't what the story was about, but before I spoke, while I was looking at Matthew, feeling nothing but anger toward him, I remembered the way he had stuck his tongue out at me, and the lard sandwiches that he brought to nursery school, and I saw in his eyes the briefest suggestion of the hope that I had seen in Mort's, and an unfamiliar feeling ran through me, a feeling that I can now recognize as compassion. If I had been grown-up, I would have said to myself, "Why, he's not as mired in the slough of despond as he pretends to be. He's just a scared little boy."

I moved back across the aisle so that I could see both of them at once. I sat on the edge of the seat, with my legs in the aisle. "Well," I said to Mort, with a smile, "I'll tell you the whole story." With those words, I felt a tiny glow of pleasure inside me, which came from the memory of the day when Mr. Beaker had first read the fable to me and the day when Miss Louisa had concocted her astounding variation on it. If she could do it, why couldn't I?

Mort wiped his eyes again and ran the back of his hand under his nose. Matthew pursed his lips and narrowed his eyes. His expression seemed to me to say, "All right, Peter. Let's see what you can do." I took a deep breath.

"It all happened in the fall," I began, "a little before supper. It was starting to get dark, and a little fox was on his way home from school. He was rowing his boat along—"

"A fox was rowing a boat?" asked Mort. It was a friendly question, not a challenge. He wasn't suggesting that he thought it impossible for a fox to row a boat; he just wanted to make sure that this fox was rowing a boat.

"Sure," I said. "Look." I looked around and found my drawing on the floor of the bus. When, earlier in the day, we had been required to draw a picture of an animal, I had drawn my favorite animal subject of that time—the fox in the rowboat. "Here, see?"

"Oh, yeah," said Mort. He had slipped his thumb into his mouth and he was half reclining now. Matthew glanced down at him and rolled his eyes.

"So," I continued, "the little fox was rowing along in his rowboat and he was excited about getting home to see his mother and father. His father was a very nice fox, who was always bringing presents home for his children."

"Cookies?" asked Mort, pulling his thumb from his mouth just long enough to ask the question.

"No, not cookies," I said. "Fox children don't eat cookies. They eat lambs."

"Oh, yeah," said Mort.

"So the fox was thinking about the nice roast lambs they'd be having for dinner, and he wasn't paying attention to where he was going. In came the fog, and before that fox knew it he was lost."

"Oh, no," said Mort. He covered his face with his hands. Matthew looked, for a fleeting moment, as if he might giggle.

"Wait," I said. "Wait. It gets better. So the little fox sat there in the fog calling and calling for his mother, but she didn't come."

"No, no, no, no," said Mort under his breath.

"And the little fox began to cry and cry, and he didn't know what to do. Since his mother didn't come, he figured that she probably didn't even notice that he wasn't at home. He thought about how she and his father and his pesty little sister were probably sitting around the table now, eating lamb and telling jokes. Calling wasn't going to do any good. Rowing wasn't going to do any good. Nothing was going to do any good. He just sat there with his head in his hands, crying and crying."

"Paws," said Matthew. I shot him an angry glance, and he pushed his face toward me defiantly.

"Why?" I asked.

"Because that's what foxes have. Paws, not hands."

"Oh," I said. "'Paws.' I thought you meant—never mind. Okay, paws." I shrugged. Matthew was right, after all. "He sat there with his head in his paws, crying and crying, and all of a sudden he started to think about the clams."

"The lambs," said Matthew.

"No," I said, with a good deal of satisfaction. "Not the lambs. The clams. You're not listening closely enough. He started to think about the clams under the water, because the little fox was cold and lost, and fog kept blowing into his face, and the darned boat was starting to leak, so the fox was having a heck of a time. He thought about the clams, and how they were all home already, in their nice little sandy beds with nothing to worry about."

Mort's lower lip began to tremble a bit.

"I know what you're thinking," I said quickly. "It's just like the other kids—they're all home now, and we're not. They get to see their mothers and eat cookies and go to the bathroom, and we don't. Well, just wait and see how this comes out."

Mort swallowed hard and nodded.

"'Jeez,' said the little fox, 'I bet the clams are happy. I wish my mother had been a clam.'"

"Me too," said Mort.

"And because the little fox was so angry and sad about all the good times that he missed because his mother wasn't a clam, he began to let out a cry that was as loud as the siren on a fire engine. At first it wasn't too loud, but the more he wailed the more angry and sad he got and the louder and screechier his wail got, and what do you think happened?"

"He died?" asked Matthew.

"No," I said. I took a breath and tried to keep the feeling of compassion alive within me. "His mother and father and sister heard him. They were looking for him all the time, and when they heard him, they rowed right to him and took him home to have dinner, and they all lived happily ever after."

Mort looked at me for a little while with his mouth hanging open.

"So do you know what the moral of the story is?" I asked. I was about to say, "The moral is: 'Never give up hope, even when you're lost,'" but I didn't get the chance, because Mort said at once, "Yeah, I get it," took a deep breath, stuck his head out the window, and let out a yell that made the bus driver slam on the brakes. The sound coming out of Mort was really remarkably like the siren on a fire engine. It rose and fell, and he could keep it up for an astounding length of time. He would pause only long enough to take another breath, and then he would launch right back into it, a little louder and a little longer each time.

"Hey, stop it, stop it," called the bus driver. "Can't you make him stop?" he asked me.

I shrugged my shoulders. "I'm just a kid," I said.

Suddenly there was a loud and frantic banging on the door of the bus. The driver and I looked toward it and saw my mother and the widow Barber and another woman, Mort's mother, banging on the door, hopping up and down to try to see into the bus, and calling our names.

I looked at Mort. An insane joy swelled within us. When our mothers got to us, we were standing on a seat, with our arms around each other, jumping up and down, and laughing hysterically. Matthew was just sitting there. When his mother reached him, he got down on the floor and retrieved his drawings. He handed them to her just as they were, crumpled into a ball, without saying a word. He started down the aisle, and when he squeezed past me, he looked at me with that sneer again, and I could tell that he was going to stick his tongue out at me. Before he had a chance, I punched him in the mouth.

6

FOR A WHOLE WEEK, I had to stay in my room from the time I got home from school until it was time to get ready to go to school the next morning. I also had to apologize to Matthew.

My mother drove me to Mrs. Barber's shop. We walked inside, and my mother said, "Hello, Mrs. Barber. Peter would like to say something to you."

Mrs. Barber looked down at me and smiled. She was wearing a white dress with puffy sleeves. Printed on the dress were yellow pansies that looked at me with expressions of stern accusation. But Mrs. Barber didn't seem to be upset with me at all. She seemed sympathetic.

"I'm sorry I punched Matthew," I said.

"That's all right, Peter," said Mrs. Barber. "I understand."

"Peter would like to apologize to Matthew too, wouldn't you, Peter," my mother said.

"Yes," I said, to the floor.

"Matthew is in the yard, Peter," said Mrs. Barber. "Why don't you go out and talk to him there?"

"Okay," I said, and I went off in the direction she showed me, through the back room and out a varnished door. I heard my mother and Mrs. Barber talking behind me, and when I paused a moment at the door and looked back into the shop, I saw that my mother was watching me. I opened the door and went out into the yard.

Matthew was sitting in a tire swing, swinging slowly back and forth, letting his feet scrape in the taupe dust under the swing. I had the feeling that he had been waiting for me. I walked up to him at once. I wanted to get this over with.

"My mother says that I have to apologize," I said.

He just kept swinging.

"So—" I said.

He just kept swinging.

"So, I'm doing what she told me I have to do. This is it. I'm doing it now," I said.

"What?" he asked.

"You know," I said. "What my mother told me to do."

I turned and walked away.

7

MATTHEW AND I KEPT OUR DISTANCE throughout kindergarten, but we wound up together in Mrs. Castile's class in the first grade. We were in competition from the first day. Mrs. Castile asked me to distribute copies of *Along Sunny Paths,* the primer that we would be reading. Matthew looked through his copy and marched right up to Mrs. Castile's desk with it.

"Mrs. Castile," he said, "I don't want to cause any trouble, but I'd rather not waste my time reading this book."

"Oh?" said Mrs. Castile.

"Yeah," said Matthew. "You see, I can already read."

"Isn't that nice!" said Mrs. Castile. "Maybe you'll help some of the other boys and girls learn to read."

"Maybe," said Matthew, "but I don't want to have to read this junk." He tried to hand the book to her.

"Matthew," said Mrs. Castile. "This is not 'junk.' These books are brand new, and there are lots of nice stories in them."

"Mrs. Castile," said Matthew, "the stories in here are too simple. They don't give you anything to think about. You know what I mean. Here, look at this one—'Quack, Duck, Quack.' That might be interesting for—"

He turned toward the classroom, looking for someone to use as an example of the "Quack, Duck Quack" level of mental development. I was on my way back to Mrs. Castile's desk with the extra books. Matthew pointed at me and sneered.

"—for Peter. In fact, he'll probably love it, but it's just too simple for me."

"We'll see, Matthew," said Mrs. Castile. "For now, I'm afraid that you will have to read the stories in *Along Sunny Paths* with the rest of the boys and girls."

"I knew it was no use," said Matthew, when he passed me on his way back to his seat. "I'm supposed to read about the duckies with the rest of you nitwits."

For a moment, I was going to hit him with my copy of *Along Sunny Paths,* but I thought better of it. I didn't want to have to go through another of those apologies.

Matthew could, in fact, read very well. So could I, and four other children in Mrs. Castile's class could read well, too. Mrs. Castile gave the six of us another book to read, *Down Dark Alleys,* and had us gather in the cloakroom during reading time to read and discuss the stories on our own. Each day she would appoint one of us as leader. I was the leader on the day that we read a story called "The Happy Clam."

"Today we're going to read a story called 'The Happy Clam,'" I said, by way of introduction. Then, emulating Mrs. Castile, I said, "Now let's see who will read the story for us." I looked around, pretending to choose someone, but in fact I had already decided to choose Matthew. "Matthew," I said, "why don't you read for us?"

The Happy Clam

Look! See the clam?
The clam is happy!
See the fox? The fox is not happy.
The fox is sad. The fox is very sad.
The clam is not sad. The clam is happy.

Oh! Oh!
Did the fox see the clam?
Yes! Yes! The fox did see the clam.
The clam is happy. The fox is not happy.
The fox is angry. The fox is angry with the clam.
What will the fox do?

Oh! Oh!
See the fox fall?
Ho! Ho! Ho!
The fox cannot get the clam!
The clam is happy. The fox is not happy.

The fox is not happy OR sad now.
The clam is still happy.
Look at that happy clam!

Things to think about . . .
1. Why was the fox sad at the beginning?
2. Why was the clam happy?
3. Why was the fox angry with the clam?
4. Why was the fox not sad at the end?
5. Will the clam stay happy?

"THE FOX WAS SAD at the beginning," said Matthew, "because there was no reason for him to be happy. The clam was happy because he was a jerk. The fox was angry with the clam because he couldn't stand to be around jerks. The fox wasn't sad at the end because he was dead. And the clam will stay happy as long as he's a jerk." He looked hard at me. "But if he ever wises up, he'll be as miserable as the fox."

Sitting next to Matthew was Mary Elizabeth Patterson. Mary Elizabeth could make a cloudy day sunny. She was a small girl with slender arms and short brown hair. Whenever I saw her in the morning, outside, before school started, she was smiling and full of things to say. When she smiled, she showed a lot of teeth. She had long, pointed canines that I thought were awfully cute. Before the day began, Mary Elizabeth and I would spend a few minutes chatting happily about the amusing things our parents had done the night before. I was quite contentedly in love with her, and I basked in the certainty that my love was reciprocated. On this day she was wearing a yellow dress with a full skirt, white anklets, and patent-leather shoes. She had been squirming on her chair throughout Matthew's reading. While he was answering the questions, she squirmed on her chair with more impatience and waved her hand in the air. When Matthew finished, I said, "Mary Elizabeth, do you want to say something?" I expected her to tell Matthew to stop being a Gloomy Gus, or words to that effect.

"I just wanted to say that I agree with Matthew," she said.

On the tip of my tongue were the words "I think you're right, Mary Elizabeth." I was even leaning forward a bit in my chair to encourage her. I caught myself before I spoke, and then I had to catch myself again before I fell off the chair. Mary Elizabeth went right on.

"I think this story shows that you just can't win," she said. She was looking at Matthew while she spoke, and the look in her eyes was admiration. I had to say something.

"Well," I said, "I guess you can't win them all. That's what my father says."

"Oh, that's just silly, Peter," said Mary Elizabeth.

Darkness seemed to descend in the cloakroom. Mary Elizabeth and Matthew were staring into each other's eyes. They looked perfectly miserable and perfectly compatible.

8

MATTHEW AND I WERE THE BEST READERS in Mrs. Castile's class, and she let us gallop through all the anthologies that the school had on hand. When reading time came around, Matthew and I would go down to the boiler room, where we had a couple of chairs and desks set up, and read together. At that time, it must have been the fashion to think of reading—or at least of learning to read—as a journey, judging from the great number of anthologies with titles derived from roads, features of roads, and roadside attractions. Matthew and I read our way through *Bridges and Tunnels, Highways and Byways, Detours and Roadblocks, Culverts and Sewers, Sidewalks and Gutters, Crosswalks and Stoplights,* and *Motels and Diners.*

At first, the atmosphere at these boiler-room sessions was tense. Matthew and I faced each other across our desks and read *at* each other. We spat out the answers to the questions, and we disagreed on the answers to all but the most trivial of them. But as the year wore on, I developed a grudging admiration for him, admiration that was mixed with pity and a strong desire to make him laugh, or at least smile. For his part, Matthew actually seemed to like me, though he continued to shake his head at some of my ideas. Matthew and I, I realized sometime in the spring, had become friends, after a fashion.

At the end of the school year, on the last day, when Matthew and I were carrying our chairs up from the boiler room, he said to me, "Peter, I want to ask you something, and I don't want you to laugh."

"All right," I said.

"Are we friends?" he asked.

"Yes," I said. "I think so."

"Then tell me something."

"Yeah?"

"Why are you happy all the time?" he asked.

"I'm not happy all the time," I said.

"Well then, why are you happy most of the time?"

"I don't know," I answered. It was an honest answer.

"Do you think I'll be happy someday?" he asked.

I looked at him. He wasn't looking at me. I thought of lying, but I didn't.

"No," I said.

We didn't say anything more to each other that day, and I didn't see Matthew again until September. I discovered, however, that he had infected me with a sympathetic melancholy that lasted well into the summer.

9

I GOT THE CHICKEN POX about halfway through the second grade, and I had to stay in bed wearing flannel pajamas with the ends of the sleeves sewn shut so that I couldn't scratch my vesicles. One day, Matthew's mother drove him to my house. My mother came into the room with a package for me, a gift from Matthew. It was wrapped in brown paper and tied with string, but I could see from the shape that it was a record. On the wrapping paper, Matthew had printed a note to me.

> Dear Peter,
> I imagine that you are feeling pretty miserable. I think you might like to listen to this record.
>
> > Your friend,
> > Matthew Barber

The record was called *The Amazing Randy the Unbreakable Record.* I was feverish and uncomfortable and bored, so miserable that my mother's hand on my forehead was almost intolerable, and I couldn't manage even to tell her to thank Matthew for the gift. My mother told me that she would play the record and let me listen to it alone.

"Call me when the first side is over," she said. She closed the door and left me with the voice of Randy, a voice that I can hear as I write this sentence.

"Ouch! Oh my! That's always a shock. No matter how carefully a person sets the needle down on me, I always feel a little pinprick. Well, hello there! I'm Randy. What's your name? (pause) What was that again? (pause) Oh! Now I've got it. That's one of my favorite names! Well, as I said, I'm Randy. I hope you like my name as much as I like yours.

"Da-da da-dum-dum-dum—
I'm Randy the Record,
Now what do you think of that?
I'm Randy the Record;
I'm round and black and flat.

"Ho-ho! Say, that was fun, wasn't it? I have rather a good voice, I think. Of course, as the years pass, my voice won't stay sweet and clear. It's going to get worn and scratchy. Well, that's life. Listen—you can help me last a little longer, but you'll have to treat me carefully: never touch my top or bottom with your fingers, only my edges; and don't go thrusting any pencils, knives, or other weapons into my hole. If you do, I could be badly maimed and slip on the spindle, which wooooould maaake meeeaaa saaoound lahhhk theeis.

"Ha, ha, ha! Well, that may sound like fun to you, but I'd be horribly embarrassed if I sounded like that, and you'd get tired of listening to it after a while, and if you weren't feeling well the sound might make you want to throw up, so don't play around with my hole, okay? Another thing: watch out for the needle. If you set it down hard or bump it or stomp around the room and make it jump, it will gaareeeahgeeeech! Uh! Jesus Christ! There's nothing worse! You know how bad chalk screeching on a blackboard sounds—well *imagine what it feels like to the blackboard!* And then a scratch like that will make me stick in that spot, so that when the needle gets there you'll find me saying the same thing over and over and (click) over and over and (click) over and over and (click) over and over and (click) over again, which would be a miserable way for me to end my days and could drive you mad. So you see that it isn't only for my own good that I tell you these things. But if you treat me right I'll give you years of listening pleasure.

"Oh, you do right by me,
And I'll do right by you.
Bo-bo ba deedle-de-dee,
Boop-boop ba doodle-de-doo!

"Ha ha! Sure hope you liked that one! Listen, there's one thing I almost forgot. Every once in a while, give me a little wipe with a damp cloth, will you? Not wet, just damp—and not too cold—oh, and not too hot. And listen, when the time comes that I'm just too old and worn to sound halfway decent, don't embarrass me by playing me for your friends, okay? I couldn't stand that. I've got my pride. Just smash me on a brick or something and tell your mother that the kid next door did it. Promise? Go on, let me hear you promise. (pause) Thanks. Thanks.

"Now let me do something for you. Get yourself into a comfortable position and tell me about everything that's bothering you. Tell me your hopes and dreams, your fears and worries, your hideous urges, and I'll listen. I'll listen sympathetically. I'll listen to you without getting tired. Maybe you think that all the other kids are having a lot more fun than you are. Their mothers and fathers never make them do the things that yours make you do. They don't have any chores to do around the house. Their daddies like taking out the garbage so much that they always want to do it themselves. I know how it is. I'm on your side. The other kids are happy as clams, and you're miserable. Don't let it get you down. When you're feeling *really bad,* just put old Randy on your record player, and when you hear me saying 'shhhhh-click, shhhhh-click, shhhhh-click,' you'll know that it's old Randy's way of letting you know that he hears you, he understands you, he agrees with you. When you've had your say, just turn me over. Now go right ahead and tell me aaaall about it. Shhhhh-click, shhhhh-click, shhhhh-click—"

10

THE COPY OF *The Amazing Randy the Unbreakable Record* that Matthew gave me was badly worn. Matthew must have played it often. I had to strain to hear Randy through the hissing and popping on the first side. The second side was marked with deep gouges that looked to me as if they had been deliberately made, perhaps with the point of a compass. I couldn't play that side at all.

When I had recovered from the chicken pox and was allowed to go outside, I smashed Randy with a brick and buried him in the back yard. It seemed the decent thing to do.

11

DURING THE SUMMER that followed second grade, I saw Matthew nearly every Saturday. My mother would drive me to Mrs. Barber's shop in the morning and leave me there for the day. At noon, Matthew and I would eat lunch upstairs, where he and his mother lived, and after lunch we would walk to the Babbington Theater, which was only a block and a half down Main Street, for the Saturday matinee.

Throughout that summer, the theater ran a series of animated cartoons before the feature. These cartoons starred two remarkable hippos. One was a kind and pleasant-looking sort, grandfatherly and a little stodgy, who drew animated cartoons for a living. This hippo was never named, but I used to think of him as Happy, because he seemed quite content and generally unruffled. Each episode began with Happy Hippo at his drawing board, puffing on his pipe and working on a fresh ink drawing of his lead character, a younger, comical, bumbling, and mischievous hippo who was also unnamed, but should have been called Hapless. As soon as Happy had drawn him, Hapless began to romp around the drawing paper, and the adventure got under way. Whatever his adventure might be in any one episode, it shared with all the others some features worth noting.

1. All the difficulties that Hapless fell into were concocted by Happy. It was he who drew the cliffs that Hapless fell over, he who made doorways too small for Hapless to get through, he who made Hapless's roof leak.

2. We were continually reminded that Hapless was a cartoon character made of ink. Sometimes, when Hapless was in a tight spot, his face drooped sadly, and then his body began to droop, and he slowly ran down into a puddle. Then from this puddle he emerged in a new form. In fact, although he began each episode as a hippopotamus, he spent most of the time in other forms, and he returned to being a hippopotamus only at the end. Often he was a chubby man in a derby hat who drove a ridiculous little car. When Hapless, as the chubby man in the derby hat, was stuck in a traffic jam, for example, he and his ridiculous little car melted into an inky puddle, and then a balloon rose from the puddle and suspended below it was a basket, in which Hapless drifted above the traffic. Of course, an enormous hawk was soon pecking at the balloon and in a minute or two Hapless was falling toward earth at his wit's end.

3. When Hapless really got into trouble, he appealed to Happy for help. In the basket dangling below the deflated balloon, for instance, when he was so beside himself with fear that he couldn't think of a metamorphosis that would save him, he got down on his knees and clasped his hands together and looked out toward us with a beseeching look. As if a camera were drawing back, the image of Hapless receded on the screen, and we saw the edges of the drawing paper, then the drawing table, Happy's workroom, and finally Happy himself, chuckling, amused by the predicament that Hapless had gotten into.

4. Sometimes, Happy simply picked up his pen and drew some help for Hapless. When Hapless was falling in the basket of the deflated balloon, Happy drew a kindly herring gull who swooped out of the corner of the page and plucked Hapless from the basket. (Later, however, the herring gull set Hapless down in another pickle. As I recall, the gull deposited him on a tiny desert island.)

5. At other times, Happy helped Hapless by drawing a likeness of himself

on the paper, joining Hapless in his adventure or misadventure. Whenever he did so, he at once became as inept as Hapless, and both of them were soon up to their necks in trouble. Happy, however, always had an out. He would draw a sheet of drawing paper around the source of their trouble—a charging lion, say—and then draw a drawing table and so on, until he had reproduced his workroom on the paper, with the predicament trapped within the edges of the new piece of drawing paper, while he and Hapless were safely outside it. Then he and Hapless would shake hands, and Happy would wink at the viewer, and the cartoon would be over.

6. And at still other times, Happy helped Hapless by drawing for him a bottle of ink and a pen. Hapless would grab the pen, dip it in the ink, and quickly draw something to help himself. Invariably, the devices that Hapless created to help himself turned out to be two-edged swords. In one episode, Hapless, a bumbling cowhand at the time, was being pursued by a charging herd of cattle. Happy drew him a bottle of ink and a pen, and Hapless drew a door in the middle of the Western vista. He opened the door, stepped through it, slammed it, and left the herd of cattle behind. He wiped his hand across his forehead, wiping away the sweat of fear, and breathed a sigh of relief. Then he looked around and saw that he was standing on a tiny platform over a bayou full of snapping alligators.

The very last Happy and Hapless cartoon that was shown at the Babbington Theater is the one that remains sharpest in my memory.

After a number of mishaps and close calls, Hapless, in his chubby-man incarnation, found himself in a rowboat, rowing across a gray bay. A storm was coming up. Already the bay was choppy, and Hapless was struggling to row into the wind. He was having a terrible time of it, and his expression showed the strain that he was under. Over the sound of the wind and the waves, we began to hear Happy's chuckling, building gradually, coming as if from behind all of us kids, as if Happy were sitting up in the balcony somewhere, where the bigger kids sat to neck and smoke.

Poor Hapless began to hear it too, and he turned toward us, stopped rowing, and looked at us with a sadness that we didn't recognize from earlier episodes. There was a scattering of nervous laughter, and all of us expected something to happen to change Hapless's situation, if not for the better, at least to make it different, at least to get this horrible look off his face. But nothing happened. Hapless just sat there, drifting, looking out at us with misery in his eyes while Happy's chuckle filled the theater.

Finally, Hapless spoke. "I don't want to do this any more," he said. The sadness in his voice was bottomless.

Kids began squirming in their seats and looking at one another. I looked at Matthew and laughed a tentative laugh, as if to say, "This is funny, right? You get the joke, don't you—even though I don't?"

Matthew gave me the sardonic grin that he had, as our friendship had grown, added to his sneer and his impassive look of disappointment.

On the screen, the wind suddenly died, and the bay was calm, though the sky was still dark. Hapless sat in the rowboat, drifting. "I don't want to do this any more," he repeated, and right before the bulging eyes of a hundred kids, he and his rowboat began to melt into the water of the bay.

It took only a few seconds, I suppose, for Hapless to disperse himself. The water lay there, undulating slowly, under a featureless gray sky. We all sat in silence for a while, and I heard some blubbering, but then Gene Autry came onto the screen, smiling and singing, and the boys and girls seemed to forget Hapless at once.

I didn't. I realized that I had spent part of every Saturday afternoon for an entire summer laughing at Hapless's misfortunes. The thought made me miserable.

12

AFTER MATTHEW AND I had put in a couple of weeks in the third grade, Mrs. Barber got it into her head that Matthew should skip a grade. I told my mother that if Matthew was going to skip a grade, then I wanted to skip a grade too. She consulted Mr. Beaker, who endorsed the idea at once.

Matthew and I were put through a series of intelligence tests. For three mornings, we sat in a tiny room near the administrative office, alone, at two desks set as far apart from each other as the room would allow, with the door of the room open so that the principal's secretary could keep an eye on us. At lunch time we would compare our answers and speculate about whether we had done well enough to meet the standards required of a student in the fourth grade.

When the intelligence tests were over, we were put through a psychological test. Both of us knew that this was important. We had heard the principal, Mr. Horne, remark to his secretary, Mrs. Torelli, while we were at work on the tests one morning, that he had no doubt that we were smart enough for fourth grade, but that, frankly, he wondered whether we were mature enough to fit in with the other fourth-graders.

We had to be tested individually, since most of the test was administered orally by Mr. Grundtvig, a fat psychologist in a brown suit who had been brought in especially for the purpose. Matthew went into the room first. He was in there for about an hour and a half. I waited in Mr. Horne's office. When Matthew was finished, he was whisked away by Mrs. Torelli before I was summoned.

I spent a while looking at pictures on cards and describing them for Mr. Grundtvig. I spent a while describing what I imagined fourth grade would be like. I spent a while describing what I imagined fourth *graders* would be like. I spent quite a while telling Mr. Grundtvig about my relatives and friends, and he took lots of notes.

"Well, Peter," said Mr. Grundtvig. "We've had quite a lot of fun talking, I think. Now we're going to play a kind of game. Do you like games?"

I was going to say no, which was the truth, but I was sure that would be the wrong answer, so I said, "Oh, yeah!"

"Well, good. This is a storytelling game." He picked up a booklet and leafed through it. "I'll read the beginning of a story, and you finish it for me, all right?"

"All right," I said.

"Here we go," said Mr. Grundtvig. "One day a man, in the middle of his life, no longer young, decided that it would be nice to row a boat across a bay. He hadn't rowed a boat in some time. When he got to the very middle of the bay, he was very tired. His hands were sore. His arms were aching. Sweat ran into his eyes. He looked around. The water was murky and gray. The man was as far from where he had started out as he was from where he wanted to go. He didn't know what to do."

Mr. Grundtvig closed the booklet and looked at me. "Well, Peter," he said, "what do you think will happen next?"

I felt very much as the man in the boat must have felt. I was midway between the third grade and the fourth grade. What I said now might be the one thing that sent me either back to the third grade or ahead to the fourth grade. I didn't care too much which happened, as long as I wound up where Matthew did. If he made it into the fourth grade, then I wanted to be there too. If he had to stay in the third grade, then I wanted to stay there.

Mr. Grundtvig cleared his throat. He had been looking at his notepad, holding his pencil ready. He looked up at me and tapped the pencil point on the pad. "Well, Peter?" he said.

I made the decision in an instant. The way to be sure of winding up where Matthew wound up was to answer as Matthew would. I pulled a long face. "It would be nice if this story had a happy ending," I said. Mr. Grundtvig began writing at once. "But it will not. I mean, in a way, we're all like the man in the rowboat—tired, confused, miserable—"

13

"SO I SAT THERE, looking at Mr. Grundtvig," said Matthew, between bites of the tuna fish sandwich I had given him, "and I said to myself, 'This is it. Everything depends on this.' There I was. I was actually in the predicament that the man in the rowboat was in. Grundtvig began tapping his pencil on his pad and he looked up at me. As soon as he looked at me, I knew what to do. I gave him the kind of story *you* would give him! You know what I told him happened at the end? The guy was carried off by a mermaid! *They lived happily ever after.* I couldn't believe it. I heard myself saying all this, but I couldn't believe it."

I couldn't believe it either. I sat looking at Matthew, who went on with his story, filling in the details, laughing, and pounding the table with his hand. My heart sank. The more he elaborated on the story, the surer I became that we would be going our separate ways. I couldn't bring myself to tell Matthew what I had done.

14

THE NEXT MORNING, my mother drove me to school. Together we went to Mr. Horne's office. Mrs. Barber and Matthew were already there. Mr. Horne talked at some length about how proud he was of Matthew and me, but after he said that both of us would be moving up to the fourth grade I was so intoxicated by the news that I missed a lot of what followed. I did, however, recover in time to hear what Mr. Horne read from Mr. Grundtvig's report, which had been the deciding factor.

Of Matthew, Mr. Grundtvig had written: "One is struck at first by his attitude of blank despondency, his apparently chronic melancholia, but one is delightfully surprised to find that this somber little fellow actually has a lively imagination and a well-developed comic sense."

Of me, he had written: "Although on the surface he appears to be unbelievably naive, with only the most frivolous and trivial thoughts, one discovers upon closer inspection that he has depth, that he harbors a profound understanding of the absurdity, the pain, the misery of modern life."

The Girl with the White Fur Muff

I have often noticed that we are inclined to endow our friends with the stability of type that literary characters acquire in the reader's mind. No matter how many times we reopen "King Lear," never shall we find the good king banging his tankard in high revelry, all woes forgotten, at a jolly reunion with all three daughters and their lapdogs . . . . Whatever evolution this or that popular character has gone through between the book covers, his fate is fixed in our minds, and, similarly, we expect our friends to follow this or that logical and conventional pattern we have fixed for them. Thus X will never compose the immortal music that would clash with the second-rate symphonies he has accustomed us to. Y will never commit murder. Under no circumstances can Z ever betray us.

> Humbert Humbert
> in Vladimir Nabokov's
> *Lolita*

Preface

BLUSHING plays an important part in the pages that follow. I do some of it myself, perhaps too much, but I should probably do some blushing here as well, because I have described Veronica McCall inaccurately. I have described her as she appears in my mind's eye: I have let myself be seduced by the image that remains there, and I have presented it as if it were accurate, have even claimed that the image was recorded and preserved with particular precision, although logic tells me that it can't be accurate at all.

In my mind's eye, Veronica is wearing—on the occasion of our first meeting—a beige knit dress made of thin, soft wool. It has long sleeves, and the neckline is a wide scoop, so wide that the dress falls off one smooth shoulder. Surely my memory can't be correct about this dress, about the fullness of Veronica's hips in it, or about the way the dress clings to her. All that must be part of a much later memory, since I met Veronica in the fourth grade.

Peter Leroy
Small's Island
December 28, 1983

1

WHEN REPORT CARDS were handed out at the Babbington Grammar School, some of my classmates fell into a whimpering terror, instinctively cowering and covering their vulnerable spots, as skittish and apprehensive as squirrels. Others began whooping and crowing, pounding one another on the back, and totting up their spoils. At the time it didn't occur to me to pity the first group, but I certainly envied the second, for my parents considered it a Principle of Child Rearing not to reward my accomplishments in school.

When I brought a report card home, I got small praise for even the best of grades, and almost nothing in the way of tangible rewards. My father would say, looking at the best report card in my class, or even in the whole school, "That's what I expected." Sometimes Gumma or Guppa would slip me a dollar, or my mother would give me a hug and whisper, "I'm proud of you, Peter," but these tokens seemed insignificant indeed beside the handsome cash prizes some of my friends collected. Some were paid for meeting certain standards, negotiated with their parents in advance, standards that were often, it seemed to me, quite low for the loot involved. Others were rewarded for showing any improvement at all; quite a few made out pretty well just for getting through six weeks without being sent to the principal's office; and still others could collect a metal dump truck or a movie pass just for compiling a decent attendance record. It didn't seem just.

However, on the extraordinary occasion when Matthew Barber and I were, after three weeks in the third grade, moved ahead to the fourth, I did get a reward: a camera, the first I had ever owned. It was small, well suited to the hands of a third-grader, but it was an unusual possession for a child in those times, a sophisticated gadget even for a fourth-grader.

The camera was made of black plastic, the kind called Bakelite. In overall shape, it was a cube, but a cube on which every edge had been smoothly rounded, as if the designer had streamlined it in case the photographer had to use it in a high wind. On each side was a vertical slide of bright metal that traveled in a channel molded into the Bakelite, so that, by moving these slides toward the top, one could separate the front and back halves of the camera to load or unload the film or to examine the interior. At its upper end, each metal slide terminated in a circular lug, through which were threaded the ends of a braided plastic strap. In the center of the back was a round window of translucent red plastic through which one could see the numbers on the paper backing of the film.

At the center of the front half was the lens, smooth and limpid, inside a crater of plastic. A short cream-colored shaft projected from a protuberance on the body. The top of the shaft was flattened to form the button that one pushed to take a picture. On the bottom of the camera was a knurled knob, also made of cream-colored plastic, that one turned to advance the film. Across the top of the camera, mounted in a channel molded into both halves of the body, was the viewfinder. When one held the camera with the viewfinder to one's eye, the forefinger of one's right hand fell quite naturally on the shutter button, and the middle finger fell quite naturally over the right half of the lens.

I loved that camera. I carried it with me everywhere for nearly a year, because holding it and looking at it reminded me that I had done something my parents regarded as extraordinarily worthy. But as much as the camera pleased me it intimidated me. A statement in the instruction booklet said, "Snapshots will capture your memories forever," and I understood at once that the snapshots I was likely to take would capture forever memories of my childish ineptitude as a photographer, the evidence of my awkwardness and uncertainty. Clearly, the wise thing to do would be to avoid using film until I had acquired some poise, if only enough so that I wouldn't take pictures I would really regret, so I put the film in the back of my sock drawer to save until I felt confident enough to use it.

For practice, I took filmless photographs, hoping that I'd become familiar enough with the camera to be able to handle it with skill and nonchalance. I trembled whenever I brought the viewfinder to my eye and tried to frame a picture. My finger froze on the white plastic button that would capture this memory forever, or would have if there had been film in the camera. I *wanted* to push the button, but some small consideration would always make me hesitate.

Maybe it would be better to aim a little higher, in case I might be cutting off the top of someone's head.

If I waited just a moment, maybe Guppa would smile.

Was I too close?

Should I wait until the sun came out from behind that cloud?
Had I remembered to turn the knob after the last picture?
Maybe I should wait for another opportunity altogether.
Maybe I didn't really want to preserve this memory at all.

2

ON THE DAY when I left the third grade, my classmates threw a party
for me. Everyone had brought cupcakes or cookies, and they had collabo-
rated on a card that said GOOD LUCK, PETER. I was pleased, embarrassed,
and moved. When it was time to go, I stood at the door with my hand on
the knob. I swallowed hard. I thought that I ought to say something.

At this point I had one of those flashes of inspiration that go off in
one's brain now and then like a flashbulb or a bolt of lightning. I said,
"I'd like to take a picture of all of you so I can be sure that I'll never
forget you."

I had all my classmates gather at one end of the room for a group portrait. I spent some time moving them around to get a good composition,
and then I said, "Okay, everybody, that looks just perfect. Now everybody smile." Everybody smiled, and I held the camera to my eye. The
familiar uncertainty gripped me, and my finger trembled over the button.
I clamped my teeth together, closed my eyes, and pushed.

"Okay, everybody, you can relax now," I called out. I wound the knob
on the bottom of the camera. "You know," I said, "snapshots capture
your memories forever."

I wasn't using film in the camera, of course, so my memories began to
fade as soon as I walked out the door.

3

I CLOSED THE DOOR BEHIND ME, and in a watery haze I walked
down the hall, away from the familiar, toward the unknown. I wasn't
crying, but there was a lump in my throat, my eyes were watering, and
everything ahead of me was blurry, indistinct. I had closed the door of

Room 218 behind me, but in a larger sense I had closed a larger door, and the echoes of its closing reverberated in the hazy corridor that lay ahead of me. I had closed the door on third grade, on a part of my childhood, forever. I was walking toward an uncertain future, and I couldn't make out where I was going.

From my right, I heard Matthew Barber's voice. "Peter," he called, "watch where you're going. You'll fall down the stairs." I felt his hand on my arm. He stopped me from going farther. "Come on," he said. "Come into the boys' room." I followed where he led me, and after I had dried my eyes and washed my face I felt better.

"I feel better now," I said. I clutched my camera a little tighter for strength, stood up straight, and added, "Let's go to the fourth grade, shall we?"

"I don't know, Peter," said Matthew. "We're probably making a big mistake. Do you think they'd let us back into the third grade?"

"Aw, come on, Matthew," I said. "We would have gone into the fourth grade eventually anyway. We might as well face up to it now. Besides, I don't think they'll let us go back—there was something about the way the door closed behind me—and the way it echoed in the hallway."

Matthew stared at the floor. "Yeah," he said quietly. "I heard that too." He sighed. "We should have left well enough alone," he said, shaking his head. "Things usually turn out wrong."

I gave him a knock on the shoulder, as if to say, "Chin up!" and said, "Baloney, Matthew! Things are going to be great! We've got a great future ahead of us!" I was beginning to believe it. "Fourth grade, here we come," I said. "Room 231, here we come!"

"Two thirty-four," he said, still looking at the floor.

"No—231," I said. From my shirt pocket I took a manila card. Matthew took a similar card from his shirt pocket. On his card was written MISS FIORE, ROOM 234. I showed him my card. On it was written MRS. GRAHAM, ROOM 231.

"I should have known," said Matthew. "I let myself get excited about this, I let myself be happy, and look what happened. I should have known. I should have known."

He walked out of the boys' room, and I followed him. He walked down the hall to the door of Room 234 while I stood in the hall watching. He never lifted his eyes from the floor, and he was still looking at the floor, shaking his head and muttering "I should have known," when he opened the door and walked in. I wondered how on earth he had been able to tell where he was going.

4

THE SCHOOL was an old one. I had begun attending it in kindergarten, and for a long time I had thought that the people who had gone to the school years ago must have been much bigger at my age than I was or than any of my friends were. Everything in the school seemed taller, wider, higher, or heavier than necessary. My friends and I struggled to climb the stairs, stood on our tiptoes to use the water fountains or the urinals, sat on the sinks to look into the mirrors. I had grown accustomed to seeing the building as too big and the boys and girls as too small.

When I opened the door to Mrs. Graham's room, I was struck at once by the fact that the boys and girls fitted their desks. Their elbows rested on the desktops, and their feet reached the floor. The fourth grade, I could see, was what the school was about. When you reached the fourth grade, you would fit. I wasn't going to fit, and everyone would know it as soon as I sat down.

Mrs. Graham was standing beside her desk. She had a book in her hand, a book with a navy-blue binding, an arithmetic book that I would soon come to regard with a deep, quiet, enduring hatred.

On Mrs. Graham's desk was a large vase made of milk glass, and in this vase were flowers, lots of flowers. I don't remember what kind of flowers, but there were always flowers in the vase, sometimes so many flowers that, if Mrs. Graham sat at her desk, I couldn't see her at all from my seat at the back of the room.

"Peter!" cried Mrs. Graham. There was so much pleasure in her voice that I felt at once that I must know her, not merely that I must have met her, but that I must have known her for a long time, that somehow circumstances had separated us, and now fate had at last brought us together again, to our surprise and delight. I was immediately as happy to see her as she seemed to be to see me.

"Hi!" I said, gleefully. She closed her book emphatically and tossed it toward her desk. It struck the vase, which tipped and rocked, and looked as if it might fall to the floor, but a boy in the front row leaped from his seat and steadied it. Before he sat down, he shook his head a couple of times and smiled indulgently. Mrs. Graham never noticed any of this, since all her attention was focused on me.

She was an enormous woman. She was not fat; she was just constructed according to a giant set of plans. Good nature and affection seemed to burn within her: her cheeks glowed red, and she approached me with the awful momentum of a locomotive under a full head of steam. She scared me to death, yet she was irresistible. I was drawn to her, and so strong was her attraction that I held my arms out as I walked toward her, as if I would hug her as I hugged my mother.

As Mrs. Graham advanced, boys and girls pulled their feet in safely under their desks. At one point in her advance she stepped on a piece of chalk that was lying on the floor, and it exploded under her shoe, sending chalk dust flying outward to form a starburst pattern that the janitor never succeeded in removing.

We didn't hug when we reached each other. Mrs. Graham stopped, took a deep breath, extended her hand toward me, and said, "Welcome to the fourth grade."

I put my hand in hers and she shook it. "Thank you," I said. I loved her at once, respected her, and feared her. I knew from that moment that I would do anything she asked me to do, told me to do, or even hinted that perhaps I should do. And I knew she'd make sure that I got through the fourth grade all right.

5

THE CLASS gave me a greeting that they had rehearsed, and Mrs. Graham pointed out a seat for me at the back of the room. I made my way to the seat in a euphoric state, for Mrs. Graham had made me feel secure, even confident. I sat down and stretched myself out nearly straight so that I could keep my feet on the floor and my elbows on the desk top. Mrs. Graham had the boys and girls stand, one at a time, and introduce themselves. Three of them, three girls, were to play particularly memorable roles in my life.

The first was Veronica McCall. She stood slowly when her turn came, placed one foot in the aisle, brought the other out to meet it, turned, tossed her head to clear her straight, dark hair from in front of her left eye, and then pushed it aside with a flip of her hand for good measure. She laughed and shrugged as if to say, "Isn't it amusing that we all have hair, but only mine falls in this odd and alluring way in front of my eye, only mine is this fine, this straight, this dark?"

She said, "Well, hello there!" and she rippled her fingers through the air. She reversed the set of steps that had brought her to her feet and slid herself into her seat. As she sat, her dress tightened across her bottom and along her legs, and I obtained a photographically precise and durable impression of the outline of her underpants.

The second was Lily O'Grady. She had hair of a color that my mother referred to as "dirty blond," though her use of *dirty* in this way may have been only partly a description of color. Lily called herself Spike. She was the class bully. She led a gang of crewcut and muscular boys named Biff, Studs, Chuck, and Knuckles. I never quite figured out which of the boys in the gang was which except for Biff, who had a scar down the side of his left cheek. It was said that Biff got this scar when Spike fought him for the leadership of the gang. (Quite a few years later, at a reunion of my class at Babbington High, I asked Biff whether that was, in fact, how he had gotten the scar. "Heck, no," he said. "It was a very democratic gang. We elected the leader by secret ballot. I got the scar while Spike and I were counting the votes.")

Spike stood slowly. She was chewing gum, and the muscles along her jaw and at her temples rippled impressively. She looked me up and down. Her head bobbed as if her neck were a coil spring. Finally, she dropped her jaw, pulled her lower lip in over her teeth, and shook her head once, in a gesture that told me, to my enormous relief, that she considered me beneath consideration. "Hi, Pete!" she shouted, though I was only a couple of feet away from her. She started to sit down, but a thought occurred to her, and she got to her feet again. "Don't worry," she said. "It's not so hard. I've been here a few weeks already, and I understand almost everything. Just keep your mouth shut and you'll be okay." She gave me a wink. I resolved to keep my mouth as shut as possible.

The third was Clarissa Bud, who made my heart ache as soon as she raised her eyes toward mine. She was small and fragile, with skin as pale and smooth as moonlight on the Bolotomy. She moved as if she were moving through water instead of air: she rose to her feet as if she were allowing herself to float upward. Her eyes were enormous, wide and surprised. Though the weather was mild, she had on her desk a white fur muff, on which she rested her left hand, rubbing the fur between her thumb and forefinger, drawing from the muff the kind of comfort that I got from clutching my camera. Clarissa seemed so frightened and retiring that she made me feel strong and bold. She was, Mrs. Graham pointed out, also new to the classroom, and in fact new to Babbington, the latest stop in Mr. Bud's progress from one important position in the food-processing industry to another. Clarissa's desk was beside mine.

"Hello, Peter," Clarissa said, so softly that when I responded I spoke in a whisper.

"Hello, Clarissa," I said. I held my hand out. To be honest, I didn't just hold my hand out, I reached for her hand. I didn't intend to shake it; I wanted to hold it. She hesitated for the briefest instant, and then she gave her right hand to me. I held it between both of mine. She kept her left hand on the muff.

"You can call me Clare if you want to," she said.

Tiny droplets of sweat formed on my upper lip. I stammered when I spoke. "Oh, th—that's okay," I said. "I th—think Clarissa is beautiful."

She blushed. So did I. I heard Spike mutter, "Oh, brother."

With the introductions over, Mrs. Graham went back to what the class had been doing before I arrived.

"Peter," Mrs. Graham said, smiling at me, her cheeks glowing, "we're just practicing our times tables."

"Oh, great!" I said, smiling right back at her, smiling with all my heart, ready to do anything to show this woman how happy I was to have been allowed into the fourth grade, to be in her classroom, to sit beside Clarissa, to have my heart ache like this. But even as I said it, a chill spread through me. I had no idea what she was talking about. I had never heard of the times tables before in my life. I smiled, but the sweat continued to form on my lip, and when I wiped it off with the back of my hand, it came right back again. When my turn came to do whatever I was supposed to do, I was going to make a fool of myself in front of all the kids that I had just met, and worst of all in front of Clarissa. My happiness would end as quickly as it had begun.

I tried not to do anything that would betray my anxiety, but something—my irregular breathing, the sweat on my lip, or the mad, twitching smile that I was struggling to maintain—must have given me away. When I glanced sidelong at the boys and girls around me, I saw that they were glancing sidelong at me, and from the *moue* Clarissa wore, the way she was stroking her muff, I thought she must know that something was wrong.

"Peter?" Suddenly I realized that Mrs. Graham was calling on me. I looked up at her.

"Yes?" I said.

"Do you know the answer?"

I didn't even know the question. I had been so firmly in the grip of my fears that I hadn't even noticed what was going on. I said, "Uh, well—"

Some tiny movement caught my eye. Maybe Spike hadn't done anything more than move her hand, but I saw it, and glanced ever so briefly at her desk. I saw, on a piece of paper, where her hand rested, the number 54. Another tiny movement caught my eye. On a piece of paper on Veronica's desk I saw the number 58. I was on the horns of a dilemma, but not for long. I didn't want to do anything that was going to offend Spike, so I decided on that basis alone to take the answer that she offered.

"—fifty-four," I said. I tossed it off as if it had been nothing.

Mrs. Graham looked at me for just long enough before she spoke so that I could tell, though no one else probably could have, that she knew how I had gotten the answer.

"No, Peter," she said. "That's not right. Seven times eight is fifty-six."

I blushed. "Oh! That's right," I said. "I guess I just forgot."

Without turning around, Spike shrugged her shoulders and covered the number she had written. Veronica looked genuinely puzzled.

6

AT THE END OF THE DAY, I made my way out the front door of the school, in a crowd of boys and girls. Mrs. Graham was standing beside the door. "Peter," she called. "I'd like to speak to you for just a minute."

She took a step toward me, advancing into the stream of boys and girls. A boy in a wrinkled white shirt and brown corduroys stumbled over her foot. Without taking her eyes off me, Mrs. Graham caught the boy with her right arm and stood him upright, gathering his books in against his chest. The boy continued on.

"You know, Peter," she said, "I've been thinking that it might be a good idea for you to practice your times tables."

"Oh?" I asked. I had had the hope that I had heard the last of the times tables, that all of us in Mrs. Graham's classroom had discharged our obligation to the times tables that day and would be going on to something else—drawing maps, perhaps, or carving swans from soap.

"Yes, I think you were just nervous today, but it would be a good idea for you to practice the times tables until you can rattle them off like that." She snapped her fingers. "Don't you think so?"

I clutched my camera tightly. I understood, if only vaguely, that she was giving me a chance to pretend that I knew the times tables, to avoid having any passing boy or girl realize that I didn't know something that I should have known. I was going to thank her and say to her simply, "Mrs. Graham, I don't know the times tables at all." But just as I was about to speak, Clarissa walked through the doorway. When I saw her, I blushed. When she saw me, she blushed and bent her head so that she was looking down at the white fur muff in which she held her hands. Mrs. Graham saw me blush and turned to find the cause.

"Oh, Clarissa," she said. "I was just telling Peter that I thought it might be a good idea for him to practice his times tables. Don't you think that would be a good idea?"

Without looking up, Clarissa said, "Yes, I guess it would." It seemed to me so beautiful a remark, spoken so liltingly, that it could have been made into a song.

"Maybe it would be a good idea for you and Peter to practice together for a while each day," said Mrs. Graham. "How would that be?"

I tried not to look at Mrs. Graham, but I couldn't help it. I was awestruck. How could she understand everything so well? How could she make things turn out so well? The woman was uncanny.

"I think that would be fine," said Clarissa. She raised her head and looked into my eyes.

"I think it would be great!" I said.

7

WHEN I GOT HOME I spent an hour sitting at the kitchen table talking to my mother about everything that had happened. My glass of milk and the cruller my mother had given me—a kind of which I was passionately fond, a thin fried cruller made of a yeasty dough twisted into the shape of a large pretzel and glazed, thickly, with sugar paste—lay untouched on the table while I went on and on. I hadn't intended to mention the times tables at all, but when I got to the end of the day and remembered Mrs. Graham's idea that Clarissa and I "practice" together, it suddenly occurred to me that I didn't want Clarissa to see me fumbling through the times tables. I had to learn them before we began practicing them, so that I could pretend to learn them quickly with Clarissa's help.

"I have to learn the times tables right away." I said. "All the other kids know them already, and I don't. I don't even know what they are, except that they're arithmetic."

"Well, I guess your father and I could teach them to you," said my mother, with little enthusiasm.

"You know," I said, picking up my cruller and using it to emphasize the good sense of what I was going to say, "Mr. Beaker could probably help me out."

"Oh, yes!" said my mother, brightening. "That's just the right idea! I'll give him a call right now." On her way to the phone, she gave me a hug and said, "You're a good boy, Peter."

8

I HAD FIGURED that if anyone could teach me the times tables quickly, it was Mr. Beaker. I was right. Mr. Beaker instituted a crash program in the times tables that very evening. He and Eliza drove up in a gleaming new Starliner, which Mr. Beaker had bought for Eliza's birthday. Eliza took all of us for a ride, and then we walked around and around the car until there was no longer enough light for us to see well.

"It's getting pretty dark," said my father, "we might as well go in. How about a beer, Dudley?"

Mr. Beaker and Eliza and my father and I went inside, but my mother stayed outside, sitting at the wheel of the car, humming a tune. Finally, my father opened the back door and called out to her, "Ella, come on inside now. Come on in and have a beer."

She didn't answer him, and he stood in the doorway for a while without saying anything else. Then we heard the car door close, and my mother's footsteps on the driveway, and then my father moved to one side and my mother came into the kitchen. She was smiling, almost laughing, acting bubbly and girlish. She seemed to me to have gone nuts out there, sitting in the car in the driveway. She hugged my father and rumpled my hair.

"Well," said Mr. Beaker with a let's-get-down-to-business air, "I've come to the conclusion that Peter can learn all he needs to know of the times tables in six days." He spread a chart out on the kitchen table. We all stood around the table, looking down at the chart. "You see, it is really only necessary for a student at the start of the fourth grade to know the times tables for the numbers one through ten." He chuckled with pleasure at the clever and efficient way he had tackled the problem. "Of course, the one-times table is trivial, so we can count that as finished right off the bat!" He was having a wonderful time with this. He made a large check mark beside the number 1. My father reached into the refrigerator and took out a couple of beers. He opened them and handed one to Mr. Beaker. "Would you like a beer, Eliza?" he asked.

"Yes, thanks, Bert," said Eliza.

"How about you, Ella?" my father asked.

"Oh, not a beer," said my mother. She turned to Eliza and said, "Let's have something more fun than a beer." She turned back to my father. "Make us an Old Fashioned, Bert," she said. My father sighed and began working on a couple of Old Fashioneds.

"Well," said Mr. Beaker, "The two- and ten-times tables are very easy, so we'll start with those. Peter should be able to master those tonight—"

He paused and looked at me.

"—if he can keep his mind on the task at hand. I'll have more to say about that later. Now the four- and five-times tables are really just versions of two and ten, so we'll take care of those tomorrow night. On Wednesday evening we'll do three and six. On Thursday we'll do seven, which is a real rogue."

He stopped to chuckle and to take a sip of his beer. My father set the Old Fashioneds in front of my mother and Eliza.

"On Friday, we'll do eight, which will be almost like a vacation. And then on Saturday we'll do nine, which is probably the toughest of them. On Sunday, we'll review them all."

Mr. Beaker stretched, as if the work were over. For him, it nearly was.

"*Voila!*" he said. "Next week, Peter will go in there knowing the times tables as well as any of them."

We were all pleased. I felt a new confidence. I was grateful for Mr. Beaker's help. Then he said, "Now, Peter, let's go to your room."

Puzzled, I followed him to my room, where I sat on the edge of the bed and he stood in front of me. He handed me a piece of paper on which he had printed the two- and ten-times tables. "Peter," he said, resting a hand on my shoulder, "if you're going to learn these by next week, you're going to have to focus your attention on the times tables and nothing else. Do you understand what I mean?"

"Yes," I said.

"We have to be *sure* that you're going to focus your attention on the times tables and nothing else, do you understand?"

"No," I said.

"Peter, you're going to have to stay in your room until you have memorized these times tables and can answer any questions about them like that." He snapped his fingers.

"What about supper?" I asked.

"Your mother will give you a plate in here," he said.

9

IN ONE MISERABLE WEEK, I did learn to answer questions about the times tables more quickly than Mr. Beaker could snap his fingers. I also learned to snap my fingers, and I learned that the pattern on the wallpaper in my room repeated every eleven inches and that the meals my mother made lost all their restorative power when they were handed through my door on a tray, the puddle of gravy around my potatoes already dark and rubbery at the edges. However, I didn't really learn the times tables very well at all. I memorized them as I might have memorized lines for a performance, and it worked pretty well. I was able to satisfy Mr. Beaker, impress Clarissa during our "practice" sessions, and please Mrs. Graham. But as soon as I had put on my performance, the lines began to slip away from me. Later, when I needed to know one of the products that had, while my mind was occupied with something else, crept into the dark unknown, never to return, I would reconstruct it from one of the ones that remained or count it out on my fingers, at least in my mind.

10

THE TIMES-TABLES BUSINESS left me skittish, afraid each day that something else was going to come up in Mrs. Graham's class that I wouldn't know, and that I'd have to put myself through another crash program. Whenever Mrs. Graham began a new lesson with the words "Now, class," I would reach for my camera and start chewing on my lower lip and praying that she wouldn't want us to learn anything I didn't already know. Mrs. Graham could see that I was anxious about something, and she became convinced that I was having trouble making friends among the fourth-graders.

She called me to her desk one day while the rest of the class was at work on a page of multiplication problems. I had finished early, but the work had required so much mental finger-counting that my head hurt.

"Peter," she said. "How would you like to have some fun and really get to know the boys and girls in the fourth grade at the same time?"

Her cheeks glowed. She was so excited by whatever she was leading up to that I immediately became excited and eager myself.

"You bet," I said.

"Well, each year the fourth grade puts on a production of *King Lear,* and this year I'm in charge. I thought that you might like to be the director," she began.

From the frozen smile on my face Mrs. Graham reasoned that I didn't know what on earth she was talking about.

"It's a play," she said. She examined my face for some sign that I was keeping up with her. She didn't find any, so she elaborated. "The boys and girls put on costumes and act it out on the stage in the auditorium." She examined my face again. "Have you ever seen a play?" she asked finally.

"No," I said, "but I know what you mean." I did have an idea of what she meant. After all, the annual production of *King Lear* was an event of long standing, and I had heard people talk about it. I had been an elf in a Christmas pageant, and I knew that a play was something along the same lines but longer and more elaborate. It wasn't ignorance that had frozen the smile on my face, it was a tiny thought that had taken root in my mind while she spoke. It was the thought that *King Lear* was going to turn out to be a lot like the times tables.

"I think that you should be the director!" she said. "It will be just wonderful. You'll get to know nearly all the other fourth-grade boys and girls that way."

"Gee," I said, "that would be great!" I meant it. It *would* be nice to get to know the other fourth-graders. "What should I do?" I asked.

"It won't be hard, Peter," said Mrs. Graham. She reached out to pat me on the shoulder, and her elbow struck the vase of flowers on her desk. I lunged toward it and caught the vase with one hand, just as it left the desk top on its way toward the floor. It was quite a feat, I thought. I hardly even spilled any water. When I set the vase back on the desk, I felt that I had in some measure repaid Mrs. Graham for the kindness she was doing me by putting me in a position to get to know the other fourth-graders. "Thank you, Peter," she said, so off-handedly that the vase might never have fallen. "I'll help you with all the work you'll have to do." She smiled at me, and a warm spot spread around my heart. She reached toward me again, and I reached for the vase at the same time, so that when her elbow struck it I already had a firm grip on it, and it barely moved. She patted me on the shoulder and said, "Everything is going to work out just fine."

11

I BEGAN MY WORK as director the very next day, full of enthusiasm but with no idea at all of what I was supposed to do. Mrs. Graham called me to her desk while the other students were working on some very tricky multiplication problems that she had written on the blackboard. I began to think that being a director was quite nice. Patiently and with a great deal of pleasure, she explained what my duties would be.

This became the pattern for the next couple of weeks. I would spend part of each day standing beside her desk, listening while she coached me in low, murmuring, conspiratorial tones, tones so low, so murmuring, and so conspiratorial that there were times when I couldn't figure out what she was saying. I didn't want to tell her that I couldn't hear her at those times, so I would just nod my head and hope that I wasn't missing anything really important.

She never told me directly what I should do. She *suggested*. I pretended to think the suggestion over and then agreed that it was exactly what should be done. I was as nervous throughout all of this as I have ever been about anything, but I was most nervous—most frightened—in the early days, and what I feared most was that when I actually began directing the fourth-graders I would do something so outrageously foolish, so third-grade, that it would ruin my chances of being accepted by them forever.

In those hours I spent standing beside her desk, Mrs. Graham and I developed a mutual understanding that was quite uncanny. I was soon able to anticipate her gestures so well that I could snatch a chair from in front of her before she barked her shin on it and move her vase out of harm's way whenever she swept her arm out to make a point. She took a protective attitude toward me, an attitude that she might have taken toward a timid and skittish kitten. I began bringing a chrysanthemum or two each day to add to the bunch of flowers in Mrs. Graham's vase. This turned out to be a continually changing bunch. Each day she added some fresh flowers and threw away a few of the oldest.

"Do you know why I keep these here on my desk?" she asked me on the day that I first brought her the chrysanthemums.

"Because they look pretty?" I suggested.

"Because they *smell* pretty," she said. She leaned toward me and spoke in her conspiratorial mumble. "This classroom stinks," she said.

I can recall the odor of the room, the odor of chalk dust, ordinary dust, the smell of wet wool that came from the coats and sweaters spread out to dry on the big steam radiators below the windows, the waxy smell of crayons left to melt on the radiators, and, quite prominently, the smell of those wonderful hard-salami sandwiches that Spike used to bring every day in a brown paper bag: thin slices of aromatic salami on spongy white bread with lots of butter. About midmorning, when the smell of Spike's sandwiches reached my desk, my stomach would begin to growl and my mouth would start to water. The memory alone is enough to make me want to break for lunch.

12

MRS. GRAHAM'S FIRST SUGGESTION was that I read *King Lear.* I did. The school used a simplified, abbreviated, optimistic adaptation called *The Story of King Lear and His Daughters,* published as part of a series called Classics Made Suitable for Boys and Girls. I read and reread the play, and I tortured my parents with recitations from it at the dinner table, at bedtime, first thing in the morning, and on any occasion that seemed to invite me to quote a line or two.

Mrs. Graham next suggested that I choose an assistant director. I think that what she had in mind was that I would choose a boy from the class, and that by working closely together we would become friends. But she could see from the speed and eagerness with which I said, "Clarissa Bud," how much I wanted to have her working with me, for during the time that we had spent together repeating the times tables we had grown quite close, and I was certain that Clarissa was not merely someone who made my heart ache but somebody I understood, someone I could trust.

13

I ALSO ENGAGED the help of Matthew Barber. Matthew wasn't enthusiastic at first. In fact, he was convinced that the production was going to be a farce.

"Peter," he said, "all of you are going to look like a bunch of idiots when this hits the boards."

"'Hits the boards'?" I asked.

"That's theater talk," he said. "You're not very familiar with the theater, are you?" he asked.

I thought of reminding him about my success as an elf, but from the way Matthew's mouth was twisted I could tell that it wouldn't go very far toward making him think that I was "familiar with the theater."

"No," I confessed.

He shook his head and let out a long sigh. "I'll never understand school," he muttered. "Look, Peter," he said, looking me in the face and putting his hands on my shoulders, "it's not going to be easy, you know. You can't just have a bunch of kids running around the stage like madmen and fools. This is a very complicated play."

"Oh," I said, "we're using a simple version, just for kids."

"I should have known," he said. "But that doesn't make any difference. It's complicated no matter how simple they make it.

This didn't make any sense to me, but I nodded my head gravely, as if I recognized that it would be impossible not to agree.

"You've got to create an atmosphere of gloom," said Matthew. "At the end, we've got to see that Lear has lost everything. You see? Did you read the play?"

"Oh, yeah!" I said. I was hurt that Matthew would think I hadn't.

"Well, don't you see what I'm talking about?"

"Well—"

"Worst of all," said Matthew, "he loses the illusion that his daughters loved him. Only when he's blind does he finally see the truth. Then he understands that Goneril and Regan think he's just a crazy old fool."

I nodded my head in the way that adults did when they meant to indicate by the nodding, "Too true, too true."

"There's no fool like an old fool," I offered. I had heard my parents say this from time to time, and considered it an example of the kind of painfully acquired wisdom that adults laid claim to.

Matthew looked at me incredulously. "'No fool like an old fool,'" he repeated. "Oh, God, this is going to be just horrible," he said. "All right, Peter. You really need my help. I'll do it."

"Great!" I said. "I knew you'd help me out, Matthew. We're going to have great fun with this, you'll see. Here."

I gave him a copy of *The Story of King Lear and His Daughters*. Matthew sneered at the book, but he did help me. In his heart of hearts, he must have been convinced that the play was doomed to failure, but part of him had decided to challenge fate on my behalf, to try with everything he had in him to make it a success for my sake. He had an apparently endless supply of ideas for staging the play, and yet he had no real enthusiasm for what he was doing. He would suggest things to me, or explain things to me, or listen tirelessly to my questions, all the time wearing a look that said, "We haven't got a chance in the world of pulling this off."

"The way I see the play is this," Matthew announced one day. "Lear is in the clam-processing business. He owns a big plant. He's worth a lot of money."

"Matthew—" I said.

"He knows he's going to die soon, so he wants his daughters to take over the family business."

"Matthew," I said, "we have to use these scripts."

"Oh, yeah," said Matthew, "we'll use those scripts, but we'll put the kids in costumes that make them look like people in the clam-processing business, and the scenery—"

His eyes lit up, and something almost like a smile formed on his lips.

"—the scenery will look like Babbington!"

"Matthew," I asked, "couldn't we just do it the regular way? Couldn't we just do it the way people usually do it, the way the book says to do it?"

Matthew gave me a look of profound disappointment. "Peter," he said, as if he were explaining something to a child, speaking as slowly and simply as he could, "you asked for my help, remember? This is our only chance to make something out of this. And it's my *big* chance. This is going to make me famous in the fourth grade." He paused and went right for my weak spot. "It might even make me happy."

"Matthew," I said, "I think this is going to get me into a lot of trouble."

14

CLARISSA took to her work with wholehearted determination, though she seemed to have no confidence in her abilities at all. Whenever I gave her a job to do, she would begin stroking her muff and looking at the floor. She'd tell me that it sounded much too hard for her, but that she knew how much I was counting on her, and so she'd try, so long as I'd agree not to be angry with her if she couldn't do the job the way it should be done. Then she would go off and do the job and come back for another, just as uncertain as ever. I was pleased to see that she had such pluck despite her fears, and I felt that working on the play was really doing something for Clarissa—she was getting to know lots of the kids in the fourth grade, for one thing. In no time at all, Clarissa had recruited a technical director, a property manager, a publicist, stagehands, a prompter, and so on.

She actually made an asset of her timidity, especially when she was recruiting someone for a job. One afternoon I watched her, clipboard in hand, walk up to a group of kids in the hall and say, her eyes wide, her voice quavering, "I need six stagehands, but you don't want to be stagehands, do you? Probably not. I don't blame you. I *do* need six stagehands, though, and I need them right away. I don't know why anybody would want to do it, really. There's no glory to the job. You'll have to work long hours, and you'll get dirty and sweaty. While the other kids are taking bows, you'll be backstage, out of sight. You'll stand there with the applause ringing in your ears and a lump in your throat, thumping one another on the back, and the only satisfaction you'll get is knowing that you've done something fine, really fine." She brought her muff up to her face and rubbed her eyes with it. Then she swallowed hard, stood up straight and said, "It's just not worth the trouble, I guess." She started to walk away, but the boys and girls quickly surrounded her, climbing over one another trying to sign up.

15

ALTHOUGH work on the play seemed to go along pretty well, I couldn't shake the conviction that *King Lear* was going to get me into some kind of trouble. I had the kind of indistinct foreboding that, on a sunny day, warns a clamdigger on Bolotomy Bay that a storm is approaching.

It was a gloriously sunny day, an unseasonably warm day for December, almost a balmy day, when Spike walked home from school with me.

"Hey, Peter! Peter!" she called. "Wait up!" When she reached me, she was a little out of breath. "It's such a nice day," she declared, flinging her arms toward the sky. "What do you say I walk you home?"

"I don't know," I said. Spike had never had much to say to me before, and I had had hopes that it might be possible for me to get through the entire fourth grade without coming within arm's reach of her.

"Come on," she said. "You and I can have a nice talk." It sounded like a command to me, so I followed her. She walked off, singing "The rain it raineth every day." When I caught up to her, she raised her arm and I thought she was going to knock me on the ear, but instead she flung her arm across my shoulder and gave me a friendly squeeze.

While we walked along, scraping our shoes on the sidewalk and chatting about this and that, I thought to myself, "Gee, this Spike is pretty nice. It just goes to show that you shouldn't judge people by reputation or appearance." I almost thought of sharing this observation with Spike, but when I tried putting it into words, it came out as, "You know, Spike, you're not the rat that everybody thinks you are," and so I decided to keep it to myself.

"Hey, Pete," said Spike, knocking me on the shoulder, "a penny for your thoughts."

"Huh?" I said.

"What're you thinking about so hard? I bet you haven't heard a word I said."

"Oh, uh, nothing," I said. "Just, uh, nothing."

"'Speak,'" she said, chewing her gum enthusiastically and giving me that big grin again.

"Nothing," I said.

"'Nothing?'" she said, widening the grin so that I could see the gum again and giving me a knock on the shoulder.

"Nothing," I said.

"Hey! That's great!" she said. "That was perfect. Maybe *you* ought to play Cordelia!"

"Huh?" I said. Then I realized what she was getting at. "Oh, I get it," I said. "Act I, Scene I. Yeah. Very good."

"Sure," she said. "I've been practicing. I think I'd be a pretty good Cordelia myself. What do you say?"

"Cordelia?" was what I said.

"Yeah," said Spike. She poked me in the stomach with her forefinger. "I'm going to try out for the part—and I sure hope I get it."

"I don't know—" I began, without knowing how I was going to finish.

"Hey, listen," she said suddenly. "I bet you haven't seen the real *King Lear,* have you?"

"Uh, no," I confessed. "Is it different?"

"The story's pretty much the same," she said. "Except it hasn't got such a happy ending." She pulled a battered blue-covered paperback book from her back pocket and looked around to see if she might get caught with it. "That part at the end where they all get together for dinner and everybody's happy again isn't in here at all." She gave me a big wink, tapped the book with her index finger, and said, "But there's a lot of other stuff in here that isn't in the other one."

"Oh, yeah?" I said.

"Yeah," she said. "Just listen to some of this." She flipped to a page with a folded-down corner. "Oswald says, 'What dost thou know me for?' And Kent answers, 'A knave, a rascal, an eater of broken meats—'"

"What's an eater of broken meats?" I asked.

Spike glared at me.

"Ohhhh!" I said. "Sure. Sure. I know." I gave her a knowing wink, although all I'd gathered from the look she gave me was that it must be another thing that a fourth-grader should know, like the times tables, and that it was probably something I shouldn't say in front of my parents.

"It gets better," she said. "'—lily-livered, action-taking, whoreson, glass-gazing, super-serviceable, cynical rogue—'"

"Wow," I said. I wanted to ask about a couple of items in that list, but instead I raised an eyebrow in the way I'd observed adults doing when they wanted to acknowledge something but didn't want to explain it to me.

Spike went on. "'—beggar, coward, pander, and the son and heir of a mongrel bitch—'"

"Hey—hey—uh—Spike," I said. "We're kind of close to my father's gas station. Maybe you should keep your voice down."

"Oh, sure," said Spike. She looked around. "Come here, come here," she said, backing into some bushes alongside the railroad tracks that ran beside my father's Esso station. "You've got to hear this one." She flipped to another page.

"The Fool says,

She that's a maid now, and laughs at my departure,
Shall not be a maid long, unless things be cut shorter.

At this Spike burst into a deep, rumbling laugh and gave me another knock on the shoulder. "You get it?" she asked.

"Oh, sure," I said. I started laughing uproariously. I screamed, "'Unless things be cut shorter!'" I had no notion in the world what might make it funny, but I exploded in another paroxysm of laughter, and tears began to run down my cheeks. I had to lean on Spike for support. "'Unless things be cut shorter!'" I howled again.

"Yeah, well, it *is* pretty funny," said Spike. She pushed me away from her and shoved the book into her back pocket again. She pushed her way out of the bushes and began walking off. I followed, repeating, "'Unless things be cut shorter,'" and chuckling.

"Hey, is this your father's gas station, right here?" Spike asked.

"Yeah," I said.

"You think your father would give us a Coke?" she asked.

"Sure!" I said.

We drank our Cokes and watched my father look for a leak in a tire. I sneaked a sidelong look at Spike and marveled at how badly I had misjudged her. I had expected, almost from my first day in Mrs. Graham's class, that Spike or one of the boys in her gang would want to beat me up sooner or later. Instead, here we were drinking Cokes and telling jokes, and she seemed to want to be pals.

By the time we got to my house, we had our arms thrown over each other's shoulders and were singing "The rain it raineth every day," like a couple of miniature drunks.

"You want to come in and have a cruller?" I asked her.

"Nah, I've got to get home." she said.

"Oh, okay," I said. I looked at her and hesitated, then finally decided to speak my mind. "You know, Spike," I said, "before I got to know you, I was afraid that you were going to beat me up or something." We both laughed. Spike looked at her shoes and scraped them back and forth on the sidewalk. "A lot of kids think you're some kind of monster," I added.

"She cannot be such a monster," muttered Spike.

"But you're not," I said. "You're nice. You've just got a bad reputation."

Spike looked up at me and shrugged. "I'm a kid more sinned against than sinning," she said.

"Well, I'll see you in school tomorrow," I said.

"Yeah," said Spike. She started down the walk. I started up the front steps. "Oh, hey," she called. "I almost forgot."

She walked back toward me, and I walked down the steps toward her. When we reached each other, she grabbed the front of my jacket in her fist and twisted it so that her knuckles dug into my chest. She put her face close to mine, so that she was looking right into my eyes, and when she spoke, her spit sprayed onto me.

"I really want to play Cordelia," she said. "And if I don't get the part, I'll break your foot with a brick."

16

THE SKY WAS QUITE DARK on the day that Veronica invited me to her house to play. It was a Saturday. Veronica called at noon. My mother drove me to her house and said that she would be back to pick me up before dinner. After I had taken my hat and coat and gloves off and said hello to Mrs. McCall, Veronica led me to the playroom in the basement.

"This is the playroom," she said.

"It's nice," I said.

The floor was covered with red and white squares of linoleum tile. A bar made of blond wood was at one end of the room, and a number of stools stood in front of it. A small pool table was in the center of the room, and to one side was a card table with four folding chairs set around it. We played Monopoly for a while, and then we worked on a picture puzzle. Veronica's mother brought us some milk and cookies and said that she had to go out to do some shopping. Veronica followed her upstairs. I drank my milk and ate a couple of the cookies. They were the kind with a small amount of peanut butter encased in a crunchy beige cookie, the two halves of which could be pried apart so that the peanut butter could be removed with the tip of the tongue. I heard the front door close, and I heard the car start and drive off. Veronica came back down the stairs. She closed the playroom door behind her and stood with her back against it and her hands behind her back. She tilted her head to one side.

"What shall we play now?" she asked, and she tossed her head just enough to make her hair swing.

"How about pool?" I suggested.

"How about Clothes Closet?" she suggested.

"Clothes Closet?" I said. "How do you play that?"

She walked across the room to a door and opened it. "First we go into this closet," she said.

I went into the closet. It was used to store toys and games and sports equipment and brooms and mops. There wasn't a lot of room. When Veronica came in and closed the door behind her, the two of us were squeezed pretty close together. It was very dark.

"Now what?" I asked.

"Now we take off our clothes," she said.

"Wow," I said. I started unbuttoning my shirt. A thought struck me. "What if your mother comes back?" I asked.

"Oh, don't worry—she won't," Veronica said. "You can't just take off your clothes all at once, you know. You have to follow the rules—"

"But what if your mother forgot something?" I asked.

"Don't worry," she said. "You have to take off what I say. Are you ready?"

"Well—"

"Take off your—shoes!" ordered Veronica.

"Veronica—"

"Are you taking off your shoes?"

"Well, yes, but—"

"Now you take off your sweater, and I'll take off my dress. Go!"

"I haven't got my shoes—"

"Hurry up, Peter. You have to keep up with me. Now I'll take off my undershirt, and you take off your shirt. Go!"

"Was that a car?"

"Hurry!"

"Yeah. I'm hurrying."

"Now you take off your pants, and I'll take off my socks. Go!"

"Maybe we should start putting our things back on, Veronica. I—"

"Oh, don't worry so much, Peter. Have you got your pants off?"

"Yes, but—"

"Good. Now what have you got left on?"

"Socks and underpants," I said. "Maybe we should start putting—"

"I only have underpants on, so you should take your socks off."

"Why don't we save this game for—"

"Peter, a lot of boys have asked me to play Clothes Closet with them, you know."

"Yeah, I guess—"

"Take your socks off."

"I am."

"Good. Now we'll take our underpants off," she whispered. "Ready?"

"Well—" I said.

"I'm taking mine off," she said. "Are you taking yours off?"

From the way she was wiggling around, I could tell that she really was taking her underpants off, and it seemed to me that it wouldn't be fair not to do as she was doing, so I said yes and pulled mine off, too.

"Do you have everything off?" she asked.

"Yes," I said.

"Here," she said. "Give me your hand."

When she groped for my hand, she touched my belly. I swallowed and reached toward her.

"Honey!" called a voice from upstairs. "I'm home!"

"It's my father!" said Veronica.

"Oh, no," I said. I began grabbing wildly for my clothes.

"Don't worry," she said. "He won't come down right away. He never does."

"Oh, what are we going to do?" I whined. "What are we going to do? What's this? Is this my shirt? This is your dress. Oh, if your father catches us like this—"

"Don't get all upset," Veronica said. There was an edge to her voice, but many years passed before I realized that the tense and breathless quality was caused not by alarm but by excitement, that part of the thrill of Clothes Closet for Veronica—perhaps all of the thrill, come to think of it—came from flirting with the danger of being caught by her father, of having him fling open the closet door, gasp, grab the nasty little boy with one hand and Veronica with the other, throw the boy out the front door, drag Veronica to her bedroom, throw her over his knees and spank her bare bottom.

"Oh, these aren't my socks," I wailed. "Here! They're yours. They don't fit me."

"Peter, the best thing to do is to stop for a minute and take a deep breath, calm down, and then just get dressed the way you do in the morning."

"In the morning, I'm not in a closet with you!" I said.

"Hello-wo!" called Mr. McCall again. "Where's my little honey-bunch?"

"He's going to come down in a minute," said Veronica. "Are you ready?"

"Yeah," I said. "I'm ready."

When Mr. McCall opened the door to the playroom an instant later, he found Veronica taking aim at the four ball while I stood holding a cue and praying silently that he wouldn't notice that my shirttail was out and my sweater was on backwards.

"*There* you are!" said Mr. McCall. "Didn't you hear me calling?"

"Oh, sorry, Daddy," said Veronica. "I was teaching Peter how to play—pool. I guess we didn't hear you."

17

WHEN MY MOTHER came to pick me up, she was excited and talkative. She had been shopping for Christmas, and among other things she had bought me a new outfit to wear during the holidays: new pants, shirt, socks, and sweater. She insisted that I try everything on as soon as we got home. She followed me upstairs to my bedroom in the attic, talking happily about how cute I was going to look and how much fun Christmas would be. I hung my coat up and took my sweater and shirt off while she spread the new things out on the bed. I unbuckled my belt and started to unzip my fly. The zipper stuck, and I glanced down at it. I could see, jammed in it, a bit of cloth, a bit of pink cloth. My hands grew cold at the fingertips. Goose bumps spread across my back. I pulled the waistband of my pants out enough so that I could see inside. I was wearing Veronica's underpants.

"What's the matter, Peter?" asked my mother.

"Uhhhhh," I said. My mind was entirely occupied by terror; there was no room for thought. "Uhhhhh," was all I could say.

"Do you feel all right?" she asked. "You look pale." I'm quite sure I did. "Maybe you should go to bed early tonight. You don't want to get a cold now, with Christmas coming."

"Uhhhhh," I said.

"What on earth is wrong?" she asked, wrinkling her brow. Then she started, as if surprised by something. Her mouth fell open a little, and she smiled a smile that was equal parts girlish and motherly. "Oh, I know what's wrong," she said.

"You do?" I asked, smiling, scared to death.

She chucked me under the chin. "I knew it would happen someday," she said.

"You did?"

"Of course," she said, slowly and tenderly. "The day had to come when you'd be embarrassed to get undressed in front of me. That's it, isn't it?"

"Yes," I said, "that's it." I was surprised to find that in fact that was exactly it.

18

IN THE MORNING, Veronica called. "Peter," she said, giggling, "I think you have something of mine."

"Yes," I said. "I do. They're in my sock drawer. Do you have mine?"

"Yes," she said. "I'm wearing them."

"What!" I exclaimed. In a hoarse and trembling whisper, I went on: "Veronica, are you crazy? What if somebody sees them?"

"Who's going to see them?" she asked. Then there passed a period of silence. It was a significant pause, and its significance was not lost on me. Veronica said, very softly, "—unless I show them to somebody."

"Look," I said, quickly, "we can switch them in school on Monday."

"You know, Peter," said Veronica, "I really want to play Cordelia."

"You do?" I asked.

"Oh, yes," she said. "I really do."

"Well—"

"I wonder what your mother would do if she knew that I was wearing your underwear?" Veronica whispered.

"Me too," I said.

"I'll see you in school, Peter," said Veronica. In her huskiest voice, she added, "I can't wait to find out who gets to play Cordelia."

"Me too," I said.

19

MANY, MANY of my fourth-grade classmates had signed up to try out for parts, and I was going to have to choose among them. When I announced which ones I had chosen, I might make a few friends, but I was likely to make lots of enemies.

The auditions were held on a Friday. I didn't sleep well the night before, and I didn't have much appetite at breakfast. My uneasiness had no real focus; it was like the feeling that some people have about ocean bathing: they know that there are nasty creatures under the water somewhere; they don't know which ones might get them, so they're afraid of all of them. I got to school by stealing from cover to cover, slinking along behind hedges, ducking behind parked cars, dashing from telephone pole to telephone pole. As soon as I reached the school, I ran up the stairs and along the hall. When I got to the door to Mrs. Graham's room, I heard my name, so I stopped outside to catch my breath and listen to what was being said about me.

Clarissa was speaking. "I'm sure Peter's going to have a hard time choosing someone to play Cordelia," she said. "It's such an important part. I think Cordelia's even more important than King Lear. It scares me just to think of playing her, doesn't it scare you?"

"Oh, no," said Veronica. "My mother told me that she was sure I would do a wonderful job as Cordelia."

"Oh, how I wish I had your self-confidence," said Clarissa. "Every time I think of playing Cordelia I shiver. I'm glad I'm working behind the scenes. I'd be scared to death if I had to play one of the big roles. I just don't think that I could do a good enough job, do you?"

Veronica spoke again, but she spoke as if she had stopped listening to Clarissa. She said, "My mother played Cordelia once, and she said she was just wonderful. She told me, 'Veronica, you go after the part of Cordelia and if you don't get Cordelia, you just forget the whole thing. The other two daughters are real snots and everybody will hate you if you play one of them.'"

Clarissa said, "I think Cordelia is just wonderful, don't you? She's kind and shy and quiet. Whenever I think of playing the part I get goose bumps all over my arms. I'm sure I could never do it. It's just such an important role. It would be too much for me."

Spike spoke, but she too seemed not to be listening to Clarissa; she was responding to Veronica. "My mother said pretty much the same thing, but not in words that I can repeat, so I figure that I better get that part. I wish Peter would get here. I want to—um—talk it over with him." She snickered and cracked her knuckles.

"Oh," said Clarissa, "I'm sure that Peter wouldn't be influenced by—"

Veronica spoke right over her. "That's not going to work, Spike," she said. "My mother has always told me that the boys buzz around the honey, if you know what I mean."

"Gosh," breathed Clarissa. In a small, hesitant, distracted voice, she asked, "Do you think that Peter would be influenced by—"

I'd heard enough. In a cold sweat, I turned and started to tiptoe down the hall. I felt a powerful hand on my shoulder, and Spike shouted, "Hey Peter! There you are! How come you're tiptoeing down the hall like that?" She turned me around to face her and looked at me with something like concern. She slowed her gum-chewing and stared into my eyes. "You're not sick or anything are you?"

"Uh, no," I said.

"Hey, that's great!" said Spike. She turned to one of her pals: Studs or Chuck or Knuckles or whatever his name was. "Isn't that great?" Spike asked him.

"Yeah," said, let's say, Studs.

"I wouldn't want you to be too sick to pick the kid who's gonna play Cordelia," she said, chewing her gum with a big wide-open smile that allowed me to see not only the wad of gum but all her teeth, her tongue, and her uvula. "You get me?" she asked, and she nodded upward, pointing her chin at me.

20

BY LUNCH TIME I was a nervous wreck. The entire fourth grade was abuzz about the auditions. It seemed to me that everybody wanted one part or another. Even one of the boys who had already taken a job as a stagehand buttonholed me to explain that he was sure he could play Edmund the Bastard and still work the curtain if I could just rewrite the script so that Edmund didn't have to be onstage at the opening of acts I, II, or V. I told him I'd have to think about it and dashed off to the boys' room.

When I got back to the cafeteria, the place was empty. I dropped my uneaten lunch into the trash can and started for the door, thinking that if I could just get to the nurse's office unseen I might be able to get her to send me home right away. Mrs. Graham was standing at the door.

"Oh, there you are Peter," she said. "It's just about time for the auditions. Isn't this exciting? I've never seen such excitement over one of these productions. You're a born leader, do you know that?" She stopped and looked at me for a moment. "Are you all right?" she asked.

"I'm not sure," I said.

"Are you going to faint?" she asked.

"Maybe," I said. "I'm not sure. I've never fainted before."

She made me sit down and put my head between my legs. She held her hand on my forehead for a while, and then she got a paper napkin and wet it with cold water and held it to my forehead. "How do you feel now?" she asked.

"I feel better," I said, "except for my stomach."

"Did you eat lunch?" she asked.

"I didn't feel like eating," I said.

She made me drink a container of milk, and that made my stomach feel better. "Okay, Peter," she said. "It's time. Don't worry. This is going to be great fun."

21

MRS. GRAHAM and I walked down the hall together. The line of boys and girls waiting for the auditions stretched from the auditorium doors down the hall nearly all the way to the cafeteria. As we walked past, I tried not to look anyone in the eye.

We passed Veronica. She was wearing the sort of thing that she usually wore, one of those clingy knit dresses, but she had added a wide black patent leather belt, she had a sheer red scarf knotted around her neck, and she had drawn a beauty spot on her cheek with a pen. She stood with her back against the wall and her head tilted to the left. Her right shoulder was raised, her left shoulder dropped. Her eyes were half shut, and her mouth was half open. "Hello, Peter," was all she said, but it was enough to make my face turn red and my knees grow weak.

Spike was right at the front of the line, waiting at the auditorium doors. She was passing the time playing jacks. She was down on the floor, scooping up jacks with remarkable dexterity, apparently immune to the tension that filled the hall. Behind her were Biff, Studs, Chuck, and Knuckles. When I reached her, Spike snatched up the jacks, stood up, and called out, "Okay! Here's Peter! Now we'll find out 'who loses and who wins; who's in, who's out—'" She stood there grinning at me, waiting for me to acknowledge that I recognized the line. I smiled weakly and nodded my head. She flung the door open for me, and I saw Clarissa standing just inside the auditorium, holding a clipboard.

"Peter!" she said. "Where have you been? We've got to get started! We're running about ten minutes behind schedule."

My legs were wobbly, and I felt a little sick. Mrs. Graham must have noticed that I was shaky: she grabbed me under the left armpit and lifted me so that my left foot was hardly touching the floor. Clarissa reached out for me, and together, one holding me up on either side, she and Mrs. Graham dragged me into the auditorium, letting the door swing shut behind us.

They led me to a seat in the front row. I sat there, staring at the empty stage. It took a while before I realized that Clarissa was talking to me.

"—and—before the rest of the boys and girls come in—I—well—" she said.

Clarissa stood silently for a moment, her hands moving nervously inside her fur muff, her head down. When she raised her head and looked me in the face, her eyes were as wide and startled as they had been when we first met. She parted her lips ever so slightly, as if she were going to speak, but then she closed them, swallowed, and looked downward. When she spoke at last, she spoke to the floor.

"Do you think it would be all right if I tried out for Cordelia?" she asked. "I know I won't be good enough, but I'd like to try. I'm usually shy in front of people, and it might help me to try out for a part in the play."

"Gee, Clarissa," I said, "I—"

"Of course, I haven't had a lot of time to practice, you know," she said quickly. "I've had other things to do."

"Oh, yes," I said. "I'm sure—"

"I'm just going to try for the fun of it," she said. "I don't even want you to pay any attention to me. Promise?"

"All right," I said.

"I could never really play Cordelia," she said. "I shiver just thinking about it, so you don't have to worry about me." She took a deep breath and giggled, and then she dashed over to the doors and swung them open. At once, she was back in the role of director's assistant, keeping a tight hold on her clipboard and her muff and meekly asking the boys and girls to file in silently and fill alternate rows and alternate seats.

"Look at them," Matthew said, taking a seat beside me. "Some of these kids would do anything for a part—anything."

I sat, stunned, while the auditions began. Clarissa asked for silence in a small voice that I wouldn't have thought anyone could hear. The auditorium hushed at once. She looked at her clipboard and said, softly, "Bobby Swanson, please."

Bobby Swanson walked onto the stage, struck a histrionic pose in front of me, making his eyes bulge out and pulling at his hair, and cried, "'Doesn't anybody here know me?'" He looked quite mad. He beat his chest and bellowed, "'This is not Lear!'"

"You're telling me," muttered Matthew.

"Okay, Bobby," said Clarissa. "That was very interesting—especially the way you made your eyes bulge out."

"Don't you want me to do some more?" asked Bobby.

"Oh, no," said Clarissa. "That's enough, I think. It was—uh—very interesting the way you made your eyes bulge out. Thank you, Bobby. Let's see Biff Parker next."

Biff jumped up, ran to the stage, and began auditioning for the part of Lear, too.

"'O, let me be not mad, not mad, sweet heaven!'" he bellowed, tearing

at his hair and stumbling around the stage. He lurched downstage toward
me and delivered the next line right in my face: "'Keep me in temper; I
would not be mad!'"

"Never, never, never, never, never," muttered Matthew.

Clarissa walked to the edge of the stage, took Biff by the arm, and led
him to the stairs at the side. "You have wonderful enthusiasm, Biff," she
said. Biff left the stage a happy boy.

I sank into my seat and avoided looking at the stage from then on.
Clarissa found something nice to say about everyone, but Matthew's
comments on the performances grew more bitter as the auditions pro-
gressed. He exercised his most cutting sarcasm on anyone who tried out
for the part of Lear. As the afternoon went on, Matthew's gestures and
his bitter laugh grew wilder and wilder, his hair flew out in all directions,
his shirt came out of his pants. He seemed to be going nuts.

I occupied myself with writing furiously on a pad that Clarissa had put
onto a clipboard for me, keeping my head down and maintaining, I hoped,
the appearance of an intense concentration that should not be interrupted,
while in fact I was just writing a description of my camera. Nearly everyone in the fourth grade must have tried out for at least one part, and Wilbur Carpenter, whose mother showed up to watch the auditions, tried out
for six, including Kent, the Fool, Edmund the Bastard, and all three
daughters. I had come to think of the auditions as an endless torture. I
didn't realize that they were over until Matthew shook me.

"Peter! Peter!" he said. "Everyone's waiting to hear who you picked!"

I looked at him beseechingly, and thought of begging for more time,
but Clarissa was on the stage and already beginning to speak in her tiny
voice. "Peter is going to announce his choices for the various parts," she
said.

I stood and made my way to the stage. I faced the audience.

"Well—" I said.

I looked at my notes.

"Well—" I said, again. I just stood there for a while, hoping that we
might have a fire drill.

"Well what?" Biff called out.

"Well—ahhhhhh—well done!" I said.

I looked at my clipboard and flipped through the pages. I said, "Um—
you know—ah—while I was watching the auditions—I—uh—couldn't
help thinking that—that watching people try out for parts is—um—a lot
like taking a roll of snapshots.

"You really can't be sure which of your snapshots is the best one on the roll until you get the film back from the camera shop, isn't that true?" Since they were disposed to agree with anything I said, there was a lot of enthusiasm for this idea. I thought of saying a few words about the intriguing X-ray machine down at the Buster Brown store, which let you see a picture of the bones in your feet right through your shoes, but I couldn't come up with a way to tie it in, so I let it go, with some reluctance.

"What I've decided to do," I said, pointing to my head, "is take this roll of film home and spend the weekend developing it to see which snapshots are the best." There were a lot of puzzled looks at this. "In other words," I said, speaking rapidly and starting for the stairs at the side of the stage, "I'll go through the notes I took on your auditions and think about them very carefully and then announce my choices next week." I began moving down the aisle as quickly as I could without actually running. I waved my clipboard at the crowd and said "Thanks for coming, everybody." I let myself out the door, and then I did start running.

Mrs. Graham burst through the doors and called out to me. "Peter! Peter!" she called, in that voice full of pleasure and excitement that was beginning to send chills down my spine. "Oh, don't run off, Peter, don't run off. Come here to me."

I stopped running and turned toward her.

"Oh, Peter, Peter," she said. "Isn't this exciting?"

"Oh, yeah," I said.

"I noticed that you were taking lots of notes," said Mrs. Graham. "Why don't we look through those together?"

"Uh—well," I said, squirming.

"Oh, you're right," she said. "We don't have much time. Here: I made a list of everyone who auditioned. I'll just read through my notes with you quickly."

The bell rang, so Mrs. Graham had no time to read through her notes with me. She gathered her things quickly and followed me outside. She fumbled in her briefcase, spilling homework papers onto the driveway, and found the notes she had taken. She gave the notes to me, and I started off for home as quickly as I could. When I looked back over my shoulder to see if anyone was following me, I saw Mrs. Graham and several boys and girls running around gathering up the homework papers.

22

I WALKED HOME QUICKLY, through back yards and along lightly
traveled streets. The sky was dark, and the wind had begun to rise. If it
had been a summer afternoon, I would have said that the rumble in the
distance was thunder. When I got home, I dashed inside and went directly to my room, where I sat on my bed holding my camera and wondering
what to do.

I heard the phone ring downstairs, but I made no move to answer it. I
didn't want to speak to Spike or Veronica or anyone else who was after a
part. My mother came to the foot of the stairs and called up to me. "It's
for you, Peter," she said.

"It's not Spike, is it?" I asked.

"Noooo," she said.

"It's not Veronica, is it?" I asked.

"Noooo," she said. She was wearing a playful smile. "It's Clarissa
Bud. She seems very eager to talk to you."

"Oh," I said, relieved. "Clarissa." I went to the hall and picked up the
phone. "Hello," I said.

"Oh, hello, Mr. Leroy," said Clarissa. "I wanted to speak to Peter."

"This is Peter," I said.

"My goodness!" said Clarissa. "I didn't recognize your voice. You
sound so grown-up on the phone. Say something else."

"Uh—what should I say?"

"That's amazing!" she declared. "You sound so strong and firm. Of
course, that's the way you sounded this afternoon, when you were on the
stage. I was really impressed. I think everybody else was, too."

"Really?" I asked.

"Oh, yes," she said. She delivered the words with lots of air, making
herself sound out of breath, as if she'd been running. "Well—how have
you been?"

"I'm still okay," I said.

"What do you mean, you're still okay?" she asked.

"Huh?" I said. I felt as if I'd heard her for the first time. I realized that
I'd been preoccupied with the idea of Spike's breaking my foot with a
brick or Veronica's showing up at the back door with my underpants in
her hand. "Oh," I said. "I—I mean nothing happened to me on the way
home from school or anything."

"Oh, that's good," Clarissa said. She sounded bewildered. Then she took a deep breath, and with even more air than before she said, "I wouldn't want anything to happen to you. I've missed you."

"You've missed me?" I asked. "You mean since three o'clock?"

"I feel as if I haven't seen you for days," she said. "I miss your smile. You have that cute little dimple."

"I do?" I said. I tried to drag the phone over to the hall mirror.

"Oh, yes!" she said. "In fact, you have one-and-a-half dimples. One on the right side, and a half on the left."

"Is that bad?" I asked.

"Oh, no," she said. "I think it's cute."

"Hold on a minute, Clarissa," I said. "I want to go look in the mirror."

I started to put the handset down, but I heard her calling to me. "Peter, wait. Don't go away. I want to invite you to dinner."

"Dinner?" I asked, and I brightened at once.

"Tomorrow night," said Clarissa. "I hope you're not doing anything then."

"Oh, no," I said. "I'm not doing anything."

23

WHEN MY MOTHER AND FATHER and I sat down that night to eat our own dinner, I told them about Clarissa's invitation. My mother was enchanted. She acquired a rosy glow, and she hugged me several times when she had gotten up to serve a dish or clear the table. My father made several remarks that made him chuckle and made my mother giggle and blush and say, "Oh, stop it, Bert."

While my mother and I were doing the dishes, I said, as casually as I could manage, "Do you think I should wear a suit?"

My mother stopped working at once. "Of course!" she said. "Of course you should wear a suit! Oh, how cute you'll look!"

We went into the living room and proposed the idea of my getting a suit to my father, who was sitting in his favorite chair drinking a beer and watching television. He thought, and said, that getting a suit just to go to dinner at a girl's house, no matter how pretty she was, was going too far. My mother suggested a sports jacket. My father said that I would probably never wear such a thing again for months, and the next time I had a use for it, I would have outgrown it.

"Why can't he wear the things you just got him?" my father asked.

"All right, but how about a necktie?" my mother asked. "Come on, Bert," she said, when he hesitated.

"Sure," said my father, grinning. "I'll lend him a necktie."

The next evening, there was lots of excitement over polishing my shoes, putting on my new corduroys and shirt and sweater, and tying my tie. My mother was teary-eyed when I was ready to go, and I wondered if there was something wrong with my outfit. My father drove me to Clarissa's house.

Riding in the car, going off to dinner at a girl's house, I felt for a short time like a young sophisticate. The feeling began to fade when my father said, as I got out of the car, "Now, be polite, Peter," and it vanished completely as soon as Mr. Bud opened the door.

"Well!" he said. "You must be Peter!"

"Yes," I said. We shook hands. I hoped that he didn't notice that my hand was trembling.

"You look as if you're ready for Christmas!" he said. Then he added "Ho-ho-ho!"

There was a mirror in their hall. As Mr. Bud and I walked past it, I took a look at myself. For the first time, I realized that except for my white shirt and brown shoes I was dressed entirely in red and green.

Mr. Bud led me into the living room, where Clarissa and her mother were waiting. Clarissa's father was a genius of sorts, a restless genius whose innovative ideas for making useful and profitable products from garbage had landed him a spot at Bivalve By-products. It was he who suggested the "Clampact" that was to become so popular: a pair of empty clamshells, gilded, rejoined by a metal hinge, a mirror glued inside one valve, the other filled with face powder. The Buds' house was larger than ours, and much fuller. Wherever it was possible to have an end table, an occasional chair, a picture, or a piece of ceramic statuary, there was one.

Clarissa and her mother were sitting on the sofa, wearing identical dresses. Clarissa's mother was wearing stockings, but Clarissa was wearing anklets with her girl-size high-heeled shoes. All of this—Mr. Bud's manner, his position at Bivalve By-products, the house, the decorating scheme, the matching dresses—made me feel completely out of my league.

Clarissa's father asked me what I would like to drink. Everything seemed so urbane that I thought he was actually asking me what kind of cocktail I would like. "Oh, nothing for me, thank you," I said, not so much because I thought that I shouldn't drink a cocktail, but because I was trying to be polite, and I knew that one of the rules of polite behavior was to refuse everything the first time it was offered. He asked Clarissa what she would like. She looked as if she were considering a long list of drinks and then finally said, "I'll have a Shirley Temple."

"All right," said her father. "Sure you wouldn't like something, Peter?"

"You know," I said, thrusting my hands into my pockets, "I guess I could use a Shirley Temple."

Mr. Bud chuckled at this, and I chuckled back, as if I had intended the remark to be funny, but I hadn't, and I felt like a fool. I tried mightily from then on to show Mr. and Mrs. Bud that I was quite grown-up for my age. I attempted some grown-up talk, drawing on what I heard from my parents. I tried several topics. The first was business.

"How's the by-product business, Mr. Bud?" I asked, rocking on my heels and taking a swig of my Shirley Temple.

Mr. Bud raised an eyebrow, glanced at Mrs. Bud, and grinned. "Not bad, Peter," he said. "How's school?"

Next I tried local politics.

"Do you think there's a chance that the mayor will come to his senses sometime soon?" I asked, as my father did when he was reading the paper.

Mr. Bud looked startled. "What on earth do you mean?" he asked.

At dinner, I praised Mrs. Bud's cooking. "Yessir," I concluded, quoting from a Western I'd seen, "this is the best meal I've had in weeks." This seemed to be pretty well received, so I pushed on, figuring to make the most of the one topic that seemed to be a success. There wasn't anything else that I could take from the Western, so I borrowed my mother's highest praise for someone else's cooking. "You must give me the recipe for these mashed potatoes," I said. This brought down the house, and Mr. Bud said, "You're a regular comedian, Peter."

So I attempted to tell a joke. I began while Mrs. Bud and Clarissa were clearing away the dinner plates and serving dessert. As soon as I had introduced the main characters, three rabbits called Phhht, Phhht-Phhht, and Phhht-Phhht-Phhht, just at the moment when I had succeeded in capturing everyone's attention, I realized that I had forgotten the punch line. While we ate our dessert, I stretched the joke out with details of the home life of these rabbits, their forebears, the rabbit village where they lived, their hobbies and favorite meals, and the mysterious illness that led to the death of the youngest of them, Phhht, and then struck the middle one, Phhht-Phhht, while my mind raced ahead to try to recover the end of the story.

Mr. Bud finally said, "Peter, maybe you and Clarissa would like to be excused."

"Sure," I said. "I'll finish the joke for you later."

Clarissa and I went into the living room and sat on the sofa. I felt that I had made an ass of myself, and when I heard laughter come from the dining room I was sure of it. To my surprise, Clarissa didn't seem to think so at all. She slid over beside me on the sofa and linked her arm with mine.

"That was a wonderful story," she said. "It's amazing how relaxed you are. I would think it must be hard for you to be in the position you're in, having to pick the boys and girls to play the parts," she said.

"It is," I said. "It really is. In fact—"

"Yes," she said with a sigh, "it must be terribly hard. I think that I'd just want to crawl into a hole and hide if I had to say to someone I knew, someone I liked, 'Sorry, but I gave the part to someone else.'"

"Yeah," I said.

"I sure know I'd hate to hear it. It makes me wish I hadn't tried out for the part of Cordelia," she said.

"I thought you just did it for fun," I said.

"Oh, yes," she said. I felt her shudder, and she reached across me to take her muff from the end table. "But I don't even know why I bothered," she said. "I know I wasn't as good as the others."

"Oh, don't say that," I said. "You were great."

"Do you really think so?"

"Oh, yes."

"But you probably want somebody prettier."

"Oh no, not necessarily," I said, too quickly. "Uh, that's not what I mean," I added.

"I'll bet you'd like to have Veronica McCall play Cordelia," she said.

"Veronica McCall?" I said. "Well, I have to think about everybody who tried out, you know. I have to be fair. I have to think about Veronica, and I have to think about Spike O'Grady."

"Spike O'Grady?" said Clarissa.

"Of course," I said. "She tried out, too."

"Well, I guess you do have to give everybody a fair chance," she said. Then, after a long pause, she said, "Well, I've made up my mind!" After another long pause and a deep breath, she announced, "I'd like to drop out of the competition for Cordelia."

"Drop out?" I said. "But I thought you weren't even—"

"Yes," she said, with a sigh. "That would make your job easier, wouldn't it?"

"Well, yes—" I began. She turned from me suddenly and buried her face in her muff. I heard something that sounded like a sob, a muffled sob. "Clarissa?" I said.

There was a pause. Clarissa pulled a tissue from her muff and blew her nose. "Yes," she said, in the smallest of voices.

"Did I hear you crying?" I asked.

"Oh, no, no," she said, still facing away from me. "Don't worry about me." She made a small choking sound.

"Maybe you're getting a cold," I suggested.

"Maybe," she blubbered.

"Peter!" called Mr. Bud. "Your father's here!"

About halfway home, I remembered the end of the joke. Phhht is dead, and Phhht-Phhht is gravely ill. In a voice cracking with emotion, Phhht-Phhht-Phhht says to the doctor who is examining Phhht-Phhht, "Oh, doctor, you *have* to save him—I already have one Phhht in the grave."

24

I WOKE EARLY on Sunday morning and sat upright in my bed thinking the situation over. My two biggest problems were Spike and Veronica. Until I chose one of them to play the part of Cordelia, I wasn't going to be able to think about the other roles. Thank goodness I didn't have to worry about Clarissa, too. Several times during my deliberations I felt a sudden rush of affection for her.

Spike wanted the part, and I was quite sure that she would break my foot if she didn't get it. Veronica wanted the part, and I was quite sure that she would show up at the kitchen door one morning and hand my underpants to my mother if *she* didn't get it. Mrs. Graham's notes weren't very helpful, since she had recommended giving the part to Wilbur Carpenter.

I tried to imagine how it might feel to have my foot broken with a brick. I tried to imagine how it might feel to explain to my parents how Veronica had gotten my underpants. I went out to the garage and found a couple of boards that fit under my armpits like crutches. I shoved my foot into one of the empty coffee cans that my father accumulated in case he might need them for mixing paint, and I tried hobbling around a bit. It was really kind of fun. My father called out the kitchen door to say that breakfast was ready. While I sat at the table dunking my toast into my cocoa and playing with the blobs of butter that formed on the surface, I pretended, silently, that I was undergoing my parents' you-have-some-ex-plaining-to-do-young-man interrogation. Veronica and her parents were there too, and Veronica's underpants, which I had been made to retrieve from my sock drawer, lay with mine in the center of the table. This really wasn't any fun at all.

I decided to give the part to Veronica.

25

AS SOON AS I had made my decision, everything else looked easy. I read through Mrs. Graham's notes again and assigned all the other parts. I sat back and took a deep breath. For the first time since I had entered the fourth grade I felt just fine. I needed someone to share this feeling with, and I had someone: Clarissa.

I telephoned her and told her that I had assigned all the parts and that I would like to come over and tell her about them. She sounded excited and pleased, and my heart ached with gratitude toward her for being so good a friend. Though the skies were gray, and a storm really seemed to be about to break, I whistled a happy tune on the way to her house, and the closer I got the happier I felt. I decided to tell her everything. "How lucky I am," I thought, "to have Clarissa to confide in."

Clarissa was smiling and blushing when I arrived. We sat at the kitchen table, and I felt relaxed and voluble. I told Clarissa about Spike's threat, and she seemed quite worried for me. She reached across the table and put her hands on mine. I told her about what had happened in Veronica's closet, and she blushed, just as I had known she would. I told her about Veronica's threat, and in her eyes I could see shock and, to *my* shock, a cold fury.

Then I told her that I had decided to give the part to Veronica.

Clarissa rose from the table slowly, with her hands still resting on it. Her cheeks grew livid.

"What's wrong, Clarissa?" I asked. "Do you think I should have given the part to Spike?"

She stood and stamped her foot. "You fool!" she screamed.

"Clarissa—"

"You lunatic!" She began stamping her foot repeatedly. She seemed to be losing her mind.

"Please, Clarissa—"

She began inhaling and exhaling rapidly, her breath howling like the wind in a nasty storm. "You treacherous villain!"

"Calm down," I commanded. I walked toward her with my arms extended, meaning to hold her and pat her on the back.

"You milk-livered coward!" she cried.

"Clarissa!" I expostulated. I was astounded to hear this kind of thing from her. I put my hands on her shoulders.

"You—you—you—" she stammered in her fury, stamping her foot as she spoke.

"But—" I began.

"You!" she shrieked, and when she brought her foot down on mine, her eyes fulgurated.

26

I GOT AROUND on crutches fairly well, but it wasn't really any fun. Most of the kids in Mrs. Graham's class signed my cast. Spike wrote, "You had it coming to you." Veronica wrote, "Thanks for everything." Clarissa signed several times. Each time she wrote, "Can you ever forgive me?"

The play was quite a success. Veronica did a creditable job as Cordelia, Spike was an excellent Regan, and Clarissa was outstanding as Goneril.

To tell the truth, I had wanted all along to play Lear myself, but I knew that no one could do a better job than Matthew, and so I gave the part to him. He was superb.

I played the Fool. Judging from the applause, I was good enough, but some people may have been applauding only out of sympathy for my broken foot.

27

VERONICA'S PARENTS threw a cast party in their playroom. They had set up a number of card tables around the room, covered with white paper tablecloths, and at each place was a fluted paper container of candy, a snapper, a paper hat, a paper plate, a paper napkin, and a paper cup with a fold-out handle. For a while, I felt a little sick, partly because I was reminded of all the birthday parties at which I had eaten too much ice cream and had had to throw up on the ride home, and partly because being in the playroom with Veronica beside me, the closet door right behind me, and Mr. and Mrs. McCall bustling around made me apprehensive, but the camaraderie was infectious, and I soon began to relax and enjoy myself. I was sitting at a table with Veronica, Spike, and Clarissa.

Spike was sitting on my right, and now and then she would pause in the wolfing down of her ice cream and cake, chuckle, and give me a friendly knock on the shoulder or punch in the stomach. I'm quite sure that Spike *would* have broken my foot when she learned that I had given the part of Cordelia to Veronica if Clarissa hadn't already broken it. As it was, seeing that my foot had been broken by *someone* seemed to be enough to satisfy her.

Veronica was sitting on my left. At one point she poked me and pointed downward. She had part of her skirt pulled up, and I saw that she was wearing my underpants. She hadn't returned them to me even after I had given her the part. When I told her the news, she had given me an extravagant hug, and while she was hugging me she whispered in my ear that she would hang on to them for a while just in case. I pulled back from her and told her not to forget that I had hers. "I guess that makes us even," she said.

Clarissa was sitting opposite me, smiling and telling whoever passed that she wished she had been able to do a better job as Goneril. She had her muff in her lap, and she stroked it like a pet.

"Say," I said. "I'd like to make a toast." The girls sat up straight. They raised their paper cups as I had raised mine.

"To Regan, to Goneril, and to Cordelia," I said, saluting each of them in turn with my cup. "I'm glad it's over, and I'm glad we're friends."

"To Peter," they answered, and we touched our raised cups. When we lowered them again, I was looking into Clarissa's big eyes. The reflection in them of the fluorescent light overhead brought on an annoying itch inside the cast on my foot.

28

LESS THAN A MONTH LATER, Mrs. Graham announced one day that Clarissa was going to be leaving Babbington and moving to Sioux City,

Iowa, where her father would be devising new uses for setae, snouts, and trotters at Pickled Pork Products, a large and nationally famous company. While Spike was at the front of the room trying to find Iowa on the map of the United States, I looked at Clarissa. She was stroking her muff again.

On Clarissa's last day, Mrs. Graham threw a party an hour or so before school ended. Clarissa hugged everyone in the class at least once. She and some of the other girls cried and promised to write to each other.

I dawdled after the bell rang, fussing around, helping Mrs. Graham straighten up, because Clarissa had stayed to help her too, and I wanted to say good-bye to Clarissa alone.

When we were finished cleaning up, we walked out to the parking lot. Clarissa's mother hadn't arrived to pick her up yet. Mrs. Graham drove off, and we were alone.

"You'll be late getting home," Clarissa said.

"Oh, that's all right," I said. "It doesn't matter."

There was a silence. Then she looked at me and said, very softly, "Good-bye, Peter."

"Good-bye, Clarissa," I said.

"We had some good times together," she said. She hugged her muff and looked off into the distance.

"Yes," I said.

She smiled and poked me with her elbow. "Remember when you tried to make Mrs. Graham think that you knew the times tables?" she asked.

"You mean you knew that I—" I began.

She chuckled. "And remember that Santa Claus suit you wore when you came to my house for dinner?"

"I wouldn't call it a Santa Claus suit," I said. I zipped my jacket up tighter.

"And I'll never forget that joke about the rabbits." She went into a fit of giggling, and her eyes began to tear.

She stopped giggling and looked hard into my eyes. "Can you forgive me for what I did?" she asked.

"Oh, Clarissa—" I said.

"You still like me, don't you?" she asked, rotating at the hips, tipping her head to one side. Her cheeks were red with the cold. A cloud of breath hung in front of her while she spoke, then disappeared while she waited for me to answer. She wasn't smiling now.

"Yes," I said.

"Will you miss me?"

I looked past her, over her shoulder. "Yes," I said.

"Will you write to me?"

"I'll write to you," I said. "I promise I will."

"Please don't forget me."

"I'll never forget you," I said.

She smiled again. "Why don't you take my picture?" She pointed to my camera, which I was holding by the strap. "You'll have something to remember me by."

"Well—" I began.

"Then you'll always remember me the way I am now," she said. "You can put the picture on your bedside table in one of those frames that stands up by itself. You can look at it each night and you won't forget me. Where do you want me to stand?"

I raised the camera to my eye and found her in the viewfinder. I had her walk backwards until all of her fit within the frame. She stood with her feet together, her legs straight, her hands in the muff. She shivered once and then smiled.

I had my finger on the button, but the familiar uncertainty came over me, and I hesitated.

"Are you finished?" she called.

Through the viewfinder, I saw her frown. She wrinkled her nose, and furrows formed across her forehead. She stamped her foot, and I pressed the button at once.

"Got it!" I called back. I brought the camera down from in front of my face and smiled. She smiled back, and I took a slow deep breath to see if anything hurt inside my chest.

Her mother drove into the parking lot and tooted the horn. Clarissa turned and walked away. I wound the cream-colored plastic knob absent-mindedly and watched Clarissa walk the length of the parking lot, get into the car, wave to me, and turn away, toward her mother, who drove off.

The next day, I began using film.

She stood with her feet together, her legs straight, her hands in the muff.

Take the Long Way Home

To be in any form, what is that?
(Round and round we go, all of us, and ever come back
    thither)
If nothing lay more develop'd the quahaug in its callous shell
    were enough.
Mine is no callous shell,
I have instant conductors all over me whether I pass or stop,
They seize every object and lead it harmlessly through me.
I merely stir, press, feel with my fingers, and am happy,
To touch my person to some one else's is about as much as I
    can stand.

Walt Whitman
"Song of Myself"

A chicken ain't nothing but a bird.

E. B. Wallace
"A Chicken Ain't Nothing But a Bird"

(recorded in New York, October 14, 1940, by Cab Calloway and His
Orchestra, including Mario Bauza, Dizzy Gillespie, Lamar Wright,
Tyree Glenn, Quentin Jackson, Keg Johnson, Hilton Jefferson, Jerry
Blake, Andrew Brown, Chu Berry, Walter Thomas, Benny Payne,
Danny Barker, Milt Hinton, and Cozy Cole)

Preface

THIS STORY WAS CONCEIVED at Corinne's Fabulous Fruits of the Sea one evening when Albertine and I had dropped by for drinks and stayed for dinner. Al always knows what she's going to have when we go to Corinne's, and since she doesn't eat fish, she always has the same thing: chicken. I study the menu, eliminating things one by one, remain undecided until the last minute, and then nearly always wind up ordering clams. During the important visit that led to my writing this story, we had been sitting at our table for a while, and I had eliminated everything on the menu but two things: chicken and clams.

"Are you having chicken?" I asked Al.

If I remember correctly, she said, "Yes."

"Maybe I'll have chicken too." I said.

She said nothing, I think.

"Or maybe I'll have clams," I said.

She said something that I couldn't quite make out. A waitress, Dianne, one of my favorites, arrived. Al ordered. I hesitated. Albertine said— and I'll be forever in her debt for this—"You have to choose: chicken or clams."

An electrifying sensation shot through me, at once frightening and exhilarating. What Albertine had said brought back to me a memory from three decades ago, when I was in the fifth grade. My work on "Take the Long Way Home" began then. Over the intervening months, the story has grown and developed in ways that I couldn't have predicted, but it is still possible to see that it began with the memory that Al's statement recalled.

Allow me a little of your time to explain what the memory was, how I changed its essentials, and why I altered them.

When I was in the fifth grade, I competed in two memorable contests. One was a contest to name a new elementary school in Babbington. The other was a contest for the affections of Veronica McCall. I lost both.

As I worked on "Take the Long Way Home," I changed, among other things, the outcome of one of these contests: the name-the-school contest. In the pages that follow, I win. Why did I change the facts? To tell you the truth, I did it just to please myself. I've thought for nearly thirty years that I should have won that contest in the first place. Surely this is one of the motives behind any fiction: the desire to correct the errors of the past. It was easy to change the outcome, so I did.

I would have changed the outcome of the other contest if I could have, but I couldn't. The reasons for my losing Veronica were so deeply rooted in fact, in history, in the social fabric of Babbington, that to deny them, to try to alter them, would have meant trying to create a new social history, and since that seemed like more than I could do, I decided to stick to the facts.

But what were the facts? These things happened to me in the fifth grade; at the time, I thought that the outcome had a simple cause: I had lost Veronica to a boy named Frankie Paretti. What did I know then about the social forces at work in Babbington? Only as I worked on the story did I come to realize that—in the largest sense—I hadn't lost Veronica to any one boy. If I hadn't lost her to Frankie, I would have lost her to someone else, because I really lost Veronica to the sweeping force of social change. As I worked, I kept asking myself, "How did it happen? Why was there such an upheaval in the social structure of Babbington that it produced the tsunami that swept Veronica from me?" Weeks passed before I understood that it was all the fault of Stretch Mitgang.

It happened like this:

Before I was born, Babbington was a stable little community, dependent on—and redolent of—the clamming industry, with some small appeal for tourists. No one living in Babbington then would have predicted that within five years a period of rapid growth would begin that would last throughout my childhood. The effects of this growth were broad and deep, both on Babbington and on me.

Most of the reasons for Babbington's phenomenal growth were not unique to Babbington: the population of the entire United States, indeed of the entire world, was growing rapidly in the postwar years, which these years were, and large numbers of people, especially young fertile couples, were choosing to live in places more or less like Babbington. However, the most important single reason *was* unique to Babbington, and that reason was Stretch Mitgang.

Mitgang, a sociologist with psychohistorical interests, moved to Babbington just a year or so before I was born. Passing himself off as a psy-

chosocial historiographer, Mitgang undertook a two-year study of the
sexual practices of Babbingtonians. His charm and good looks made it
easy for him to ingratiate himself with Babbingtonians of all stripes, so he
was able to gather reams of data, thousands of anecdotes, tens of thousands of tall tales, and quite a few firsthand experiences. When he had
gathered the material he needed, Mitgang disappeared. A couple of years
later, he published the results of his research under the title *Seafood and
Sex: a Study of Life in a Coastal Town.*

In his book, Mitgang included the data, history, and logical cement
that readers expected, but he also laced the book with anecdotes about
Babbington and Babbingtonians that were, for their time, quite frank
(and probably exaggerated), and he also included photographs that were,
for their time, frank to an extreme (and probably staged). *Seafood and
Sex* has been out of print for years, but if you take the trouble to track
down a copy, you will understand why it quickly became a best-seller
and why the book itself became a primary reason for Babbington's rapid
growth.

Mitgang waxed Whitmanesque in his enthusiasm for the general good
health of the citizens, the "unflagging vigor that they bring to the day's
labor and the night's delight." This he attributed to the generally salubri-
ous effects of bracing salt air. He went on to praise the "mesmerizing
seductiveness of its women, at once shy and bold, endearingly naive and
shockingly inventive, teasing and complaisant." These qualities he attributed to the aphrodisiac effects of moonlight on the bay. In describing the
men, Mitgang returned again and again to their "sturdy thighs, priapic
grandeur, and remarkable endurance," which he attributed to the habit of
hard work and to the eating of clams. That did it. As soon as the book
was published, outsiders began flocking to Babbington, and the population began an accelerating rise.

The newcomers moved into a town that was already sharply divided
culturally. Clamming had always been important to the town, but after
the War of 1812, for reasons too complex for me to explain here, chicken
farming and processing became an important secondary industry. In the
early years of this century, there occurred a series of riots during which
clamdiggers attempted to drive chicken farmers out of Babbington. Most
historians refer to the period during which these riots occurred as the
Chicken Purge; however, the clamdiggers attacked the chicken farmers
with, among other weapons, the tongs that they used for harvesting clams
from the bay, and because of this unorthodox use of the clam tongs, this

unpleasant period is sometimes referred to as—and I apologize for this—
the Tong Wars.

Call it what you will, it was an ugly time in Babbington's history, one
that just about everyone would rather forget. But it had such a powerful
effect on the culture of Babbington that it can't be—and, I think, must not
be—forgotten. At the time, the clammies claimed that runoff from the
chicken farms was fouling the bay, and there was probably some truth to
the claim, but it was not the real reason for the animosity that they felt
toward the chicken farmers. I think we can find the real reason if we read
between the lines of a passage in *Our Town and Its People,* a social studies text that all fifth-grade Babbingtonians were required to study, a text
commissioned by the Daughters of the Tong Wars. Of the chicken farmers that textbook said, in part:

> Chicken farming is easy work, suitable for people who cannot do
> much else. As a group, chicken farmers are a happy-go-lucky lot.
> Like the birds they raise, they pass most of their lives eating, sleep-
> ing, and copulating. They live in blissful ignorance of time and tide.

I infer from this passage that the clammies were simply jealous of the
chicken farmers. The chicken-farming culture seemed to offer a life that
was easier, happier, and more exciting. Their own lives were hard, sometimes miserable, and often dull. But most of all, the chicken-based culture must have seemed sexy.

Well, when Mitgang's book appeared, it gave the clam culture reason
to think of itself as far sexier than the chicken culture. One might expect
that the animosity would, as a result, have disappeared, but any good psy-
chohistorian would be quick to point out that things are rarely as simple
as that. The anti-chicken attitude in Babbington *might* eventually have
disappeared if *Seafood and Sex* hadn't brought so many outsiders into the
town. These newcomers, remember, had been attracted to Babbington by
Mitgang's descriptions of the clamming culture, so they arrived eager to
embrace this culture, to penetrate its mysteries, to become part of it. (I'm
told that it wasn't unusual during this time to see half a dozen new Babbingtonians dogging the steps of a native, trying to learn to walk like a
clamdigger ashore.) Sadly, among the aspects of clam culture embraced
by the newcomers was the anti-chicken-farming prejudice.

Now here comes the strange irony of all this, the truth-is-stranger-
than-fiction part. Most of the land available in Babbington for building

the houses that the newcomers would live in was in the northern half of town, away from the bay, the part of town to which the chicken farmers had been driven so long ago. This part of town had come to be known as Babbington Heights. As newcomers moved into Babbington, the chicken farms gave way to tracts of new houses, one very much like another, and most of the chicken farmers collected their money from the developers and went off to the Midwest. The people who moved into the tract houses, lured by the promise of seafood and sex, tried to emulate the Old Babbingtonians but found that the *real* Old Babbingtonians treated them as if they'd been born and bred in the Heights, as if they'd sprung from generations of chicken farmers.

When my parents finally saved enough money to buy a small house, they moved from my grandparents' house on No Bridge Road, not far from the heart of Old Babbington, to one of the small houses built on a former chicken farm in the Heights.

Perhaps it was inevitable that the people in the Heights, stung by the rejection of the Old Babbingtonians, should band together and reject the people who rejected them. That is what they did. They turned against the old clam-based culture and developed a nostalgic affection for chicken farming, for a past and a way of life that they had never known. Like most converts, they quickly became zealots. Within a year or two, there was hardly a household in the Heights that didn't have its small flock in a little homemade coop out in the back yard. Most people kept laying hens, but some specialized in roasters or fryers, one or two kept fighting cocks, and several had flocks of homing chickens, which they would allow to walk around the block a few times in the gathering dusk of a summer evening, summoning them home with elaborate whistle signals when night fell. I admired the ability of the whistlers, and my father became one of the best of them, but I never cared for those chickens. I was friendly with the boys and girls in my neighborhood, but my roots were in the other culture—the bay owned my heart and my imagination.

FIFTH-GRADERS are not noted for their tolerance. When the population growth forced the town to build a new central upper elementary school, and boys and girls from all over Babbington were thrown together in that new central upper elementary school, they quickly took sides, as if they were choosing up for a mammoth game of dodgeball. I had grown up with a foot in each of the cultures; I tried to remain aloof from this tribalism, but it didn't take long for me to see that—at least for the time being—I couldn't. I could see the way it was going to be. If I was going to have any friends in school, I was going to have to choose one camp or the other. Veronica certainly saw that this was the case, and she began to grow impatient with my reluctance to choose. Finally, on the day when the winner of the name-that-school contest was announced, just a few minutes before the announcement itself, Veronica put her ultimatum to me, in terms nearly identical to those that Albertine was to use thirty years later. She touched her hand to my cheek and said, "Peter, you've got to choose: chicken or clams." I chose clams, and Veronica chose chicken, and away she went.

YOU SEE HOW DIFFICULT it would have been for me to change that outcome without changing Babbington, my past, my feelings for my family, and so on. However, all of the foregoing seemed to me far too complex to include in the story of a childhood romance.

What to do? The solution that you'll find in the pages that follow was not the only possible one, but working it out gave me great satisfaction. I compressed everything. Since Mitgang and *Seafood and Sex* were to blame for my losing Veronica, I cast Stretch Mitgang in Frankie Paretti's role, and I used sex instead of societal forces as the reason for my losing Veronica. Then, since I really hated to see myself lose, whatever the reason, I had myself drop out of the contest instead. And finally, since my loss to Frankie Paretti still stung a bit after all these years, I cast him as an especially unattractive infant. That the satisfaction I gained from doing this to Frankie was ignoble bothered me only a little, and only for a little while.

Peter Leroy
Small's Island
June 15, 1984

1

THIS IS THE STORY of two contests in which I competed in the fifth grade. One, probably the more important, was a competition for the love of Veronica McCall. This was a competition that I sponsored, but I was never a serious contender in it myself at all, which is probably as it should have been, since I didn't really understand what prize was at stake, did not, to tell a truth that I would have been too embarrassed to tell at the time, even want to understand what prize was at stake, because I did understand that it was a variety of love for which I hadn't yet developed an appetite.

In the manner of a chowder, which is a complex and subtle mixture of elemental foodstuffs, the emotion that we call love is a bewildering and varied concoction of more elemental emotions: lust, friendship, curiosity, guilt, and fear, among others. Tastes in chowders vary from person to person, from nation to nation, from region to region; one's own taste in chowder changes over the course of one's lifetime, and it may even shift from day to day. So it is with tastes in love. Some like theirs chock full of voluptuous scarlet tomatoes; others prefer something rarer, more exotic, heady with saffron; and still others like theirs bland and sturdy, with cream and potatoes.

My tastes and Veronica's were different because I was two years younger than she, and at the time they were an especially important two years. Those two years represented the Gulf of Puberty, not so wide a gulf, but one where the waters can be treacherous, and where the fog is often so thick that one can't see from one shore to the other. When I finally began to get a fuzzy notion of what Veronica wanted from a boyfriend (however fuzzy her desires might still have been) I began looking for someone who might be able to take the job away from me.

The other contest seemed much simpler on the surface, but I soon found that I had underestimated its demands. Not long after I had entered it, I found myself wishing that I could withdraw from this one too. It was the contest to name the new school.

Because of a rapid increase in Babbington's population, a new upper-elementary school was being built at what was almost the geographical center of Babbington, and boys and girls from all over town would attend the fourth, fifth, and sixth grades there. The three small existing elementary schools—two old ones in the old town and one fairly new one in Babbington Heights—would be used only by children in the lower grades.

Work on the new school had begun the year before. During the summer, when it looked for a while as if the school might actually be completed before the fall, the announcement of the name-the-school contest appeared in the *Babbington Reporter,* and it sent a ripple of excitement through the upper-elementary-school population of Babbington.

"Did you see this?" I shouted when I arrived at Raskol's with the paper.

"Yeah," said Raskol. "Margot and Martha burst in here with it in the middle of breakfast. My father was just slipping a soft-boiled egg into his mouth with his soup spoon when they flew into the house, wham, bam, no knocking, no hellos, all squeals and excitement. God, his face got so red and swollen I thought his head was going to blow up—barroom! Egg yolk was dripping from the corners of his mouth. He grabbed that broom handle he keeps beside his plate and smacked it on the table, right on the edge of Little Ernie's oatmeal bowl. There was oatmeal all over the table, all over Ariane's slip, and all over me, too. My first thought was, *Maybe I should call the cops,* but then my second thought was, *Maybe I should call an ambulance.* But it all worked out all right because my father is such a pushover for those two. As soon as he saw them, he said, 'Hey, how're my girls?' and he wiped his mouth on his sleeve, tossed the broom handle into a corner, and squatted down so that the two of them could jump into his arms. He's out on the dock with them now, thinking up names. They've got about sixty entries already written out."

"Sixty?" I exclaimed. I had imagined that I would enter one name, one top-notch name, one name that was the product of weeks of satisfying effort, the one name that survived after I had rejected hundreds of others as second-rate or worse, one name of such transcendent aptness that it couldn't lose. It didn't strike me as appropriate to send in every name that popped into my head. When I saw the stack of papers that Margot and Martha and Mr. Lodkochnikov had beside them I said as much, taking care to direct my criticisms at the Glynns only, suggesting indirectly but as clearly as I could that Mr. Lodkochnikov probably disapproved as strongly as I did, but was just indulging their childish impropriety because he was a kindly sort.

"No, Peter," said Margot. "You're wrong. Martha and I talked this

Coming soon

TO MUSGRAVE SWAMP
A GREAT NEW SCHOOL FOR BABBINGTON . . .
AND A GREAT OPPORTUNITY FOR YOU!

Hey, kids! Here's the chance of a lifetime! As most of you know, un-
precedented population growth here in Babbington has put a real strain
on the sewer system and is threatening the clam harvest in the Bay. Not
only that! Our schools are crowded to the bursting point. That's why
we're building that spiffy new school in the area near the Saltaire development, the area that some of your parents and grandparents might call
Musgrave Swamp. Some of you reading this will get to go to the new
school when it opens in September. AND some lucky boy or girl out
there will get to name the school! The name of the winner will be en-
graved on a plaque that will be displayed inside the school forever!

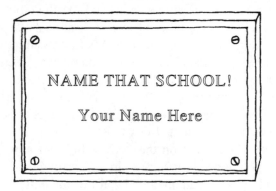

NAME THAT SCHOOL!

Your Name Here

That's right! One of you has a chance at immortality. Just think of
it, generations of schoolchildren not unlike yourself will think as they
pass through the portals of the school, "Wow! Whoever that is whose
name is on that plaque must be pretty important!"

All you have to do is write your name and address on a piece of paper, along with your name for the school. Send it to the Babbington
Board of Education, and wait for the decision of the judges, which will
be final. Enter as often as you like. Be sure to visit the new school on
Saturday, August 1. Once you see the place, you're sure to get lots of
good ideas for names!

over for a long time, and Mr. Lodkochnikov agrees with us, too, don't you, Uncle Bunny?"

"Uncle Bunny?" I repeated, soundlessly.

"Well," said Raskol's father, shrugging, "I got some reservations—"

"But you mostly agree with us, don't you," asserted Martha, "that what it comes down to is this—it's not the name that pleases you or me that's going to win; it's the name that pleases the judges, whose decision is final."

"There I agree with you," said Mr. Lodkochnikov.

This was a shattering but indisputable truth. "You're right," I admitted.

"And the more names you send in," said Martha, "the better chance you have of sending in one that they'll all like."

"You're right about that too," I said. I abandoned immediately the approach that I had intended to take and adopted theirs. Over the course of the next five or six weeks, we submitted, among the four of us (five, counting Mr. Lodkochnikov, whose names went in under Margot or Martha's sponsorship), more than a thousand names for the school. Margot spent afternoons in the library hunting for ideas for names on old maps of Babbington ("Bolotomy Bay School," "Musgrave Swamp School"); Martha was especially adept at deriving names from the names of animals and birds ("Herring Gull Elementary School," "One-clawed Crab Elementary School"); Mr. Lodkochnikov contributed a few, but none of us thought they were likely winners ("Unfinished School," "School of Hard Knocks"); and Raskol proved to have an uncanny knack for coming up with phrases that linked the school with aspects of everyday life in Babbington ("Slow Leak School," "Foggy Day School"). Compared to theirs, my names were, well, lackluster. They had the virtue of accuracy, but one was much like another, and none, it seemed to me, offered anything that would make the judges sit up and take notice, nothing that would make them say, "That's it! That's the name we want!"

2

THE NEW SCHOOL OPENED on schedule, although the building wasn't finished. On the first day, in the middle of the morning, all of us were herded into the auditorium to hear the principal, Mr. Simon, explain the rules that we would have to follow. It was with nervous anticipation that we shuffled through the hallways to the auditorium, because all of us assumed that once Mr. Simon had finished explaining the rules, he would announce the winner of the name-the-school contest.

Scaffolding was arranged on the sides of the auditorium, and dozens of workmen stood on it, working on a tangle of wires, pipes, and ducts that would, perhaps, be concealed by a ceiling someday. No carpet was on the floor yet, and some of the seats hadn't been installed, so some of the sixth-graders had to stand in ranks at the back of the hall where the seats should have been. The whine of the workmen's electric drills and saws and the blows of their hammers echoed in the hall.

Principal Simon stood at a lectern on the stage. When the auditorium was full, he blew into a microphone.

"May I have quiet, please?" he asked, raising his eyes toward the scaffolding and looking around the room. Some of the workmen had heard him and noticed his look. They stopped work, elbowed their co-workers, and began shushing one another, and gradually the noise stopped.

"Thank you," said Mr. Simon. "We'll try to get through this as quickly as possible. Then Mr. Simone, our new superintendent of public schools, will talk to you." Mr. Simon nodded in the direction of Mr. Simone, and a thrill of anticipation ran through all of us, as if we had been wired together. Mr. Simone must be the one who would announce the winner. Mr. Simon shuffled through some papers on the lectern, cleared his throat, and spoke to us with measured simplicity.

"Now, boys and girls, as you can see, the school is not quite finished yet." Roars of laughter came from the scaffolding, a couple of hoots, and then much shushing. Mr. Simon ignored it and went on. "Because the school is not quite finished, we are going to have to try to stay out of the workmen's way." One of the workmen made a remark that no one but his fellows beside him could make out. They roared.

"I have made a list of some of the things that we will have to do to stay out of their way. I hope you will listen very carefully."

We all listened carefully, even the workmen on the scaffolding.

"Do not walk under ladders," Mr. Simon began. He went on, citing reasons for not walking under ladders, offering anecdotes that illustrated the misfortune that could befall a person who did walk under ladders, and then went on to another rule. While he spoke, we, and the men on the scaffolding, listened less and less carefully. It was the sort of thing we had heard before. All of us, at least all of the kids, wanted to get to the announcement of the winner of the name-the-school contest. When Principal Simon finally finished, he asked whether there were any questions.

Matthew Barber raised his hand, but a much larger boy beside him quickly pulled it down and held Matthew in his seat so that he couldn't raise it again.

"All right, then," said Mr. Simon. I took a deep breath and held it. My heart was pounding. All around me, boys and girls took deep breaths of their own and held them. The auditorium was eerily quiet, except for the muffled rumble of our pounding hearts. "In just a minute," said Mr. Simon, "Mr. Simone is going to—"

I swallowed hard. I wiped my palms on my pants. "This is it," said Raskol. His jaws were clenched, and he was slowly striking his fists together. A sigh came from somewhere behind me, and Kevin McManus, in front of me, crossed himself and bowed his head.

"—explain your room assignments and your lunch, gym, art, music, and recess schedules to you," said Mr. Simon. A unanimous groan escaped from us. "Well," said Mr. Simon, "I know that you've been sitting still—or some of you have been *standing* still—for a long time. What do you say we have a little seventh-inning stretch? Why don't we have a game of Simon Says?"

Mr. Simon led us all in a spirited round of Simon Says. The workmen joined in too, making their scaffolding shake, and inspiring rippling laughter among all of us on the floor. A boy named Stretch, a sixth-grader, won. He was a tall boy, dark and muscular, with wavy black hair and thick black eyebrows.

Mr. Simone came to the lectern and stood there for a while, waiting for quiet. After much shuffling, coughing, twisting in seats and shushing, he got it, and he began.

"We all enjoyed that very much, didn't we?" he asked. There was a scattering of yeses and yeahs, one or two low-toned noes, and one excellent imitation of a fart, which came from Spike O'Grady.

Mr. Simone pushed ahead, apparently deaf to any signs of dissent. "This will be a lot like Simon Says too. I want all of you sixth-graders whose last names begin with *A* through *K* to stand." No one stood. We weren't that stupid.

"Well?" said Mr. Simone at last.

"You didn't say 'Simon Says,'" came a voice from the scaffolding. There was thunderous laughter at this, and a group of workmen began slapping at one of their number with their hats, presumably the one who had called out.

"Oh," said Mr. Simone. "Well, this will be like Simon Says without my saying 'Simon Says.' We'll call it Simone Says. Whatever I say, you will do." Then his playful tone disappeared, he glared at us and said sternly, "I hope you understand."

Spike emitted a rasping and resonant noise from the side of her mouth, but, unfortunately, Miss Rasmussen, the girls' gym teacher, alerted by Spike's first offense, had taken a position just behind the row where Spike sat, and as soon as Spike began her delivery Miss Rasmussen pounced on her, grabbing Spike by the right ear and pulling her to her feet. She dragged Spike from the auditorium in this fashion, and all of us became silent and attentive. I found myself involuntarily reaching for my ear, as if it were sore. Mr. Simone began giving orders.

"All those of you who are in the sixth grade and whose names begin with *A* through *K* stand up, or, if you are already standing, remain standing, and, of course, if your last name begins with *L* through *Z* and you are now sitting, remain sitting, or if you are now standing, sit down," said Mr. Simone. There was some confused mumbling, and a number of sixth-graders who had been sitting stood, a similar number who had been standing sat on the floor or scrambled for vacated seats, and a few looked to the heavens, or to the scaffolding, for help.

One of the sixth-grade boys called out, in an exaggeratedly deep voice, as if it were the voice of God, "Simon says, 'Sit down, Mitgang.'" Stretch, the dark-haired boy who had won at Simon Says, sat down suddenly, as quickly and surely as he had responded in the game.

"Now all of you who are in the sixth grade and whose last names begin with *L* through *Z* stand up," said Mr. Simone. They did. "All the *A*-through-*K*'s move to this half of the auditorium, and the *L*-through-*Z*'s move to that half." After several minutes and a great deal of pushing, shoving, and mock-accidental stepping-on-of-feet, this was accomplished. "Now, all the *A*-through-*F*'s move to the front half of their half of the auditorium, and the *G*-through-*K*'s move to the back half of their half of the auditorium." This sort of thing went on for nearly an hour, until Mr. Simone had divided each grade into groups of classroom size.

3

AN ASIDE. So much depends on chance. The coincidence of our having last names that began with the same letter of the alphabet, or at least with

letters that were close in the alphabet, meant that certain of us would remain in each other's company throughout most of every day for the next
couple of years. The population of Babbington continued to grow rapidly
during that time, and school building could not keep pace with the
growth, so Mr. Simone continued to shuffle the students' schedules to try
to squeeze us into what space was available. Each group of twenty-five
or so of us would sit in the same classrooms together throughout fifth and
sixth grades; we would go to gym at the same time, go to lunch together,
go to recess together, write at the same time, draw pictures at the same
time, grow anxious about tests and book reports and science projects at
the same time and then, when we reached junior high school, during the
most overcrowded period for Babbington's schools, we would arrive at
school and leave school at a time unique to our group, since Mr. Simone
developed a bafflingly complex system for moving students through the
school in groups, a system that became more complicated as the schools
became more crowded.

The lives of the boys and girls in one of Mr. Simone's groups were
aligned so precisely after a while that we became closer than most sib-
lings. My age, since I had skipped most of the third grade, should have
made me feel a person apart from my classmates, most of whom were a
year and a half older than I, some of whom were more than two years
older. However, the bond that Mr. Simone created seemed so strong that
I decided the difference in our ages didn't matter; I felt as if I had been
aged by being one of them. On that score, I was, as I mentioned above,
wrong.

4

ANOTHER ASIDE. It is, I think, quite possible that during the next several years, the most important part of our education came from learning to
follow Mr. Simone's schedules, with their complex branchings:

> All those who have music on Tuesdays and Thursdays skip ahead to
> page six for your Monday and Wednesday afternoon schedule.
> Those with music on Mondays and Wednesdays turn back to page
> two for your Monday and Wednesday afternoon schedule.

alternative paths:

> During the twenty-two minutes allotted for lunch, you may (a) eat
> lunch, (b) cavort in the school yard, (c) play dodgeball in the gym-
> nasium, or (d) work in the study halls held in rooms 112 or 124, but
> when the period is over, you must all assemble by group in the au-
> ditorium.

and dependent relationships:

> If you take wood shop on Tuesdays and Thursdays during the first
> half of the year, you must study either French [see note on page 12]
> or the Tonette on Tuesdays and Thursdays during the second half of
> the year.

It is indisputably true that the generation of students who learned to follow Mr. Simone's schedules or others like them has produced a large
number of adults who are remarkably adept at writing long and intricate
computer programs and long and intricate sentences that establish relationships among ideas so widely separated that one wouldn't have imagined that a chain of reasoning could have been forged long enough to link
them. I think that there is a cause-and-effect relationship in there somewhere.

5

AS MR. SIMONE divided us into groups that morning in the auditorium,
I began to guess what the groups meant. I couldn't have guessed then all
the implications of the division, but I guessed that the boys and girls in a
group would be in the same classroom. Other rumors about the meaning
of the groupings circulated through the auditorium, including the idea that
one group would be sent to a reform school, and that another contained
the finalists in the name-the-school contest, but I decided that the boys
and girls who remained with me were going to be my classmates: these
would be the boys and girls with whom I'd be closest, at least in school.
In the very first division, I was separated from the Glynns and from Matthew Barber. When Mr. Simone finally stopped, I was in a group with all

the *L*s and the first half of the *M*s. Raskol Lodkochnikov was in my group, and so was Veronica McCall.

6

OVER THE NEXT FEW WEEKS, Veronica and I saw a great deal of each other, not only at school, but after school, usually at her house. I was pleased and flattered by Veronica's attentions, and I enjoyed showing off for her when we studied together. I enjoyed less the domestic tone that Veronica gave to our afternoons. The McCalls' neighbors, the Parettis, had an infant child, Frankie. Very often, when I arrived, I would find that Veronica had volunteered to give Frankie an airing. Walking side by side, very much as if we were his parents, we would push Frankie around the neighborhood in his carriage. We would stop when someone wanted a look at him, and Veronica would beam when he was praised (which wasn't often, for Frankie was a singularly unattractive baby, the kind that makes people, when they poke their heads under the hood of the carriage, gasp and say, "Oh, my!"). Veronica worried about whether Frankie was too cold or too warm and whether he was developing as he should. I hid from her my conviction that he hadn't a brain in his head. Now and then, Veronica, playing at our being Frankie's parents, would nuzzle me and suggest that perhaps we should have "another baby" so that Frankie wouldn't be lonesome. My stomach grew cold when she asked me if I thought we should give it a try. At the time, I thought that the coldness was caused only by the prospect of bringing into the world another baby like Frankie, but the truth is that the sexuality Veronica had discovered on the other side of puberty scared me to death. I was to begin to recognize that truth one afternoon late in September.

7

ON THAT AFTERNOON late in September, Veronica and I were walking home together after school. It was a Wednesday, and Veronica ordinarily had a piano lesson after school on Wednesdays, but Veronica's piano lesson had been canceled. Mr. Getchel, the music teacher, had not come to school because he had cracked a tooth while using his teeth, as my mother had told me never to use them, in an attempt to remove the cap from a tube of toothpaste.

Veronica was quite nervous about the social studies test that we would have the next day, a test based on the first three chapters of *Our Town and Its People,* a history of Babbington that all fifth-graders were required to study.

"We can study together," she suggested.

"All right," I said.

"I'll ask you questions that might be on the test," she said.

"I think I should ask you questions instead," I said.

"How come?" she asked.

"Because I know the answers better than you do," I said. "You're the one who needs to study."

She burst out laughing. "You're a funny guy, Peter," she said.

"I am?" I asked.

"You sure are," she said. "What's the sense of asking me the questions if I don't know the answers? I'll just sit there saying nothing, won't I?"

"Well—"

"Or else I'll just answer them wrong, and that isn't going to get me anywhere, is it?"

"No, I guess it isn't."

"But if I ask *you* the questions, then I'll learn the answers from you."

"I guess you're right," I said

"Of course I'm right," she said.

I didn't want to argue with Veronica, but in a corner of my mind I was beginning to form a vague hunch about how children came to have the vacant look that Frankie usually wore, and that hunch made me wonder whether any child that Veronica bore might not wind up with a version of Frankie's vacant look.

We turned the corner of Veronica's block, and she stopped short. A red convertible was parked at the corner, several houses away from Veronica's. Veronica held a forefinger to her lips. She leaned toward me and whispered, "That's Jack's car."

"Who's Jack?" I asked.

"He's—" she began, but she stopped at once. She looked steadily into my eyes for a moment, and I could see from the way she drew her eyebrows together that she was making a decision. Finally she said, "Come with me, but don't make a sound."

She led me to the back door of her house. I stood behind while she opened the door, slowly and silently. We stepped soundlessly into the kitchen, and Veronica began closing the door as slowly and silently as she had opened it. From upstairs, as from a great distance, came a shriek from Mrs. McCall, a squealing, crazy sound that might have been made by a madwoman or a frightened piglet. Veronica and I looked at each other. "You want to see?" she asked, whispering into my ear.

"See what?" I wondered. I wanted to go home. I wanted to stay in the kitchen and ignore any sound that came from upstairs. I wanted to see. I wanted to go home.

Veronica tilted her head to one side and raised her eyebrows, calling for an answer. I swallowed, but I said nothing.

"Come on," she said, noiselessly, just moving her lips and beckoning with a finger. She led me from the kitchen into the dining room. She started up the carpeted stairs, tiptoeing with great care, keeping to the edge of the stairs nearest the wall. I followed her, my heart pounding, fear gathering in my throat like a cat's fur ball. Whatever was going on up there, it was, I was certain, none of my business. To get caught even tiptoeing up the stairs like this would mean trouble, and whatever Veronica had in mind for us to do when we reached the top of the stairs was going to mean more trouble. Ah, but curiosity is a powerful force. Ignorance is so bleak a state that we are willing to risk a great deal to get out of it. Ignorance seems cold and wet and gray and foggy; knowledge seems warm and sunny and golden and clear. I followed Veronica as if she were leading me out of the darkness into the dawn.

We reached the top of the stairs. The door to Veronica's parents' room, where Jack and Mrs. McCall were, was closed, but Mrs. McCall was speaking, or making sounds, in a falsetto voice, a voice that made me think she and Jack were playing a game. Veronica and I had reached the top of the stairs, and we stood outside the door now. The thought occurred to me that Jack and Mrs. McCall might burst out of the room, intending to continue the game on the stairs or in the living room. Suppose the game involved running up and down the stairs? Veronica tugged my hand, and I realized that I'd been standing for some time on the landing, without moving, staring at the door. Veronica led me to the door to her room. She opened it and pulled me inside.

"Veronica," I said, as quietly as I could. "Maybe I'll go home now."

"Oh, shut up," she said. "Don't you want to see them?"

"No, I don't think—" I began, turning away.

"They're naked, stupid," she whispered. She giggled.

To explain the effect that Veronica's statement had on me, I must describe the toy gun that I had received as a present the preceding Christmas. It was shaped like a bazooka, the antitank weapon that fired a rocket. This bazooka gun, as I called it, fired Ping-Pong balls. The barrel of the gun was in two parts: a larger cylinder in the front slid over a narrower cylinder behind. One loaded a supply of balls into a magazine and then, by sliding the outer barrel forward once, loaded a ball into the inner barrel and filled the space in the barrel behind the ball with air. The ball was pushed by the air all the way to the muzzle, where the ball itself functioned as a stopper because a rubber ring fixed inside the muzzle, a ring with an opening just slightly smaller than the diameter of the ball, prevented the ball from leaving the barrel. However, when one suddenly pulled the outer barrel backward, the air in the chamber behind the ball was compressed, and when the pressure reached a sufficiently high level, the ball was forced suddenly through the opening in the rubber ring and exploded from the muzzle. The firing was accompanied by a wonderfully loud *whoomp,* and the ball flew out with impressive velocity. Since a Ping-Pong ball has little mass, air resistance would slow its flight quickly, so the gun was actually a reasonably safe toy. (At least it was a *physically* safe toy. It was probably extremely harmful psychologically, but during the time that I'm recalling, children were apparently regarded as immune from psychological harm.) My friends and I devised a nasty little game with this bazooka gun. One player would be chosen as shooter, another as target. The target would stand up against a wall, facing the wall. The shooter would walk several paces away from the target and aim the gun at the back of the target's head. The object, for the shooter, was to make the target flinch (cringe, shudder, or otherwise respond out of fear) between the time of the *whoomp* and the time that the ball struck the target's head. The object for the target was not to flinch. Being a good target was much more difficult than being a good shooter. Raskolnikov was remarkably good at this game, in both roles. I was quite bad at it, especially as target. The worst part was the waiting. The impact of the ball grew more and more forceful in the mind until it was as powerful as a punch from one of the boys in the gang that Spike O'Grady led. When I finally heard the *whoomp,* I could never help myself: the muscles across my back tightened automatically, my shoulder blades snapped inward, and my neck snapped back, as if I had already received the blow. Then, *smack,* the ball would strike me, but feebly, harmlessly. The laughs followed. It was the laughter, not the ball, that stung.

Veronica's remark struck me like the Ping-Pong ball from the bazooka gun. As Veronica and I mounted the stairs and slipped into her room, I began to understand, somehow, somewhere in the back of my mind, that whatever Mrs. McCall and Jack were up to was something that they wouldn't want me to know anything about, something that I wasn't supposed to know anything about, and something that in my heart of hearts I didn't *want* to know anything about.

"They're naked *(whoomp)*, stupid *(smack)*," she whispered. She giggled. That stung.

"Oh, yeah," I said. "I knew that."

Of adult nudity I knew nothing at first hand. At my grandparents' house, I had studied, very carefully, the nude photographs of May Castle that I had found in a desk drawer in the bedroom that had once been my father's. I had seen, briefly, usually looking over another boy's shoulder, in a book that sometimes materialized in the boys' room, photographs of nude men and women with black rectangles over their eyes, but these photographs were more puzzling than revealing. The people were always facing not quite the right way, or the photographs had been cropped just a fraction of an inch before the point at which they would have provided the curious viewer with some real information. The pictures implied a great deal, but without the experience that would have helped me to interpret them, with only my imagination to complete a curve, extend a line, illuminate a shadow, sharpen the fuzzy focus, the possibilities multiplied so quickly and assumed such grotesque forms and enormous proportions that my head began to reel.

The second floor of Veronica's house was an attic, expanded and made suitable for bedrooms by dormers that ran the length of the house at the front and rear. The stairs led to a small landing, off which there were two doors. One led to Veronica's parents' bedroom. The other led to Veronica's bedroom. Under the eaves, there was space for storage. This arrangement was typical of the houses built in Babbington during the postwar population boom. My house, and the houses of most of the other boys and girls I knew, at least in Babbington Heights, resembled Veronica's, differing only in rotation and scale.

Access to the storage space under the eaves was provided by sliding doors crudely constructed of thin sheets of pressed wood fibers that were sold under the trade name Masonite, with a simple finger hole drilled through each door to allow one to get a grip on it and slide it in its track to one side.

Slowly and silently, Veronica slid the door in her room open enough so that we could squeeze through. She got down on her hands and knees and crawled in. I followed her.

The floor of the storage area was simply a few pine boards nailed to

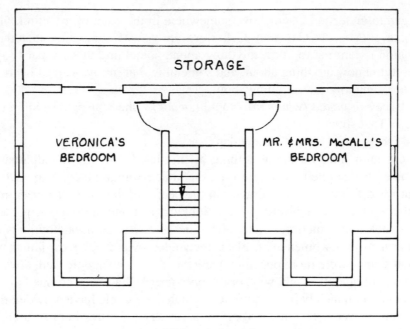

SECOND FLOOR

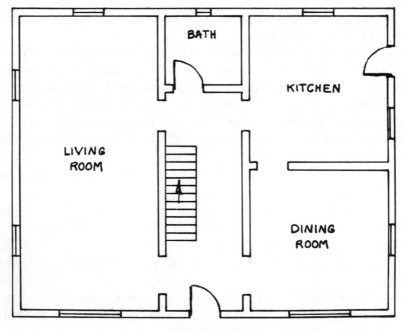

FIRST FLOOR

the joists. To our left as we crawled along, there was no floor at all; the joists were exposed, and below them was the plasterboard of the ceiling below. I knew this because as soon as I put my hand out in the darkness of this tunnel, I missed the boards and felt my hand slip into dark nothingness, but then my hand struck the plasterboard, and I recognized it for what it was from familiarity with the attic at home, where I slept.

Very slowly, Veronica crawled along toward the light that we could see ahead of us, coming from the finger holes in the doors to the eaves storage in Veronica's parents' bedroom, from which the voices of Jack and Mrs. McCall came now in low rhythmical waves, sometimes resembling the involuntary grunting sounds one makes when one has been rowing a boat for quite a while and has to put a strong effort into each stroke, at other times more like the startled exclamation one makes when one is taken by surprise by some physical contact, at first frightened and then relieved, as when one feels the impact of a Ping-Pong ball on the back of one's neck and realizes an instant later that it was only a Ping-Pong ball, nothing more.

After what seemed a very long time, Veronica stopped behind the door, where she could see into her parents' bedroom through the finger hole. Light fell on her face through the hole. She wore a rapt, curious expression, but there was also in it a trace of anger—no, more than anger. It was a trace, apparent in a certain steadiness in her eyes, a twist in her upper lip, of hatred.

A car door, muffled but unmistakably a car door. The front door. No doubt about it, the front door. "Hello-wo! Hey, where's my honey?" It was Mr. McCall.

"Oh, my God," said Mrs. McCall, quite softly, and apparently quite calmly.

"Jesus H. Christ!" said Jack, and I could tell that he said it through clenched teeth.

Veronica turned toward me. I couldn't see her face at all, but the light behind her lit her dark hair with a thin, golden aureole.

"Quick! Grab your clothes," said Mrs. McCall. "You hide under the eaves. I'll get him out of the house, and you slip away."

I backed up as quickly as I could, and Veronica scrambled toward me. We had barely managed to crouch behind a cardboard carton marked OR-NAMENTS, when the door at the other end of the closet slid open, and Jack crawled in, carrying his shoes and socks and pants.

Mrs. McCall called out, "Hi, Honey. I was taking a nap. I'll be right there." A couple of minutes later she went downstairs. We heard muffled voices from downstairs, then the front door opened and closed, and the car started and drove off.

Jack slid the door open. Light flooded into the closet. Veronica and I shrank behind the carton and waited. He closed the door. We heard his footsteps on the stairs, rapid footsteps. We heard him open and close the front door. We waited for a minute or so and then slid the door open and crawled out into Veronica's bedroom.

"I'd better get home," I said. I started for the door at once. Veronica didn't say a thing. When I reached the front door, I turned and looked back upstairs. Veronica was standing at the door to her parents' bedroom, looking in. She turned toward me.

"Come on back, Peter," she said.

"I really better get home, Veronica," I said.

"They're probably not going to be back for a while," she said.

"I can't, Veronica," I said. I was trying not to whine, trying to keep myself from saying, in whatever way, "I'm still a little boy, Veronica." I said, "I have to go home and study for the social studies test."

I ran all the way home. In my mind was a burning question, and it was probably the same burning question that was in Jack's mind while he hid under the eaves: "How am I going to get out of this?"

8

MORALE in the new school sank daily. The continuing construction made things difficult for everyone. Whenever the site of construction shifted, groups of students would be shifted to clear the area. When the cafeteria floor was being laid, we had to eat lunch in the gym, and the gym classes were held in the corridors. Teachers taped paper over the glass in the classroom doors, but still the thunder of sneakers would distract us now and then. We were never quite sure from one day to another, and even during a single day, where we were supposed to go next. However, for the students the most unsettling part of all this was that since the school wasn't finished, the choosing of the winner of the name-the-school contest was continually postponed. Not only did we suffer the disappointment of not knowing who the winner was, but, worse still, since the deadline for submitting names was extended again and again, there was the need to come up with more and more names. Some boys and girls developed more or less constant headaches. I ran out of ideas. Over and over again, I tried scrambling the elements of the names that I had already submitted in the hope that I might come up with a winning combination. Like words repeated too often, my names began to sound meaningless and stupid to me, and I decided to ask that all my entries be withdrawn, so that I'd be spared the disappointment of losing or the embarrassment of having one of my ridiculous entries win. I went to see Mr. Simone one day during my lunch period and asked to have my entries back.

"I'm going to pretend that I didn't hear what you said," he said.

"Why?" I asked.

"Because nobody likes a quitter, my boy."

"Oh," I said.

"So you just get those ideas about withdrawing from the contest right out of your head."

"Yes, sir," I said. He showed me to the door.

"And as far as I'm concerned, none of this ever happened, okay?" He smiled quickly and held his hand out for me to shake. I shook it, with little enthusiasm, and left.

Several innovations were introduced to raise the spirits of the students. Among these was the Young Tars. Membership in this group was limited to boys and girls who achieved certain academic standards, excelled in athletics, fawned over their teachers, or had influential and insistent parents. The Tars wore nifty sailor suits that caught the fancy of everyone in the school. Well, nearly everyone. The elitist selection process, which the faculty and administration had designed to make other students try their darnedest to earn admission to the Tars, created a large and angry group of students who hated the whole idea of the Young Tars and every now and then a couple of them leaped from behind a privet hedge and beat the bejesus out of a Tar who was on the way home.

The duties of a Young Tar varied from rank to rank and from week to week. Among other things, we directed traffic at street corners near the school; kept boys and girls in line on their way to lunch or recess, when they left school, and while they waited for their buses; ran errands for teachers; clapped erasers; distributed announcements; carried messages; hung exhortatory posters in the halls; interpreted Mr. Simone's schedule changes for students who were baffled by them; and washed the car of Mr. Summers, the science teacher who was put in charge of the flotilla.

Within the ranks of the Tars, the fawners usually held the higher positions (Commodores or Admirals), followed by the ones with influential parents (Captains or Lieutenants), those who did well at athletics (Ensigns or Petty Officers), and those who did well academically (Seamen, Bay-men, and Swabbies). I would have been in the last group, but fortunately for me, when the first uniforms were being handed out, it was discovered that Mr. Summers had ordered one of the two Commodore outfits in my size, instead of a size that would fit Robby Haskins, who was to have been a Commodore. Since this fact wasn't discovered until all the Young Tars were backstage in the auditorium minutes before we were to be pre-sented to the school as paragons, I became a Commodore by default.

One of my regular duties as a member of the Young Tars was monitor-ing the boarding of the school buses at the end of the school day. This responsibility meant that I spent some time each afternoon with Porky White, who was at that time driving a bus for the town of Babbington. I remember well the first afternoon that I spent talking with, or listening to, Porky, while we sat in the bus he drove, Bus Six, waiting along with the other bus drivers for the bell to ring, ending the school day. It was a day early in October, a clear, bright afternoon. Talk had turned, as it is likely to turn in any conversation with Porky, to women. He asked me: "You got a girlfriend, Peter?"

"Well—" I said.

"You can tell me," he said. He looked over my head, at the other bus drivers, and grinned.

I answered, with a little hesitation, "Veronica McCall."

"Wow!" Porky said. "I'm impressed. You go right after first prize, don't you? She's quite a little number."

"She's cute, isn't she?" I asked. I was glowing.

"Cute?" said Porky. He raised his eyebrows and looked at each of the other drivers in turn. "Hey, open your eyes, Peter. She's more than cute, if you know what I mean. I bet you've got a lot of competition from the other guys."

"Competition?" I asked.

"Sure," he said. "A guy has got to be eternally vigilant if he doesn't want to lose his girl. You know, there's always somebody who wants to take your place."

"There is?" I asked.

"And it's when you think that you don't have anything to worry about that you probably have the *most* to worry about," Porky said.

"Why is that?" I asked.

"Well, when you start thinking you don't have anything to worry about, you start taking her for granted."

"Oh."

"You stop sending her flowers—"

"Flowers?"

"You stop saying those sweet nothings she likes to hear—"

"Sweet nothings?"

"And pretty soon you start seeing signs that she's bored."

"Bored?"

"Sure. You have to remember to keep up the romantic touches, because when you get right down to it, it's usually not *you* they like—what they like is *romance.*'

"Romance?"

"Of course, Peter. Before you know it, some other guy is sending her flowers, some other guy is whispering sweet nothings to her, and pretty soon another mule is kicking in your stall, you know what I mean?"

"Yeah," I said. I wondered whether Jack had sent flowers to Mrs. McCall.

"When was the last time you took her out for dinner somewhere with candlelight?"

"I'm only in the fifth grade," I said.

"Oh, yeah," said Porky, shrugging. "Well, not dinner, then. When was the last time you took her—"

"I've never taken her anywhere," I said.

"You don't take her out?" asked Porky.

"No," I said. I couldn't decide whether Porky was pulling my leg or whether an important facet of fifth-grade life had been entirely hidden from me. "None of the boys my age take girls out," I said. Porky smiled and patted me on the head. He winked at one of the other drivers. "Do they?" I asked.

I didn't know what to think. Certainly none of the boys I knew took girls out. Certainly none of the girls I knew *went* out. Or did they? Suppose they did go out, but they never told me about it. It might be that they had been keeping this going-out business from me because they knew I wasn't ready for it. I had an early bedtime, after all, even on weekends. Perhaps the boys and girls who went out didn't have to be in bed until a couple of hours later than I did, and perhaps they were accustomed to rendezvousing, of a Saturday night, at the Gilded Peacock, where they ate egg rolls and spare ribs and danced the merengue while I was asleep. It was possible, even likely, that they kept their nightlife secret from me out of kindness. They didn't want me to feel left out. Of course, I *was* left out, but they couldn't help that, and if I didn't *know* that I was left out, at least I wouldn't *feel* left out. It was kind of them to keep all this from me, in a way. Not only was it kind, but it was really quite amazing. To think that they could lead such wild lives after dark and manage to conceal all of it from me. I'd never even had a hint that all this was going on. None of my friends ever betrayed any of it. Veronica certainly never gave the slightest—Veronica. Veronica. Did she want to be part of this, did she want to go dancing at night at the Gilded Peacock? Of course she did. The poor thing. I was going to have to start taking her out.

9

IF I WAS GOING TO START buying Veronica flowers and candy and taking her out on dates, I was going to need money. I received a small allowance from my parents, quite a small allowance: twenty-five cents a week. Of course in those days—and the days that I'm recalling *were* those days—a quarter was worth something. Something, but not enough. I was going to have to get a job, and the first thing that occurred to me, doubtless the first thing that would have occurred to any boy my age in a situation like mine, was a paper route. The boy who delivered the *Babbington Reporter* looked at me with incredulity and glee when I asked him whether he ever thought of retiring from the newspaper business.

He recovered quickly. "Nah," he said. "It's too exciting."

I walked alongside him while he delivered the papers and tried to collect from each customer. The *Reporter* was published on weekdays only; customers paid twenty-five cents a week for it, delivered. For two or three hours I walked the route with him and worked to persuade him to give it up. My argument ran along the following lines, which I'd based on comments I'd heard Mel Allen make before a broadcast of an old-timers' game: there comes a time when the veteran has to step aside to give the rookie a chance, has to recognize that the river of life is flowing on and it's time he drifted on with it, has to recognize that someone else may need the work more than he does, that there are other kinds of work that he can do because he is older, and that it is meet and right that he do that other work, whatever it may be, and let another boy deliver his papers.

"All right," he said, after he had delivered the last paper. "You win. I'll sell you the route."

"Sell?" I asked.

"Sure. Let's say a dime a customer."

"Well, I—"

"You have to give me all the money I'm owed, too."

"Owed?"

"Yeah. Not everybody pays on time. Didn't you notice?"

"No," I said. I had been too occupied with the task of convincing him to surrender the route.

"You don't know much about the newspaper business, do you?" he asked.

"No," I confessed.

"You'll learn," he said. He pulled the strap of his newsboy's bag over his head and thrust the bag at me. "It's a deal then, right?"

"Right," I said. I was so pleased to have the job that I accepted his terms without bargaining, without even considering that bargaining might be possible, establishing that day a habit of thought that has made me pay too much for most of the things I have bought since.

I borrowed, from Guppa, the money to buy the route and pay the bills of all the customers who were late in paying. I was to pay Guppa back at the rate of a penny per customer per week, but I was determined to collect all the old debts in the first week. When I stopped at the home of the first deadbeat on my list and she told me that she couldn't pay me because she didn't have the right change, I stood speechless in front of the door for a moment before I remembered that I had change.

"I can give you change," I said.

"Of twenty bucks?" she asked.

"Oh, no," I admitted.

"You better try me next week," she said. She closed the door. I got onto my bike and rode to the next stop on the route.

I soon found, to my surprise and disappointment, that not only did I have a hard time getting my customers to pay me, but even when they did pay me I didn't get to keep the twenty-five cents that they paid for the *Reporter.* I had to pay the *Reporter,* in the person of their agent, Mr. Creeley, who threw the bundle of papers into our driveway every afternoon, four cents for each issue on delivery and somehow get the money from the customers. From the first day, I was sinking into a hole. Fortunately, Porky had an idea about this problem too.

"You've got to look at it this way," he said. "What are your customers paying you for, or I should say, what would they be paying you for if they were paying you?"

"The paper," I said, trotting all my naïveté out for Porky to chuckle at.

"Oh, no they're not," said Porky. He chuckled at my naïveté and tousled my hair. "If they were just paying for the paper, they'd pick up a copy at the corner store, but they don't. You see, you're not selling the paper."

He paused to unbutton his pants and tuck in his shirt, providing, through this business, time for me to wonder what on earth he was getting at, so that when he made himself clear I would say to myself, "Ah-ha! So that's it."

"You're selling service," he said. "The service of delivering the paper to them. If they're not paying you, it's because they think they're not getting enough service."

"But I'm never late," I protested. "And I—"

"I know, I know," said Porky. "You're going about it completely wrong. You're just doing the job the way it's supposed to be done. You're not late, you don't miss a day, you don't complain, you don't cause any trouble. They think your job must be easy for you—too easy. You notice I didn't say that they think they're not getting *good* service. I said that they think they're not getting *enough* service. You see what I mean?"

I did see what Porky meant. I saw it very clearly, and I took action almost at once. On the next collection day, I delivered all the papers about an hour later than I usually did. I bandaged my right arm from the hand up to the elbow, smeared dirt on my cheek, and put a Band-aid on my forehead. With the paper, I delivered a halting apology for being late. As if reluctantly, I allowed it to be understood, in response to their questions, that an enormous dog had attacked me just as I had begun the route, knocking me off my bicycle and scattering the papers, and that I had lost time picking up a new batch of papers, having my cuts and scrapes bandaged, and getting the first in a long and painful series of rabies shots. Not only did I collect from every customer, but I took home far more in tips than I earned on my markup.

I began giving outstanding service, or the illusion of outstanding service, every payday and on any other day when an opportunity presented itself. On rainy days, I rolled the newspapers in wax paper. I learned to ask about customers' children, grandchildren, pets, arthritis, or whatever else interested them. I often apologized for the paper itself, anticipating the complaints of the customers that an issue was too thin, that the news on the front page was all bad, or that three words had been misspelled in a single headline, and I offered to knock a penny off the price of such defective issues and absorb the loss myself on the grounds that it embarrassed me to charge full price for "a rag like this."

On one occasion, inspired beyond anything I'd done before, I tore the front page of one copy and put it at the front of the stack in my canvas bag. At each customer's door, I would pull the torn copy from the bag and say, "Oops, can't give you *this* one," then add, with a wink, "I'll have to give that one to somebody else." They loved it. Of course, when I got to my last customer, Mrs. Blynman, I had no other copy for her. To Mrs. Blynman I said, "I can't give you this. It's torn. I'm going to ride my bike downtown to the *Reporter* printing plant and get you a fresh copy."

Mrs. Blynman didn't say anything. I started down the walk. Suddenly I turned and ran back to her door.

"Oh," I said. "Before I go, could you call my mother and tell her I might not get home for dinner, Mrs. Blynman?" I asked.

Mrs. Blynman said she would. Again I started down the walk. Again I turned suddenly and ran back to her door.

"And ask her to save me a piece of her birthday cake, would you please?" I said. Mrs. Blynman swallowed hard, insisted on taking the torn copy of the *Reporter,* and pressed a dollar bill into my hand.

I collected on Thursdays. Each Thursday afternoon, when I got home, I would spread the money out on my bed and count it. I kept a ledger, and I also made a graph that showed how much profit I had made each week. On a slip of paper in the back of the ledger, I calculated how long it would be before I had enough money to take Veronica on a date. I paid Mr. Creeley with the change and with the oldest, dirtiest bills, and I kept the newest, crispest ones for myself. On occasion, when my mother was ironing, I would get my capital out and press it. It was on one of these occasions, while I was ironing my money, that the thought ran through my mind that I had enough to buy a model plane kit with a real gas engine.

How strange it is that one's mind works independently of one's efforts to direct it, that the solution to a knotty problem eludes one through hours of concentrated effort and then appears unbidden but certainly welcome while one is running to the dock with the last of the trash cans, hoping that the trash boat will wait. Only when the image of the model plane kit appeared in my mind did I understand that I would rather have a model plane than go on dates with Veronica McCall, and the question returned: "How am I going to get out of this?"

The next morning, while my classmates and I were seated in our classroom, holding manila cards with new schedules on them, puzzling through the schedule and Mr. Simone's explanation of it, the door opened, and into the classroom walked Stretch Mitgang, the boy who had won at Simon Says on the first day of school, the boy who hadn't been certain about whether he should stand or sit. He stopped just inside the door and surveyed us. From his bravado, the defiant way he chewed his gum, his slouch, the way he hooked his thumbs in his pockets, I understood why he had come into our classroom. He had been sent back, thrown out of the sixth grade. From the way his eyes rested on Veronica and the way she turned abruptly away from him and tossed her hair, the way she pouted and pretended not to have seen him at all, I understood that Stretch might be the answer.

10

I MAY SPEND a good deal of time in confused indecision about what I ought to do next, but when I have at last seen which way is the right way, I run right along it. The next day, in the cafeteria, when Stretch Mitgang passed Veronica and me, I asked her, "Why does he wink at you like that?"

"Did he wink at me?" she asked. She smiled and looked in Stretch's direction; then she turned quickly back toward me and twisted the smile into a scowl.

"Yes," I said. "He winked at you."

"He's probably just being friendly, or he's teasing," said Veronica.

"Oh, no," I said. "It's more than that. He thinks you're quite a little number."

"Do you think so?" asked Veronica. The smile returned.

11

"STRETCH! WAIT UP!" I called. I had overheard our teacher, Mrs. Collingswood, talking with Stretch about his work. I knew that he was having a difficult time with everything, but that he was particularly bad at arithmetic. He looked morose.

"Stretch, I've got an idea for you," I said.

"Yeah?" he asked. He still looked morose, but his eyes flickered with a small hope.

"Yeah," I said. "I think you ought to study with someone and do your homework with someone. If you do that, it will help you keep your mind on your work."

"I do have trouble with that," he said. "Are you going to work with me?"

"I'm afraid I can't," I said. "I'm too busy with my paper route. I was thinking of Veronica."

"Veronica?"

"Sure," I said. "That way, you'll be doing both of us a favor: me and you. You'll do better in arithmetic, and you'll be able to keep an eye on Veronica for me. See, I don't get to spend much time with her now that I have my paper route. I'm getting a little worried that some other mule might start kicking in my stall, you know what I mean?"

"No," he said.

"Never mind," I said. "It doesn't matter. Just try studying with Veronica and see if it helps."

"All right," he said. "I can ask her the problems and she can give me the answers."

"I think she should ask you the problems instead, and you should figure out the answers," I said.

"How come?" he asked.

"Because she's better at arithmetic than you are," I said. "You're the one who needs practice."

He expelled one sharp laugh. "That's a joke, right?" he asked.

"A joke?"

"Yeah. Say—you're not making fun of me, are you?"

"Oh," I said, "now I see what you mean. You mean, what's the sense of Veronica asking you the problems if you don't know the answers? Is that it?"

"Yeah, that's right."

"You and Veronica are going to get along really well, Stretch," I said. In a corner of my mind, I did a little further development work on my vague hunch about the contributions of Frankie Paretti's parents to the vacant look that Frankie wore and arrived at a more coherent theory, a theory that allowed me to predict that Veronica and Stretch would be likely, if they were to have a child some day, to have one about as bright as Frankie, a theory that was to be confirmed several years later, during a high school biology class devoted to the work of Gregor Mendel.

"Would you do me a favor when you go to Veronica's?" I asked.

"What?" asked Stretch.

"I was going to get Veronica some flowers, but I don't have time now.

It's already late for me to be starting my route. Here's a dollar. Stop at Anderson's on the way to Veronica's and get whatever you think she'll like, okay?"

12

VERONICA AND STRETCH began spending some time together, but they didn't seem to be making much progress. Veronica seemed, now that she was getting a closer look, not to see anything attractive in Stretch. I was close to giving up, letting Veronica rob me of my childhood, of my innocence, resigning myself to spending my money on dates and never being able to set enough aside for a model airplane with a real gas engine, when I saw the poster for the roller-skating party. The whole plan came to me at once. I would invite Veronica to the skating party. She would be delighted, flattered, and thrilled. Not only was the roller-skating party likely to be appealing to Veronica for itself, but this was a high-school roller-skating party, sponsored by the junior class to help raise money for the traditional junior class barge for the annual Babbington Clam Fest. Veronica was sure to consider it, as I did, a sophisticated event. I would fall ill on the day of the party. I'd ask Stretch to escort her. At the party, Veronica would fall in love with Stretch and drop me like a hot potato. I would be able to buy the model airplane.

I saw Veronica next in the cafeteria, where she was buying her lunch. She slid her tray along the shelf formed by stainless steel tubes and took a plate of a macaroni dish called American chop suey, a bowl of boiled green beans, and a bowl filled with cubes of green Jell-O. "Do you want to go to the high school roller-skating party?" I called out to her. Veronica stopped and spun around. Her eyes were wide with pleasure. Her mouth was open. Her Jell-O was quivering. She put her tray down on the rack and ran to me and took both of my hands in hers.

"Do you mean it?" she asked.

"Sure I mean it," I said, with the confidence that a well-wrought scheme could give a boy my age at that time.

"I've always wanted to go to one of those skating parties," she said. She hugged me, right there in the cafeteria, with everyone watching.

"Oh, Peter," she said. "I can't wait. I bet I can skate just as well as any of those big girls."

"You can?" I asked, bemused. The idea of actually skating, it suddenly occurred to me, had not been part of my vision of the evening. As I had seen it, Veronica would be happy enough just to be there, to sit somewhere with Stretch and eat popcorn, drink root beer and orange soda, and watch the high school boys and girls perform intricate and fluid routines that had required most of their high school years to perfect.

"Just wait till you see me skate," she said.

I looked at my hands, and since they looked awkward just hanging there at the ends of my arms, I began wringing them. I was worried that perhaps Stretch couldn't skate. If in fact he couldn't skate, Veronica wouldn't be likely to fall in love with him at the skating party.

"Oh, no," said Veronica.

"What?" I asked. She looked concerned.

"You can't skate, can you?"

I nearly told her that it didn't matter whether I could skate or not, but I thought better of it in time. I doubt that pride would have allowed me to admit that I couldn't skate anyway.

"Well," I said, "It isn't that I *can't* roller-skate. It's just that I'm—I'm a little rusty."

I risked looking her in the face. There were signs that she might smile, that all might be well, if I could just say the right thing now.

"But it's like riding a bicycle or doing multiplication," I said. "It comes right back to you. I just need some practice. Of course, I won't be as good as you are, but I'll bet we'll look pretty good together."

Her face had lit up, and she gave me a quick hug. "We can practice together!" she said. She began to hop up and down. "I'll get my mother to let you come along to one of my lessons. After my lesson is over, you and I can practice together for a while."

"That would be great," I said. To preserve the illusion that I would be taking her to the skating party, I was going to have to practice with her. I felt the sinking feeling that I have always felt when I know that I am getting myself in over my head, but I felt at the same time the other emotion that accompanies my diving into the dark waters of overreaching: an intoxicating self-confidence, all the more intoxicating because it is groundless. After all, since I had never roller-skated before, I had no reason to believe that I was not a roller-skating prodigy, awaiting only the sensations that would rush through me when the wheels of my skates first touched the floor to unlock the grace and power that lay within me.

13

"HEY, you made the right decision," Porky told me. "You're going to have a great time." I had told him that I had invited Veronica to the skating party and that I didn't know how to skate. I had not told him that the skating party was part of a plan to swap Veronica for a model airplane. Porky punched my shoulder in the good-natured way that men do when they're going to start talking about sex. "Do you know what those roller-skating parties are like?" he asked me.

"No," I admitted.

"Everybody meets at the high school," he said. "You ride to the roller rink in a school bus, and everyone sings songs and tells jokes and has a wonderful time. In the back of the bus, they might do a little (he made the motions of puffing on a cigarette), a little (he made his hand into a fist and made the motion of drinking from his thumb), a little (he hugged himself and twisted from side to side). Then, at the rink, you skate and skate, and you take breaks for Cokes, and sometimes you walk out to the parking lot for some air, and a little (he made the motions of puffing on a cigarette), a little (he made his hand into a fist and made the motion of drinking from his thumb), a little (he hugged himself and twisted from side to side), and then you skate some more. You can have a hot dog or another Coke. Then everybody gets onto the bus again, and you ride back to the high school. This time, if the kids on the bus take care of the bus driver, he might take the long way home. You know," said Porky, wearing an odd grin. "I'm going to be driving one of the buses to the roller rink and back. It might be arranged for me to take the long way home."

I had a good idea what he meant. How? How did I know anything about taking the long way home? It was in the air. Just as a house, especially an old house, has an ambient odor that is only temporarily disturbed by a chowder simmering on the stove or a chicken roasting in the oven and soon returns to its more or less constant composition, of which we, the inhabitants of the house, are ordinarily unaware, noticing it only when we have been away for some time and return and inhale the comfortable odor of home, so a community, especially an old and established community, has an ambient *Weltanschauung* that may be temporarily disturbed by the arrival of outsiders or by the ideas in an influential book, but eventually returns to its more or less stable composition, of which we, the residents, may be unaware until we have been away and return and hear in a conversation the comforting ideas that were in the air around us when we were at home. One of the ideas in the air when I was a boy was the idea of taking the long way home. It was enough in the air so that I knew approximately what it was about.

I didn't say anything in response to Porky's suggestion. I just laughed. He winked and poked me in the side. I confided to him my fears that I might make a fool of myself when I tried to skate.

"Don't worry about it, Peter," said Porky. "It's like anything else: if you convince yourself you can do it, you can do it."

"You can?" I asked. I was young, but not so young that Porky's statement didn't strike me as preposterous. And yet, so strong within me was the irrational hope that he might somehow be right, that all it would take for me to turn in a creditable performance on roller skates was my convincing myself that I could do it, that I was poised for conversion, eager to believe Porky if he could provide even the flimsiest reason for my doing so.

"The thing to do," Porky said, "is to imagine yourself doing what you're going to try to do. You close your eyes and picture in your mind what you're going to do. You picture every detail, from the first moment when your wheels hit the floor to the last spectacular spin and the applause of the crowd, and then when you really start to do it, when you glide onto the floor, you'll feel as if you've already done all of this before, so it won't be such a big deal anymore. You won't be nervous at all. I do it all the time."

I sat up straight. This was it. He was going to give me the evidence.

"Say I'm bowling, and I've left myself a tough split. I just take a few seconds to close my eyes and imagine myself making the split. I feel the ball in my hand. In my mind, I start my approach. I can feel the whole thing—my feet sliding toward the foul line, the release—and I can see the pins standing there, the ball rolling toward them, the hook, the way that it strikes the pin just right, the pin kicking across and striking the other. Then I'm ready. A calm spreads through me the way the smell of dinner spreads through a house. I'm ready. I *think* I can do it, so I *can* do it."

It was a raw and drizzly afternoon. Porky and I were sitting in Bus Six, waiting for school to get out. Joy rushed through me. I believed Porky. I knew from the testimony of many people, including my father and Porky's father, that Porky was a great bowler. If he had tried to convince me that this I-think-I-can technique had won him the love of beautiful women, I would have known that it didn't work, but bowling was quite another story. It was easy for me to believe that it worked for bowling. And bowling, after all, was a lot like roller-skating.

14

VERONICA'S ROLLER-SKATING LESSONS were held at a big, drafty indoor rink, a Quonset hut made of corrugated metal. The metal had rusted in spots, and from these spots brown and orange streaks ran down the corrugations. The parking lot was mostly mud, with a clamshell island here and there, and Veronica's mother cursed under her breath as the car pitched across the lot, tossed like a boat on a day when the bay was choppy. The entrance was a plywood shed stuck onto one end of the metal building. Over it was a sign that had once been brightly painted in red and yellow. The paint had faded and peeled, so that the appearance of the sign belied its claim:

FUNTIME ROLLER RINK

The door was loose on its hinges. The girl at the ticket counter was chewing gum and reading a comic book. Veronica's mother passed a card to the girl, and the girl cut a notch out of it with a conductor's punch. Then she looked at me. I had brought ninety-five cents with me. Neither my mother nor I had had any idea what it would cost me to rent skates and skate for a while with Veronica, so my mother had told me to call and ask. I hadn't wanted to do that, for a reason that persists to this day: I don't want to appear to be ignorant of the ways of the establishment I'm patronizing. I dislike calling a restaurant, for example, to ask whether they will accept a personal check as payment for a meal. If the answer is yes, I become convinced that when I write out my check at the restaurant, the waiter is sure to say, in a voice that carries to the dimmest and most intimate corners, "Say, I'll bet you're the guy who called this afternoon to ask whether we take personal checks, aren't you?" And if the answer is no, then I'm sure that when I pay with cash or a credit card, something in the way I handle the money or the rapidity with which I produce the card will bring on that booming voice anyway. So, rather than call the Funtime Rink to make the inquiries myself, I got Raskolnikov to call for me. Armed with the information that he procured, I was able to push my ninety-five cents at the girl with some confidence, bothered only by the small fear, which I have never outgrown, that between the time I have learned what to do at the establishment and the time when I actually walk through the door, all the rules will have changed; if I attempt to pay the restaurant bill in cash, the waiter will look at me with shock and embarrassment and whisper, "I'm sorry, sir, but we no longer accept American money."

"What is this for?" asked the girl.

"Rent skates," I said. "And skate for an hour."

"Oh, that's just right," she said. "It comes to ninety-five cents."

"Yeah, I know," I said, relieved, pretending a familiarity with roller-skating that I did not have, hoping that the girl would assume that I frequented other, larger, more glamorous roller-skating rinks and was, therefore, familiar with the going rates.

"Oh, you must be Peter!" said the girl, clearly not deceived. "Your uncle called this morning to find out how much it was going to 'set you back' to go skating here."

"My uncle," I said, trying to smile.

"Yes, he told me it was your first time skating, and you wanted to impress your girlfriend, and he wanted to make sure you had a good time. Is Veronica your girlfriend? Veronica's a really good skater. Is she going to teach you? I'm sure she can teach you a lot."

"I really just need practice," I said, weakly. I started for the door that led inside.

"How did your uncle get that nickname, Rascal?" the girl asked.

"Oh, it's a long story," I said. I kept on walking.

Veronica put her skates on and rolled out onto the floor of the rink. She looked just terrific, skating around the rink as if she were the only one on it, and to my eyes she was. I couldn't really imagine why she was taking lessons. What could any lessons teach her beyond the things she was doing already? She wore a tiny skater's dress that hugged her at the top but had a skirt that flew outward whenever she turned, displaying her legs and her panties. I tried to maintain an appearance of detached interest in the sport without betraying the uneasy feeling I got each time Veronica skated backwards past us with her little skirt flipped up over her little bottom. As she skated, I began to understand what Porky had meant when he had said that she was quite a little number, and I began to understand that Veronica was growing up in a way that I wasn't. At the same time, I became more and more convinced that I would be able to acquit myself quite well when I went out onto the rink. I began to wonder why I had ever worried about being able to skate. Watching Veronica, I could see that it was so much easier than I had imagined, and it was clearly lots of fun, such a delight to zip around like that, to whirl, to spin, to glide along with one leg stretched out in the air behind you. I was going to have a ball.

Then Veronica's teacher arrived. As soon as I saw him, I knew that he was Jack, the Jack who had been forced to hide in the storage area under the eaves in Veronica's parents' bedroom. It took a moment longer for me to recognize that he must be Stretch Mitgang's older brother. I couldn't have estimated his age then, but I would guess now that he was twenty-two. He had jet black hair, heavy eyebrows, a clear and piercing gaze, a craggy jaw, a heartwarming smile, and straight teeth. Just watching him glide across the rink made me feel confident; surely Jack must have taught Stretch to skate.

Mrs. McCall put her hand on my knee. "Oh, here's Jack," she breathed. "Hi, Jack!" she called out. She waved at him with her other hand, and squeezed my knee so hard that I turned toward her with some alarm, wondering what I had done to upset her.

"Isn't he cute?" she whispered to me. He didn't seem at all cute to me. After all, he was a grown man.

"He's handsome," I said. "Veronica's cute." I paused. Distractedly, I corrected myself. "She's more than cute, if you know what I mean," I said. "She's quite a little number."

Mrs. McCall looked at me. She seemed to be noticing me for the first time.

"Why, you're right," she said. "She is, isn't she?" She looked out across the rink. For quite a while she said nothing, just watched Jack and Veronica. Jack swooped up behind Veronica and gave her a pat on the rump. Mrs. McCall muttered, "My God."

For several minutes, we watched Jack and Veronica cavort around the rink. Jack would grasp Veronica between the legs, his large hand forming a seat for her, her tight nates settling into his palm, his fingers reaching up toward the small of her back. I thought that Mrs. McCall might pass out. She breathed in short, shallow draughts, and she had begun languidly to massage my knee, as if she were trying to make up for the pain she had inflicted earlier. At last Jack put Veronica down, and he began directing her through a series of slow, precise exercises. Mrs. McCall sighed and said, "I'm going outside for a cigarette. You want to come?"

"Sure," I said.

When we reached the parking lot, Mrs. McCall took a package of Kools from her handbag, and asked, "Do you smoke?" Before I could speak she put a hand to her forehead and shook her head. "Of course you don't smoke," she said. "What am I thinking of? I must be losing my mind. You're a little boy." I looked at the ground. "Oh, I didn't mean it that way," she said. "Peter?" I looked up. She let a long stream of smoke out through her puckered lips. She took another long pull at her cigarette and let the smoke out. "You're very—advanced—for your age," she said.

"Well, I read a lot," I said.

She smiled and patted me on the shoulder. "So you think Veronica is quite a little number, do you?"

"Yes," I said. I felt my ears redden.

"And Jack is handsome," she added.

"Right," I said.

"What about me?" she asked. She raised her eyebrows and tilted her head, waiting for an answer.

I knew the answer, if only by imitation. It was a statement that had shocked me when I heard my mother repeat it one Sunday morning at breakfast. She and my father had gone to a party, some couple's anniversary party, the night before, and my mother was in an effervescent mood that Sunday morning. She actually danced around the kitchen while she made breakfast, humming and singing, and she recounted the entire evening, while my father stared at the paper and drank his coffee and I watched and listened wide-eyed and open-mouthed. I caught my mother's delight in the memory of the evening before, the dancing, the toast with real champagne, the canapés, the high spirits, the flirting, and though I was shocked I was also proud and pleased when she repeated, giggling, what a man, some other woman's husband, had said to her.

"You look sexy in that sweater."

Mrs. McCall choked and burst out laughing. "Oh, thank you, Peter," she said.

It was the truth. She was, I guess, about thirty-five at the time. She had dark hair and large, bright eyes. She was voluptuous. Her lips were full, and she used a bright red shade of lipstick. She had large breasts, a rounded belly, wide hips, and a lively bottom that could have been the inspiration for the tight skirts that came into fashion a year or two later. The sweater she was wearing, a white cardigan, very snug, with the top buttons open to display her cleavage, did make her look sexy. It was the truth, but I didn't understand why it was the truth; my notion of sexy went no further than the décolletage of the sweater. I had no appreciation of what the décolletage was designed to inspire, what ultimately it was intended to offer. I wished that I had said nothing. I wished that my mother had said nothing. I wished that I could go home.

Veronica called to me. She was standing in the doorway of the plywood entry. Jack stood behind her with a hand on her shoulder.

"Come on, Peter," she said. "We can practice together."

Inside, Mrs. McCall helped me lace my skates.

"All right, Peter," she said at last. "You're as ready as you'll ever be." She stood up and gave me a pat on the shoulder. "Good luck," she said.

Jack skated to the railing in front of us, all power, skill, muscles, chin, and teeth. "Hey, good morning, Mrs. McCall," he said. He gave an odd emphasis to the words *Mrs. McCall,* and he smiled broadly and winked at her.

I told myself to do what Porky had told me, to imagine myself doing what it was I wanted to do. I stood at the railing, closed my eyes, and summoned all the strength of imagination that I could muster, and in a single brilliant instant I was able to imagine everything that was going to happen.

I would say, "Well, here I go!" and I would push myself onto the floor and be startled by the sensation of having lost all control over my feet. My right foot would insist on rolling farther and farther forward while my left rolled slowly backward. I would flail my arms as falling people do, as if imitating the herky-jerky rotation of the wings of an ornithopter. And I would, of course, fall. I would land on my right buttock, hard, my eyes locked on Veronica, and I'd watch her expression shift from surprise to concern to hilarity to embarrassment and back to hilarity. I would scramble to my knees and look over at Mrs. McCall, who would be trying awfully hard not to laugh, and at Jack, who would be roaring, so forgetting himself in his exuberant amusement that he had flung his arm around Mrs. McCall and was kneading her shoulder through the soft angora sweater. I would struggle to my feet and try to make myself move in Veronica's direction. Try as I might, I would not be able to make myself move on a course that would get me to her side. Weak with laughter, she would finally come to me, put her hand on my waist, and try to show me how to change direction. The smallest movement would upset my balance, and at any moment, even when standing still, I would be on the verge of falling down. I would clutch at her, to keep from falling, and fall anyway, often taking her down with me. I would discover in the tumbles a surprising pleasure, and I would discover in the laughter an analgesic for the embarrassment of not being able to skate, for not being graceful and confident, for being, in that puzzling way, so very much younger than Veronica. I would begin to play for the laughs, and Veronica and I would wind up having a wonderful time. She would begin to anticipate my falls, and she would prove to be so at ease on skates that she could even play the clown. She could fake losing her balance herself, go through a wild parody of my attempts to recover my balance, recover hers at the last instant, make it look as if both of us had recovered, then give me a little nudge and send me sprawling. Jack and Mrs. McCall would be beside themselves with laughter, flinging their arms around each other in uncontrollable glee when Veronica resorted to simply holding me up and guiding me around the rink as if I were stuffed. When Veronica and I finally made our way back across the rink to where they were seated, they would stand and applaud us, Veronica would stop and deliver a graceful swanlike curtsy, and I would bend at the waist and fall in a heap.

"Bravo!" Jack would shout, when I had a grip on the railing again at last.

"Oh, Peter, you were so funny!" Mrs. McCall would say, gasping for breath, dabbing at her eyes with a handkerchief. "I haven't laughed so much in I don't know how long."

"You were hilarious, kid," Jack would say. He'd pat me on the shoulder and add, "You're really a good sport."

Veronica would put her arm through mine and snuggle up beside me, and when I looked at her I would know that she was pleased with me, that she liked being with me, and that it would be quite possible for Veronica and me to be great friends once she'd transferred her lusts to Stretch.

"Here I go!" I announced through clenched teeth. I pushed myself out onto the floor. Porky White turned out to be right; everything happened just as I had imagined it would.

15

THE SKATING PARTY was scheduled for a Friday night. During school that day, I began to exhibit signs of illness. By the end of the day, I had made all the arrangements. I told Veronica that I was coming down with a twenty-four-hour virus and I was sure that I would begin vomiting at about the time that the skating-party bus left the high school lot. She was terribly disappointed, but she accepted Stretch as a substitute escort, since the party meant so much to her. Stretch was surprised. I gave him the tickets and lent him two dollars to make sure that he and Veronica had a good time.

By the time the school day ended, only one thing remained for me to do. On the way home from school, I sat in the seat right behind Porky, and I told him most—but not all—of the story.

"What?" said Porky. "You mean another guy is taking your girl to the skating party? Hey, don't worry. I'll keep an eye on them. I'll make them sit right up in the front of the bus and I'll keep the lights on the whole way back. And I'll drive straight back to the school, too. He's not going to get away with anything while I'm driving."

I opened *Our Town and Its People* and removed from it a new five-dollar bill. "Here, Porky," I said, handing it to him. "Do me a favor. Take the long way home."

16

I told my parents that I wasn't feeling well, and I went up to bed right after dinner, at about the time that Jack was dropping Stretch and Veronica off at the high school parking lot. I lay in my bed and tried to form in my mind a clear image of what Veronica and Stretch were doing.

Three buses were waiting in front of the high school when they arrived. They got out of the car, and Stretch's father drove away.

"Which bus should we take?" Stretch asked.

"I don't know," said Veronica.

A line of very big boys and girls stood at the door to each of the buses. Boarding the first bus was that sad group of boys and girls who remain awkward throughout adolescence, who never find a cure for their acne, who either can't lose weight or can't gain weight, who are too tall or too short, too smart or too outspoken. Since Veronica and Stretch were so out of place, so much younger than the others, they probably belonged on that bus. Boarding the second bus were the clean-cut boys and girls with whom my mother would have wanted me to ride if I had taken Veronica. The third bus, however, was Bus Six.

"Oh look, this is Bus Six," Veronica said. "It's the bus Porky White drives. Let's get on this one."

They did.

"Let's sit in the back," said Veronica.

"Sure," Stretch said. "Anywhere you want."

The back of the bus was filled with smoke, loud talking, and boys and girls in leather jackets. Veronica and Stretch walked into the smoke, and one of the boys said, "Get lost, kids. These seats are taken. You're on the wrong bus."

"Yeah, I guess we are," Stretch said. He grabbed Veronica's sleeve and turned to go.

"Shut up, stupid," said one of the girls, punching the boy on the shoulder and grabbing Veronica's other sleeve. "They can sit right here," said the girl. She pulled them onto the seat beside her, where in fact there was plenty of room for them.

"I think you kids look so cute," the girl said.

"What's your name, cutie?" asked another boy. He reached from behind Veronica and put his hands on her shoulders, brought his face next to hers. His breath was dank and sour.

"Veronica," said Veronica. Her voice sounded a little hollow, but she smiled when she gave her name, and after she had spoken she tilted her head upward bravely and batted her eyelashes.

"And what's your name, kid?" the boy asked.

Stretch stuck his chin out and said, "Stretch," in a voice as deep as he could manage.

"That's it, Stretch, don't be afraid of him," said another girl who was leaning over the back of the seat in front of them. "He's just a big jerk. Knock it off, Sal," she said to the big jerk.

Sal didn't say anything to her, but he gave her a weaselly, calculating look. Then he gave Veronica a squeeze, pulling her back toward him. He bent his head downward and in a stage whisper asked her, "Veronica, you want a little drink?"

The girl in front of them looked furious. "If you don't leave them alone, I'll never talk to you again, Sal," she said. Her teeth were clenched, and so were her fists.

"Hey," said Sal. "Don't get all upset with me. Stretch and Veronica are here because they want to play with the big kids." He snapped Stretch's ear. "Isn't that right?" he asked.

"Oh, sure," Stretch said.

"There you are," said Sal. He flipped his hand in the air in a gesture that meant: "There you have it; there can be no further argument; the evidence that you have just heard is so conclusive that any unbiased observer would agree that the matter is settled."

The girl pounded her fists once on the back of the seat and said "Ooooh!" She spun forward again, away from Sal, and slumped down so that her head was hardly visible. Sal made with his free hand a gesture, the meaning of which, "Fuck you," I didn't learn for another couple of months.

By the time the bus reached the skating rink, Stretch and Veronica knew the names of most of the boys and girls around them, their breath smelled of bourbon, and their cheeks were flushed. They emerged as the stars of the evening. They were certainly the best skaters there, and the girls were able to admire Veronica without feeling jealous, since she was so much younger than they, only a child, while the boys were able to toss her around like a basketball, and they lined up for an opportunity to do so. Finally, the lights began to flash, and the skaters drifted off the rink, removed their skates, and boarded the bus. Shortly after Porky pulled out of the parking lot, the lights inside the bus went out. Stretch and Veronica peered into the darkness around them, squinting to try to make out just what the older boys and girls were doing. When Stretch put his hand on Veronica's thigh, I smiled, stretched out in the cozy warmth of my bed, and fell asleep.

17

THE WINNER of the name-the-school contest was announced about a week later. Since some ill feeling had developed toward the judges and the school administrators during the long time that had passed since the contest began, Mr. Simone decided that it would be a good idea to make a grand occasion out of the award ceremony. Invitations went out to all our parents to tour the completed school and then gather in the auditorium to learn the winning name and applaud the student who had submitted it.

I was sitting with Raskol, Margot and Martha, Matthew, and Veronica and Stretch; Stretch was on Veronica's right and I was on her left. My parents were beside me. When Mr. Simone stepped up to the podium, everything inside my chest and abdomen seemed to vanish, leaving only a cold hollow.

"The time has come at last," said Mr. Simone. He looked at a sheet of paper, and then he looked out over the audience. "Will Peter Leroy please come up onto the stage?" he said.

Veronica squeezed my hand. I stood. I walked sideways out of the row of seats, and somehow I walked down the aisle and up the stairs to the stage and across the stage to Mr. Simone's side.

"It wasn't easy to pick a winner," Mr. Simone said. "There were many, many good names submitted. I wish you could have seen some of the meetings we held when we were trying to pick a winner. Some of us liked names that had to do with nature and that sort of thing. Others liked names that gave you a sense of Babbington's past. One that I happened to like was 'Unfinished School.'" He waited while the adults laughed. "But we couldn't seem to agree on a name that *all* of us liked," he continued. "Finally, I said to the other judges, 'Look, the school is nearly finished. The kids have been waiting for months. We've got to choose. Let's go through all the names once more and see if there isn't one that all of us can at least tolerate.' Well, I'm happy to be able to say to you that there *was* one name that none of us really hated." He turned aside and accepted a bronze plaque from Mr. Simon. Then he turned to me. "Peter," he said, "yours was the winning name. Perhaps you would like to read it to the people." He handed the plaque to me. In a voice tight with pride and nervousness, I read:

Babbington Central Upper Elementary School
(Named by Peter Leroy)

Applause filled the hall. Raskol clasped his hands together and waved them over his head. Veronica and Stretch got up and slipped out the side door. At the door, before they left, Veronica paused, turned, and waved; Stretch gave me a salute and a wink. I held the plaque over my head. I felt the dizzying happiness that I later felt when I turned round and round, guiding my gasoline-powered flying model Piper Cub in a wide circle at the end of its tether.

Call Me Larry

Though we do not wholly believe it yet, the interior life is a real life, and the intangible dreams of people have a tangible effect on the world.

James Baldwin

Are there perhaps other worlds more real than the waking world? . . . Often we have before us, in those first minutes in which we allow ourself to slip into the waking state, a truth composed of different realities among which we imagine that we can choose, as among a pack of cards.

Marcel Proust
The Captive
(translated by C. K. Scott Moncrieff)

Eric Kraft . . . looks exactly like my mind's-eye picture of Peter Leroy: wiry build, wacky smile, bright eyes.

Susan Orlean
"Getting Serial"
The Boston Phoenix

Preface

MY RELATIONSHIP with Larry Peters is a complex one. In the simplest terms, I owe my livelihood to him, but, far more than that, I owe to the series of adventure novels in which Larry has appeared for some thirty years—and to their pseudonymous authors—the discovery of an avenue to a feeling of artistic freedom without which I might never have managed to write any of my personal history, adventures, experiences, and observations.

In the pages that follow, I have tried to narrate the origin of that relationship and explain its complexity. I fear that in the process I may have slighted the authors of the original Larry Peters books. That was never my intention. Because I know far too well how much effort goes into the writing of even the thinnest books, I would never intentionally belittle anyone who attempts it.

Peter Leroy
Small's Island
December 10, 1984

1

I WAS BARELY ADOLESCENT when I first encountered Larry Peters, the eponymous hero of a series of books called, collectively, The Adventures of Larry Peters. My maternal grandmother, Gumma, gave me the first book in the series, *The Shapely Brunette,* as a present and a consolation, when I was sick, confined to bed, on my birthday. I had one of the childhood diseases, but I can't recall now which one it was: measles, mumps, chicken pox, or the twenty-four-hour virus. These illnesses were not so bad, I thought. The discomfort that they brought was part of growing up, each made one a little more grown up, and the knowledge that one gained from them ranked in the upper third or so of things that were, at that age and time, important to know: if one did not know at first hand what the pain of mumps was like, one was not an initiate into a certain shadowy nook of childhood experience that those outside it wanted to enter. That it might be nice not to have to be initiated into that particular corner of childhood experience at all did not occur to me then. It would have been more painful, at the time, to be excluded from it, and so I welcomed the mumps, the experience of mumps, the knowledge of mumps.

There was even an aspect of illness that I enjoyed. I liked having to stay in bed for hours on end, left to myself, left to amuse myself. At that time, before my mother became an independent businesswoman, she was at home for most of the day, cleaning the house and cooking. She would come into my room from time to time to see if I needed anything, but for most of the day she was busy with her own occupations, and so I had time to myself, time to think, time to let my mind wander, time just to enjoy being alone; and when my mother left the house, as she did for at least part of each day, to go shopping or do other chores or to visit a friend, I had the house to myself. I had formed the habit, at an early age, of reading in bed, so it was a treat to have all day to do it, in my own bed, in my own room, and, best of all, in a silent and empty house. In the morning, my mother would give me breakfast in bed: toast and cocoa, hot cereal with evaporated milk, or graham crackers broken into milk. I would listen to the radio while I ate, usually to a program called "Bob Balducci's Breakfast Bunch," which was supposed to originate from a restaurant, Bob Balducci's, famous for its pancakes and waffles. The program was a variety show, with singers and comedians, and with guests who spoke on subjects that they knew at least something about. All of that was interesting enough, but my favorite part came late in the program, when Bob Balducci and his sidekick, Baldy the Talking Dummy, had the people in the audience—a group that seemed, from his interviews with representatives of it, to consist entirely of grandmothers—stand beside their chairs and perform calisthenics. My mental image of this performance was so vivid and so hilarious that on some mornings it made me laugh until I cried. I was careful to set my tray on my bedside table as soon as Baldy the Dummy announced in his everlastingly ebullient style, "Now it's time to get up off your (pause) chairs!" I knew that if I didn't set my tray aside, I was sure to spill my breakfast when I began laughing. When Bob Balducci signed off, I would sit up, with several pillows propped behind me, and read.

At noon, I'd have clam chowder, tomato soup, or chicken noodle soup with saltine crackers that I would either break into pieces and scatter over the top of the soup or eat in single bites that I alternated with spoonfuls of soup, and I would listen to the radio while I ate, listening at this time of the day to soap operas, my favorite of which was "Mary Backstage, Noble Wife." After lunch, I would read some more, play with my plaster Babbingtonians, listen to the radio, and doze.

I should explain about those plaster Babbingtonians. At Jack's Twenty-Four Hour Jokes, on the southwest corner of Bolotomy and Main, one could buy, and most of us between the ages of nine and twelve did buy, model kits called Virtues 'n' Vices, which contained red rubber molds and plaster of Paris, with which one could cast figures that represented the Cardinal Virtues and the Seven Deadly Sins. I had quite a collection of these figures, most of them imperfect, with holes where bubbles had formed when I filled the mold, or with an arm glued ineptly back on after I had broken it in the unmolding. From the first, I had noticed resemblances between the figures and various people around town. In fact, I found that by making a few simple modifications, working with one of my mother's emery boards, a Popsicle stick, and some fresh plaster, I could construct, out of Wisdom, Courage, Temperance, Justice, Faith, Hope, Charity, Pride, Covetousness, Lust, Anger, Gluttony, Envy, and Sloth, convincing likenesses of nearly everyone I knew or noticed. A little work with some tempera paint made the likenesses even more convincing. I enjoyed manipulating these model Babbingtonians, pairing them, grouping them, imagining conversations and arguments among them. (Years later, I learned that Jack sold other molds as well, but only to older boys and girls, molds from which one could cast figures of men and women that could be combined in interesting sexual positions. When I learned this, two thoughts came immediately to my mind: first, that it must have taken much greater skill than I possessed to unmold these figures and, second, that modifying them to make them resemble Babbingtonians must have been more complicated than modifying the Virtues 'n' Vices had been.)

At night, during times when I was ill, I would put on my plaid flannel bathrobe and join my mother and father for dinner, and then I would return to bed to read some more, draw pictures, write notes to friends I wasn't able to visit or see in school, put my plaster Babbingtonians away, listen to the radio some more—most often to mystery programs—and doze. There are certainly worse ways to spend one's days.

2

I WAS ENCHANTED by that first Larry Peters adventure, *The Shapely Brunette,* from the moment I opened the book. On the front endpaper was a map of the area where Larry lived, a seacoast town called Murky Bay. The town of Murky Bay was situated on the shore of the bay called Murky Bay, and in Murky Bay were hundreds of islands, among them one called Kittiwake Island, where the Peters family lived. On the back endpaper was a map of the island itself and the floor plans of the Peters house and the workshops where Mr. Peters and the employees of Peters's Knickknacks worked in secrecy to develop the gewgaws, trinkets, baubles, bric-a-brac, curios, gimcrackery, and brummagems that were the Peterses' bread and butter. I spent quite some time with the maps and floor plans before I began reading the book, and I returned to them often while I was reading it. There was something about those maps and floor plans that invited the mind to wander, to meander among the islets as one might in a rowboat, to prowl around the house looking for hidden nooks, to imagine the conversations one might have with a companion while meandering among the islets or hiding in a nook. The maps and floor plans were detailed enough to seem to depict real places, and yet they were vague enough not to impose on me the limitations of reality, since I knew that they *didn't* depict real places. They permitted—even invited—the fabrication of imaginary details, and if one accepted the invitation, as I did, reality did not intrude with the stern demands it made from day to day: the invented details had only to fit the empty spaces provided for them and be in keeping with the details that were already there; they did not have to be verifiable. Often, later, while I was rereading one Larry Peters adventure or another, the stories themselves seemed too specific; at such times, I found myself returning to the endpapers, and I began making up new stories for myself. Surely, I thought, these schematics were deliberately designed to encourage this kind of dreaming, and surely the stories were intended only to give one an excuse for sitting still for long hours, imagining new goings-on on Kittiwake Island, imagining the voices across the Peterses' dinner table, the debates that must have taken place in the knickknack workrooms, and so on.

The frontispiece to that first book showed two boys, Larry Peters and his friend Rocky King, square-jawed American boys, standing side by side in a fierce wind, the collars of their windbreakers or flight jackets up, their hair blowing in a style that became popular in men's clothing advertisements much later in my life. Rocky was holding a large pair of binoculars to his eyes and peering into the darkness. In that darkness, one could see a lighted window, and in that lighted window, one could make out, if one studied the illustration closely and carefully enough, a shapely woman, presumably the brunette of the title. Larry was reaching for the binoculars, and under the illustration was a line from the book: "Come on, Rocky," Larry pleaded. "It's my turn."

I READ *The Shapely Brunette* twice that day, and a third time the next day. Then I read every other Larry Peters book that had been published. From then on, I waited impatiently for new books to come out. I was hooked on Larry Peters, and I wanted my friends to share my enthusiasm. I wanted them to read the books, to read them as thoroughly as I had read them, to absorb them as I had, so that we could use them in our friendship, use them as a constant, a given, in our conversation together, add them to the context of our conversations for the same reasons that one adds manure to garden soil: so that the plants will flourish, grow thick and intertwined, flower profusely and brilliantly. But most of my friends didn't share my enthusiasm for Larry Peters, his adventures, Kittiwake Island, or the habit of mingling reading with dreaming. They didn't notice every-

"Come on, Rocky," Larry pleaded. "It's my turn."

thing that I noticed. Most didn't even recognize, in the frontispiece to *The Shapely Brunette,* the image of the shapely brunette in the lighted window.

"Wishful thinking," said Raskolnikov. "That's just a way of drawing. The artist uses a few quick strokes of the pen to suggest that the shade is down without inking in the whole shade. We had that in art class already. It's just an artist's trick. It's not really meant to represent anything. You only see a woman there because you want to." He jabbed me in the ribs.

3

I RETURNED to the Larry Peters books again and again because the Peters family, Kittiwake Island, Murky Bay, and the ambience of potential adventure were so fecund a ground for the imagination. The adventures themselves became, for me, only the trellises on which each book grew. The stories were there to hold the books together, prop them up, but that function, although useful, perhaps even necessary, wasn't interesting; it could have been fulfilled by any story, as far as I was concerned, any story at all. The vines that grew on these trellises were much, much more interesting, and part of the interest that I took in them came from the fact that I was partly responsible for making them grow. Certainly the author, Roger Drake, was responsible for planting them and fertilizing the ground they grew in, but it was I who sent tendrils off at unpredictable spots, who sent the vines wandering in several directions, who made them blossom.

I didn't dislike the adventures, of course, but their attraction faded quickly. They were exciting to read the first time, considerably less exciting the second time, and not particularly exciting at all after that. Exactly the reverse was true of what each book told me about Larry, his home and family, his surroundings, and his friend Rocky King. These were matters that on first reading seemed to be only part of the background for the adventures, and a sketchy background at that, but that became more and more interesting as I read and reread.

The reader was not given much direct information about the personal, the private side of Larry's life. Now and then, a tantalizing piece of information would pop up in the course of an adventure, but more often there were simply gaps in the narrative that invited one to fill them. For example, in the adventure called *Bamboozled,* Larry and Rocky and Mr. Peters chase a mysterious prowler across the island, dashing through a labyrinth of bamboo that Larry has planted to baffle such prowlers. During a long and complicated night, the three become separated in the maze and are lost for several hours while the prowler makes his way to the knickknack works, rifles the file cabinet containing the plans for next year's line of gewgaws, and makes his getaway in the Peterses' speedboat. When, finally, the boys and Mr. Peters are reunited and realize what has happened, Mr. Peters pounds them on the back, assures them that they did their best, tells them that he's counting on them to track the prowler down while he and the designers come up with a new line of gewgaws, and then says, "Boys, it will be dawn in another hour or so, and we've got quite a day ahead of us. What do you say we get an hour's sleep, have a swim and a shower, and put away one of your mother's famous hearty breakfasts?"

That is the end of the chapter. The next chapter opens with Larry and Rocky crouched outside a boathouse, peering through a window at a gang of thugs in the employ of a rival knickknack company. But for me, a great deal happened between the chapters. I had, ever since Mr. Beaker first taught me to read, been in the habit of filling whatever gaps appeared in whatever I was reading. The adventures of Larry Peters seemed to have been written just for someone who had developed this habit, just for me. The books were full of gaps, some small, some big enough to wander in for days at a time. I filled this particular one with a conversation in Larry's bedroom, a swim, a glimpse of Larry's sister Lucinda in the shower, a breakfast of blueberry pancakes and sausage, the boys' goodbyes, their running out of gas on the way across Murky Bay, the Coast Guard's towing them to the town dock, a friend who lent them a jalopy (an amusing fellow who was always trying to get Larry's sister to go to the movies with him), a dented fender, a flat tire, a Pullman diner, a redheaded waitress with freckles and teary eyes, and much, much more.

4

THE PETERS FAMILY seemed, to me, quite rich, rich in all the ways that I would have considered a family rich at that time. They owned a whole island, after all. They had a maid, about whom I will have more to say later. They owned three boats: a working boat, a barge really, that they used for carrying freight from the mainland, and, in *The Missing*

Garage, used to transport an entire Esso gas station; a sailboat, a lean blue sloop that Larry was permitted to sail by himself and on which Larry's sister enjoyed sunning herself; and a speedboat, a mahogany Chris Craft speedboat with a twelve-cylinder engine. On the mainland, they owned a small piece of waterfront property in the town of Murky Bay, where they had a dock, a boathouse for the speedboat, and a garage in which they kept a Jaguar Saloon and a war-surplus Jeep.

Everything that the Peterses did was of an order different from anything my family or the families of any of my friends did. My father might spend most of a Saturday changing the oil and filter in our aging Commander, trying to devise a scheme to make my mother's washing machine stop walking across the cellar floor, or painting the garage, but Mr. Peters was likely to spend a Saturday tied up in the hold of a sinking ship, rappelling down a rock face in pursuit of some bric-a-brac smugglers, or conducting delicate negotiations for the purchase of some fine amber in Lübeck.

And the meals! Every time the Peters family sat down to a meal, it seemed to be the kind of meal that I associated with festivals and celebrations and funerals. If they were having breakfast, they drifted into the dining room one by one, and each filled a plate from a sideboard laden with oatmeal, pancakes, bacon, sausages (sometimes two kinds), coffee, cocoa, milk, juices, sticky buns, crumb cake, crullers, bran muffins, bagels, kaiser rolls, English muffins, toasted rye bread, toasted raisin bread, jelly doughnuts, white mountain rolls, corn muffins, salt sticks, bialys, and fruit. Marie, the maid, would fix eggs any way anyone wanted them. At home, my father usually started the day with white toast, coffee, and a couple of cigarettes. My mother rarely had more than coffee. I usually had a bowl of graham crackers soaked in milk, sometimes a cup of cocoa and toast.

Dinner at the Peterses' was always a big deal: baked ham, turkey, a roast beef, bowls of potatoes and vegetables, everyone talking away and eating like mad. Of course, they had to eat a lot when they could, because most of the meals at the Peters house were never finished. No sooner would they get their plates heaped with food and eat a few healthy bites than someone would begin shooting at the house from a low-flying plane, an explosion on the mainland would rattle the windows, or Marie would announce the arrival of a mysterious stranger. Dinners were sometimes interrupted in my family, too, but the interruptions seemed to me, at the time, less likely to lead to anything interesting: the heating pipes would begin making metallic knocking sounds, but upon investigation we would find no dark-eyed waif tied up in the cellar, banging on the pipes to rouse some help, only air in the radiators; we'd be startled by a knock at the back door, but it was never a mysterious stranger, only the Mr. Doughboy delivery man, running late on his route; a flash of light would fill the room, and a moment later an explosive crash would rattle the windows, but it would only be a summer thunderstorm, and in those days I didn't find a summer storm as exciting as an exploding gimcrack factory.

5

LARRY WAS NEVER BORED. That is, he was never bored within the books. I knew from experience that everyone my age was bored for a significant amount of time every day. It may have been the absence of boredom that made me truly understand how much of Larry's life was missing from the Adventures of Larry Peters, that made me begin to understand how distorted was the picture of Larry's life that we, the readers, Larry's admirers, were allowed to see. It seemed safe to assume, for example, that the Peters family ate dinner every evening, or nearly every evening. Logic told me that not all of these dinners could be interrupted by events that were part of one adventure or another. There had to be dinners when no one had much to say, when Larry poked at his peas with his fork, watched a skin form on his gravy, and didn't hear his father asking him what he was daydreaming or moping about.

Not only was Larry never bored within the books, but he was always busy. He was always working on one project or another, and taking the trash out was never one of them. Larry seemed very clever to me, as he must have to all readers, as he was intended to seem, and yet for all his cleverness, for all the things he knew, for all his work on one arcane project or another, he managed to be an all-round guy. He could make a good showing in a fight, even against hired thugs, run like a deer when the situation required it, climb cliffs or warehouse walls, tap phone lines, swim, fish, play chess. In fact, I had the idea, an idea encouraged by most of the things that occurred in the books, that there was probably nothing a boy my age might *want* to do that Larry *couldn't* do. If Larry never sang or danced or played the clarinet or baked a soufflé or cast sculpture in bronze or flew an airplane, it wasn't because he couldn't, it was simply because he didn't feel like it or because the occasion for doing so hadn't yet arisen in one of his adventures. In fact, I now recall that he *did* bake a soufflé and fly an airplane in *The Aerobatic Sous-Chef.*

6

LARRY'S FRIEND, buddy, *copain,* comrade, Rocky King, was the perfect pal for someone like Larry—or for someone like me. He was big and strong, older, a young man more than a boy. He had a past about which we knew little, other than the fact that he had lost his parents at an early age and had had to shift for himself, a necessity that had toughened him. When he first appeared on the scene, in that very first book, *The Shapely Brunette,* it was to come to Larry's aid, much as Arthur comes to the aid of Guyon in *The Faerie Queene* (Book II, Canto VIII). Larry was in an out-of-the way section of Istanbul, on the trail of some smugglers:

> He walked quickly along the wet streets, his footsteps echoing against the squalid houses on either side. Now and then he thought that he caught sight of a face in one of the windows, spotted a puff of smoke exhaled behind a shutter, or heard a murmured remark as he passed. Then, from an archway to his right, came a small voice, a small voice straining to sound strong.
>
> "Hey, what's your hurry?" asked the voice.
>
> Larry snapped his head around and saw, in the shadowy archway, the face of a girl no older than he. Her hair was straight, the color of a fawn's ears, and it needed combing. Her eyes were bright, even in the darkness, but they looked out from deep recesses darkened with kohl. She looked terribly tired, despite her smile, despite the way she tilted her head so that her pointed chin showed to best advantage. She reached out toward him.
>
> "It's cold," she said. "Wet, too. Why don't you come inside?"
>
> "I'd like to," said Larry, "but—"
>
> He stopped himself. He had to be careful. He had almost let slip the fact that he was searching for a gang of Turkish gewgaw smugglers. He had to remember that he couldn't afford to trust anyone.
>
> "It's warm inside," she said. "We can have fun together."
>
> She spread the shawl that she had wrapped around her, opening it

as an angel might spread her wings. In the shadows, Larry could just make out the pale whiteness of her skin. As if in a dream, he moved toward her.

"Hold it, sailor," said a strong voice behind Larry.

A hand as strong as the voice gripped his shoulder and held him back. Something in that grip, something strangely fraternal, told Larry that the hand that held him back was the hand of a friend, an ally.

"Get lost, sister," said the unknown friend to the girl in the shadows.

The girl closed the shawl around her, twisted her mouth into a sneer and then spat on the paving stones at Larry's feet, turned and disappeared through a dark doorway. From the same doorway, a stocky, swarthy, unshaven man emerged. Clearly, this man was no friend. In his hand was a cleaver. Larry heard a metallic click behind his ear, and the strong arm of his unknown protector pushed him to one side, against the stone building. From an open window somewhere above him Larry heard the sharp, staccato notes of a zither. Larry's mysterious ally was silhouetted against the light from a street lamp, and Larry could see that in one strong hand he held a revolver.

"Get lost, Bud," snarled the strong but oddly friendly voice of the young man who had come to Larry's aid.

Larry saw the swarthy man bare his teeth, then retreat into the shadows, and Larry heard a door close.

"Come on, kid," said the friendly stranger. "Let's get out of here."

Later, when they sat in the relative safety of a rough waterfront café, warming themselves over steaming mugs of cocoa, Larry struggled to find the words to thank the young man who had come to his aid.

"I don't know how to thank you," he began.

"Forget it, kid," said the smiling young man.

"I don't even know your name," said Larry.

"Call me Rocky," said the young man, smiling broadly and extending his large and callused right hand across the table.

"Call me Larry," said Larry, smiling as broadly as he could, reaching across the table to shake Rocky's hand and knocking the young man's cocoa into his lap.

Certainly Rocky impressed Larry and the reader with his strength, his predisposition to act, to do something about whatever situation arose,

even if he did not often take the time to consider whether what he was
doing was in every respect, in all its ramifications, right. More surprising,
however, and, for me at least, more welcome, was the fact that Rocky was
continually impressed by qualities of Larry's that the reader may not have
thought impressive, qualities that many readers—this one, certainly—
may have possessed themselves but counted as nearly worthless since
their playmates and schoolmates considered them of little value, may
even have counted them as shortcomings before they saw that Rocky admired them in Larry. Among these was Larry's indecisiveness, which
Rocky took as laudable evidence not merely of Larry's ability to see all
sides of a question and all the consequences of an action, but also of his
feeling that he had an intellectual obligation to do so.

"We'll go in through the French doors," said Rocky, "get the will
out of the safe, make our getaway through the topiary garden, and
then call your father from the pay phone back at that godforsaken
gas station and beanery we passed out there in the middle of nowhere."

"I'm not sure that's the best plan, Rocky," said Larry, his eyelids
lowered in an attitude of thought. "What if the will isn't in the safe?
Or suppose there are *two* safes in the house? We know that these
people are quite rich, and if *I* were quite rich and had a big house
like this, I'd have two safes: one for jewels and one for cash and
valuable papers. Now the *obvious* thing to do would be to put the
one for jewels in a bedroom, or in a dressing room, and put the one
for valuable papers in the library. But if I've learned one thing
about Kurt Politzer, it's that he's too smart to do the obvious thing.
The safe in the library here probably doesn't have any valuable papers in it at all. In *fact,* I wouldn't be surprised if the papers were in
the safe in the dressing room."

Suddenly Larry's face lit up, and he began shaking his head in an
attitude of grudging admiration for their adversary.

"No," he said. "No. There are *three* safes. Of *course.* The safe
in the library has nothing valuable in it at all. There is a *third* safe,
and it's probably tucked away somewhere where no one would expect a safe to be. In the kitchen, maybe. Or in the nursery. Or in a
bathroom. I'll bet that's it! The safe *we* want is in a *bathroom.* I'll
bet I even know which bathroom it is: it's the guest bathroom, the
powder room, and I'll bet it's on the ground floor. Perfect, *perfect.*
All the most valuable papers are in a place that most people, certain-

ly most thieves, would think wasn't safe at all: *behind the mirror in the powder room.* Oh, there are probably *some* papers in the safe in the library, some nonnegotiable stock certificates, passports, things like that, so that a thief who broke into *that* safe wouldn't look for *another* one, would just figure that the jewels and other valuables were in a safe-deposit box. Wait! *A safe-deposit box!"*

Larry snapped his fingers, and a group of dogs began barking.

"Of course, Rocky!" he shouted.

Suddenly, floodlights lit the grounds of the Politzer mansion.

"The will isn't in the house at all!" said Larry. "It's in a *safe-deposit box* somewhere!"

"Come on!" chuckled Rocky, with a barely perceptible note of urgency. "Let's get out of here before those dogs tear us apart."

Rocky also admired Larry's academic talents. He never ceased to be amazed at how quick and clever Larry was, not that Rocky was less quick or less clever, but Rocky's talents and knowledge were more restricted to practical areas: he could overhaul the engine in the Jeep with only a nail file and a can opener as tools, and he could find the best place to get a cheap and decent meal in most of the world's ports; yet Rocky, although he was older than Larry, seemed to know a lot less about the things one might be expected to learn in school than Larry did. This shortcoming of Rocky's wasn't explained, but I decided that it must have to do with that past of Rocky's about which we knew so little. I supposed that in his past there had been a reform school, from which Rocky had run away before he'd had a chance to pick up much long division or world history. Rocky's ignorance of what one learned in school gave Larry the opportunity, frequently, to explain something to Rocky that would impress the heck out of him and would make the reader, who was likely already to know what Larry explained, feel all the more like Larry and to think of himself as in some ways a leader or even a protector of big, friendly, uneducated lugs like Rocky.

7

LARRY'S FATHER was everything a boy might hope for, a real paterfamilias, who considered himself in control, who entertained few doubts

about himself, who assumed that he was the true head of the Peters
ménage. But beyond that, his work made him unusual as fathers go: he
was an artist of sorts. His artistic impulses had two manifestations. One
was the knickknack business, of course, and that could be considered one
of the practical or applied arts; the other, the purer manifestation, was his
making life interesting for himself and for his family.

Mr. Peters was able to do many things, and he got many things done.
He was well known and admired for many of the things he did, but others
of the things that he attempted did not have the results that he or anyone
else involved in the endeavor might have hoped for, except that they always resulted in a richer, more various, more interesting life for the Peterses. Within the Peters family, not an eyebrow would be raised if Mr.
Peters announced, over dinner one evening, that in the morning everyone
would begin building a raft so that the family could chart the course of the
Gulf Stream during their vacation, or that he had a plan for a sling that
could be hung inside a suburban garage, onto which the suburban motorist could drive his car, and which, thanks to an ingenious system of gears
driven by the car's rear wheels, would rock the motorist's colicky infant
offspring gently to sleep, or that he intended to import minks to the island,
where, since there were no predators, they could be allowed to run free
and would breed quickly, making the Peterses wealthy beyond imagining.

And yet, as unpredictable and impracticable as Mr. Peters's schemes
may sometimes have been, he had a steady, responsible side too. The
business savvy he displayed as the head of a world-renowned knickknack
design firm was a world apart from the world of late nights, cheap wine,
and strong cigarettes that is so firmly established in the popular notion of
bric-a-brac designers. The knickknack business, as portrayed in the Larry
Peters books, was a tense, competitive, cutthroat business, much more exciting than most businesses that my father or the fathers of my friends
were in or were ever likely to get themselves into. Mr. Peters had moved
his family to Kittiwake Island because he needed secrecy, he needed a
place where he could develop his designs without his competitors' learning about them before they were released. However, his competitors were
a ruthless, unprincipled bunch who would stop at nothing to steal his designs or sabotage his plans: that's how the adventures arose.

Mr. Peters was inventive, a leader, a loving father, and more. He was
something that most fathers of my acquaintance were not: a dignified
man. One could see, too, that he bore as if he were a block of granite the
cares that can fall on any family, taking the full weight, so that life should

rest lightly on the shoulders of the others. The reader saw this quality at once, at first meeting, when Mr. Peters was introduced in his study in *The Shapely Brunette:*

> Larry knew that he would find his father in the tiny attic study to which Edgar Peters retired when he needed to think and work undisturbed. Larry stopped outside the door and knocked. Everyone on Kittiwake Island knew that Edgar Peters was not to be burst in upon when he was concentrating in his attic retreat.
>
> "Just a minute," said the voice of Marie, the maid.
>
> Larry waited impatiently, snapping the nails of the thumb and middle finger of each hand together in his eager agitation. From behind the door came muffled conversation, the sound of something scraping along the floor. At last the door opened, and Marie, flushed, breathing heavily, the rounded tops of her ample breasts heaving above the neckline of her little black chintz uniform, stepped out of Edgar Peters's attic asylum.
>
> "Oh, it's you Larry," she said. "Your father is deep in thought. I was just straightening up around him and—"
>
> She turned suddenly and looked back into the little hideaway. She scampered back inside and emerged with her feather duster.
>
> "—dusting," she finished, flourishing the feather duster. She giggled and started down the stairs.
>
> Larry stepped inside his father's narrow lair. Gewgaws were everywhere—along the radiator, on shelves, and tossed indiscriminately on the floor. The walls were lined with cartons of letters from correspondents around the world, all on the subject of knickknacks, the bread and butter of the Peters clan. Just inside the door were displayed documents declaring that Edgar Lawrence Peters was a member of the National Institute of Bric-a-brac Designers, an honorary member of the *Institut des Fabricateurs des Bibelots,* and an honorary fellow of the Royal Academy of Curio Makers. He had won awards from the Gewgaw Fanciers and the Chatchke Mavens, among others. On the knickknack ladder, Edgar Peters was tops.
>
> Crammed into one corner, positioned to take advantage of the light from the only window, was a rickety table that served Mr. Peters as a desk. To the casual eye, the desk, heaped with market research reports, rough sketches, and prototypes of next year's line of gimcrackery from the Peters group, suggested a disorganized and

haphazard thinker, but Larry knew that his father possessed a fine analytical mind, and that the disarray was deliberate, calculated to disarm visitors.

Dressed in one of the rumpled tweed suits that he wore in the belief that they gave him a learned air, Edgar Peters was mussing his thick sandy hair with one hand and tracing the lines of an intricate sketch with the other.

Larry wanted his father's attention, but he was reluctant to disturb his concentration, so he stood across the table from him, fidgeting.

Father and son shared the most pronounced Peters family features: a wiry build, a wacky smile, and bright eyes. Larry shared his father's affectations too: rumpling his hair now and then as if absent-mindedly, and dressing in professorial tweeds, usually a herringbone suit, though Larry's tweeds were often considerably spotted with oil paints, which Larry considered a bohemian touch. Mr. Peters thought the boy lacked polish.

Edgar Peters looked up from his work at last. He peered at Larry over the top of his glasses, as parents of adolescents (parents who wear glasses) will sometimes do. "Oh, Larry," he said. "What's up, son?"

Larry chuckled. "You certainly were deep in concentration, Dad," he said. "You didn't even know I was here. I'll bet you never even noticed that Marie was in here, trying to straighten up and do some dusting."

Mr. Peters reddened, and Larry wished that he hadn't said anything, for it was apparent to him that his father was embarrassed by his being, as Larry's mother so often said, "in another world" when he was concentrating on a gimcrack design.

"Yes—well—I—I—" Mr. Peters's voice trailed off, and he rumpled his hair. "Did you want something, Larry?" he asked.

"Can you spare a minute to take a look at my latest project, Dad?" asked Larry.

Edgar Peters removed his glasses and slipped them into his jacket pocket. He rubbed the spatulate indentations on either side of his nose. "I could use a break," he said with a weary sigh. "These damned sketches are giving me a headache." With a sweep of his hand he indicated the plans that covered his desk.

"Aren't they any good?" asked Larry.

"On the contrary," said Mr. Peters. "They're more than good. They're brilliant, innovative, ambitious." He let out another weary sigh. "That's the problem." He indicated the clutter on his desk. "These are the sketches for next year's line. Your Uncle Hector thinks we can make bivalves the next knickknack rage, bigger than the little rococo courtiers we've done so well with, bigger than the black ceramic panthers, bigger even than the flamingos. Perhaps he's right, but frankly it's an enormous risk. Who can really be sure what piece of bric-a-brac people will want next? And these are supposed to be made of glass. I'm not even sure that we *can* make these in glass. Even if we can, tooling up will cost us a fortune." From the clutter on the desk he produced a glass clam, a hand-blown prototype. "Here, look at this one," he said.

He handed the clam to Larry, who examined it closely, racking his brain for something to say about it.

Edgar Peters waited for a bit, expecting that his son would make a comment or ask a penetrating question. When the silence had grown embarrassing, Mr. Peters cleared his throat and spoke in Larry's stead.

"First," he said, "will anyone *buy* a glass clam? I doubt that clams have widespread appeal. Second, look at how complex this is: the valves are actually hinged. Look at this! A glass hinge." He snatched the clam from Larry and flipped it open, impatiently, breaking the glass hinge. "Can you imagine what these are going to have to sell for? Well, enough of my worries. Tell me what you've been up to."

8

THE READER COULD BE SURE, at the beginning of any Larry Peters book, that Larry would soon be up to something interesting, for Larry shared his father's ingenuity for creating amusing diversions, devising interesting endeavors. Often, these were obviously derivative: after his father suggested building a raft to chart the Gulf Stream, Larry suggested casting adrift bottles containing questionnaires about the weather conditions and curious local customs of the areas in which they would eventually wash ashore; inspired by his father's car-rocking idea, Larry developed the "dry land sailboat," a dinghy on a platform decorated with a cardboard sea, which would fit within one half of a two-car garage and could be rocked by a near relative of the mechanism his father had designed to rock automobiles.

(The "dry land sailboat" was the basis for the subplot in *The Thief of Time.* In that book, Larry entertained hopes that he and Rocky might go into business for themselves with this device, but, sadly, their hopes were shattered when Harrison Whitehead, one of the world's most distinguished brummagem designers, a mainstay of the Peters outfit, was killed during the testing of the prototype when the mock-up two-car garage filled with real exhaust fumes from the real car that Larry and Rocky and Lucinda had brought over from the mainland to drive the mechanism. The incident was reported in the Murky Bay *Daily News* under the headline, "Boating Accident Leaves One Dead.")

Others of Larry's projects were more original: his planting most of the island in bamboo and hacking out intricate pathways through it (in *Bamboozled*) remains my favorite, and I remember with fond admiration his success in persuading Lucinda and several of her pubescent friends to dye their hair auburn and participate in a tableau vivant based on John William Waterhouse's *Hylas and the Nymphs* (in *That Crazy Redhead*).

In each of the Larry Peters adventures, the plot of the adventure itself turned somehow on the latest of Mr. Peters's or Larry's inventions, preoccupations, or avocations. For a reader who was familiar with the series and its conventions, one of the pleasures of reading any new volume came from trying to anticipate the way in which Larry's current interest would figure in the resolution of the mystery, the capture of the crooks, the unmasking of the spies, the rescue of the hostages, or whatever other satisfactory resolution would conclude the story. Take, as an example, *The Phantom Island,* the eleventh novel in the series. In the first chapter, Larry assembles his family in the living room for the unveiling of a painting that he has executed on one of the living-room windows.

"Well, let's have a look at it," said Edgar Peters, with furrowed brow. He threw a protective arm across the shoulders of his wife, Antonia.

Larry arranged his family in a semicircle facing the draped window. Hector, an old mustard-colored dog, followed feebly after them, made his way to a spot just in front of the drapes, groaned, and fell to the floor.

Mrs. Peters spotted some spatters of paint on the rug. She gave a weary sigh. "Oh, Larry, why must these projects always make messes of one sort or another?" she asked.

"Don't worry, Mom," Larry said impatiently. "I'll clean it up. I promise. Lucy, will you do the honors? Just pull the cord over there, and the drapes will part."

Lucinda fumbled around behind the drapes until she found the cord. She struck a pose of some dignity and tugged gently; the drapes began to open but stopped after an inch or two. She gave a less gentle tug.

"Something's jammed," she muttered.

She wrapped the cord around her hand and gave a vigorous yank, and the entire assembly tore loose from the wall and fell to the floor at her feet, along with some plaster.

"Darn it!" she cried, leaping out of the way.

When she stepped on his tail, Hector, the old mustard-colored dog, howled and began to struggle to his feet, whimpering.

"Oh, Heck," wailed Lucy. "Did I step on you? I'm sorry."

She reached down to comfort the old fellow, her tiny shorts riding up to expose an eye-catching crescent of the smoothly rounded underside of her tight pubescent buttocks as she did so.

Larry indicated the painted window with a flip of his hand. "*Voila!*" he said.

Mr. Peters cleared his throat. It often occurred to him that if it wasn't one thing it was another; if a radiator wasn't leaking, for example, the wysteria was dying. A little sigh escaped from Mrs. Peters. Hector whimpered and fell to the floor again, rolling over on his back so that Lucinda could scratch his flabby belly, but her attention had returned to the painting.

"It's very—creative," Mrs. Peters said haltingly. "Very creative. It must be wonderful to be able to come up with these ideas."

"It's intended to keep the mind alive," said Larry. "Say you walk into the living room, full of the cares of the workaday world, and you glance out the window." He demonstrated. "Before, you would have seen a familiar view that offered you no escape from your own tedious life because there was nothing interesting in it."

"You're telling me," muttered Lucy.

Mr. Peters shook his head and stared at his shoes. He wondered why young people were so easily bored with life and what he might do to stir up some new excitement.

"Before," said Larry, "you would have seen nothing but the gray waters of Murky Bay. But now you see something interesting, and you have a whole flock of things to wonder about." He began sug-

gesting questions, indicating details in the painting as he did so.
"What island is that? How did it get there? Who built the hotel?
Why would anyone build a hotel on a little island like that? Why
was it abandoned? Is anyone living there now? If so, who? And
what about that rowboat, that sunken rowboat at the end of the dilapidated dock?"

I read this passage for the first time with a pleasure that only Larry
Peters initiates could share, for my familiarity with the conventions of the
series led me at once to the conclusion that this painting would in some
way offer a clue to the mystery that was going to unfold as the novel pro-
gressed, that this was one of the conventional problems in a Larry Peters
story, one of the formal elements that shaped a Larry Peters story, and this
knowledge made me feel that I was a participant in the unfolding of that
story. A hundred pages or so later, my anticipation was rewarded.

Rocky rolled onto the grass and let out a long sigh. "All right, all
right," he said. "Have it your way."
"Oh, Rocky," said Lucinda, "it's not that I don't want to—it's
just that I'm afraid I'll get pregnant."
"I told you Lucy," said Rocky. "You don't have to worry about
that if the moon is full. Jeez, you've got me all frustrated now."
Lucinda sat up and rested her head on Rocky's shoulder. Her
heart pounded with fear and desire. "Oh, heck," she thought. "Why
don't I just let him? The moon sure is full. Whenever it peeks
through the clouds it lights up that oval island out there as if it were
daytime."
She ran her tongue into Rocky's ear, and she rubbed her hand
across his chest. He held her head with one strong hand and kissed
her, thrusting his tongue deeply, violently, into her mouth. With his
other hand he tore her shorts open and reached inside, his fingers
probing roughly, poking and prying. Lucinda's eyes opened wide
with surprise, with the shock of an unexpected pleasure, and in the
moonlight the oval island seemed to flash like the silver underbelly
of a gigantic flatfish. All at once Lucinda was struck by the realization that something was very wrong.
"Rocky!" she shouted, pushing herself away from him and wrig-
gling from his grasp.
"Oh, God, what is it now?" moaned Rocky.
"That island!" she cried.

"What about it?" wailed Rocky, striking the grass repeatedly with his fists.

"It's coming closer!"

Rocky leaped to his feet and peered out over the bay. There was no doubt about it. In the moonlight, he could see a wake behind the island. The entire island was moving toward them, and it was moving fast.

"Come on," he said. "We've got to get help!"

9

LARRY'S MOTHER was entirely occupied with domestic affairs, although she didn't actually do much work. Marie did most of the cooking, though Mrs. Peters had several dishes for which she was famous: her chow-chow relish, piccalilli, one-eyed Egyptians, hoppin' John, and pigs-in-blankets were family favorites. Marie made the beds, did the laundry, ordered supplies for delivery from Murky Bay, and generally bustled around, wisecracking, pushing dust around, and offering down-to-earth advice. Employees of the knickknack works did the heavier maintenance chores. Mrs. Peters was the domestic manager. She organized everything. It was clear to me from the start that although there was a surface dottiness to her character, she made everything in the Peters ménage work. None of the Peterses could be described as level-headed, but Antonia Peters possessed the levelest of the Peters heads. She was the only member of the Peters family who could be counted on, when six or seven things were happening at once, to pick out the one thing that most needed immediate attention. Consider the situation in *The Camel's Back*. One morning, after Lucinda has brought the workers from shore to the island on the Peters barge, a resounding crash, coming from who-knows-where on the island, rattles the windows in the big old Peters house. At that moment, the family is gathered in the dining room, eating breakfast.

"My goodness!" cried Mrs. Peters. "What was that?"

"It was a crash of some kind," said Larry. "Would you pass me the sausages, Dad?"

"Do you think it might have been serious?" asked Mrs. Peters.

"Oh, I doubt it, dear," said Edgar Peters. He put his fork down

and reached for a platter of link sausages. He stopped before actually raising the platter, however. "Did you want the link sausages,
Larry, or the sausage patties?" he asked.

"Gee, I'm not sure," said Larry. "What kind are you having,
Sexpot?" he asked Lucinda in the wisecracking tone that brother and
sister used with each other.

"I'm going to have one of those cute little links," she replied
saucily. "They're just about the size of your—"

"I think we should investigate," said Mrs. Peters. Her brow was
furrowed with concern.

"I haven't had any complaints yet, Green Eyes," Larry asserted
cockily, passing the platter of link sausages to his sister.

"Stop teasing, you two," said Edgar Peters in the kindly tone he
always used with his son and daughter. "Antonia," he said to his
wife, in the reassuring tone he often employed when speaking with
her, "I'm sure that if anything serious has occurred, my brother
Hector will be here shortly to tell us all about it."

"The only reason Larry hasn't had any complaints," said a tall,
handsome young man who suddenly stepped through the doorway
to the dining room, "is that he hasn't had any customers."

"Rocky!" squealed Lucinda. She leaped from her chair, upsetting
her glass of prune juice, and ran to Rocky. She threw herself at the
smiling young man, winding her arms around his neck and her long,
honey-colored legs around his waist. She began covering his face
with kisses.

"Hey, take it easy, Hot Stuff," said Rocky, cupping her tight pubescent buttocks in his large and muscular hands. "I've had a long,
hard night."

"Did you learn anything about that swarthy stranger, Rocky?"
asked Edgar Peters, in the sober tone he employed when there was a
problem to be solved.

"Dear," said Antonia Peters, "I really think that before we do
anything else we ought to investigate that crash." There was a petu-
lant tone in her voice, which Edgar Peters interpreted as meaning
that she felt she was being ignored.

"Now, dear—" he began, thinking that it might be best to humor
her and investigate the crash, so that they could get on to more important things.

"Hey, I heard that too," said Rocky. With Lucinda still wrapped
around him, he made his way to the sideboard, where he took a

piece of raisin-bread toast from a silver toast caddy. "There was a lot of dust and debris falling out of the air in the vicinity of the design building." He winked at Larry and said, "I figured it was one of your projects, Larry."

"I really think that we—" began Antonia Peters, but just then Hector Peters, Edgar Peters's brother, burst into the dining room, dragging behind him, covered with dust from head to toe, Ignatz Steinmetz, the brilliant European gewgaw designer who had become, in two short years, one of the most valuable members of the Peters team.

"Edgar!" cried Hector. "We're ruined!"

"There you are, Antonia," said Edgar Peters, reaching out to pat his wife's hand in a reassuring manner. "I told you that if the crash was serious Hector would soon be here to tell us about it." He turned to his brother, his eyebrows drawn together in a look of grave concern. "It's serious then, Hector?" he asked.

"Steinmetz," said Hector Peters, "tell him what you told me."

"Ruins!" cried the world-renowned designer. "Everything is in ruins!" When he gesticulated, and he gesticulated extravagantly, dust flew from his laboratory coat. His left cheek was badly scraped, and his hands were trembling. "We were working on the new models, and Entwhistle said, 'How about a cup of coffee, Iggie?' and I said, 'Sure, why not?' and then—*kerwhammy!* The roof falls in and the whole place is a shambles!"

10

LARRY'S SISTER, Lucinda, was as cute as a button and smart as a whip. She and Larry loved trading wisecracks; in fact, I realize, reflecting on the Peterses now and bringing to mind my feelings toward them when I was a boy, that the wisecracking and playful teasing among them was meant to serve as a sign of the love they felt for one another, something I didn't understand at the time. To me then, it seemed no more than a part of their exciting and unpredictable style, but even if I considered it no more than an element of style, the wisecracking was one of those constants of the Peters household that persisted beyond the adventures, and was therefore one of the truly valuable aspects of the books and of life in the Peters family. There was little wisecracking in my family, and I came to think that there would be a good deal more fun and immeasurably more panache if only there were more wisecracking. The Peterses' wisecracking seemed to be one of the few things that I might translate from Larry's life into mine.

"Peter," said my father one morning while I was musing along the foregoing lines, "would you bring me an ashtray?"

"Ash and ye shall reshieve," I said.

My father gave me a pained look, and I came quickly to the conclusion that there are, essentially, two kinds of families, wisecracking families and nonwisecracking families, and that it had been my unfortunate lot to be born into one of the latter.

Whenever Lucinda entered a scene, I began to smile as I read, for I knew that something interesting was going to happen. She was a year younger than Larry, but since girls mature more quickly than boys, she easily held her own in their amiable tussles, both verbal and physical. (The ages of the characters in the Larry Peters adventures were never given. The only references to age that I can recall were relative: we were told somewhere in one of the early books that Lucinda was a year younger than Larry and that Rocky was three years older. After considerable reading in the literature, I've concluded that Lucinda and Larry, given the different rates at which they matured, were both somewhere in late-early to early-middle adolescence and that Rocky was just postadolescent. I could be wrong.)

Lucinda's character was wildly variable. She'd act like one of the guys at one time, grow shy and retiring at another, become brazen and sarcastic, headstrong, cautious, and who-knows-what-all by turns. Her appearance was never described in full, and even the fragments that the reader was given now and then, glimpses, as it were, through a curtain parted by a puff of a summer night's breeze, were vague, more tantalizing than satisfying. This vagueness was, I concluded, deliberate and wise, since the reader was, thanks to the lack of details about her appearance, allowed, even encouraged, to construct his own Lucinda from bits and pieces of girls he knew, or a girl he had merely glimpsed—at the beach, say, dropping a strap of her bathing suit down over her arm, rubbing suntan lotion onto her shoulder absentmindedly while she stared out across the surf toward the shimmering horizon, or stretched out on the foredeck of a lean blue sloop, wearing red-rimmed reflective sunglasses, reading a paperback book the title of which one could not make out, or perhaps perched with a group of friends on the varnished handrail atop the railing that ran along the boardwalk, raising her right leg to scratch, just at the edge of the line imprinted by the elastic of her bathing suit, the irregular red welt of a horsefly bite—for these books were in one respect truly masterly pieces of work: they provided a context for the fantasies of adolescent boys, a context so reassuring that the timidity and fear that ordinarily attended those fantasies nearly disappeared when they were entertained within it. One's parents and other adults, who seemed at times to be regarding one with lancet eyes, eyes that penetrated straight to that abscess where one's guilty urges maturated, did not go to Kittiwake Island.

If the bond between Larry and Rocky became for me the paradigm of friendship, and it did, what existed between Larry and Lucy made me wish for that special relationship that can exist only between a brother and sister. What is it that makes that relationship what it is? It is, I suppose, partly narcissistic. Here is an interlocutor who understands all your references, who shares your habits of speech, who even sounds a bit like you. Here is a girl who reminds you of yourself. Here is your companion, if your ages are close, as Lucy's and Larry's were, in growing up. I didn't have to envy Larry for his having Rocky, the older male friend, who had seen so much more of the world than Larry had, who could teach him the things that a worldly older male friend can, since I had Raskolnikov, who showed every sign of growing up to be a lot like Rocky, but I envied Larry very much for his having Lucinda, the younger sister, together with whom he was able to learn so much by trial and error, as was the case in *No Laughing Matter*.

"What was that?" whispered Larry.

"I didn't hear anything," said Lucinda.

"I think someone's coming," said Larry. "I'm sure I heard someone laugh out there in the dark." He switched his flashlight off. He and Lucinda stood silently in the darkness.

"I don't hear anything," said Lucinda.

"I'm sure now," said Larry. "I heard someone laugh, and I heard footsteps, the footsteps of two people, two heavy people, on the gravel outside." Larry took Lucinda's hand and squeezed it. "We've got to hide," he said. "I wish I could remember where that ladder was. We could hide in the hayloft above us if we could find the ladder, but I'm afraid we might miss our footing in the dark and make a noise. If only I could risk turning the flashlight on for an instant. Wait a minute! There was a wooden box of some kind around here, wasn't there?"

"Larry, are you sure someone's out there? I didn't hear anything," said Lucinda.

"Lucy," whispered Larry. "I've found the box! Hurry! Climb in here. If they find us, there's no telling what they'll do to us!"

The urgency in her brother's voice was clear. Lucy moved quickly and soundlessly to the box and climbed inside while he held the lid open. The box was narrow and shallow, just about the right size, Lucy reflected as she climbed in, for a coffin. The thought sent a shiver down her spine. She stretched out in the box and Larry climbed in and lowered the lid.

"There's not much room in here," said Larry. "I don't think I can squeeze beside you. I'm going to have to lie on top of you."

"That's okay," whispered Lucinda. "It's pretty comfortable. Somebody has put a blanket and pillow in here."

"That's a stroke of good luck," said Larry.

"Hey, what are you doing?" asked Lucinda.

"I'm just trying to find a comfortable position," said Larry.

"If you make yourself any more comfortable, we're going to have to get engaged," said Lucinda.

Larry stifled a laugh. He and Lucinda loved trading wisecracks like this.

"It's pretty hot in here, isn't it?" said Larry.

"It sure is," said Lucinda. "What are you doing now?"

"I'm just trying to get these hot clothes off."

"Larry, let me out of here!"

"It's not safe out there, Sis."

"It's not safe in here either, Brother."

11

MARIE, THE PETERSES' MAID, made my heart go pit-a-pat the moment she first appeared in one of the adventures, pushing the kitchen door open with a beautifully rounded hip, stepping into the dining room on those long and luscious legs, carrying a tray of blueberry pancakes, just as, I'm sure, she made the hearts of most of the boys who read the Larry Peters books beat faster whenever she appeared. Marie never figured very prominently in the adventures themselves, though she would pop in now and then. Ordinarily, she was left at home when the pace of the action picked up, and we wouldn't see her again until the end of the book, when the adventurers—tired, possibly injured, but always victorious—returned to Kittiwake Island and sat down to another big meal. Most of my ideas about Marie came from outside the books themselves, from other sources and from my imagination. There were, however, one or two scenes in which Marie appeared that have remained sharp and clear and brilliant in my memory. I am willing to bet a sizable sum that any reader of the Larry Peters books will recall one of those scenes immediately and vividly if I merely end this sentence with the phrase *tub of Jell-O*.

In *The Flying Aspidistras,* Kittiwake Island is invaded by a squadron of thugs and goons in the pay of an evil manufacturer of rubber house plants who is planning to move into the gewgaw business, and Marie and Larry are bound hand and foot and set adrift in a leaking rowboat. As the water in the rowboat rises, and Larry and Marie confront the likelihood that the next few minutes will be their last, Marie tells Larry that what makes her saddest is the thought of the many things she hoped to do in the life that she had imagined still stretched out before her like a long highway, with mysterious stretches hidden behind curves or over hills, with forks and crossroads where she might have, on impulse, veered from the broad, well-traveled way and so on.

> "Well," said Larry, "I guess that road into the future has come to a dead end." He laughed bitterly, and then his voice softened. "I'm sorry that you won't get to do all those things, Marie," he said gently.
>
> "So am I," said Marie. Her voice caught, a shudder ran through her, and she swallowed hard.
>
> "Say," said Larry, forcing a lighthearted tone into his voice, "suppose you could do just *one* of those things. What would it be?"
>
> "One?" asked Marie. "Oh, my goodness. One? I don't know, I—"
>
> "What's the first one that pops into your head?"
>
> "Oh, well," said Marie. "The first one that pops into my head? I—oh, I don't know—I—well—I've always thought it would be fun to—you know that big claw-foot tub in my bathroom?"
>
> "Sure," said Larry. He blushed as soon as he had spoken, for he had on many an evening climbed the apple tree outside the window of Marie's bathroom in the hope of catching a glimpse of her while she bathed in the claw-foot tub to which she referred, and had, in fact, succeeded on a number of occasions.
>
> "Well, I've often thought that it would be fun to draw a nice hot bath in that tub and then stir in—oh, you'll laugh at me."
>
> "No, Marie, I won't," said Larry. There was so much genuine

compassion in his voice that Marie was able to continue without embarrassment.

"Well," she said, "I'd stir in about—oh, I guess, two or three doz-
en packages of Jell-O."

"Jell-O?" asked Larry. His heart had begun to beat at a faster rate.

"What's your favorite flavor?"

"Raspberry," said Larry, in a hoarse whisper.

"I'd stir in all that raspberry Jell-O and then slip off my night-
gown and settle into the tub."

"Oh my God," said Larry. His heart beat pit-a-pat.

"I'd rest my head on the edge of the tub and lie there in the warm
water and just relax while the water cooled and the Jell-O firmed
around me—"

"Oh," said Larry. "Pit-a-pat, pit-a-pat," said his heart.

"—shaping itself to every inch of me—"

"Ah," said Larry. His heart was beating now with a small, sharp
pain, as if a thorn had lodged in it.

"—and perhaps I'd fall asleep. When I woke up, I'd be enveloped by Jell-O, snug in a tub of Jell-O, resilient raspberry Jell-O,
molded to me, embracing me as no lover ever could, as not even a
hundred lovers could embrace me at once."

A sound something like a sob came from Larry.

"And then, very softly, I would call out, 'Help. Help me, Larry.'"

"What?" asked Larry. "What?"

"And you would open the door of the bathroom—"

"I would?"

"—and you'd be holding—now, don't laugh—"

"What would I be holding? What?"

"A spoon."

"A spoon. Oh, my God, a spoon."

"Not a big spoon. A little spoon, a demitasse spoon."

12

I THINK THAT MOST READERS of the Larry Peters books dreamed of
being a friend of Larry's, of being found washed up on Kittiwake Island
one morning, carried to the big house on an improvised litter, nursed back

to health by Marie and Mrs. Peters, and then adopted into the Peters circle. The attitude inspired in me by the Larry Peters books was fundamentally different. I didn't want to be *like* Larry Peters; I wanted to *be* Larry Peters.

I wanted his chum Rocky King to be my chum on exactly the terms that existed between him and Larry. I wanted his brilliant and unpredictable dad to be my dad. I wanted his fussy, cuddly mother to be my mother. I wanted Marie to turn down my sheets. I wanted to sit up at night, after everyone else was asleep, and trade confidences and wisecracks with my saucy sister Lucy. I knew that this was, in all the ways that most people would have considered important, impossible. But I understood even then that there were ways in which it was not only possible but, for me, necessary, necessary in a way that only the things we truly want to do, truly derive pleasure from doing, are necessary, however complex and demanding they may be. If Roger Drake had been able to imagine Larry and all the rest of them and the context for them, surely I could manage to imagine myself as Larry, could imagine a complete and consistent enough set of details to fill the chinks in Mr. Drake's portrait of Larry with details about myself, to have Larry say what I would say during the breakfast conversations on the mornings when there was no adventure to interrupt, when the Peterses could stretch out and relax, putter in the garden, read the papers, listen to a record, play the piano, go for a swim.

I spent a lot of time within the Larry Peters books, playing at being Larry, but I never thought of myself as escaping into them, never thought of myself as retreating into them to get away from a world that wasn't what it ought to have been, never thought of myself as making my way across Murky Bay in the hope of finding something better or leaving something worse behind, never, that is, until my great-grandmother died.

13

GREAT-GRANDMOTHER LEROY was ill for months, but I didn't realize how seriously ill she was until Grandfather moved her downstairs from her rooms in the attic. She moved into the room across the hall from what had been my father's bedroom when he was a boy and was now the bedroom I used when I visited. She never left the bed. For several weeks

before she died, she didn't speak. Sometimes when I visited, I sat beside
her bed for an hour or so and talked without even pausing for a response.
I knew that she wasn't going to say anything, so I just talked on and on,
quicker and quicker, to keep the silence from settling over her like a
shroud. When I ran out of events at school, episodes with my playmates,
things I had learned, and things I had heard or seen, I recounted for her
episodes from the Larry Peters books, and when I came to those gaps between scenes, between chapters, when the action in one chapter ended
and the action of the next, set somewhere else, hadn't yet begun, I filled
those gaps, as, years earlier, I had filled the gaps in my understanding of
the Leroy family history when I had recited it for her in her attic rooms,
with sawdust—that is, with episodes that I made up on my own, as one
uses sawdust to fill the cracks in the bottom of a wooden boat. Throughout all my chatter, Great-grandmother never said a thing.

But then, one afternoon, Great-grandmother suddenly interrupted me,
as if she had heard enough at last. I was startled by her voice. I hadn't
expected to hear her talk at all, but I must have had in the back of my
mind the idea that if she were to speak, her voice would be as thin and
tired as her face had become. Instead, it was nearly as strong as it had
always been, and it deceived me into thinking that she had suddenly gotten better.

"Peter," she said. "I have a present for you."

"You do?" I glanced around the room. "Where is it?" I asked.

"Upstairs," she said. "You go up and get it."

I went upstairs and opened the door to her rooms. Something strange
had happened to these rooms while she had been out of them. Left alone,
the things there had begun to claim ownership. The chair where Great-
grandmother used to sit and carve coconuts to represent Leroys had become the strongest personality in the room now, and it sat in command,
dark and heavy, in front of the windows, silhouetted against the curtained
light. I looked around, but for a while I couldn't find anything that looked
like a present. Then, on one of the shelves that held the coconuts, I saw a
box, nearly cubical. The box wasn't wrapped, or even tied with ribbon,
but it was taped shut, and when I took it from the shelf, I found, written on
the top, in pencil, the words FOR PETER.

From the heft and size, I was certain that the box held a coconut. A
lump formed in my throat, and tears filled my eyes. I decided at once that
Great-grandmother had carved a coconut to represent herself, and that by
giving it to me she was telling me that she expected to die. I lifted the lid
gravely, slowly, holding my hands symmetrically, palms parallel, fingers

extended, raising the lid directly upward and slowly setting it down to one side, for I had begun to serve as an altar boy at the Babbington Episcopal Church and had developed an exaggerated sense of ceremony. Great-grandmother's coconut heads looked so like one another, and I was so completely prepared to find one carved in Great-grandmother's likeness and to feel grief at the sight of it, that for a moment or two I didn't recognize that the coconut represented me. Not only had Great-grandmother carved the coconut in my likeness, but she had carved me laughing, though the faces of the other Leroys were tight-lipped and stern. I hurried downstairs, smiling.

Great-grandmother was chuckling when I came into the bedroom. "I always meant to get around to you," she said.

"Thanks, Grandma," I said. "Is it all right if I take it home with me?"

"Of course it's all right, Peter," she said. "You can have all of them."

This gift brought with it a pleasure so buoyant that it was dizzying, almost frightening. I kissed Great-grandmother, and as soon as I left the room where she lay I could feel the lightness of my delight lifting me from the floor, feel myself drifting upward as easily as a soaring bird, up the stairs to her room, where I spent the rest of the afternoon drifting on the air there, so dense with memories and dust, and playing with my heads.

WHEN I CAME DOWNSTAIRS much later, with the head of Black Jacques under my left arm and my own under my right, the door to the room where Great-grandmother lay was locked, and my parents were in the living room with Grandfather and Grandmother, making plans for the funeral.

THAT NIGHT I lay in bed, wakeful and anxious and hurt. Everything seemed wrong. Everything seemed confused. My thoughts were turbid, roiling, like wrack stirred up by a storm. I couldn't make sense of them, and I couldn't drive them away. Then, at last, I saw through the murk a heartening yellow light, and after a while I could see that it was coming from the windows of the Peterses' living room, where everyone was gathered to trade wisecracks after dinner, where no one good was going to die, where things were as they ought to be, and since there was a rowboat handy, I stepped into it, shoved off, and began rowing. With each stroke, my mad and disappointing world receded, and from Kittiwake Island I could hear Lucinda calling me, calling me to come in now, to come in off Murky Bay and join them in the living room, and she was calling me Larry.

14

SOME EIGHT YEARS LATER, on a cold February afternoon during my
sophomore year at Hargrove University, I sat in Cranston Library, trying
to study for a mathematics examination. The library was overheated; I
was sitting in an overstuffed leather wing chair, the type of chair that I
have, ever since my days at Hargrove, thought of as the only type of chair
proper for a library. Snow was falling outside, and the air in the library
was heavy with the odor of wet wool, wet leather, old books, painted
steam radiators, and students, many of us dozing over our studies.

I stretched, yawned, and decided to take a break from my work to read
a letter from a high school acquaintance, Robert Meyer, a boy who had
passed through Babbington High School almost unnoticed, but who had
this year done a daring thing for that time, taken a year's sabbatical from
college to be on his own in Europe. As soon as he reached European soil,
Robert began writing to everyone who had ignored him in high school.
He wrote long, tedious letters full of strained insights, accounts of unlikely sexual encounters, and snatches of the local language. I received at
least one a week.

When the first of his letters arrived, I had no idea who Robert Meyer
was, and it wasn't until I began hearing from friends who had also received letters from him that I was able to retrieve a blurry face from my
memory of high school, someone rushing past in the hallway, mumbling a
greeting, but averting his face and hurrying on, someone still sitting in the
stands after a football game, alone, at one end of the upper row of
bleachers, while the rest of us headed for the gate, the parking lot, cars,
pizza. I looked him up in my yearbook, but his photograph was no more
help to me in recalling Robert just a year after we had been in school together than the photographs of my other classmates would be twenty-five
years later. Though I was happy to receive any mail, even letters from
Robert, they grew wearying after a while, and so when one arrived I delayed opening it for a little longer than I had delayed opening the last.
This one had been in my book bag for several days. I tore open the thin
blue envelope, unfolded the letter and read.

*"Ich bin nun endlich in München und sitze hier in meinem Zimmer bei
Frau Brenner in der Schellingstrasse,"* the letter began.

The heat, the odors, and Robert Meyer's prose style put me to sleep
nearly at once. I had been sitting with my feet up on a table, and I had
leaned backward in the chair until it rocked on the back legs only. When I

woke, I was sitting on a dilapidated wooden dock, the sort of dock from which you are certain to pick up splinters in your feet if you walk along it barefoot. Rusty nailheads projected from pilings where boards had once been attached. Other boards, half rotted, hung at odd angles. Beside the dock was a rowboat, a sunken rowboat, resting on the sandy bottom in a foot or so of water. An old line, green with slime, still made the rowboat fast to a piling at the end of the dock. I was barefoot, and I was playing a game with the surface of the water—the same game that I used to play when I let my feet dangle over the stern of the *Rambunctious,* Big Grandfather's boat: I was trying to bring the soles of my feet as close to the surface of the water as I could without touching it. It was day, but the day was foggy. It was summer, and I was wearing only a pair of shorts and a short-sleeved shirt. A wavelet touched my heel, which meant I'd lost another round, and I kicked my feet and ran my toes through the water. It was still and warm. I was nine or ten.

Faintly, I began to hear something through the fog. As the sound grew stronger, I thought I recognized it, but I couldn't be quite sure. It might be only the lapping of waves, but the water was still. It might be laughter, but who would be out in the fog, laughing?

"Are you all right?"

A young woman with dark hair stepped out of the fog and brought her face near mine. I found myself sitting straight in a leather chair, my back pressed firmly along its back, my legs flat along the seat where the dock ought to have been, my lower legs against the edge of the cushion, and from around me I heard a sound that I thought I recognized, a sound that might be laughter, but I saw no people; a sound that might be the lapping of waves, if there were waves inside a building. Certainly I *was* inside a building, but I was looking at the ceiling, and if the evidence of my eyes was to be believed, the ceiling had been moved around to occupy the plane ordinarily occupied by a wall. Some sort of practical joke? Not likely, I thought. A trick of the mind, the not-quite-fully-awake mind. Transpositions of this sort were, I knew from my several attempts to read *À La Recherche du Temps Perdu,* not uncommon illusions upon awakening; in the misty margin between sleep and wakefulness Marcel might seem to recognize the architecture and furnishings of his room at home, only to find, as he came slowly to his senses, that the uplifted forefinger of day had rearranged the furniture, the windows, the doorways, and the walls, and transformed his bedroom into a hotel room with a view of the sea.

(Since it has occurred to me just now and is such a fine illustration of the fundamental truths one sometimes finds in fiction, I will mention briefly a comparable anecdote that Porky White told me many years later. He and his wife, Marcella, had traveled to a small lakeside village somewhere in New England for a wedding. The ceremony was intimate and touching, and the party that followed was long and exuberant. Porky retired in wonderful spirits, more than a little soused. "In the middle of the night," he told me, "I get a message from my unconscious: 'Porky! Wake up! You have got to take a piss, and you have got to do it right now,' it was saying. Quiet as I can be, I get out of bed, step out of the bedroom into the dark hallway, turn right, turn right again into the bathroom, walk to the toilet, reach into my shorts and pull out my pride and joy, yawn, and let myself go. Instead of the basso splashing I usually hear under these circumstances, I hear an odd, hollow, splattering sound, and this incongruity wakes me up. I discover that I'm not in my own house, of course, I'm not in my bathroom, and I'm pissing onto the caned seat of a fine old bentwood chair.")

"Oh, sure," I said to the young woman with dark hair. "I'm fine. I just dozed off." I yawned and stretched and rubbed my eyes. I thought that some fresh air might be in order, and I tried to get up. Only then, when my body told me that gravity was pulling from the wrong direction, did I realize that the chair and I were lying on our backs on the floor, and that the laughter was real, directed at me. I scrambled to my feet, righted the chair, and stacked my books and papers, trying not to raise my head all the while, so that I wouldn't have to see any of the people who were laughing at me. I made my way, with what I hoped was dignified haste, through the doors of the main entrance and out into the bright sunlight. The sun was so bright after the library that I closed my eyes against it for a moment and reeled with a dazzled dizziness. In the iridescent images in my mind's eye I saw a piece of a persistent memory of part of a dream, no more than a snapshot, but a clear and intriguing snapshot: that moment of sitting on the old dock.

15

AS TIME PASSED, the snapshot stayed in my mind. I could recover the picture of myself sitting on the dock whenever I wished, just by closing my eyes and willing it to appear. I assumed that it was a memory, but unlike most memories, the picture became clearer with time, more detailed, more precise. I could feel my sensations better, more clearly, as time passed. At the same time, however, much about this memory made little sense to me, and explanations eluded me. Where was I? How did I get there?

I had my suspicions. My maternal grandmother, Gumma, was a believer in recurring dreams that passed from generation to generation, dreams that arose from acts of such power that they inspired emotions too strong to die in a single lifetime. She claimed to have one herself, a dream about rushing along a curving corridor, opening a series of doors, and falling after she opened the last one. She was convinced that this derived from something terrible her grandmother had done. My mother had one, one that I had learned about when I told her, years before, about a dream that I had had while I tossed restlessly during a bout with one of the childhood diseases, something that made me feverish.

It was a dream in which nothing happened. There was a featureless landscape; it might have been a desert or tundra. In the foreground was a post, and from the post a line of some kind dangled. The post, and, even more than the post, the line dangling from it, made me feel miserable, nauseated, frightened, horribly empty, as if something terrible had happened and things would never be right again. When I told my mother about this, I did so reluctantly, because during this restless and feverish time I had, by assembling in a careful, step-by-step, logical fashion the few facts I knew, the rumors, assertions, wild claims, and flights of fancy I had heard, and the mystifying hints in a pamphlet my mother had left in my room, arrived at a clear theoretical understanding—which in form resembled the instruction sheets that came with the model airplanes I had become fond of building, an insert-part-A-into-part-B understanding—of what men and women did when they "went to bed together," and had discovered, by way of looking for an experimental method to test my theory, masturbation. I had a hunch that my unsettling dream might have something to do with that.

"Oh, Peter," said my mother. "I have that dream, too."

"You do?" I asked.

"Oh, yes. But I know why."

"I think I know why, too," I said, looking at my hands.

"It's because of the rowboat."

"The rowboat?"

She explained a painful memory. One Sunday when she was a little girl, Gumma and Guppa had organized a picnic on one of the islands in the bay. Friends had traveled to the island in boats, and after a while the children had wandered away from the adults to amuse themselves. The amusement for the youngest children consisted of throwing sand and pebbles into a dinghy that Garth and May Castle had used to row from their sloop to the island. The rowboat was tied to a piece of driftwood that the Castles had thrust into the sand. In time, the children succeeded in sinking the dinghy, and they cheered when it settled to the bottom. When it was discovered, none of the adults had been particularly angry, in fact most had thought the incident funny, but my mother had felt ashamed of her part in the business, and she insisted that a sudden wind had arisen and blown the sand and pebbles into the dinghy while the children watched, helpless and aghast. As time passed, she became more ashamed of the lie than of the act it was meant to hide. She thought that the recurring dream showed the piece of driftwood and the line leading into the water. I thought for a while that my sitting-on-the-dock memory might have been a more precise version of my post-and-line dream, but I have never been a believer in such things, so I continued to look for another explanation.

I thought that the dock might be on Small's Island, but things were not quite right. For one thing, I was not quite myself in this scene. For another, the island was not quite Small's Island. I was reminded of the eerie feeling Raskol had described so many years before, when he told the Glynns and me about his crawling through a culvert into what he took to be another world. Finally, with all the force of the truth, the explanation hit me. I was, in this snapshot, the young Larry Peters, but not quite the young Larry Peters with whom I was familiar. I was the young Larry Peters as he would have been if *I* had been the young Larry Peters. Sitting on the dock, I was Larry Peters before the adventures began, before the family had prospered, when Larry's father was still struggling to make his gewgaw business go, Larry Peters at a time of his life about which Roger Drake had told me nothing, at time when I was free to construct any Larry I wished. Something else struck me at nearly the same time. The picture of myself as the young Larry Peters that I had in my mind was becoming clearer with time, rather than fading, because it was not a memory: I was making it up.

16

MY ABILITY TO IMAGINE myself as Larry Peters improved with time, and I must admit that I used it now and then to get away. And I have continued to do so. I'm just old enough now—as I write these words I am forty years and thirty-eight days old—to be able to admit without embarrassment that I never really abandoned most of my childhood habits and interests, certainly not the pleasant pastime of slipping into the character of Larry Peters.

For several years, while I finished college and took a master's degree in molluscan biology, my version of Larry developed without any apparent assistance from me. He simply sat in that comfortable corner of my mind, on Kittiwake Island, which came to resemble Small's Island more and more, and a life grew around him while I neglected him, as beach grass will grow in sand under the worst conditions. Whenever I rowed out to the island to see what he was up to I was surprised to find how much more I knew about him, and how much more there was to know about him.

From time to time, I began jotting down my thoughts about Larry, conversations that he might have been involved in before the boundless summer in which all the adventures seemed to occur, or after that summer, when he went off to college, or later, when he returned to the island.

Albertine and I married, and, as most people who can read do at some time or other, often in their youth, I began to want to write a book. And, as most people do who begin to want to write a book, especially those who begin to want to write a book in their youth, I wanted to write a book about myself. Unlike many people who want to write books about themselves, I was embarrassed to admit it, even to myself, and so I cast about for a way to write a book about myself without seeming to. I didn't know exactly what I was going to put into this book if I was going to avoid putting in anything about myself, if I was not going to admit that it was ego that made me want to write a book at all, that my only reason for wanting to write a book was to cry out in an acceptable way, "Look at me! Over here! Look at me! Watch this: no hands! See? Wait, wait! Look at this! I can do it with my eyes closed! Watch!"

Had I simply been willing to admit all that, however, I would have written, had I managed to write a book at all, a chaotic, pointless, formless book, because I hadn't more than the foggiest, inchoate notion of what I was like. It took nearly twenty years for me to discover what my books should be like, and during all that time I wrestled every day with big, powerful ideas, ideas that were much bigger and stronger than I. How apt that time-worn image for struggling with a big idea is, the image of grappling, grasping, clutching, twisting, trying to hold on to a squirming, powerful, slippery idea that strives to elude you, to get out of your clutches. I wrestled with form and style and tone and argument, and the book grew larger and more diverse, more populous, more anarchic.

What headaches I gave myself over this. What pits of despair I threw myself into. How difficult I was to live with. What a pest I was at parties. More and more often, to get to sleep at night, to escape the big ideas, I would make my way across Murky Bay to trade wisecracks with Rocky and Lucinda and Marie.

17

ONE SUMMER NIGHT, when my struggles had only begun, Albertine and I were sitting on Big Grandfather's front porch. We had been spending the summer with Grandfather, in his house. Grandmother had died during the year, and our presence in the house was supposed to cheer Grandfather up, to keep the place from echoing with sorrow and loneliness. We felt that we hadn't succeeded, and we had become convinced that we couldn't have succeeded, that we should have known that Grandfather felt the loss of my grandmother too strongly for us to make him forget it for long.

However, of an evening, the three of us would sit on his front porch, on the glider, or in metal chairs that were suspended on springs within metal frames and wheezed when we rocked in them, and I would tell my grandfather stories about things that had happened at work. I was working right down the street, in the boatyard that was once Cap'n Leech's, then Leech's son's, and is now Raskolnikov's. Crazy and amusing things happened there; crazy things happen wherever pleasure boats are moored near working boats, because people who think that boats are for fun and people who think that boats are for work each think the others are crazy. I was a college student at the time, so of course I thought everyone was crazy. My grandfather and Albertine and I would sit and rock and drink gin-and-tonics, and I'd tell my stories, and sometimes I would make Grandfather laugh. When I made him laugh, I'd add to what I had told him, embellish, improvise, mimic, burlesque to make him laugh again, because, after all, I was supposed to try to cheer him up.

On that night, it had grown late, and the three of us had grown quiet. We would be going upstairs to bed soon. Out of the darkness, Grandfather asked me what I wanted to do with myself. I told him what I had told only Albertine before, that I wanted to write a book, and in the confessional safety of the darkness, the security of this familiar setting and sympathetic audience, I felt myself ready to try to tell him all about the book, the impossibly big book, that I wanted to write.

"That's good," he said, before I had a chance to say any of that. "That's very good. Make sure that there's a laugh on every page."

I stopped myself. I took a sudden cheap pity on him, who didn't need or want it. Instead of telling him anything about the book I wanted to write, I indulged him—or so I thought. I'm not sure now exactly how I answered him, but I must have said something like, "That's an interesting idea."

And in the darkness I smiled to myself a shameful, condescending smile, and decided that it would be too difficult to explain to Grandfather why I didn't want laughs, why laughing seemed to me reprehensible in this miserable world.

In truth, I learned only much later, explaining would have been too difficult because I didn't understand that the main reason I considered laughter inappropriate was that my circle of serious friends considered it so, walked with their eyes down, their heads bowed by the misery of life. To expect happiness was insane; to want happiness was arrogant and selfish. I had come to regard having a good time, laughing without irony, singing anything but the blues, dancing of any sort as childishly foolish, betrayals of one's unwillingness or inability to face up to the horror that is Life. To indulge in any of the foregoing whoopee, I had to be drunk, but my drinking, even if it led to laughing, singing, and dancing, was not of the variety that makes a young suburban matron, leading her grinning husband to the door, wonder why she wasted the money having her hair done for this terrible night, makes her turn to her hosts and say, "He thinks he has to drink to have a good time. I'm sorry about the tray of glasses." No, it was the variety that makes a dark-eyed model stub out her Camel and say to her hosts, before she drags the young painter or poet or sculptor or playwright or filmmaker or novelist off, "Only bourbon dulls his pain."

I couldn't have explained to Grandfather then that I wanted the respect of all those very serious people, people for whom it was an axiom that no serious thought could lead to laughter, real laughter, and since I couldn't explain, I yawned and said, "Are you ready for bed, Al?"

Albertine and I went up to bed, and when we got in and pulled the sheet over us and lay quietly in the dark, I heard Grandfather on the porch, rocking his chair and making the springs wheeze, tapping his foot, and whistling the tune to "Rarotonga," and then, suddenly, loudly, he began to sing:

> Come on, honey, come with me
> Sail away, across the sea
> To Rarotonga,
> Where the nights are longa
> And our love will grow much stronga.
> Oh, honey, *won't* you come alonga,
> Across the sea
> To Rarotonga—
> With me?

A neighbor slammed her window down, as she had done on another evening, when Albertine and I had stayed on the porch too late with friends and I had begun to talk too loudly about the nature of things. Grandfather stopped singing, and I heard him come into the house. In a little while, when he came upstairs, I heard him chuckling, and so ignorant was I of the way life really is that I thought his sorrow must have driven him mad. I didn't understand at all that the memories accumulated during years of happiness could weigh enough to balance so large a loss, or that the mind will sometimes find a way to free the heart from pain.

18

ALMOST FOUR YEARS LATER, Albertine and I were sitting in Dudley Beaker's living room one evening. We had come for dinner, and we had been having a wonderful time. The conversation had been lively, and Eliza had, I think, genuinely enjoyed our youthful volubility. Albertine and I were so full of ourselves and of each other just then that in conversation we never really confronted a subject directly: we could only talk about its relationship to, meaning for, effect on, or even irrelevance to, ourselves.

It was late now, and the four of us had moved from the dining room to the living room, where we sat sipping cognac, which I was trying very hard to learn how to sip, and talking, talking, talking. Mr. Beaker had been, throughout the evening, urging me to take a position that had opened at the Babbington Clam Council, a position as an assistant copy writer. I had restrained myself, throughout the evening, from telling him that a position as an assistant copy writer at the Babbington Clam Council seemed ridiculous to me. Talk had turned to Burton Calder, whose new novel, *Burning Wind,* had everyone talking, including me. Finally, because the hour was so late and the meal had been so good and I had known Mr. Beaker and Eliza for so long and I had had too much to drink, I confessed.

"You know," I said, and I paused to gather all their attention, "that's what I'd really like. I'd like a *Burning Wind.* I'd like to write a big, fat book, bigger than *Burning Wind.*" (Just as an aside here let me ask what it is about being young that makes us want to do things that are difficult beyond anything we know, beyond the level of difficulty that we have even learned how to *imagine,* and in some cases, of which mine is one, makes us so burn to do them that we never let go of the desire to do them until at last we have done them or have failed in the attempt? Albertine's answer, when I posed this question to her, was, "We were all asses in the past," but she was busy at the time, going over the accounts, and she may not have given it much thought.)

Mr. Beaker, perhaps because he had endured with equanimity and restraint an evening of youthful ambition and egotism that must finally have had an effect like that of eating too many jelly doughnuts, and because he had endured my coolness toward the work at which he had labored for so long, work that he had hated when he had done it but had come, in the fullness of time, to regard as his apprenticeship, work that had been necessary and valuable, rose, stretched, yawned, looked down at me, and said, deliberately, "Ahhhh, but Peter Leroy will never do that."

He gave me a twisted smile, drank the last of his cognac, and got our coats while my heart sank and snow fell on my future. We said our goodnights, and we all kept our smiles on, but after that night I never spoke frankly to Mr. Beaker again.

19

NEARLY EIGHT YEARS LATER, I was earning my living as a writer: writing advertising copy, brochures, recipe booklets, press releases, answers to inquiries, and requests for brochures and recipe books. I was working for the Babbington Clam Council. It was, I told myself, an apprenticeship, and when asked about my work, I was quick to enumerate the many things I had learned from it. I tried not to admit to myself how much I enjoyed the work, how happy I would probably be if I were to stick at it. Instead, I spent my evenings, and stolen hours at work, trying to write that big book, and trying not to believe that Mr. Beaker might have been right, that I would never do it. But the harder I worked, the more confused and uncertain I became. I filled cartons with fragments, but of what complete construction they were fragments was not clear, and often when I should have been wrestling with a big idea I was wandering around Kittiwake Island.

Sitting at my desk one morning, I opened a letter from Robert Meyer, who was still wandering from place to place, accumulating degrees, writing letters, and, by his own account at any rate, breaking hearts. He had enclosed a clipping from the *International Herald Tribune,* an article about clams based on a press release that I had written.

In the space of a single moment, my life's work was determined, for on the reverse of the clipping were several classified ads, in one of which a name caught my eye: Larry Peters. The publisher of the Larry Peters series was looking for people to write new installments, not only new adventures for Larry, but installments for other series as well. By responding to the advertisement, I learned that the several series of books for boys and girls published by this house were written by people working from character dossiers and plot outlines that the publisher himself supplied. When I had read the books as a boy, I had believed that they were written by Roger Drake, whose name appeared on the covers, and it never occurred to me that there might be many "Roger Drakes," that the Larry Peters stories were the product of several hands, that the Roger Drake whose name appeared on each of the books was himself a work of fiction. Those stories that had appeared over the years, those stories of which I had been so fond, in which I thought I had found so much more than met the eye, beneath the text of which I thought I had been able to read a richer text about the way Larry lived with his family and his friends, the way he understood things, the way he felt about things, had been built on a deception.

Only after a careful rereading and a good deal of thought did I understand that underpinning my reading of the Larry Peters adventures, the only foundation beneath them, was what I had wanted to be there, nothing but what I had donated to Larry from *my* past, from *my* imagination. To a great degree, the Larry Peters I knew, the Larry Peters I had once wanted to be, had always been *my* creation, was even, perhaps, me.

I GOT THE JOB advertised on the back of the clipping that Robert sent me, and for the last nine years I have been the only Roger Drake. Since the series had become dated in its topical references and in the props that the succession of earlier Roger Drakes had used, my first task was to revise all the earlier books, in sequence. Thereby, of course, I got the opportunity to bring the books more in line with what I had imagined them to be, and even to insert here and there some of the episodes that I had imagined occurring in the gaps between adventures. I have also written eight adventures that are entirely my own, and the income from the Larry Peters books that I've written, added to what we make from the hotel (which is small for the effort involved) has allowed Al and me to live quite comfortably for the last five years or so, or at least would allow us to live quite comfortably if we had any sense about money at all.

I am often asked whether the Larry Peters books that I have written are autobiographical. They are and they are not. It's not surprising, I suppose, that the characters in my version of Larry Peters have acquired some of the habits, expressions, and physical characteristics of people that I have actually known. Larry's friend Rocky King has become more and more like my friend Raskol. Lucinda and Marie exhibit aspects of most of the girls and women I ever had any interest in. Larry's father and mother seem to be composed of equal parts derived from the depictions of them in the earlier Larry Peters books, my own parents, and both sets of my grandparents. I have also included details and props from my life in Larry's: the kittens that live beneath the Peterses' front porch are the very kittens I pursued on my grandparents' lawn the day that Mr. Beaker introduced Eliza Foote to us, the day that my mother fell out of her lawn chair. The alabaster busts of Peterses that reside in lighted niches in the wall along the staircase are derived from the coconuts my great-grandmother carved to represent Leroys. In that capacious summer during which all the adventures occur, there is room for everything, and nothing changes much once it has been admitted into Larry's world. So, at the top of the Peterses' house, my great-grandmother lives forever, unchanging, still strong, playing the part of the matriarch of the Peters bunch, offering the guidance that so often holds the key to the solution of the mystery in each book.

The publisher has complained from time to time that the changes I have made in the series have led to the misperception of the books as being intended for adult readers, rather than for adolescents, and that the "adventures" I write for Larry are not really adventures. Well, I never thought that the Larry Peters books were intended only for adolescents, and I never thought that the adventures were very important. I try, I do try, to include in each episode something that will build suspense, but I find that as I work on, say, the stealthy approach of saboteurs who are bent on destroying the prototypes for next year's line of Peters knick-knacks, my attention is easily diverted to, for example, Larry and Lucinda, who are having an interesting conversation about love and jealousy while they sit on the lowest limb of the apple tree out beyond the gazebo. Larry's adventures are more likely to be little adventures of his growing-up, which turn out to resemble the little adventures of my own.

Yet there is, I hope, mystery of a sort. My friend Raskol—who has spent a lifetime tinkering, who has a poet's admiration for the machine that does its job with the fewest parts, the computer program that does its job with the fewest commands; who has an irresistible itch to find out how a thing works; and who can see a complex thing whole, as if he were looking at the designer's drawings, as soon as he takes the lid off it—once gave me the highest praise I've received for any of my Larry Peters books. He said, and this is all he's ever said about my work, "I like the way everything snaps together at the end."

Making everything snap together at the end is what makes the writing of each Larry Peters book an adventure for me; it provides the small part of writing them that is play. I've tried, most of the time, to make an object or an idea control the book, like a cotter pin, say, that appears and reappears unexpectedly—at the bottom of a drawer, in someone's pocket, hanging improbably on a gold chain—and snapping into place at the end as the pin that holds the whole gadget together. Not everyone likes that sort of thing, of course, and many of my readers have written quite persuasive letters asking for fewer cotter pins and more laughs.

20

AND THEN, some four years ago, I was sitting in Corinne's Fabulous Fruits of the Sea one night, talking to Porky White, complaining along familiar lines.

"It still isn't enough, Porky," I said. "Now that I'm Roger Drake, I ought to be satisfied, but I'm not. I still keep trying to write that big book about myself, that book as rich and various as a good clam chowder, loaded with useful and interesting information, hilarious anecdotes, recherché allusions, philosophical speculations, intriguing stories, clever word play, important themes, striking symbols, creative sex, intricate diagrams, mouth-watering recipes, big ideas—"

"Yeah," said Porky, "but you want to know something?"

"What?" I asked.

"I don't think that the guy I'm listening to now is ever going to do that."

My heart sank.

"Don't get me wrong," said Porky. "I mean just what I said: the guy I've been listening to for the last hour is never going to write it. He takes himself too seriously, much too seriously to do what you're always talking about doing. His ego is too tender, and he protects it too well. He's too afraid of making a mistake. He's afraid of making a fool of himself, afraid of falling on his face in print, afraid that people are going to laugh at him."

There was a danger of my bursting into tears. To hide my face from Porky, I brought my beer mug up and drained it slowly. Porky signaled for two more.

"Let me give you some advice," he said. "You don't have to take it."

"Okay," I managed.

"What you need," said Porky, "is a new dummy. You've got a dummy called Larry. Now you need another dummy. Let the dummy write the big book."

Porky held his hand up in a gesture that meant I should hear him out.

"Years ago," he said, "I used to listen to Bob Balducci on the radio. You probably don't remember him. He was a ventriloquist, and he had a dummy named Baldy. Baldy used to say the craziest things, insulting things, embarrassing things, stupid things. I don't remember any of them now, but they were crazy things. He used to break me up. Sometimes, though, Baldy would go a little too far: he'd say something too stupid, or too embarrassing, or too insulting, and you know what he'd say then? He'd say, 'The big guy made me do it.'"

Porky laughed long and loud at the memory of this remark.

"And you know what Balducci would say to that?" he asked through his laughter, and answered himself at once. "He'd say, 'Don't listen to him—he's only a dummy.'"

He laughed long and loud again, and then he pulled his handkerchief out of his pocket and blew his nose twice. He shrugged.

"Maybe I'm not making myself clear," he said.

But he had made himself so clear that my heart had begun to go pit-a-pat and I couldn't speak. I just sat there wearing a wacky grin.

The Young Tars

Of these treacherous instructors, the one destroys industry by declaring that industry is vain, the other by representing it as needless; the one cuts away at the root of hope, the other raises it only to be blasted. The one confines his pupil to the shore, by telling him that his wreck is certain, the other sends him to sea, without preparing him for tempests.

Samuel Johnson
Rambler, No. 25

Do you know what it is I dislike about writing?—All the scratchings out and touchings up that are necessary . . . . It's the power of revising that makes writing such a colorless affair . . . . That's what seems to me so fine about life. It's like fresco-painting—erasures aren't allowed.

Lafcadio, in Andre Gide's
Les Caves du Vatican (Lafcadio's Adventures)
(translated by Dorothy Bussy)

Preface

I WOULD NEVER have written this story if Porky White hadn't insisted on it. Not long after I finished *Call Me Larry*, Porky threw a party to announce the addition of Frizzlin' Fritters to the menu at his Kap'n Klam family restaurants. At one point in the evening Porky and I found ourselves standing side by side at the bar, waiting for fresh drinks, eating fritters. On the whole, these fritters were not bad. Like all the other items on the Kap'n Klam menu that are not actually billed as clams (the Baked Stuffed Stuffin', Marvelous Mush, Krumbs Kasino, and Bubblin' Broth, for instance), they were flavored with the secret concentrate that Porky had developed, Klamessence. Porky asked me what I was going to work on next.

"I'm not sure," I said.

"Tell the story of the Young Tars," he said.

I shuddered and said, "No, thanks. That's one of those dark, gritty bits at the bottom of my life that I'd just as soon forget. Every time I face an audience, there is a moment, just before I start to read, when the memory of that night returns, every detail. My palms start to sweat and I look out at the people sitting there, waiting for me to start, and I find myself wishing that I'd had the foresight to lock the doors so that they couldn't get out. No thanks."

"Peter!" he exclaimed. "I really am surprised at you. That's kind of a narrow, self-centered way of looking at it, isn't it?"

"Perhaps," I said, "but remember that this is *my* personal history—and so forth."

"Not entirely," he said. "There are other people in it, aren't there?"

"Come on, Porky," I said.

"Come on, nothing. This is important to me. The Tars may have been nothing but dark, gritty bits in your life, but in mine those dark, gritty bits had silver linings."

"I know," I said, "but—"

"But me no buts," said Porky. "Just look around this room."

I did. Dozens of young men and women, models made up to appear to be of high-school age, the age of most of the help at the Kap'n Klam restaurants, circulated around the room, passing drinks and platters of Kap'n Klam specialties. The uniforms they wore were identical to the uniforms we Tars had worn years ago, just as the ranks that Kap'n Klam workers carried were the ranks we Tars had carried years ago. The Tars had been the inspiration for the nautical touches and organizational scheme that were so much a part of the Kap'n Klam success.

"I'll make you a deal," said Porky, his eyes atwinkle. Leaning toward me, grabbing at my shoulder, he said, "I'll tell you what Klamessence is if you'll write the story of the Young Tars."

"Not a fair bargain," I said.

"What's not a fair bargain?" asked Albertine. She draped herself on my shoulder and took a sip of her martini.

"I'll tell him what Klamessence is if he'll write the story of the Young Tars," said Porky.

"Is that the story with the 'prendergast' in it?" asked Al.

"Yeah," said Porky, and he chuckled. "Come on, Peter."

"Oh, go ahead and write it," said Al. "How long can it take?"

"All right," I said. "I'll do it." For, after all, why not? It does explain why I'm uneasy before an audience and why I no longer carry a pocket notebook.

"Okay, then," said Porky. "Come here."

He motioned us into a huddle. Al and I drew closer, so that the three of us formed a tight circle.

"All the items that say 'klam' have real clams in them," said Porky. He raised his right hand. "I swear they do. But all the rest of the stuff has Klamessence in it. That's the *real* secret of my success. That's how I get people who don't like clams to eat at a Kap'n Klam joint—Klamessence." He looked over his shoulder, turned back toward us, lowered his voice. "Klamessence is chicken fat—schmaltz. People go into a Kap'n Klam, eat an order of Baked Stuffed Stuffin' with Klamessence, and leave saying, 'Gee, I never tried clams before, but they're *good*. They taste like chicken.'"

Peter Leroy
Aluminum Commodore (retired)
Small's Island
September 25, 1986
(Last revision October 16, 1991)

1

ON THE NIGHT BEFORE the first official meeting of the Babbington Flotilla of the Young Tars, I paced the floor of my attic bedroom, certain that, the next day, as the first official piece of business at the first official meeting, I would be demoted from the rank of Commodore, probably all the way down to Swabby. The likelihood of my being demoted didn't worry me half as much as the likelihood that I wouldn't take it well. I had prepared some remarks for the occasion and copied them into a small spiral-bound notebook that I could carry in my pocket, at the ready in case I needed to prompt myself while I was taking the demotion like a man.

Pacing the floor, reading from the notebook by flashlight, I rehearsed the remarks.

"You know," I said, adopting a puzzled look to indicate that sometimes, as on this occasion, the occasion of my demotion, the world was just too illogical, too crazy, for me to understand, "I always thought that there must have been some mistake when I became a Commodore."

Here I paused, for I was certain that there would be laughter, relieved laughter, when the other Tars saw that I wasn't going to cry or to punch Robby Haskins, who would, I was equally certain, be elevated to Commodore in my place. I continued in an all-kidding-aside tone: "I never thought that I was really worthy of the rank. I hate to be demoted, of course, but I have to admit I'm pleased to see that I was right all along. I wonder why the *rest* of you took so long to find out."

I paused again for laughter. I felt reasonably certain that there might be a couple of sighs of relief here too, perhaps a couple of grunts of grudging admiration for my ability to shrug off disappointment, to take whatever fate dished out on the breadline of life.

I shifted, next, to an offhand manner and chummy tone meant to show that we could all relax now, secure in the knowledge that Peter was going to be all right, that he wasn't going to fall apart over anything like this. I figured that if I got this far in my remarks without having to run from the room, then we would in fact be able to relax, and I would be able to make a good job of the offhand manner and chummy tone. "You know," I said, "I'm reminded of something my grandfather often says. Every now and then, he'll say, 'Easy come, easy go.' I never really understood what that meant until today. Now I understand what it means, and I've got the Young Tars to thank for that."

I planned another pause here, because I thought that there might be some self-congratulatory applause from the assembled Tars.

"It means," I went on, "that when you get something you didn't really work for, you don't really deserve it, since it came to you so easily. And since you don't really deserve it, you're probably going to lose it as easily as you got it. Easy come, easy go. I don't want to take up too much of your time, and I know that we all want to raise a glass of cream soda to the new Commodore and grab a couple of cupcakes, but let me give you an example.

"Suppose you're walking along one day on your way to school, and you find a dollar bill on the sidewalk in front of you. You bend over and pick it up. What do you do with it? Put it in the bank? No. Turn it in to the principal? Uh-uh. Stick it into the Red Cross box outside the nurse's office? Heck, no. I'll tell you what you probably do. You probably stop at the candy store and spend the dollar buying wax teeth for the whole gang. Later, when you get home after school, you tell your mother how lucky you were.

"'Hey Mom!' you shout. 'I found a dollar on the way to school!'

"'Aren't you lucky!' she says. 'Where is it?'

"'Huh?' you say. 'Oh, I spent it on wax teeth.'

"She gives you a look you've seen before, and suddenly the truth hits you. You realize that the dollar is gone and you'll never get it back again. You're left standing there with a mouthful of wax teeth and an empty pocket, wondering how you can sum up the lesson you've learned. Well, the next time you find a dollar and spend it on wax teeth, or the next time a mixup in uniforms makes you a Commodore until a new uniform comes in and you're demoted to Swabby, I hope you'll shrug and grin and say what my grandfather would say: 'Easy come, easy go.'"

I was sure there would be applause after these remarks. I planned to drop my head and, with a swift movement I'd been practicing all week, slip a set of wax teeth into my mouth. When I raised my head, shrugged, and grinned, I would, I hoped, ignite a blaze of esteem and good humor in the heart of every Tar. The Tars might, I thought, gather around me to shake my hand and punch my shoulder and clap me on the back. It wasn't inconceivable, it seemed to me, that they might hoist me onto their shoulders and carry me around the room for a while, singing "For He's a Jolly Good Fellow." There was even at least a slim chance that, in a frenzy of admiration for my gumption and my ability to take the long view of things, the Tars might rise up in a body, demand in a single voice my reinstatement as Commodore, rip the insignia from Robby Haskins's uniform, and drum him out of the flotilla.

2

OF COURSE, things rarely happen as we expect they will. I wasn't demoted. Instead, Robby Haskins was elevated beyond Commodore, to the newly created rank of Commodore of the First Water. (I had, as I mentioned in my demotion speech, become a Commodore by accident, when Mr. Summers confused Robby Haskins's sizes with mine and ordered a Commodore's uniform to fit me. Haskins, a short, fat boy, called by some of my schoolmates Blubby Fatskins, had at first tried to get into the uniform that had been made to fit me, but some of the Tars had begun to snicker, and he had quickly abandoned the attempt. Instead, he put on the uniform of a Swabby, the lowest rank; in fact, he put on the Swabby's uniform that would have been mine if Mr. Summers hadn't confused our sizes.) Although I thought that creating a higher rank was a neat solution to a difficult problem, and although I was grateful to Mr. Summers for allowing me to keep my rank, I was surprised to find that I was disappointed at missing the opportunity to show that I could take a demotion like a man and eat whatever fate could dish out. I should have realized that the Tars would provide other opportunities.

After Robby's advancement had been applauded and we had drunk the cream soda and eaten the cupcakes, Mr. Summers called for quiet, had us sit cross-legged on the gym floor, in a rough circle around him, and outlined his vision for the Young Tars.

"Lads," he said, "today we have begun a great journey, the voyage of the Tars."

Excitement rippled through the group; this sounded like fun.

"Now, you might be asking yourselves," he continued, "'Where are we going on this journey?' Well, the answer to that question is, 'It doesn't matter.'"

There were some puzzled looks; I wore one of them.

"Look at it this way," he said. "We've just left port. We're somewhere at sea. We're surrounded by fog, and we can't see where we're going. We can't even see where we've been. I say, 'Great!' You may think, 'That's a crazy thing to say,' but hear me out. If we can't see where we've been, then we're not shackled by tradition, are we? No, we're not. If we can't see where we're going, then we're not limited by the blinders of narrow purpose, are we? No. Well then, what the heck is our destination? Our destination, lads, is the horizon, and the horizon is all around us, so we can't miss it! On the other hand, the horizon is unattainable, so it doesn't really matter whether we get there! And that's my point," he said.

We all perked up at this, hoping for a break in the fog.

"We're going to make this voyage together, over the bounding main, through fog and storms, and wherever we go we're going there together— wherever the winds of fate may blow us!"

He swept his hand outward, in the approximate direction of the row of windows above the bleachers behind me. Most of the Tars followed his gesture with their eyes, hoping, I think, that they might spot something on our horizon. Some twisted around to look in the direction toward which he had gesticulated. A few stood and peered that way.

"Together," said Mr. Summers. "Together. We're going 'Onward, ever onward,' because that's our motto. It's the journey that counts, lads, not the destination, and we're embarking on that journey together."

I'm sure that none of us had any real idea what Mr. Summers was talking about, but he certainly made it sound exciting. The idea of a boat trip began to form in my mind, all the Tars on deck, peering into the fog, trying to figure out where we were. This idea was not a metaphor as I understood it; it was quite literal. This seemed to me to be what Mr. Summers was getting at, that the Tars would eventually have a boat, probably quite a large sailing vessel, a schooner, say, on which we would make many an exciting voyage.

"Are you with me?" asked Mr. Summers suddenly.

"Yes, sir!" I shouted at once. My enthusiasm for the ocean voyage that I'd seen through the fog had me primed, and the words shot from me before the others had opened their mouths. Their yesses and you-bets and yeahs were hearty enough, but my "Yes, sir!" was by far the strongest endorsement, and I think the others envied me my quickness.

Mr. Summers was clearly pleased and moved. He swallowed hard and blinked a couple of times. When he spoke again, there was a catch in his voice. "Thanks, lads," he said. "I'm glad to know you're with me. Together we can really enjoy the trip."

He bowed his head, and a reverential silence fell over the assembled Tars. We were, I thought then, mutually awestruck by an ill-defined sense of some kind of mission. After a long moment, Mr. Summers lifted his head, took a deep breath, and brought his hands together sharply.

"Well!" he said. "Let's get down to work. On a ship, everyone has a job, you know, and I've got a job for every one of you, and I want you to know that every job is important. Every job. I mean that. Every Young Tar has a job, and every job is important. As far as I'm concerned, the jobs that all you Tars have to do are equal, whether you're at the top of the heap, like Commodore of the First Water Haskins, or you're at the bottom of the heap, like Swabby Heywood."

Robby Haskins beamed. Bones Heywood, the skinniest boy in the fifth grade, a pale boy with freckles, looked into his lap.

WHEN Mr. Summers began assigning jobs, the fog that hid the Tars' course began to lift a little. Most of what we were to do involved keeping the school shipshape and our schoolmates in line. Despite what Mr. Summers had said, there *were* differences among the jobs. Robby Haskins's job boiled down to keeping his hair combed and standing up straight when he was in uniform, but the Swabbies, Baymen, and Seamen had jobs that actually involved work: cleaning erasers and washing blackboards, picking up papers on the school grounds, washing Mr. Summers's car, and so on.

I was one of the Tars assigned the task of attempting to keep order among the boys and girls who rode buses to and from school. They were to enter and leave the buses in a safe manner, without jumping. They were to walk to or from the bus, not run. They were not to shout. They were not to make rude remarks about the teachers or the administration. They were not to ridicule the bus driver, and they were not to sneer at the Tar who was monitoring them.

"If anyone breaches these basic rules of good conduct," said Mr. Summers, "I want to know about it. I want names. I want details. I want to know the time and place of the transgression. I want the names of witnesses. I want each of you to carry a small notebook—"

I was already carrying a small notebook, the one in which I had written my easy-come-easy-go speech, so I perked up at this remark, recognizing an opportunity to distinguish myself. I whipped out the notebook and waved it at Mr. Summers.

3

AN ASIDE. From the time I became a Tar, I think I knew, without understanding it, that from a Tar's point of view the real reason for being a Tar was not to perform the services to the school that the Tars were supposed to perform, not to provide the model of comportment and achievement that the Tars were supposed to provide, not to learn the ways of seafaring men, but to gain a position in a hierarchy, a position above one's fellows. I say that I knew this from the start because I can recall so vividly the emotions I felt when I thought that I would lose the rank of Commodore, and because I can recall with equal vividness the petty satisfaction I took in producing my notebook, in having this small advantage over the others, an advantage with a value within the structure of the Tars far beyond its worth in society at large.

(I don't mean to belittle the value of carrying a notebook. Society is a vast edifice with many nooks and crannies where notebooks are necessities. The gas-meter reader couldn't do his job without his notebook; Albertine couldn't run the hotel without hers. I only mean that, within most social structures, carrying a notebook does not give one rights and privileges over one's fellows. One does not expect, for example, when waiting in a line for a movie, that if one flourishes one's pocket notebook, the others in line will fall away and call out, "Step aside, please. Here's a guy with a notebook. Let him go to the head of the line.")

I was eager to use the hierarchy of the Tars to elevate myself above my fellows. I wanted to be declared and *certified* superior to anyone Mr. Summers could round up who was willing to be certified inferior to me. I was certainly not alone in this desire for rank; if it hadn't been widespread, there could have been no Young Tars. The first evidence of how well Mr. Summers understood this desire came when he demoted all the girls—in effect—by kicking them out of the Tars and into the newly created Tars Auxiliary. All of us Tars, to our shame, stood taller at once.

One more aside, a related one. Although I attained the rank of Commodore through a fluke, today (the day of my composing this sentence, a still, hot one in my forty-first August, one of those when the bay is oleaginous and the sun buttery), I see that there was a sense in which I *earned* the rank of Commodore, earned at least the right to keep it: I earned it by enduring the expectation of losing it, and it may be that no other experience so makes us deserve to feel that a thing is ours as enduring the fear that it will be taken from us.

4

PRODUCING the notebook earned me my second job, a job within the structure of the Tars this time.

"Now there's an example for the rest of you," boomed Mr. Summers. "Commodore Leroy has already got his notebook! Good for you, Commodore Leroy!"

Mr. Summers paused a moment, and I could see that he was thinking.

"You know," he said, "I think you deserve something special for being so well prepared. You're going to have a special job. You're going to take notes. You will be our Scribe."

"Yes, sir," I said. "I'll keep the log."

"The log!" said Mr. Summers. "Excellent, Commodore Leroy. The log. That's exactly what you'll do: keep the log. I knew you were right for the job. You have a way with words. You've got good handwriting, too, and you can spell."

THE WORK of the Scribe had, I soon learned, two aspects. The keeping of the log was straightforward and really quite simple. All it required was careful observation, the ability to write legibly, and the ability to find the right word, or at least the almost-right word, quickly enough to keep the taking of notes moving along at or near the pace of the meeting. The other part of the job was the compiling, editing, mimeographing, collating, and stapling of the Tars Manual, and this turned out to be far from simple.

When Mr. Summers first presented me with the manual, it was in a box.

"Here, Peter," he said. "These are some notes for the Tars Manual."

"The Tars Manual?" I asked.

"Yes indeed!" said Mr. Summers. "We're going to have a nice fat manual that tells each and every Tar what to do and how to do it—how to be the best Tar possible, what to do at the Tars meetings, how to raise money for Tars events, how to play Tars games, and so on. We'll have the Tars Oath in there, and the official Tars Hymn, the history of the Tars, some chanteys for Tars to sing when they're off watch and just sort of hanging around the quarterdeck or whatever, and much, much more. We are going to have, in one handy place, just about everything a Tar needs to know."

"Wow," I said.

"As Scribe," said Mr. Summers, "one of your jobs will be to get the manual into shipshape condition so that we can have it typed up and mimeographed for each of the lads. Can you type?"

"Not the real way," I said. "I can't use all my fingers. But I know how to use a typewriter, and we have an old one at home."

"Good, good," said Mr. Summers. "Then you can type the manual too."

I opened the box. It was filled with papers of many varieties. There were sheets of lined composition paper, typing paper, sheets from a legal-size yellow pad, envelopes, sheets from a telephone message pad, scraps of brown paper bags, file cards, pages torn from a small spiral-bound notebook like mine, matchbooks, paper napkins, and, as Mr. Summers had said, much, much more. On each scrap of paper, Mr. Summers had written something that he wanted included in the Tars Manual.

"Now some of these are just rough ideas," said Mr. Summers.

He took one from the box and read it to himself. A smile came to his face, the kind of smile one sees on the face of young parents when they look at their infant child while it is sleeping. He shook his head slightly, as if he had to hand it to himself for having conceived so good an idea as whatever idea he had found on the scrap of paper in his hand. He returned it to the box and patted the stack of papers as he might have patted a son on the head.

"This is only the beginning, remember, Peter," he said. "Think of your work as a journey—"

"Yes, sir," I said. The fog that had figured so prominently in Mr. Summers's vision of the Tars' future was beginning to thicken again. "What should I, um, do with all of this?" I asked.

"Just type it up. That's all you have to do," he said. "There's some pretty good stuff in here, some fine stuff, some really fine stuff, but it has to be typed, that's all. Nothing to it."

I looked at the box of papers, on which Mr. Summers's hand still rested affectionately. What Mr. Summers wanted struck me as more than I was capable of doing, even as something that was in some way wrong for me to do. These were Mr. Summers's ideas, and from the way he handled them it seemed likely that he wasn't going to want me messing around with them. I would be a lot better off, I thought, not even to *begin* messing around with them.

"This job might be too hard for me," I said.

"Look, Peter," said Mr. Summers. He gripped my shoulders. "Look out there." He swept his hand toward the windows again. "The future is out there. Somewhere. The future of the Tars." He squeezed my shoulders. I tried to smile. "Who knows where we'll go from here. Who knows what the Tars might become." He squeezed harder. "What do you think of that? Exciting, isn't it?"

"Sure," I said. "Great." I smiled, but his squeezing my shoulders was bringing tears to my eyes.

"And wherever the Tars may go, whatever they may do, whatever they may become, they'll look to their manuals to guide them!"

"Ow!" I cried.

"Oh," he said, relaxing his grip. "Sorry, Peter. I get a little carried away about the Tars sometimes, I suppose. Still, I just can't help being enthusiastic about this. Just think of it, Peter," he said, and in his enthusiasm he reached again for my shoulder. When he saw me flinch, he stopped himself and held his open palms out to show me that he wasn't going to grab me again. "Hundreds—*thousands* of Tars, Peter, dressed in their uniforms, standing tall, learning the Tars Oath from a manual that you, Commodore Peter Leroy, typed."

5

"PETER," called my mother from the bottom of the stairs, "are you still up?"

"Yes," I called back to her. "What time is it?"

"Why, it's after midnight," she said. I heard her begin climbing the stairs. I stood and stretched and looked at the clock beside my bed. The face was a blur. I rubbed my eyes. They stung.

My mother appeared in the doorway. She too was a blur. The door frame wobbled a bit, and my mother swayed within it.

"Why Peter!" she said suddenly, clearly alarmed. "You're asleep on your feet."

She rushed to me, steadied me, held me in her arms, and guided me to my bed, where she sat me down on some of the papers from Mr. Summers's box of notes for the Tars Manual.

"This is really too much," said my mother, holding her hand to my forehead and rocking me gently. "They really are giving you too much homework. It's terrible! A boy has to sleep!"

"This isn't homework," I said. "My homework's all done. I finished it right after dinner."

"Oh, Peter," said my mother, "you're pushing yourself too hard. Is this a science project or something?"

She looked around the room. I had papers everywhere—in neat piles on the floor, on my dresser, on my desk, on the window sills, on the lamps, on my bed, on my bedside table, tacked to the walls. I had found that there was a lot more to it than typing. The box of notes contained so many contradictions, repetitions, vague ideas, and false starts that I still seemed a long way from typing despite all the work I'd done.

"No," I said, "it's—"

She gave me a look in which sympathy was mixed with sternness. When she spoke, her tone was similarly mixed.

"It's not another of those Larry Peters stories, is it?" she asked.

"No," I said. "It isn't that. Honest."

The writing of Larry Peters stories had been the subject of a good talking-to from my father not long before. New books in the Larry Peters series appeared at a pace too slow to satisfy the desire of an addict like me, so I had begun trying to write stories about Larry on my own. When, full of pride in my undertaking and in myself for undertaking it, I told my parents what I had begun, my mother had at first been pleased.

"Oh, Peter," she said. "What a wonderful idea. Maybe you'll be able to sell them to the Larry Peters people."

The idea that I, an eleven-year-old-kid, might be able to sell stories to the publisher of the Larry Peters series was, I knew, preposterous, and my mother would have agreed that it was preposterous if she'd thought about it, but it was a pleasant dream, so neither she nor I bothered to think about it. We let ourselves dream it, instead.

"Wouldn't it be fun if one of the adventures was in Babbington?" I said.

"Oh, that *would* be fun," said my mother.

"I could put my friends in it, and myself too," I said. "We could *all* be in it."

"You can't do that, Peter," said my father.

"What?" I said.

"You can't do that. You can't go putting people into stories."

"Why not, Bert?" asked my mother.

"It's not legal," said my father. "You can get arrested for that sort of thing."

"Oh, Bert," said my mother.

"Oh, Bert, nothing," said my father. "People can have you arrested for putting them into a story."

"Why?" I asked.

"Why? Because they can, that's all. They've got the law on their side." Emphatically, he stuck his fork into a slice of meatloaf. With his thumb, he pushed the slice off the fork onto his plate. "Pass me the potatoes, Peter," he said.

"Why would they want to have me arrested?" I asked, passing the mashed potatoes. "My friends would be happy to be in a Larry Peters story."

"Don't be so sure," said my father, wagging his fork at me. "Look, I'll give you a for-instance. Suppose you put *me* in a story and you put in this conversation we're having right now. All right. Now, I'm tired. I've had a long day. Whitey's damned son Porky spent all afternoon trying to get me to put money into some foolish restaurant he wants to open. I'm bushed, and I don't feel like listening to any more crackpot ideas. So in your story, I'm going to look like a cranky, grouchy, old—" He searched for a noun.

"Killjoy," my mother offered.

"Grump," I suggested.

"Yeah," he snarled. He bent to his meatloaf and potatoes.

"Oh, Bert," said my mother, "I'm sorry you had a bad day. Tell us about it. Tell us about Porky and his restaurant."

"Ella," said my father, "forget the jackass and his restaurant. And you, young man," he said, in an I-don't-want-to-hear-another-word-about-it tone, pointing his fork at me, "forget about writing Larry Peters stories. You've got plenty of homework to keep you busy, and if that's not enough, there are plenty of things you can do around the house."

So, I stopped writing Larry Peters stories, but I didn't stop *thinking* about writing them, and as a result the time I spent in bed before I fell asleep became, for me even more than for most adolescents, a time of guilty pleasures, when my thoughts would turn both to girls and to stories. Since I was already developing the tastes that are today so broad that there is almost no girl or woman in whom I do not see some touch of beauty, almost no book in which I do not find some good idea, some admirable phrase, there were very many girls and very many stories for me to think about, and, of course, the aftermath of these thoughts was guilt, since these were forbidden territories through which I wandered in the dark of my attic bedroom.

Not only did I have to bear all the fearful guilt derived from my awakening interest in sex, but I had a growing load of guilt from my awakening interest in my imagination, and that, I could see, was potentially far more dangerous an obsession. Sex occupies a territory of the mind that has been mapped rather well over the ages; during our personal wanderings there, each of us leaves regions unexplored, but the species has poked into every nook and cranny. The territory of the imagination is another story. The universe of the imagination expands much faster than the physical universe. Even at eleven, I could see that my imagination was, much like the foggy future of the Tars, a place without visible boundaries, perhaps with no boundaries at all, a place where I could get lost if I wasn't careful. My wanderings there, most often while concocting a Larry Peters story, were thrilling but sometimes frightened me a little. When my father warned me to give up thinking about writing Larry Peters stories, it had an effect on me far worse than the effect that he might have produced by saying, "And you, young man, you cut out that masturbating, understand? If you need something to keep your hands busy, there are plenty of things you can do around the house."

I did try, though. I tried to stop even thinking about writing Larry Peters stories. I thought about girls instead. They were the only thing that could pull me back from the misty unknown. I tried, very deliberately, to anchor myself to memory—to the remembered image of one girl or another—and thereby keep myself from drifting off into the fog of imagination. It rarely worked for long. I would bring to mind Caroline Thurlow, for example, and try to concentrate on the nape of her neck, on the rounded prominence of the vertebra there, the wisps of hair, and find that soon she and I were crawling through brambles, trying to reach the mountain hideout of the gang that was holding Larry Peters for ransom.

Therefore, my mother's question, "It's not another of those Larry Peters stories, is it?" aroused in me some guilty embarrassment.

"No," I said. "It isn't that. Honest."

"Well, then, what is all this, Peter?" she asked.

"It's supposed to be the manual for the Young Tars," I said. "I have to get it into shipshape order, because I'm the Scribe now."

"The Scribe!" said my mother. "Why that's wonderful! Why didn't you tell me?"

"Well," I said, "I wasn't sure that I wanted to keep the job. I thought it might be too hard for me."

"Oh, but you've decided to keep it now, haven't you Peter?"

"Well, I—" I began.

"Good for you, Peter," she said. "I just think it's wonderful that you're in the Tars and that you're a Commodore, and now Scribe!"

"I know," I said.

"And you look so good in your uniform. Your father said so, just yesterday." She glanced at my clock. "Well, it wasn't just yesterday any
more," she said. "It was the day before yesterday. He said, 'You know,
Peter really looks good in a uniform. Some men can really wear a uniform, and some just can't. You know what I mean, Ella? Some guys, you
put them in a janitor's uniform and they look like the admiral of the fleet,
and other guys, you put them in an admiral's uniform, and they look as if
they forgot their brooms.'

"He's right," she said. "I always think your father looks especially
nice when he goes off to work in a nice clean uniform, the way he has
"Bert" stitched over his breast pocket and "Esso" on the back. You know
who *really* looks good in a uniform though? Dudley."

My mother looked into the distance.

"During the war," she said, "he looked really—"

She sat without finishing her sentence. She was still. She looked
straight ahead. In the quiet, a long time seemed to pass, and I began to
feel as tired as I was.

Yawning, I asked her at last, "Really what?"

"Hmmm?" she asked, as if surprised that I was beside her, surprised
that I had spoken.

"Dudley looked really what?"

"Oh. Handsome. Dashing. You should get to bed, Peter."

"What about all these papers?"

"I'll put them in a neat pile," she said. "You get into bed."

6

I DID MANAGE to get the manual organized before the next meeting,
and with my mother's help I even managed to get it typed. After I eliminated all the repetitions and notes that seemed too sketchy to include it
didn't amount to much: six-and-a-half pages.

"Maybe we should have used wider margins," said my mother. "I'll
type up a cover for it, and we'll add a back cover too. That should thicken
it up some."

The covers helped, but the manual still seemed a skimpy thing, and I
hoped that Mr. Summers wouldn't be too disappointed by it.

The Tars meetings were held on Thursday evenings, in the gymnasium of the school known as "the old school," because it was the oldest school building in Babbington. When I arrived at the gym, Mr. Summers and Robby Haskins were standing in the circle painted on the floor. Mr. Summers was holding a toy gun. I recognized it at once because I had one myself. It was a model of a bazooka. It fired Ping-Pong balls. An involuntary shudder ran through me at the sight of it, prompted by memories of the nasty game my friends and I played with mine, standing one another against a wall, facing the wall, as targets, and teasing the target to make him flinch in fear between the firing of the gun, *whoomp,* and the impact, *smack,* of the Ping-Pong ball, feeble and harmless though the impact was. At those who flinched, we laughed, and the laughter was mortifying. This toy bazooka seemed an odd thing for Mr. Summers to have, and I wanted to ask him why he had it, but I said nothing. The rest of the Tars were in the bleachers, hanging around, waiting for the meeting to begin. I walked onto the floor, carrying the manual and the box of notes.

"Ah," said Mr. Summers when he spotted me, "here comes Commodore Leroy with the manual."

"Yes, sir," I said. I corrected myself: "I mean, 'Aye, sir.'"

"'Aye, sir'?" asked Robby.

"Aye, sir," I said. "A Tar is supposed to say 'Aye, sir,' when answering a Tar of superior rank—to indicate agreement, that is."

"Was that in my notes?" asked Mr. Summers.

"Aye, sir," I said.

"Well, good," he said, surprised again by one of his own ideas. "I'd forgotten that. It's good. Very good. It's nautical."

"Aye, sir," I said.

"Is that the manual you have there?" he asked. His eyes lit up.

"Aye, sir," I said.

I handed it to him.

"Is this all of it?" he asked.

"Aye, sir," I said. "My mother and I added covers to make it thicker."

Mr. Summers looked at me with his eyes narrowed, as if trying to decide whether I was making a nasty joke.

"I should have used wider margins when I typed it," I said. "It would have been longer."

"Well, that's all right," he said. "This is just a beginning. 'Onward, ever onward,' remember that. I've got some more notes for you. Commodore of the First Water Haskins, get that bag of notes, will you?"

"Okay," said Robby.

I corrected him: "'Aye, sir.'"

"That's right, Haskins," said Mr. Summers. "We've got to start doing things by the—"

He looked at the pages he held in his hand and thought better of using the word *book* for them.

"—by the manual," he said.

Robby brought me a brown paper bag filled with more scraps of paper on which Mr. Summers had written notes for things that he wanted added to the manual. I looked into the bag and pulled out and read one or two of the pieces of paper.

"Mr. Summers," I said, "some of these are notes about things that are already *in* the manual. Here. Here's one about the Tars Traits. I already typed the traits."

"Good for you," said Mr. Summers. "They're in here, then?" he asked. He began flipping through the manual.

"Aye, sir," I said. "The four Tars Traits, page three."

"Good, good," he said, turning to page three and scanning the list of traits.

"Where will I put this one?"

"What does that one say?"

"'A Tar does what he's told,'" I read.

"Just add it at the end," said Mr. Summers.

"But it seems kind of important," I said. "I mean, it seems more important than 'A Tar never wears a dirty uniform,' and that's the First Trait now. Maybe we should make that the Fifth Trait."

"You might be right. But it's all typed, and it doesn't really matter. Just add it at the end. Take the easy way out."

I didn't say anything, because I knew I couldn't obey Mr. Summers. My mother and I had discarded many sheets of paper in the process of trying to make the manual neat. I liked the look of it, and I would have been a happy Tar if it had been cast in bronze just as it was, but if it was going to change, then it couldn't change for the worse. I was going to have to retype the whole thing. I told myself that I wouldn't really be disobeying Mr. Summers. After all, 'A Tar does what he's told' wouldn't be one of the traits until I had typed it.

"Say, there—chin up, Commodore Leroy," said Mr. Summers. "Remember what I told you. It's the journey that counts, not the destination, remember? Enjoy the journey. We've got quite a voyage ahead of us. You have to expect some changes along the way. You have to learn to take what fate dishes out without letting it throw you, if you know what I mean. As we Tars travel over the sea of life, we're going to run into some storms now and then, and we can't let them make us seasick, can we? We can't let ourselves be tossed overboard by the tossing waves. A Tar has to keep his feet in a storm, Peter."

He planted his feet and mimed keeping his balance on a rolling deck. Again there appeared on his face that look of being surprised by one of his own ideas.

"A Tar rolls with the swells," he said.

"Aye, sir," I said. I pulled out my notebook and jotted it down, with a note to make it Trait One and renumber the other ones.

The meeting that followed was the first ever conducted according to the manual, and it was a mess. Mr. Summers's thinking about the conduct of the meetings was, as he had said of all his ideas for the Tars, only a beginning, and I was beginning to see that that meant "vague" and "foggy."

"Commodore of the First Water Haskins," commanded Mr. Summers, "call the Tars to order."

"Okay," said Robby. I could see that he was going to have to be trained for some time before he met the Tars Standards.

"Aye, sir," I corrected him.

"Oh, yeah," said Robby. "Aye, sir."

"That's good, Haskins," said Mr. Summers. "You pay attention to Commodore Leroy. He knows the manual. He knows how to do things the Tars Way."

Mr. Summers gave me a nod, and I began to feel stirring within me something that I couldn't identify as either an emotion or an idea, something warm and thrilling, something that made me feel that I was standing steadier, that I could roll with the swells. It was power.

At that moment I understood for the first time that in any organization, whether there are two members or a thousand, there is more to the distribution of power than meets the eye, even the eye of a member. The outward and visible system of ranks may offer no clue to the invisible system of power. I was right about that in general, I think, but I was wrong in supposing that I understood the specific invisible system of power within the Tars organization. (Sometimes, when I bring my young self to mind this way and see the little guy brightening because he's concocted a half-baked idea, I wish I could reach out across time and tap him on the shoulder and say, "That's good, Peter, but there's more to it. Wait and see.")

I had decided, reasoning from my insight into the nature of power, that whether I wound up carrying the rank of Commodore or Bayman wouldn't have mattered, so long as I had become—as I had—Scribe.

That was, it seemed to me, where the real power lay. I had it, and I was going to use it.

"All right, guys," Robby called out. "Line up."

"No, no, no," I called out. I waved my arms and shook my head and strode to a position in front of Robby. "That's not the way you do it. Everybody back into the bleachers," I said. "We've got to do this right. We've got to do it by the Manual. A Tar does things by the manual." As soon as I said it, I knew that it belonged in the manual, as one of the traits, say number three.

To the Tars in the bleachers, I said, "Now go back to doing what you were doing just before Robby—just before Commodore of the First Water Haskins—told you to line up."

There followed some shuffling about, some discussion, and some disagreement among groups of Tars about what they had been doing just before Robby told them to line up, but finally everyone—even the parents who had come to watch—assumed exaggerated versions of the positions they had been in and engaged one another in exaggerated versions of the conversations they had been having.

To Robby, I whispered, "Now you say, 'All right, me Swabbies, hit the deck!'"

"All right, me Swabbies," bellowed Robby, "hit the deck!"

"Okay," I called out to the Tars, "all you Swabbies run onto the floor and line up facing us."

To Robby, I whispered, "Now you say, 'All right, me Baymen, hit the deck!'"

"All right, me Baymen," bellowed Robby, "hit the deck!"

"Baymen," I called out, "run onto the floor and line up in front of the Swabbies."

We continued in that fashion, moving up through the ranks, until all the Tars were lined up in front of us, each Tar standing in front of a Tar of the next lower rank. Something struck me. The Tars were also lined up by height and weight. The shortest, fattest Tars were in the front. The tallest, thinnest were in the back, lowly Swabbies. This seemed an odd and amusing coincidence, and I thought of pointing it out to Mr. Summers, but something prevented me. Call it a hunch if you like; it was as if someone had tapped me on the shoulder and said, "Better wait and see, Peter. There may be more to this than you think."

"All you Tars of the First Water," called Mr. Summers. "Into the coach's office." He pointed toward the door with his toy bazooka. "For a humility session."

7

DURING THE NEXT WEEK, I spent all of my spare time and much of the time that I should have spent on homework working on the manual. The source of our problems had become clear during the first meeting. Mr. Summers had many ideas about things that he wanted a Tar to do and be, and he had many ideas about things that he wanted to have happen during a Tars meeting, but his thinking on most of these topics other than the hitting-the-deck and lining-up procedures had ended with the initial idea. The manual stated that a Tar should salute a superior Tar, but didn't specify how or when. It said that the assembled Tars should recite the Tars Oath to begin each meeting, but there was no oath. Tars were supposed to practice "skills useful in a seafaring way of life," and "learn salty expressions and gestures," but these were not described.

Because the manual had so many gaps, Mr. Summers spent most of the meeting nonplussed and spluttering. Whenever he wasn't certain how to do what the manual said should be done, he would turn smartly on his heel to face me and ask crisply, "Commodore Leroy, what do we do next?" and I would say, "Well, we'll have those procedures worked out for next week's meeting."

Going by the manual, we used only thirteen minutes to get through the meeting. After that, we hung around in the bleachers, ran up and down the stairs, and slid back and forth on the gym floor in our socks until our parents arrived to pick us up.

I was embarrassed for myself, for Mr. Summers, and for the Tars, and I was determined not to let this happen again. Every evening, I spent hours rewriting the manual to fill the gaps and make the necessary repairs. I couldn't just add things at the end as Mr. Summers had told me to, but I knew it wasn't right to disobey him, so I included as part of a description of the duties of the Scribe "to retype the manual as often as necessary so that it looks neat and finished." Mr. Summers never noticed.

I began to see and admire in myself some of the stick-to-itiveness that I saw and admired in my grandfather, but my parents became concerned about my spending so much time alone in my room.

"Peter," my father called up the stairs one night, "what are you doing up there?"

The suspicion in his voice was unmistakable. I almost gave him the answer that was becoming my automatic response to his calling up the stairs to ask me what I was doing: "Nothing." More and more of my pur-

suits in the time after dinner were becoming private. My room had become a sanctum, where privacy was defended by secrecy. This was my
island. My parents already resented the isolation I was establishing for
myself, already suspected me of spending my solitary time in unhealthy,
illegal, or useless pursuits. "Nothing," as an answer wasn't enough to satisfy my father, although he wouldn't have been satisfied by most of the
truthful answers either. He didn't want me to write Larry Peters stories or
even to think about writing Larry Peters stories. He wouldn't have wanted me to lie on my bed daydreaming. He wouldn't have wanted me to sit
in my room with the lights out, watching the neighbors across the street,
and I spent quite a bit of time doing that. Often, when I said that I was
doing nothing, he would call up to me, "Well, if you're doing nothing,
then come on downstairs and watch television with your mother and me."

"I'm working on the Tars Manual," I called back to him, truthfully.

"Oh," he said.

Was that disappointment in his voice? Perhaps. He may have been
telling my mother that I was becoming a stranger in my own home, that I
treated the place as a hotel, that there was no telling what sort of mischief
I was getting into up there in my room for hours, that sometimes I sat
there with the lights off, that he was tired of hearing that I was doing
"nothing," that he was going to get a straight answer from me or know the
reason why.

"How's it going?" he asked. There was no suggestion of disappointment now. Approval, even pride, came through clearly.

"It's getting there," I said, "but it's a lot of work."

"Well, don't keep at it too long. You've got to learn when to quit."

"Aye, sir," I muttered.

"What did you say?" asked my father.

"I said, 'I sure will,'" I said.

(I've never crawled into bed, but the verb *crawled* brings to mind such
a good image of the utterly exhausted person, too tired to get into bed in
the normal manner, too tired even to walk across the room to the bed,
dragging himself across the floor like a weary lizard, that I've often been
tempted to use it even though I don't know from experience what crawling into bed is like. Now, I think, is the time.)

I crawled into bed. Too tired to sleep, I lay awake in the dark for a
long while, my thoughts crawling through the fog of my tired mind,
bumping now and then into a figment of my imagination. Just before I
fell asleep I came upon an idea, another important lesson from the Tars,
the idea that I could get my father to permit me to do almost anything if it

was done for, or in the name of, a cause of which he approved. I could even write Larry Peters stories—if they went into the manual.

8

I ARRIVED at the gym well before the start of the next meeting. The doors to the school hadn't even been opened yet. I ran around to the boiler-room door and tapped on its wire-reinforced window with a rock to wake Mr. Griswold, the janitor, a huge bear of a man whom I never saw anywhere but in the old school, usually in the basement. Now and then, if I stayed at school late for some reason, I would see him pushing a broom along one of the hallways, pushing piles of a bright green sweeping compound that was stored in the basement in huge pressed-cardboard drums. Once, Babbington Bivalve By-products had delivered to Mr. Griswold a dozen drums of a new product, KlamKleen, that the company hoped would replace the green sweeping compound, which, I suppose, school janitors all over the country then used. KlamKleen was a white powder made from finely ground clamshells. "Another Useful By-product from One of Nature's Most Versatile Creatures," the slogan on the barrels proclaimed. The powder rose in choking clouds as Mr. Griswold swept, drifting on the air currents in the old building and penetrating to every nook and cranny, requiring the closing of school for a thorough vacuuming. Eleven unopened drums of KlamKleen still stood in the storage room.

To my surprise, it wasn't Mr. Griswold who came to the door; it was Porky White.

"Hi, Porky," I said. "How come you're here?"

"I'm the night janitor now," he said. "I talked Grizzly into hiring me so that he could sleep. He pays me half of what he gets paid. I've got to get some money together to open a restaurant."

"I heard about that," I said.

"Interested in investing?" he asked.

"Well," I said, "I—"

"That's okay, Peter," said Porky. "I was only kidding."

"But I'd like to invest," I said. "I've never invested in anything before."

"Thanks, Peter," said Porky, "but, really, I was only kidding." He paused. "You don't really have any money to invest, do you?" he asked.

"I got a savings bond for my birthday," I said. "Twenty-five dollars. Would that be enough?"

"It's a deal," said Porky. He held out his hand, and I shook it. "You're the first official investor."

"The first?" I said. "Wow."

"Hey," said Porky, "you're pretty early, aren't you? The meeting doesn't start till seven-thirty."

"I wanted to make sure that I was the first one here," I said. "I want everything to go the way it should this time."

"Ahhh," Porky said, folding his arms over his stomach. "A perfectionist."

"A perfectionist?" I asked, of myself as much as of Porky. "I guess you're right," I said. "I am a perfectionist, I suppose."

TODAY, nearly thirty years later, I know just how right Porky was. I am a perfectionist, and my quest for perfection has been the source of some of my happiest productions, some of my worst headaches, and a certain gurgling racket in my stomach that is, I suppose, the flourish announcing an incipient ulcer.

Perfectionism is, according to my old friend Mark Dorset, a characteristic of one of the two basic styles of human endeavor. These styles are, according to Mark, "movin' on" and "stayin' put." Mark ought to know, I suppose. He has been trying for most of his adult life to describe how, and figure out why, people do the things they do. (Perhaps you have in your library *How Come You Do the Things You Do?*—the book derived from Mark's public television series of the same name, an analytical tour de force that rambles across a vast range of human endeavor, from cathedral-building to bartending; or perhaps you have on your coffee table *Wit, Grace, and Style: Recognizing the Best of Human Endeavor from Its Artifacts*, a book filled with beautiful photographs and epigrammatic snippets of text, now in its fourth revised edition, which, employed as a coffee-table object, is as important an element in modern interior decorating as Picasso's drawing of Don Quixote and Sancho Panza.)

Mr. Summers carried the movin' on style to the point of drifting. Obviously, I work in the stayin' put style. Here I am, still in Babbington, trying to maintain a crumbling building against decay, against time, still rowing the waters of Bolotomy Bay that I rowed when I was a boy, still walking the streets I walked as a boy, retracing my steps in my memory, still in love with the woman I fell in love with when I was sixteen. Those who stay put, Mark says, are usually perfectionists. We're the ones who will hold on to a leaky old boat in the belief that someday we'll get the old tub fixed up just the way she ought to be. We're the ones who would gladly spend the second half of life in leisurely reconsideration of the first. We like our journeys short. We prefer having the end in sight when we set out, and that keeps us close to home and makes us shy of fog. We often have only one really big idea in an entire lifetime; if it arrives early, we're likely to spend a lifetime working on it, trying to get it right, trying to fill in all the details, fill every gap, stuff every crack. This idea may come to define us so completely that we are able to work up numberless meta-phorical variations on it, find that it reaches every nook and cranny of our life as the KlamKleen dust did, find that it flavors the whole of ourselves, as the flavor of clam appears in every spoonful of a good clam chowder, find that we try to incorporate every experience in the expression of this idea, as a clam (a paragon of stayin' put behavior if there ever was one) draws into its siphon just about anything that will fit and tries to turn it into clam, a form of being that must seem, to a clam, perfection itself.

WHEN MR. SUMMERS ARRIVED, I explained that I wanted to run through the new procedures with the Tars before the actual meeting began.

"I think it would help make the meeting run smoother if they knew what to do before we asked them to do it," I said.

Mr. Summers looked down at me and squinted, in a manner that was becoming familiar, examining my expression for any sign of humorous intent.

"You do understand that the first meeting was, well, just the first meeting, don't you?" he asked. "We had to start somewhere."

"Aye, sir," I said. "I know that, but I want the meeting to be perfect." I stood a little straighter and said with new pride: "I'm a perfectionist."

"Well, Peter," said Mr. Summers. "Perfection is something we poor mortals shall never see, I'm afraid."

"But," I said, "I figure that if we just try to make each meeting a little better—"

"Oh, no," he said. "Not that. Not 'Every day, in every way.'"

"'Every day, in every way'?" I said.

"Yes," said Mr. Summers.

"'Every day, in every way' what?" I asked.

Another of those squints.

"'We're getting better and better,'" said Mr. Summers.

"*That's* the idea!" I said.

He twitched, then shuddered as if he had been hit by a Ping-Pong ball from a toy bazooka gun.

"That was my father's motto," he said. "He used to say it when he
came to the breakfast table in the morning. He'd pound himself on the
chest or pound me on the shoulder or squeeze my mother—she was quite
a plump armful, my mother—and he'd say, 'Every day, in every way,
we're getting better and better.'"

"Maybe we should use it as the Tars motto," I said. "What do you
think?"

"I thought the motto was 'Onward, ever onward.'"

"Oh, sure. But I can just rewrite that part and then retype it all and it
will look just as if that was always—"

"No, Peter," said Mr. Summers. "You know what the poet says, don't
you?"

"Well—" I said, unsure which of the poet's sayings Mr. Summers
might have in mind. "The poet" was a device my father sometimes used,
so I recognized it at once. "The poet" might not be a poet at all. My
father's saying, "You know what the poet says, don't you?" was a way of
introducing something he didn't want to be quoted as having said, like
"Don't fart into a tailwind," or something the author of which he didn't
know.

"'The moving finger writes, and having writ moves on,'" Mr. Summers said. "'Nor all your piety nor wit can lure it back to cancel half a
line.' That's what the poet says."

"Well, it's really not *that* hard," I said. "It's a nuisance, but—"

"No, Peter," he said.

"But it would give a Tar something to cling to in rough seas."

"No, Peter."

"Aye, sir."

WHEN the Tars began arriving, quite a few of the parents who had driven
them to the school came into the gym and took seats in the bleachers. Apparently they had decided that if the meeting was only going to last for
thirteen minutes they might as well wait until it was over instead of going
home and coming back.

"Attention!" I called out. "I want to talk to all the Tars before the
meeting begins. Please! May I have your attention, all you Tars?"

Gradually, the Tars and their parents stopped talking and turned their
attention to me.

"Thanks," I said. "This won't take long. I just want to go through the
meeting procedure with you before we actually start the meeting. I think
things will go a lot more smoothly if we all know what we're supposed to
do before we start doing it."

Laughter. Behind me, Mr. Summers cleared his throat.

I cleared mine, too, and said, "I've been working on the Tars Manual all week—"

"Oh, that reminds me, Peter," said Mr. Summers. "I've got some more notes for you. Things to add."

I turned to look at Mr. Summers. "Things to add?" I said.

"Nothing really important, just part of the development of the Tars," he said. "You have to learn to take these developments in your stride, Peter. You can't just sit in the sand like a clam. You've got to move on—"

"Like the moving finger."

He gave me another of those squints. "Yes," he said. "You could say that."

He stepped forward and addressed the Tars and parents in a raised voice.

"We all have to learn to leave the past in our wake, to move on, to go where the wind blows us, and roll with the swells. I'd like to say a few words about that before Peter continues. Many of you are in my science classes, so I know that you've seen that wonderful film of bean plants growing."

All of us had. In the fifth and sixth grades, we left our ordinary classrooms for instruction in certain subjects that, I suppose, required talents ordinary teachers did not possess; these included music, art, and science. Everyone, at one time or another, saw the film that Mr. Summers was referring to; it was one of the attractions of elementary science instruction, along with the model volcano that actually erupted and the frank and baffling description of reproduction among bivalves. The bean-plant film had been made by photographing a pair of bean plants at one-hour intervals. The plants sprouted, grew, flowered, and bore beans in a few minutes, dancing jerkily to the ragged rhythms of short-lived phenomena, such as shifts of light and wind.

"You know how those bean plants move this way and that way," Mr. Summers said, bobbing and weaving in demonstration. "They don't know where they're going, but they keep *growing*! Well, that's the way it's going to be for us Tars. We may lean off to the side sometimes."

He leaned to the side; many of the Tars leaned in a similar manner.

"We may be knocked around by the winds of change."

He reeled as if buffeted by wind; most of the Tars reeled along with him, and a couple of the parents rolled their shoulders sympathetically.

"We may wander a bit, like a ship without a compass."

He took a few steps in the manner of a drunk trying to walk a line; there was some movement of Tars toward the floor, presumably to try walking in that manner. I held my hands up to stop them, and they obeyed, reluctantly.

"But we keep growing, like those bean plants! We keep *growing* and we keep *going*! That's what the Tars' Motto means!" he said.

I cleared my throat. He snapped his head around to give me a keep-your-mouth-shut look.

"—we're *growing*, and we're *going*! Onward, ever onward!'"

"Ye gods," I said, under my breath, in just the way my grandmother did when something struck her as too illogical and wacky to understand.

Mr. Summers stood silently for a moment, breathing deeply. Droplets of sweat glistened on his forehead. "Tars of the First Water," he said at last, "into the coach's office. Humility session." They waddled off, and Mr. Summers shouldered his bazooka. "All right, Peter," he said as he turned to go, "get on with the meeting."

I SPENT A WHILE teaching the remaining Tars the salute that I had worked out in the evenings, in my room, in front of my mirror, late at night.

When I had first tried saluting, what I saw in the mirror disappointed me, even after an hour of practice, even though I could deliver a crisp salute that seemed to me nearly as good as those I saw delivered by drill teams in the parades for Memorial Day, the Fourth of July, the Clam Fest, and Labor Day. I was disappointed because my salute was *nearly* as good as theirs, but not *as* good. I wasn't sure why my salute fell short of the drill-team ideal, but I could see that it did.

When I tried the salute on my parents and asked them what was wrong, they were no help at all. My father beamed at the sight of me in my uniform, saluting. "Smart!" he said. "Very smart. You've got just the right snap there, Peter."

"But what's wrong?" I asked. "Something's wrong, but I don't know what it is."

"Why, I don't think anything's wrong at all, Peter," said my mother. "I think you look very dashing. Doesn't he, Bert?"

"Well," said my father, chuckling, "I wouldn't use that word, but I know what you mean, and I'd say you're right." He gave me a grin and wink that meant, between men in those days, "Women sure are a funny bunch, but where would we be without them?"

"Why wouldn't you use the word *dashing*?" asked my mother.

"Well," said my father, "it's not a word I would use, that's all. I wouldn't say about a guy, 'He looks dashing.' It would sound stupid for me to say something like that."

"What *would* you say?" asked my mother.

"Oh, I don't know," said my father. "I'd—oh—I don't know, I probably wouldn't say anything. Come on, Ella, don't make an issue out of this."

"I think he looks dashing," said my mother. She spun around and walked into the kitchen.

My father snorted, dropped into his chair, and picked up his paper. "There's nothing wrong with the salute, Peter," he said. "It's—"

We looked at each other for a moment.

"It's okay," he said, and raised his newspaper.

I went upstairs, saluted in front of the mirror, and went to work, modifying the salute until I was happier with it. In the process, I learned three new lessons.

First, I learned that no one close to me, certainly not my parents, could give me an honest appraisal of anything I did.

Second, I learned that by sufficiently deviating from the norm, one can hide the shortcomings of what one does, for a time, by claiming to be working in a new area entirely. As an immediate consequence of this lesson, I developed a Tars salute, a salute *sui generis*, a salute outside the standards by which a drill team's salute would be judged.

Third, I learned that if I got away with the Tars salute, if I was capable of hiding the deficiencies in what I did by appearing to be doing something outside conventional forms, outside conventional criticism, then the real truth of the matter was that no one could give me an honest appraisal of anything I did but myself.

"LET'S TRY IT just once more," I called out to the Tars in the bleachers. "Right arm straight out to the side. I want you to *fling* that arm out smartly. Now *bend* at the elbow and bring your hand forward in a nice smooth arc. Slowly, slowwwwwly. Keep your fingers extended; keep your palm parallel to the floor. Then right in here, everybody do any old thing you want, anything at all. That's it. Okay, now bring your hand in to the shoulder, that's it, now *whip* that forearm up! You've got to stop, *bang*, at forty-five degrees. Now *zoom* your fingers to your forehead, like a rocket! Let's try it once more."

The Tars of the First Water emerged from the coach's office and shuffled into their positions in the ranks. "That's all the practice we have time for, Peter," said Mr. Summers. "We've got to start the meeting."

"Oh," I said. "Do you think we really have to? Maybe we should just spend this week practicing, and then we could have a perfect meeting next week."

"No, Peter," said Mr. Summers. "We have to start the meeting now."

"Aye, sir," I said. To the Tars, I called out, "That's all the time we have for practice tonight. We have to start the meeting. But practice at home during the week, okay? And keep this in mind: 'Every day—'"

"Peter."

"Aye, sir. Now, Tars, you remember how the meeting starts. Robby's going to call you to the floor by rank just the same way we did it last week. Why don't you just pretend that you're hanging around and talking the way you were last week, and then as Robby calls your rank, you take to the floor. Good luck."

I stepped aside, and I was surprised and pleased to see that the Tars took my suggestion quite literally. Not only did they pretend to be chatting and otherwise killing time while waiting for the meeting to begin, but their pretending took the form of duplicating the chats and the forms of killing time that they had employed the previous week. This week, though, they made a much better job of it. They were more polished. Their laughter was more ebullient, their pranks were more boisterous, their confidential whispers were more mysterious, their games were more competitive. We were getting somewhere.

9

"PETER!" my father called from the foot of the stairs. "What are you doing up there?"

His voice startled me, and I reacted like a guilty party. I pushed aside the paper I was writing on, covered it with my science book, grabbed some other pages of the Tars Manual, and spread them in front of me.

Then I recovered. I reminded myself that I had, at least technically, been doing something of which my father approved. I had been working on the Tars Manual. "I'm working on the manual," I said. There was, however, a tremor in my voice. I hoped my father wouldn't notice it.

"Are you really, Peter?" he asked. He must have noticed the tremor.

"Yeah," I said. "I am." I decided to take the big step, to see whether my father would accept the reasoning that I had accepted, whether he would legitimize what I was doing. "I'm working on a whole new section. It's called 'Tales for Tars.'"

"'Tales for Tars'?" asked my father. I heard a note of suspicion in his voice.

"That's right," I said. I let a long sigh escape me and rubbed my temples as if I had a headache. "This is going to be a section of stories that

Tars can read at night, when they're off watch and hanging around on the afterdeck or lying in their bunks. It's a lot of work, though, and it's giving me a headache." I was using a tone and style that I'd learned from my mother. She used it on the telephone, when she was describing one of the tasks she particularly disliked—cleaning the oven, defrosting the refrigerator, bringing the fall clothes out of the storage closets under the eaves in the attic—and even though she was talking on the telephone, she would include the gesture of rubbing her temples, bringing her right hand to her forehead, masking her eyes, so that she could rub her right temple with her thumb and her left with her middle finger.

"Well, Peter," said my father (and from the note of sympathy that I could hear beneath the sternness on the surface I knew that I'd been successful, that he'd accepted my writing "Tales for Tars" as a legitimate part of my working on the manual), "sometimes you have to just grin and bear it. I remember when I was on the baseball team, in high school—"

My father went on to describe for me the pain he'd felt when he'd had to run laps and his annoyance, even anger, when the coach demanded, as he always did, one more lap. I listened with a guilty pleasure, because the tales I was writing for the Tars were, of course, about Larry Peters, and the headache I felt was of a different order from the one I got when I had to reorder the Tars Traits, or rewrite the procedure for the Tars meetings.

10

ANOTHER ASIDE. I was surprised and, I must admit, annoyed, to discover, as I described my guilty feelings about working on the "Tales for Tars," deceiving my father by disguising work I *wanted* to do as work I *had* to do, how little my attitude toward work that brings pleasure has changed. I *still* feel guilty when I'm doing such work, still feel that if I'm having a good time I must not be working hard enough, still feel that work that brings pleasure can't be real work. One of the most persistent and pernicious of the wrong ideas I learned in school, an idea reinforced by my father's attitude toward his work at the gas station, and by his attitude toward the avocations my grandfathers pursued—Guppa's tinkering, Big Grandfather's boatbuilding—was the idea that work, real work, was not a pleasure. One might derive a little backhanded pleasure from seeing a job done at last (pleasure of the I-keep-hitting-myself-on-the-head-because-it-feels-so-good-when-I-stop variety, the kind of pleasure celebrated in beer commercials: "Hey, you made it through another day on that lousy job! It's time to pop open a frosty Lethe and forget the whole dirty business!"), but, according to my father and to many of my teachers (I exclude half a dozen magnificent ones), the pleasure didn't come from the work itself. I'm sorry that they never knew what pleasure comes from working well, that when you're working as well as you can you're inclined to giggle, and that when you find yourself, once in a rare while, working better than you ever thought you could, the feeling is so euphoric that a tingle runs across your back and you have a suspicion that you might be growing wings.

11

AT THE NEXT MEETING, I began to see a pattern, a structure, developing. A Tars meeting had three parts: a rehearsal, the meeting itself, and free time.

The rehearsal was, all things considered, my favorite part of the meeting. One might contend that the rehearsal wasn't really part of the meeting at all, but I would disagree. I think that the rehearsal period stood in relation to the meeting as a preface stands in relation to the work that follows it or as an hors d'oeuvre stands to the meal that follows it. What is the nature of the prefatory relationship? The preface stands apart from the work, *hors d'oeuvre*, but is related to the work, since it prepares the mind for the work, and the two together—the work and the preface to it— are components of a larger work: the volume in which they both appear. The hors d'oeuvre stands apart from the meal, but is related to the meal, since it prepares the palate for the meal, and the two together—the meal and the hors d'oeuvre—are components of a larger work: the evening's dining *tout compris*. The rehearsal period became an important part of the Thursday evenings that were given over to the Tars. I liked the rehearsal because I led the Tars then. They looked to me for guidance since I was the only person in the old gymnasium who had an up-to-the-minute copy of the manual. I was the only one who knew the latest revision of the oath, the only one who knew on any given evening how many traits there were and what their relative importance was. I was the only one who knew the latest system of ranks and privileges. I was often the only one who knew what rank a given Tar held from one Thursday to the next.

While Mr. Summers had the highest-ranking Tars in the coach's office for their humility session, I kept the other Tars hopping, running through new maneuvers, reciting new rigmaroles, and, above all, polishing and polishing the stable elements. I wish I could say that the rest of the Tars enjoyed this part of the evening as much as I did. They groaned and moaned and hooted and howled each time I handed out a new version of the manual. Since Mr. Summers was was moving on while I was trying to perfect the past, he was always a step ahead of me, and at the end of the the rehearsal I often had to announce that most of what the Tars had just practiced would be changed next week. I began to worry about a mutiny.

"Next week," I said, one Thursday, "I'm going to collect your old manuals and give you a brand-new manual with some exciting new changes in it." Grumbling, groaning, hooting, howling.

"But listen," I said, impulsively, optimistically. "There's going to be something special in it. A whole new section called 'Tales for Tars.'"

I can't say that this made them any happier, but I can say that it made me miserable. For weeks thereafter I tried to get even one of the tales into a condition that I would consider ready for the Tars to read. I couldn't seem to do it. Mr. Summers got wind of my promise and began asking about it every week.

"Not ready *yet?*" he might say. "That's too bad. You're not trying to make it too perfect, are you Peter? Remember that a Tar knows when to say 'good enough.'"

"Aye, sir," I said.

To the Tars as a group, he said, "I hope that all of you will remember that. I'm sure you've probably heard your parents say something like, 'Anything worth doing is worth doing well.'"

Indeed I had—not my parents, but Guppa. I remembered him in his cellar, raising the last coil he had had to wind for the radio he was building me, and saying, "If you're not ready to do what has to be done the way it should be done, then you're not ready to do it at all."

"Well," said Mr. Summers, "I certainly don't want to suggest for a moment that your parents don't know what they're talking about. No, sir. A Tar always keeps his ears open when his parents are talking. However, a Tar takes what he hears with a grain of salt. A Tar knows that sometimes good enough is good enough."

This sounded a lot like my father, who had told me that one of the big lessons in life was "knowing when to quit."

Mr. Summers looked at me, and he said, "A Tar knows that nobody's perfect, that perfection is an unattainable goal, and that although he pursues perfection, he will never reach it any more than he will reach the horizon on the vasty sea. He knows that anything he tries to do will fall

short of the ideal, and, knowing that, he knows when to quit. He knows
when to say, 'Ahhhh, the heck with it. Nobody else will notice.'"

12

WHAT QUALITY was it that made me resist Mr. Summers's order to
abandon my perfectionism? Stubbornness? I suppose it was, at least in
part. Pride? Certainly. I was proud of my role, responsibilities, and accomplishments as Scribe of the Tars, and I resisted Mr. Summers's efforts
to alter my definition of the job and its standards. Rebellion? Sure. My
resistance probably marked the first grumblings of incipient adolescent
insubordination. More than any of these, though, perfectionism itself
made me resist Mr. Summers. Mr. Summers was sloppy and headstrong;
there was about him and the organization he had created a messiness that
I couldn't tolerate. The Tars were not a shipshape outfit.
    Perhaps perfectionism is a real human trait, genetically transferred, not
a habit, not something learned. Perhaps it's a Leroy family trait, one of
those that skips generations. Certainly there are similarities between perfectionism and the qualities I admired in my great-great-grandfather,
Black Jacques Leroy—his dedication to his dreams, his persistence in
making them come true, qualities he demonstrated in developing and producing what may have been the best beer ever brewed, the legendary Leroy Lager, the beer that Emily Dickinson praised, in a generous gesture of
self-parody, in a poem she sent to Black Jacques for publication on one of
his labels:

    I taste a Lager better brewed—
    From Tankards scooped in Pearl—
    Than all the Vats upon the Rhine
    Might offer this New England Girl!

    Inebriate of Lager, I—
    And Debauchee of Pilsner, too—
    Reel—from Inn to Tavern—aye—
    In search of Black Jacques's perfect Brew—

    It is still a strong attribute of my character, but I'm not now the perfec-
tionist I was in my Tars days. As I've aged, my increasing awareness of

the fact that the number of days left to me is decreasing has worked against my perfectionism. So has my increasing awareness that many people find perfectionists annoying, a lesson I probably should have learned from the groans of the Tars each time I began passing out a revision of the manual. However, at the time when I was Scribe of the Tars, I was so much a perfectionist that I began rewriting the log.

13

"PETER," called my father from the foot of the stairs. "What are you working on? Homework?"

"No," I said. "I finished my homework."

"Are you working on the Tars Manual?"

"No," I said. "I've got that finished too. I'm working on the log."

"The log? What do you mean?"

"Well," I said, aware that what I was doing could be considered ridiculous, was likely to be considered ridiculous by anyone I knew, and was certain to be considered ridiculous by my father, "I'm—um—trying to make it a little—better."

"Better?"

"Yeah," I said. "Whenever I look back at the early meetings, I see a lot of places where things could have gone better, and I remember things I left out, and I think of things that would have made the meeting smoother or more fun, and the rules have changed a lot since the early meetings, so—"

"Peter," called my father, "wait a minute, wait a minute." He began walking up the stairs. "Do you mean to say that you're *changing* the log?"

"Well," I said, made wary by his tone, "yes."

"You can't do that," he said. He stood behind me, looking over my shoulder at the work on my desk. He reached over me and picked up the spiral-bound notebook in which I was writing a revised version of the log. "Peter," he said, exasperation and surprise driving the anger from him, "you just can't do this. A log is—well—it's something sacred, it's like history. It *is* history. You can't rewrite history, can you?"

I didn't say anything. I just sat there, looking at my desk top, letting my eyes drift out of focus.

"Of course you can't," he said. "It's wrong. It's—well—it's just wrong. You know what the poet says, don't you?" I didn't answe

"Well?" asked my father. He poked me on the shoulder. "Do you?"

For a moment I thought of saying, "Every day, in every way, we're getting better and better," but decided against it. "I guess not," I said.

"'The moving finger writes, and having writ moves on,'" he said. "That's what the poet says."

"Oh, yeah," I said. "I have heard that."

14

I GREW DEPRESSED. I lost the will to work. I wanted to grab that moving finger and say, "Hold it a minute. Don't be in such a hurry. There are some messes to be cleaned up before you go rushing on," but it seemed to be impossible. What was the sense of working on the manual if it would never be what I wanted it to be, would never be perfect, would never reach a point where I could say, "Okay, that's it! That's just the way it should be. Now let's not change anything." We perfectionists are reluctant to let go of our projects while we see in them the slightest flaw, but if we do pronounce a thing finished at last, we expect it to endure forever, immutably perfect. When the garden is at last laid out and planted just right, we never want to see any weeds. When the fence is completed, we never want to see any rot. When we get the Tars Manual just right, we never want to see another revised edition.

I couldn't eat. I lost weight at an alarming rate. My parents tried to get me to eat by making meals that appealed to me (scalloped potatoes with ham were a favorite then, but they tasted like paste), or by pushing snacks on me (especially sandwiches made with cream cheese and grape jelly). They also tried to "get my mind off my work."

Getting one's mind off one's work was, in my family, regarded as absolutely essential to mental—and even physical—health. (In later life, I've more often felt just the opposite, and have used work as a way of getting my mind off, say, plumbing problems, or taxes, or the barking of the poor dog that, when Albertine and I lived elsewhere, before we moved to the splendid quiet of Small's Island, some neighbors of ours bought for their children, in an apparent effort to demonstrate how long a dog could be made to bark by leaving it tied on a short tether without food, water, or affection.) In my family, the most desirable way of getting one's mind off one's work was to take a vacation, but the most convenient one was to watch television.

"Peter," said my mother, and I started as if someone had thrown a rock through my window. I hadn't heard her come up the stairs or come into my room. There she was, beside me, with her hand on my shoulder. "My goodness, Peter," she said. "You're a nervous wreck. Didn't you even hear me come in?"

"No," I said. "I—I—was trying to work on the—well—on the manual—or—I don't know—anything."

"Oh, Peter," said my mother. "This is terrible. You're worrying too much about this work. You'll give yourself the collywobbles."

"I will?" I asked.

"Of course you will. Now you just set that aside for the rest of the night and come on downstairs and watch television with us. You can make some popcorn, and we'll watch a show, and you'll get your mind off your work. 'All work and no play makes Jack a dull boy,' remember."

I followed my mother downstairs. My father was sitting in his favorite chair, drinking a beer and watching a comedian, a rubber-faced guy with a crewcut and heavy, black-rimmed glasses, teeter atop a wobbly ladder, holding a bucket of sloshing paint and a dripping brush. I smiled. It was good to be reminded that things could be worse.

I went into the kitchen. From a cupboard I took a package of the popcorn favored in my family at that time, a kind that came in a plastic pouch that was divided vertically into two rectangular pockets. The smaller of these pockets, the one on the right side of the package, held a rectangle of solidified vegetable fat that resembled an elongated bar of soap. The other pocket held just the right amount of popcorn for a family a little larger than ours. I tore open the section that held the fat, and, squeezing from the bottom, ejected the bar from the package into the largest pot from my mother's set of waterless cookware. I cut off a quarter of a stick of butter, peeled the wax paper from it, and put the butter into a saucepan over a low flame to melt. When the fat began to smoke, I tore open the section that held the popcorn and poured the kernels in. I covered the pot and shook it vigorously until the kernels had nearly stopped popping. I removed the lid then, so that I could watch while the popping of the last tardy kernels made the mass of popcorn rise and fall as if it were breathing, heaving a sigh. I poured the popcorn into a gray earthenware bowl with a pale blue line around the lip. I drizzled the butter over the top in figure eights. I shook salt onto the popcorn from the kitchen salt shaker, part of a ceramic salt-and-pepper set shaped like ears of corn. I had won them at a carnival. I carried the bowl into the living room and put it on the coffee table, a pine table supposed to imitate a cobbler's bench of colonial times. I sat on the floor beside it and watched, without real interest, while the guy with the crewcut and a woman with a wide mouth and a loud voice tried, with clownish ineptitude, to put floral wallpaper onto the walls of a set that represented a living room similar to ours.

My mother put her hand on my head and stroked my hair. "You mustn't let little things bother you so much," she said. "Why, when you're grown up you probably won't even remember any of this."

15

ON MY HONOR as a former Tar, I swear that I will not shirk from shouldering whatever share of the responsibility for the downfall of the Tars I should shoulder. A Tar stands tall, after all, and doesn't pass the buck. However, I'm not going to be reticent about Mr. Summers's part in the collapse, either. After all, a Tar is nobody's patsy and doesn't get stuck holding the bag.

Pledged as I now am to a full, fair, and frank disclosure, I'm forced to say that Mr. Summers deserves all the blame, since even the blame for my small mutiny must ultimately be laid at his feet.

I WAS NOT the only Tar who decided he had had just about enough when Mr. Summers introduced the metallic ranks. The original Tars ranks ran from Commodore at the top down through Admiral, Captain, Lieutenant, Ensign, Petty Officer, Seaman, and Bayman, to Swabby at the bottom. When Mr. Summers introduced the notion that a Tar could be "of the First Water" within his rank, none of us minded. It gave us something new to shoot for. A kid who couldn't meet—or even keep track of—the shifting requirements for advancing from, say, Petty Officer to Ensign could at least aspire to becoming a Petty Officer of the First Water. From my vantage in front of the Tars during the rehearsal period, watching when they took the floor by rank, I may have been the only person other than Mr. Summers and Robby who noticed (and I doubt that Robby noticed much of anything, come to think of it) that only a heavier-than-average Tar ever advanced into the upper ranks, and that within each rank only the chubbiest were ever recognized as being of the first water.

Then Mr. Summers introduced a parallel ranking of metals, from Gold at the top down through Silver, Platinum, Copper, Aluminum, Iron, Lead, and Zinc, to Tin at the bottom, which could be added, he claimed, to any of the regular Tars ranks and even combined with "of the First Water." There was some grumbling at first over the confusion introduced along with the new ranks, but this subsided after a while, after we had tried the sound of some of the names of metals with the ranks we bore and found that they had a nice ring to them. Some were especially plangent. I was taken with the sound of "Aluminum Commodore of the First Water Leroy," and I immediately aspired to it.

Soon, however, I saw the truth. The metallic ranks merely reinforced the policy of fat favoritism I'd seen in the basic ranks. No lowly, skinny Swabby ever became a Gold or Silver Swabby; none ever got beyond Lead, and there were lots of thin Tins. No exalted, overstuffed Commodore or Admiral was ranked lower than Aluminum. Mr. Summers referred to Tars of the topmost ranks as the Precious Metals, and during rehearsals he skimmed these boys, the shortest and fattest of the Tars, from the ranks at large, and, shouldering his Ping-Pong bazooka, marched them off to the coach's office for private instruction in leadership, navigation, *esprit de corps,* and humility.

The beginning of the end, that important point in any history, a point apparent only in retrospect, came when something occurred that was simply mystifying at first: just as I was about to begin the rehearsal one Thursday night, the door of the coach's office opened and Robby Haskins walked out, silent and glassy-eyed. He walked across the floor and into the bleachers. He sat there among the rest of the Tars. Mr. Summers said nothing when he emerged with the Precious Metals, but it was clear to all of us that for some reason Robby had been demoted in fact if not in rank. He took the floor with the Swabbies. Though he still wore the uniform of a Commodore, it hung on him like a hand-me-down from an older, fatter brother.

Others of the Precious Metals took over Robby's duties. When Mr. Summers took to the floor at the beginning of a meeting now, he was surrounded by a swarm of short, fat Tars. He had one short, fat Tar to carry his note cards, another to hold the box of medals and pins that he was going to award, another to carry his ballpoint pen, and so on.

Later, at the trial, Mr. Summers asserted that he had established the Precious Metals as an experiment, because he'd seen that a system of ranks and privileges gave him a means for gaining the undivided attention of boys who, when they sat in his science classroom, often stared out the windows for long periods of time and paid no attention to him at all. He had, he claimed, developed a theory that he could, by using a hierarchy like that of the Tars as a system of rewards and punishments, accomplish something that he had begun to despair of ever accomplishing inside his science classroom: actually teaching something that the children in his charge would remember. To test it on a small scale, he had chosen a group of Tars by weight and set out to teach them humility. He had, he said, tried to explain his theory and methods to some of the other teachers, but they had pooh-poohed it. Several had, he complained, not merely ridiculed his ideas, but had suggested to him, with leers and chuckles, that his theory was nothing but a pederast's cloak.

"MR. SUMMERS," I asked, after the meeting ended, "what happened to Robby? Did he do something wrong?"

"Yes, Peter, he did," said Mr. Summers, in a voice with the timbre that I've long recognized as exactly right for grave pronouncements, one that I've often wished I could produce when a situation warrants it, as more and more situations have since I've assumed the responsibilities of an adult and, therefore, have required more and more often the services of lawyers and plumbers, professionals who are alike in practicing a mystery in the manner of medieval guildsmen, guarding jealously the tricks of their trade, and charging the client for every second of their time, including time spent correcting their own mistakes. That grave voice combines the voices of the bassoon and cello, and there are times when only that voice will do, as, for instance, when I'm forced to say, "Albertine, I'm afraid we're going to have to sue the plumber."

"What did Robby do?" I asked. I had been puzzled by this question throughout the meeting, because the manual didn't specify any rules that Robby might have broken. Most of the manual was, in fact, given over to the procedures for the meetings, and since Robby's offense had been committed *outside* the meeting, in one of the humility sessions, it couldn't have had anything to do with those procedures. The only other section of the manual that might be construed as a set of rules or laws, it seemed to me, was the list of Tars Traits. "Did he violate one of the traits?" I asked. Then, exhibiting a trait of my own, one that has become more prominent over the years, I attempted a little humor to camouflage the gravity of the situation, as my mother used to add a spoonful of sugar to her spaghetti sauce to diminish the bitterness she found in the taste of tomatoes. "Did he refuse to roll with the swells?" I asked, grinning.

Mr. Summers's eyes widened. His nostrils flared. His jaw muscles rippled. The veins in his neck stood out. His face reddened. After a long and terrible silence, he said, in a voice made tense by his effort to control it, "What do you mean by that, Peter?"

"I just—I—I didn't really mean anything—I was just making a joke," I said.

"Making a joke. Oh, yes. You're quite the humorist, aren't you? You weren't just 'making a joke,' Peter. You were being sarcastic, weren't you?" he said, accusing, not asking. The veins in his neck were more swollen, his face redder.

"Sarcastic?" I asked, shaken.

"Yes," he said, "sarcastic. It seems to me that often, much *too* often, there's a hidden meaning in what you say."

"I don't know what you—"

"Oh, yes, you do. Oh, yes, you *do* know," he said at once. "You know very well what I mean, Peter. Are you going to tell me you don't remember the way you said that you and your mother put covers on the manual to try to make it thicker? Hmm? Do you think I don't know that you were mocking me when you said it would help make the meetings run smoother if the Tars knew what to do before we asked them to do it? Ha!"

The way Mr. Summers was treating me baffled, hurt, and angered me. I knew that I would begin to cry if I didn't get a grip on myself somehow. "Mr. Summers," I began, "I—"

"Don't 'Mr. Summers' me that way," he said, twisting the left side of his mouth in a sneer. "I know what you mean by that. 'Mr. Summers. Mr. Summers.' I know what you mean. I know what you mean when you say, 'Aye, sir,' too. 'Aye, sir. Aye, sir.' It's all in the way you say it. You're saying you think there's something wrong with me. You're questioning my leadership. You think I don't know what you think, but I do. I know just what you think—you think you're pretty smart, that's what you think. You think you're a lot smarter than everyone else, don't you, Peter?"

I was still baffled and hurt, but now anger had taken the upper hand, had taken a firm grip on me, a grip like that of an instructor, say a tennis instructor, who grips one's arm and pushes it firmly in a direction it does not really want to go. Anger gripped me and pushed me in a direction I didn't really want to go, pushed me past one of the milestones on the road from childhood to adulthood. In an instant of bitter recognition (which, in memory, resembles heartburn) I saw that Mr. Summers had perverted the relationship that should have existed between us, that he was using his status as an adult, an adult in a position that was supposed to command my obedience and respect, to hurt me, make me feel small, insignificant, and wrong for being what I was. However, some sweet came with the bitter. Mr. Summers's anger had taught me that I could fight back with humor.

"Aye, sir," I said. Mr. Summers's head really seemed about to explode. A wonderful calm came over me. I looked Mr. Summers in the eye, and, drawing on whatever gland it is that secretes *chutzpah*, I grinned.

"Nobody likes a wise guy, Peter," he said, his lips trembling. "A Tar does not act like a wise guy."

"I'll add that to the traits," I said.

Instantly, all the blood drained from Mr. Summers's face. It was, for me, an exhilarating sight. Whatever else might happen, the blanching of Mr. Summers marked a victory, a small victory certainly, one likely to be reversed by a punitive counterattack, but a victory never to be forgotten.

16

FROM EXHILARATION came inspiration. All I mean by that is that the exhilaration I felt at having stood up to Mr. Summers put me in a state of mind that encouraged the development of an idea that came to me at about the same time. Inspiration is, I think, nothing more than the name we give after the fact to the arrival of those of our ideas that turn out well. On this subject, Porky asked me not long ago, "Where the heck do our ideas come from, after all? What makes them take one form rather than another? You know how it is some days—nothing seems to go right: the computer-controlled microwave deep-fat fryers I ordered will not boil oil no matter how high I set the thermostats, and every time I try to call the manufacturer I get an answering service. My mind isn't working any better. Every idea I get is like a cold French fry. On other days, the sun shines, life is glorious, people are lined up twelve deep outside Kap'n Klam shops all over America, and my mind leaps and darts. Even bad ideas shimmer in the sunlight like foamy wavelets, you know what I mean? But get this: the interesting ideas, the ideas that are worth pursuing, are as likely to have been dragged out of the sludge of one of those dull days as to have come gliding in on the surf of one of the brilliant ones. Now I ask you this: on which days am I inspired?"

Weeks earlier, I had been in a state of mind that had made me fear demotion, made me fear losing status in the Tars, and I had thought of resigning as a way of saving myself from worse disgrace. Now my state of mind was very different from what it had been then, and the idea had come to me that I could accomplish much more by resigning than merely making the best of a bad situation. The will to work returned because I had a reason to work. I knew what I was going to do. I was going to make the manual perfect, and when it was perfect I was going to make sure that no Scribe-come-lately could change it. I was going to carve it in stone. I was going to bring my journey as Scribe to an end.

First, I made "A Tar does things by the manual" the foremost Trait, and from there on everything fell into place, though it still took an awful lot of work. I spent every night working on the manual, trying as hard as I could to make it exactly what I wanted it to be by the next meeting, including the only one of the Tales for Tars that seemed to me anywhere near ready for the Tars to see, the one I'd found myself working on most often, the one I called "Mutiny."

17

ON THE NIGHT of the last meeting of the Young Tars, I arrived at the school very early. Porky let me in, and we went upstairs to the office together, where I ran off copies of the manual on the mimeograph machine. Porky helped me collate and staple them, and we carried them to the gym, where Porky took a position at the door, so that he could give a copy to each Tar as he arrived. I took my position in the circle in the circle at the center of the floor. I paced nervously within the circle, taking care not to leave it.

When most of the Tars had arrived, I called for attention, and after the usual (and, according to the latest and final version of the manual, required) shushing, elbowing, and rude noises, I got it.

"I know you're all unhappy about getting *another* version of the manual," I said.

There was a rowdy uproar at this, with raspberries.

"All right, all right," I said, holding my hands in the air to signal for quiet. "I promise you—"

I was drowned out by the groans and hoots of boys who had been made too many promises of the sort they knew they were going to hear. I laughed, and they laughed with me—well, they laughed, anyway.

"I promise you," I shouted above them, "that this is absolutely the last Tars Manual you will ever receive."

Wild whooping and screaming greeted this announcement.

I said, "We're going to conduct this meeting strictly by the manual."
I held my copy of the manual high.

"A Tar does things by the manual," I called out.

Mr. Summers walked in just then, carrying his Ping-Pong bazooka, and made his way down the steps to the gym floor. When he was within ten feet or so of me, I saluted him. I tried to put into my salute the tone of sarcasm, of mockery, of insolence, that I had put into my saying "Aye, Sir," the week before.

Mr. Summers returned my salute with what looked to me like a nasty glance, but I smiled.

"Precious Metals," he called out. "I want you in the coach's office for a humility session." The Precious Metals scrambled down from their seats in the bleachers and waddled across the floor to the coach's office. Mr. Summers turned to me. "Humility is something *you* could use a good dose of, Peter," he said.

"Aye, Sir," said I.

"Impudence takes many forms, Peter, as I see you've learned. Learn this too: Pride goeth before a fall."

"Aye, Thir," said I. I couldn't resist, and I was new at this nasty game. My understanding of subtlety was not well developed.

Mr. Summers sneered. He handed me a sheet of paper. "I want this added to the manual," he said. He paused. "Don't rewrite the whole thing—just stick this on the end." He twisted his mouth into a grin. "It's the official Tars court-martial procedure," he said.

I took the paper from him, saluted again, and said, "Sir, it's—"

He turned and walked to the coach's office, herded the last of the Precious Metals inside, and slammed the door.

"—too late," I said. I crumpled the sheet of paper into a ball and tossed it over my shoulder.

I PUT the Tars through their paces. With every moment that passed, I felt myself drawing closer to the completion of a phase of my life, a phase that I would think of thirty years later as characterized in a significant and memorable way by my involvement with the Young Tars. My excitement and happiness grew. I began to feel the pride that comes with the satisfactory completion of something, a feeling that has since become one of the sustaining emotions of my life, the feeling that makes me rub my hands together, grin, sigh, and say to myself, "At last it's finished, and it's perfect—well, as close to perfect as I can make it."

I didn't *try* to make my feelings show, but they influenced, inevitably, my tone of voice, my gestures, and my carriage, for I was not then any more than I am now able to keep my emotions out of my style. The message in the style I used with the Tars was as clear as the message in the style I used with Mr. Summers. Without quite understanding what I was doing, I was using style to communicate an idea, the idea that things were reaching some kind of conclusion, something like perfection, a pleasure of a yet-to-be-determined kind. The Tars saw it, understood it, and returned it. The rehearsal was shipshape. The Tars were spiffy. Our ship was coming into port.

When we had finished the rehearsal, and the last echoes of the Tars Hymn died away, I held my hands up for silence. The idea that something was up hung in the air, and I got the quiet I wanted.

"This is the time when we would usually end the rehearsal and call Mr. Summers and the Precious Metals out to start the regular part of the meeting," I said, heart pounding, palms sweating. "But tonight I have kind of a surprise for you. You remember that I told you this would be the last version of the Tars Manual," I said.

I held it over my head.

"Well I meant it."

A resounding cheer.

"And now I'm going to prove it to you."

Silence.

"I want everybody to turn to the last page in the manual."

Flipping of pages.

"The very last page."

When everyone had turned to the last page, I began reading.

RESIGNATION OF THE SCRIBE
If the Scribe resigns, there will never be another version of the manual.

"Wait a minute, Peter," Porky interrupted. "Are you really going to resign now, or is this just practice?"

"I'm really going to resign now," I said.

"Well, this may be kind of a technical point," said Porky, "but if you're really resigning, shouldn't you do it in the real meeting? This is just the *practice* for the meeting, isn't it?"

"Not any more," I said, beaming, enormously grateful to Porky for

playing the straight man this way. I flipped back to the beginning of the
manual and read:

```
Tars meetings are held on Thursday evenings.  The meeting
officially begins when the Scribe walks out to the middle of
the gym floor and stands in the painted circle.
```

I looked up at Porky and grinned.

"That's good," he said. "That's very good. Very, very good. I'm
gonna get Mr. Summers out here," he said, chuckling. "I've got to see
what he thinks of this. Just wait a minute, Peter, okay?"

"If I wait, I might chicken out, Porky," I said. "I've got to keep going."

"All right," said Porky, jumping from the bleachers and trotting across
the floor, "but try to stretch it out."

From the pocket of my bell-bottom Tars Trousers, I took my spiral-
bound notebook. I flipped it open and began reading from it a revised,
final version of the remarks I had first prepared months earlier. "You
know," I read, adopting a puzzled look, to indicate that the world was
sometimes just too illogical, too crazy a place for me to understand, "I
always thought Mr. Summers was making a mistake when he made me
the Scribe." This was received with a little uneasy chuckling. I continued
in my practiced all-kidding-aside tone: "After all, I only got the job because I happened to be carrying a notebook. I won't make that mistake
again."

I tossed my notebook over my shoulder as I had tossed the court-martial procedures. A little more uneasy chuckling.

"Now that I'm going to resign, I want you to know that, all things considered, I liked being Scribe, but I have to admit that I've got better things
to do than change the order of the traits again—"

There was laughter at this, we-know-just-what-you-mean laughter.

After a pause, I added, "—and again—"

They roared.

After a longer pause, I said, "—and *again*."

I brought down the house.

Porky arrived at the door of the coach's office and reached for the
knob. He stopped. He seemed to be confused by what he saw through the
pebbled glass. I decided that I'd better keep going while I had a good
head of steam.

"Before I actually resign," I said, "I'd like to take this opportunity—
my *last* opportunity—"

Porky leaned closer to the window. He shaded his eyes with his hand. He turned the knob slowly.

"—to read you the story I wrote for you," I went on. I flipped through my copy of the manual to the "Tales for Tars" section. The Tars were playing the part of an eager audience. It would be fair to say that the gymnasium was hushed.

Porky pulled the door of the coach's office open. Into the hush came the sound *whoomp,* then *smack,* then *yow!* Then laughter.

"It's—um—called 'Mutiny,'" I said. I turned in the direction of the coach's office. So did everyone else.

"What the hell is going on?" said Porky, into the doorway.

Mr. Summers's voice came from the office. We could hear the anger in it, but we couldn't make out much of what he said, just "—discipline— humility—your own business." Then *whoomp, smack,* and *yow!* A Ping-Pong ball bounced through the doorway, and the door slammed shut.

"It starts on—uh—page thirty-nine of the manual," I said, turning back toward the bleachers, "and—I'd like to—"

No one was paying any attention to me. Porky picked up the Ping-Pong ball and walked back toward the bleachers. His mouth was open.

"I'd like to—um—read it to you," I said, almost as distracted as my audience.

A group of parents wearing quizzical looks gathered around Porky. He sctratched his head and began talking in a low tone. I listened. Every-one was listening. I heard, as well as I remember, "—a nut—some kind of gun—Ping-Pong balls—lined up bare-assed—kind of jostling and jig-gling—like a row of piglets at a feeding trough—or maybe more like a row of 'Spaldeens'—"

Porky's audience looked toward the door of the coach's office. *I* didn't seem to *have* an audience anymore. "Well!" I said. "What do you say we get started?" I slapped the manual with my open hand, but no one seemed to hear me. Everyone was still looking toward the door. "Larry had had about as much as he could take of summer camp," I read, as loudly as I could.

The door of the coach's office opened, and Mr. Summers stuck his head out. He looked at the cluster of parents and then pulled his head back in. The parents looked at one another.

"Larry had made the mistake of becoming Camp Historian," I went on, almost shouting.

The door of the coach's office opened again, and the Precious Metals began filing out. They looked the way they always did after a humility

session: humiliated. Their eyes were down, and they shuffled along. Mr.
Summers followed, walking stiffly, his demeanor stern.

"Pervert!" called one of the mothers in the front row.

Mr. Summers twitched. "I beg your pardon," he said. "I must have
misheard you—"

"Humiliator!" cried another of the parents.

Other voices rose from the crowd, one by one, and some of the braver
Tars joined in, too. Memory can be tricky, of course, but I seem to hear
them calling—

"Ridiculer! Mocking your Scribe's unwillingness to cut corners!"

And all the people assembled in the gym cried, "Shame!"

"Demeaner! Heartlessly belittling your Scribe's conviction that there
is a right way of doing things!"

And everyone cried, "Shame! Shame!"

"Treacherous instructor! Falsely counseling that good enough is good
enough!"

And they all cried again, "Shame! Shame! Shame!"

—but maybe I'm wrong about that. Wishful thinking may be rewriting
my memory. Maybe they were calling something else, something like:

"*Prendergast!*"

Another father had cried out, leaning over the railing at the base of the
bleachers, shaking his fist.

Mr. Summers looked puzzled. Frankly, *everyone* looked pretty puzzled. "I'm not quite sure that I understand you—" he began, but the red-
faced fury of the man made him close his mouth in mid-sentence, and he
began inching along the wall.

Porky whispered into the ear of the red-faced man, who said, "Oh,"
and frowned in embarrassment. "Sorry," he said. "I mean, 'Pederast!'"

Mr. Summers shook his head and said, "Now, *just a minute!*"

But more voices came from the crowd—another, and another, and another. Mr. Summers turned to me. His hair was wild, his eyes were wide.
He seemed to want me to tell him what was going on.

I shrugged. "I didn't do it," I said. "Honest."

A murmurous bunch of parents began advancing from the bleachers.
Mr. Summers took one wild look around the gymnasium and broke into a
run. In a moment he was up the stairs and out the door to the parking lot.
A spooky silence filled the gym for a moment.

"Well," I said, returning to the manual and "Mutiny." "Where was I?"

My words were lost in a wild outburst. Everyone surged toward the
door through which Mr. Summers had fled—everyone, that is, but me.

I WAS LEFT STANDING THERE, alone, in the middle of the gym floor, in the painted circle, baffled. I looked at the manual in my hand. I knew now, for certain, that I was holding the last version. My work was over. There wasn't even any need for me to resign. Still, I'd gone to a lot of trouble to make my resignation memorable, to give it wit, grace, and style.

I started again at the beginning. I delivered my entire speech and read my entire story, to an empty house. The story was—well, let's be frank—it wasn't ready. It really needed more work—much more work. The ending had lots of problems. Mr. Winters, waspish ruler of the Young Salts Summer Sailing Camp, was cast adrift in a tiny dinghy by mutinous Salts. It was a *fitting* end, but hackneyed. Even I could see that. I'd tacked it on in haste, rushed it, and I regretted it. When I finished, I looked up at the empty seats, and I was, I'm willing to admit now, glad that there wasn't a Tar in them.

My resignation speech was another story altogether. I had put *plenty* of time in on that, worked and reworked it, polished and buffed it. It *was* ready. Every little pause, every inflection, every nuance was exactly as it should have been. I couldn't have done it any better if I'd practiced for another week, and *that* ending was, I'm forced by honesty to say, perfect—just perfect.

"So," I said, "the next time you find a dollar and wonder how to spend it, the way Larry did in the story, I hope you'll shrug and grin and say what my grandfather would say: 'If you're not ready to do something the way it should be done, then you're not ready to do it at all. If you're going to buy wax teeth, buy them for the whole gang.'"

I'm sure that if there had been any Tars left in the gym, they would have loved it. They would have laughed at the funny parts and applauded me when I finished, and when I passed out the wax teeth they would certainly have come swarming out of the bleachers to gather around me and shake my hand and punch my shoulder and clap me on the back, and I have no doubt, no doubt at all, that if they hadn't been out there chasing Mr. Summers into the night they would have hoisted me onto their shoulders and carried me around the gym a couple of times, singing "For He's a Jolly Good Fellow."

Years later, that's just what happened, at the end of the Larry Peters novel that I called—but you've guessed already—*Mutiny*.

(TO BE CONTINUED)